THE
OTHER
WOMAN

LAURA WILSON

Quercus

First published in Great Britain in 2017 by Quercus
This paperback edition published in 2018 by

Quercus Editions Ltd
Carmelite House
50 Victoria Embankment
London EC4Y 0DZ

An Hachette UK company

A CIP catalogue record for this book is available
from the British Library

PB ISBN 978 1 78648 524 3

10 9 8 7 6 5 4 3 2 1

Typeset by CC Book Production

Printed and bound in Great Britain by Clays Ltd, St Ives plc

To George William Harding (1939–2015)

oh bear what have you done

ONE

'You wouldn't think anything bad could happen here,' says DC Gina Walton of the Norfolk constabulary. 'It's gorgeous.'

'There was a break-in reported a few weeks ago.' DS Ian Sullivan switches off the ignition and there's a slight hiss of pressure equalizing as the air con stops. 'Nothing taken, apparently, so I suppose they were disturbed. It's Georgian, at a guess.' Sullivan takes an interest in architecture. 'The vicar must have lived here. Originally, I mean.' To the right of the house, with its perfect proportions, understated grandeur and purple wisteria, is a square-towered church in the middle of a stone-walled graveyard. Aside from this, and the cottage and outbuildings in several well-tended acres of grounds, there are no other structures; except for the odd stand of trees, the view across the fields is uninterrupted.

It's early June, almost dusk. It's been unnaturally hot for the time of year: the weather broke yesterday, a terrific thunderstorm with rain bouncing off the tarmac which made everyone say, 'There goes the summer,' but then the weather repaired itself, resealing them in heat.

Inside the house, a dog barks. 'Bet it's a black Labrador,'

Walton says. 'People who live in houses like this always have black Labradors.'

There's a row of dumpsters by the churchyard wall, incongruous primary-coloured plastic. Rubbish from the Summer Fair, Sullivan thinks. He's seen it advertised on posters and flyers. Crafts and face-painting. Dog show. Pimm's.

'Odd to build a church such a distance from the rest of the village,' says Walton. 'You'd have to walk half a mile to go to a service.'

Sullivan remembers reading something about this once, but not the actual content. 'I think it might have been to do with the plague. Six bedrooms, would you say?'

Walton nods, abstracted. Sullivan can see, from the expression on her face, that she is engaged in preparation, as he is – the talk is just cover, while they tune themselves, like radios, to the right level of spontaneity and compassion for the news they are about to deliver. Sullivan hates this part of the job: the split second before you say the words when they guess from your face why you're there, and how you'd give anything not to have to say it and they'd give anything not to have to hear it; then the bewildered denial, the growing comprehension, the wait for the anguished spasm of the face, the tears . . .

When Sullivan's delivered death messages before, it's been in slab-grey housing estates or grimy streets where mothers with scraped-back hair and bad complexions swear at their toddlers, where junk-food wrappings litter the pavements and half the locals are on drugs. Here, the very air seems prosperous, ordered and calm. But, Sullivan reminds himself, bad things can happen anywhere.

He opens the car door.

SIX MONTHS EARLIER

TWO

Sophie stared at the returned letter. YOU SMUG BITCH in red, furious capitals, right across the paragraph about their trip to New Zealand and the skiing holiday in Zermatt. It was as if the words were shouting at her, drowning out the brisk jollity of 'Ding Dong Merrily on High' carolling from her laptop, and spoiling her private pre-Christmas ritual.

She hadn't meant to look at the letter, but it had come out of the desk drawer with the list of people who'd sent them cards the previous year. Most of them liked her round robins, she knew. They wrote little notes like 'We always look forward to hearing all your news' underneath the signatures and kisses.

It had happened two years in a row, now. The first letter, visible in the open drawer, had been returned with YOU'RE SO BLOODY PLEASED WITH YOURSELF scrawled over the news about Poppy's distinction in Grade 5 Violin and Alfie's better-than-expected mock A-level results. Sophie glanced down apprehensively, as if the thing might levitate by its own malicious agency and come to rest on her lap.

She wasn't sure why she'd kept the returned letters. When she'd shown them to Leo, he'd made a joke about an old-fashioned troll, ugly and stupid, who probably lived under an actual bridge. This troll wasn't *that* stupid, though – he or she obviously knew where to put an apostrophe.

Sophie had tried to work out who'd sent the letters back. They'd been sent in new envelopes, the address typed on what seemed to be an old-fashioned typewriter with a thick, serifed font. The first one had come from Harlow in Essex, and they didn't know anyone who lived there. The second had come from Scunthorpe, and no one they knew lived there, either. In fact, Sophie couldn't imagine who *did* live in Scunthorpe. She wasn't even sure where it was.

She'd considered having a Hamilton family Facebook page with a Christmas message instead, but the children had vetoed it. Besides, proper Christmas cards, with a letter inside, were so much nicer. Not everyone had email and anyway, you couldn't put an e-card on your mantelpiece. Of course, their cards weren't family photos. Sophie drew the line at such narcissism – in any case, she'd never get Leo to cooperate, or the boys, despite the fact that they took selfies and uploaded them on social media all the time – and someone needed to keep up the old traditions, so Highland cattle in the snow, robins, and religious subjects by old masters were the order of the day. It was a good way to keep in touch with people they didn't see often – or in some cases, it had to be admitted, at all.

At this time of year, Sophie always reflected on just how fortunate she was. Not in a smug way, though. Never that. Just thankful – although, God knew, she'd worked for it. Even with help from Imanuela (the Romanian au pair) and Mrs Palmer (the twice-weekly cleaner – local, bulky, and of indeterminate age), the sheer level of organization needed to keep the household going – not to mention the shop she'd opened a couple of years ago with her friend Melissa – was exhausting. However, it was undoubtedly true that she and her family didn't have to worry about money. They lived in a lovely house in a beautiful part of the country, Leo had a good job in the City (it was just a pity that he had to be in London all week), and – more importantly, because it was something money couldn't buy – everyone was healthy.

Sophie had always felt that her round-robin letter struck just the right balance. Wanton showing off was out, as was the false modesty of the humblebrag; what she was doing was simply reporting the facts. She *had* had a new kitchen last year – although not the whole thing as the small room where they kept the freezer still needed redecorating – and they *had* had a trip to Rwanda to see the mountain gorillas, and the yacht – named *Alzapop* in a play on the children's names – *had* needed a refit. And it hadn't all been wonderful. The upheaval when the builders were in had been horrendous; an ominous crack had appeared in the lining of the swimming pool; Zac had somehow managed, on his fifteenth birthday, to set fire to his bedroom, and last month Dexter the black Labrador had inexplicably eaten a pair of her knickers, necessitating a visit to the vet.

She'd definitely put that last one in: if she played down Leo's rage when the dog had puked all over the hand-knotted Chinese rug she'd just bought for the hall it made quite a funny little story, especially the bit when the vet asked if she wanted her underwear back.

Stuffing the defaced letter back into the drawer, Sophie resumed typing. *We were on tenterhooks waiting for Alfie's A-level* *results, but we needn't have worried – four A*s. He's got into his father's alma mater, Cambridge – Economics at Clare, if you please – but he's having a gap year first, travelling the world. At the moment he's in America, and he plans to go to Borneo in the new year to work on a marine life conservation project. He'll also get a British Sub-Aqua Club Sports Diver qualification. Poppy continues to excel at school, passing all her exams with flying colours. She's doing well with her music too, and is now, aged eleven, the youngest member of the school orchestra . . .*

If only Poppy were not so anxious, Sophie thought. She worried constantly, and regarded anything less than perfection as a failure. Even as a young child she'd become tearful and disconsolate if her colouring had gone over the lines.

Still, Poppy was both clever and conscientious – unlike Zac. Sophie paused, wondering how to parlay her middle child's irresponsibility and general lack of attention to anything except *World of Warcraft* into sensitivity and endearing quirkiness. At least she could write that he enjoyed school, which was true – the problem was that he never seemed to do any work. Each report sent Leo into a fresh paroxysm of fury about money wasted on school fees, with threats to take him out of Oddham's and send him to the local comprehensive if he didn't get his act together.

There's never a dull moment with Zac around – he continues to entertain and confound us. No. Too easy to read between the lines.

She deleted the sentence. Perhaps a glass of wine might help. The bottom right-hand corner of the screen said 19:35 – definitely past wine o'clock. Poppy (who could be judgemental about her parents' drinking) was in her room doing her homework. Zac (who'd probably ask if he could have some) was in his room, too, doing God-knew-what.

8

Sophie wandered out of her study and down the hall into the new kitchen, where she poured herself a glass of Domaine Pélaquié Côtes du Rhône (recommended in the *Telegraph*: 'like crushed crimson velvet, but also pleasingly fresh'). She drank half of it leaning against the counter, then topped up and returned to her study. She'd start a fresh paragraph and come back to Zac later.

Leo is . . . What? Leo was Leo. That was what she loved about him. He was there, dependable and calm – well, except when he had a go at her about spending or Zac's behaviour sent him into a spin. Stolid. That was the word for Leo. It sounded dull and thick – suety, almost – but it was a good word, four-square and reliable. It was the reason she'd married him. What he'd offered had been so utterly different to the rackety bohemianism of her existence with her mother, the desperation dressed up as spontaneity with countless house moves and Margot's endless different men, chaos presented as fun and excitement and not being like other people. All Sophie had ever wanted was to be like other people, and Leo, with his public-school background, Cambridge degree, good job and traditional parents, was a perfect specimen.

Leo was security and comfort, a bulwark against loss and calamity. Not only that, but he was funny, too, and tender – and if, after nineteen years, the excitement had rather left the bedroom, that was only to be expected. In any case, Leo had never expected her to swing from a chandelier – he was, and remained, a sweetly conventional lover.

Not that she was going to write any of that, of course. Perhaps she ought to park Leo, too, for the time being, and say something about Margot. As far as she knew, her mother didn't have lovers any more, apart from an occasional visit from the old hippie who lived in the next village. Margot's Suffolk cottage, on the rare occasions Sophie visited, seemed ever more cluttered and untidy, and, judging by her behaviour when she'd come to stay for a few days in the summer, she was growing increasingly vague. She'd kept putting things in odd places: wristwatch down the side of the sofa, keys and coins in the salad drawer of the fridge. She was on three different types of medication but seemed to have no idea about how many tablets she was supposed to take or how often, and had insisted, when Sophie'd tried to get to the bottom of it, that she was making a fuss about nothing. Now, guilty that she'd given in too easily, Sophie decided it would be best to leave Margot out of the letter entirely. After all, nobody wanted to read a list of health problems.

She drank some more wine and made a note to remind herself to add bits about the Senegalese child they were sponsoring and how Poppy and her friends had raised money for the local animal sanctuary. She'd really been looking forward to writing the letter this evening – it usually went like a breeze once she'd got started – but she couldn't get into it, somehow, knowing those angry, spiteful scrawls were still in her desk drawer.

It was no good. Sophie shut down her laptop, drained her glass, and stood up. Reaching inside the drawer, she extracted both letters, and, crumpling them in her fist, went down the hall to the sitting room. The fire wasn't really necessary – the central heating was perfectly adequate – but Imanuela had laid it anyway, and all Sophie had to do was set a match to the twists of newspaper at the bottom. She waited until the flames were starting to lap at the edges of the logs, then dropped the two balled-up pages onto the top. They were consumed in a few bright seconds, reduced to flakes of ash that drifted out onto the hearth.

It was what she should have done in the first place – what Leo had suggested she do. She should have listened to him, although it hadn't seemed to matter so much when she'd thought the letter was just a one-off. Now there were two, and perhaps there would be another after Christmas, and then another the following year, and another . . . But they were nothing, after all. There and gone. The hater, gone up in smoke.

That was better. Sophie went into the kitchen to fetch another glass of wine. When she returned, she found Dexter stretched out on the rug in front of the blaze. Hearing her, he lifted his head for a moment, then settled back with a happy sigh.

They couldn't touch her, whoever they were. Sophie made herself comfortable in the armchair and contemplated the restful, elegant room she'd created.

Everything was all right, and Christmas would be wonderful. She'd carry on with her letter tomorrow.

THREE

'Margot's getting more absent-minded.' Leo was standing in front of one of the sitting-room windows, staring out at the pond and jingling the change in both his pockets so that his trousers were drawn tight across his buttocks. 'The day before she left, I found her spooning Mrs Palmer's instant coffee into a mug with a teabag already in it. I'm starting to wonder how long she's going to be all right living on her own.'

'She keeps telling me not to fuss.' Sitting on the sofa with her cup of coffee and looking at Leo side-on, Sophie could tell, both from his stance and his semi-detached tone of voice, that he didn't really want to talk about her mother. Neither did she. Having got through both Christmas and New Year without mishap, she was tired. Some praise, she thought, would have been nice – whether for the artfully arranged swags of beribboned pine up the staircase, the lights and the splendid tree; or for the lavish meals, delivered on time with no help from Imanuela, who'd gone home for a week; or for organizing the annual New Year's Day buffet lunch for local friends and Leo's parents; or – better still – for all of it. He'd bought her a lovely bracelet for Christmas, but he hadn't *said* anything, and usually, he did. She realized now that this annual speech, short and heartfelt, about how much he appreciated 'all the things you do for us', was just as important as the present. He'd told her, the previous evening as they were going to bed, that he wanted to get back to London early, and now, lunch over and the lift to the station beckoning, she had a feeling of incompleteness. 'Actually,' she added, trying to keep her voice light, 'she asked me if *you* were all right.'

'Did she?' Leo carried on staring at the garden.

'Yes, she did. Are you all right?'

'Mmm.' Leo did some more jingling.

'You just seem a bit . . . well, distant.'

'Do I?' Still he didn't turn round. 'Just tired, I suppose.'

He did look it, she thought. Although not particularly tall, and certainly not fat, he was solid, with – usually – an upright posture, but now his broad shoulders were slumped and there was a weary look, bruised and pouched, about his eyes. This was no good. They weren't having a conversation, just saying words as if they were two strangers thrown together by chance and trying to fill the empty space between them. They had, she now realized, spent almost no time alone together (unless you counted time spent asleep), in the past ten days, and pretty much all of their conversation had been purely logistical, the whirl of activity – meals, outings, party-going – masking the lack of intimacy. I love you, she wanted to say now. I love you, and I know how hard you work. Yes, she wanted praise, but more, she realized, she wanted the familiar feeling of time well spent, things well done, of being part of their team of two that made it all possible. Sensing that any display of affection would receive only a perfunctory response, she said, 'Alfie seems happy, doesn't he?'

'Bigger.'

'Well, yes. He's filling out.'

'When's he off again?'

'A couple of weeks. He's really excited about it.'

Leo sighed repressively. 'I suppose I'd better sort out some more funds for him.'

Sophie searched for something to change the subject. It would be a mistake to mention Zac. The previous day, Leo had left his Porsche in the driveway with the key in the ignition, and finding Zac behind the wheel and about to start the thing up hadn't done much for father–son relations. Poppy had been a source of annoyance, too, announcing on Christmas Eve that she'd decided to become vegetarian.

More to break the impasse than anything else, Sophie put down her coffee and went to join him by the window. She watched the rain dripping off the nearest clump of trees for a moment before saying, 'All a bit soggy, isn't it?'

Leo shrugged.

'Shame we didn't get any snow.'

'I keep telling you.' Leo sounded irritated. 'We're too near the sea.' He shifted his weight slightly, leaning away from her, and said, 'I met that friend of yours when I was out with Dexter.'

'Which friend?'

'You know . . .' Leo thought for a moment. 'Scruffy. Mid-fifties. Got a Border collie.'

'Oh, you mean Belinda. The dog's called Robbie.'

'Does she live round here?'

Sophie nodded. 'Over towards Brancaster. She told me she used to live somewhere right on the coast, near Cromer, but she had to move because of the erosion.'

'Silly place to buy a house.'

Sophie pictured an asphalt road leading off a precipice as the spray plumed above unstrung and swaying telegraph poles, whole cottages capsizing and bungalows drowning as the waves tore chunks out of the cliffs. She didn't think Belinda had ever actually described any of that in the two or three years she'd known her, but it was hard to remember – like all conversations between dog walkers, theirs tended to be fitful, the rhythms constantly interrupted by the need to throw balls, pat heads and deploy 'poo bags'. 'I don't know if it was actually *hers*,' she said. 'I mean, I don't know her that well.'

'She was at Miles and Melissa's party,' said Leo, as if this meant that Belinda and Sophie must be bosom chums.

'Yes, she was. Actually, that was a bit embarrassing. I know she wasn't wearing a uniform or anything, but I had the impression that she wasn't a guest – that they'd paid her to hand round the canapés and things. I wasn't sure if I was supposed to talk to her or not.'

'Was she? Working, I mean.'

'I don't know. I meant to ask Melissa about it afterwards, but I forgot. But if Belinda's a bit hard up, I wondered if she'd like a few hours in the shop.'

She knew, even before she'd finished saying it, that she'd made a mistake. Leo reacted instantly, as though she'd flicked a switch. 'Jesus, Soph! We are *haemorrhaging* money. Over forty grand a year in school fees, and we'll have to go on supporting

Alfie for Christ knows how long, and there's all of *this*. Every time I set foot in this place, there's more expense.'

'"This place" is your home, Leo.' Sophie laid a placating hand on his arm. '*Our* home. If things aren't going well at work . . . You haven't said anything, so I assumed—'

'Yes, you assumed.' Leo twitched away from her. 'You take it all for granted.'

'No, Leo, I don't. But if you don't tell me—'

'Tell you what?'

Bewildered, Sophie fumbled for words. 'If you're . . . I don't know . . . in trouble . . .'

'I'm not "in trouble",' he mimicked. 'I'm not one of the children.'

'Then what . . . ? Please, Leo, I don't understand.'

'No, I know you don't. You just stand there all . . . *glossy* . . . and expect me to deliver.'

Stung by the injustice of this, Sophie said, 'Leo, that's not fair. We agreed that I'd stay at home and bring up the children, and we agreed to move here from London. We both thought it would be better, and it is. And there's the shop. We'll soon be—'

'What, in profit? No, you won't. The shop *loses* money, Sophie. You can't even cover the overheads, never mind paying your-selves a wage.'

'That's because we've only just started.'

'It's been eighteen months, Soph. Be realistic. It's a hobby. You've got that girl doing all the real work. You and Melissa just swan about buying up bits of fancy tat.'

'Firstly, we need Megan. Secondly, it isn't "fancy tat", it's good quality; and thirdly, it sells – we did really well in the run-up to Christmas. Those tapestry cushions we got in, and the hand-printed cards, and—'

'Yes, fine, but what about *after* Christmas? Nobody buys anything in January, and now you're proposing to take somebody else on!'

'That's not fair. You were all for it when we started.'

'I didn't realize how much it was going to cost me. Neither did Miles – and we're *still* bankrolling the bloody thing. And there's Imanuela, as well.'

'I can't do without her, Leo. Not while we're still getting the shop on its feet.'

'Which it's never going to be, as far as I can see. Imanuela can't stay forever, Soph. Apart from anything else, we always said we'd turn the cottage into a holiday let.'

'I know, but not *now*!'

'Why not now? If you got rid of the shop and concentrated on that, at least we'd have a realistic prospect of more money coming in.'

'Yes, but it would cost money to do it up, and that would be more outlay.' Sophie had never liked the idea of a holiday let. All right, the cottage – currently occupied by Imanuela – was tucked behind the garages and the outhouse, and had its own little patch of garden, but she didn't like the idea of having to be constantly on hand for demanding strangers. She expected Leo to have an argument for this, but instead – and more disconcertingly – he just stared at her for a long moment before turning back towards the garden. 'And,' she continued, 'there'd be endless fuss from the Historic England people if we started changing things.'

'No, there wouldn't. It's only the house that's listed, not the cottage.'

'Well, even if it isn't listed, it's still going to cost money, isn't it?'

Sophie waited for a response. Surely, after all that, he wasn't going to just give in about the holiday let? And if he was, what had the conversation actually been *about*?

'It's just . . .' Leo rubbed a hand across his face. 'I feel I'm knocking myself out to pay for all this stuff that we don't really need. How much was Christmas, for example?'

'I'm perfectly capable of economizing, Leo. If you'd just *said* . . . And we don't have to go away over Easter, and—'

'Of course we don't *have* to! We don't *have* to do or have any of it. I feel like a hamster on a wheel – we've got something, now we've got to have something else, and something else after that. The goalposts keep moving. I don't feel . . . I don't know, *connected* to myself any more. Not in control. Everything's got away from me and I can't see the *point* of any of it.' Leo's face seemed to lose all definition, and, for an awful moment, Sophie thought he was going to cry. 'I'm sorry, Soph.'

Sophie didn't know what to say. She felt terrified. What was he trying to tell her? He patted her clumsily on the shoulder. 'It's not that I don't appreciate you, and Christmas was lovely, but it's just . . .' Leo shook his head as if his thoughts had defeated him. 'Look, I'd better go upstairs and sort a few things out. You must be tired, too, after all that hard work – I can get a taxi to the station, if you like.'

'No!' The word burst out, too loud, too sudden. 'I mean, it's fine. I can take you.'

'OK, then. Thanks.' Leo gave her a tight little smile and left the room.

As she drove home in the dusk, Sophie felt very alone. Getting out of her Mercedes SUV at King's Lynn station, Leo had said all the right things, but now, for the first time since they'd moved to Norfolk, she felt abandoned, as though the place were an island with life going on somewhere else. Which Leo's weekday life did, of course. She'd never really known much about his job. At first she'd tried to understand, even read books with titles like *How the City Works*, but the subject remained stubbornly opaque. She'd always paid attention when Leo talked about the stresses and strains – that was only fair – but she never felt that she had much to contribute beyond a sympathetic ear. Which was all he'd ever seemed to need . . . But what had he wanted from her a couple of hours ago, in the sitting room? That stuff about getting and spending – had he actually meant that, or something entirely different?

Sophie looked out of the car window at the vast expanse of land, sombre and flat, dotted with gaunt trees, the only sign of habitation the square grey tower of a distant church. At the end of it all was the fraying coastline, with its banded, crumbling cliffs. Sophie imagined Belinda's house toppling into the waves with her inside, screaming through a broken window into the wind, and accelerated, shuddering. Once she was back in the warmth, light and safety of the Old Rectory, she'd feel better.

She always told people that she loved the sea. What she didn't say was that what she loved wasn't being in the sea, or even on it. The yacht tended to make her seasick, especially if she were down in the cabin. Tablets made no difference, and there were too many things on the deck to trip over. The neatness of the *Alzapop*'s interior, the varnished wood and the way everything fitted neatly into place, appealed to her – if only it would *stay still*. What she really enjoyed was watching the ocean from the shore and feeling safe from its immensity and power. As a child, cartoons of desert islands with their single palm trees had upset her. The jaunty captions had never compensated for the image of the lone figure, marooned and ragged, doomed to die in isolation, always supposing that he (and it was always a 'he') wasn't obliterated by a tidal onslaught.

It hadn't been a good start to the year. All that stuff Leo had come out with about not being in control . . . It's all very well for him, she thought irritably. He didn't understand. Having money meant that you *were* in control – that was the whole point of it. During her childhood, Margot's lack of funds and haphazard housekeeping had meant that she'd often come home from school to an empty fridge. There'd been times, too, when they'd had to run away in the middle of the night, leaving half their stuff behind, because they'd owed too much rent. All across north London, the pair of them had camped out in the spare rooms of friends in a jumble of sleeping bags, ashtrays and the debris of meals, with sheets hastily strung across the windows for curtains, hissing gas fires and tussocky, littered gardens – 'Isn't this *fun*, darling?'

No, it hadn't been fun. It had been utterly miserable. Happiness was a settled home with a full pantry and the ability to pay bills on time, and Leo could only talk like that because he'd never known anything different.

Was it only a general dissatisfaction, though, or was there something else? Sophie swatted at the thoughts that buzzed round the edges of her mind. She'd always worked hard on her appearance. Diet, exercise, hairdresser, manicurist, beautician – although her dark-brown hair showed no grey as yet, and her olive skin was smooth. Perhaps she should think about some Botox, as well, and maybe some new lingerie. People often felt a bit low after Christmas, didn't they?

Still. New year, new start. She and Melissa needed to have a good chat about the shop, work out how to up their game. It wasn't as if she didn't have plenty of ideas. And the dining-room curtains needed cleaning, and Poppy needed some new shoes . . . She'd make a list when she got home. The image of herself sitting in her study, practical and organized, was soothing.

Everything would be all right, Sophie told herself. Leo was bound to perk up once he was back in the swing of things – he was going shooting with Miles and the others next weekend, and he always enjoyed that. There'd been no returned round-robin letter, either. Perhaps the person who'd sent them back the two previous years had seen the error of their ways – or just grown up a bit. Sophie imagined the nameless, faceless, genderless person clouded in shame, and felt compassion for the unknown individual, and pleasure at herself for feeling it.

These reactions saw her home, and the sight of 'their' church seemed to underline the rightness of them.

FOUR

'. . . and Dexter went absolutely ballistic – you know how much he hates cats. He shot straight across the road, taking me with him, and if Belinda hadn't been there, I don't know what would have happened.'

Leo, gin and tonic in hand, prodded the recumbent Labrador with his toe. 'Bad dog. Who's Belinda?'

'*You* know. Dog walker. The one with the collie. It was a few days ago – we were talking about what Alfie's been up to in Borneo, and I wasn't paying attention. Dexter nearly dragged me off my feet.'

'What would you do if you actually caught a cat, Dexter?'

Sophie got up to put another log on the sitting-room fire. 'He'd probably die of shock.'

'Or even a kitten? You'd get scratched . . . or bitten. Bitten by a kitten, you silly old thing.' Leo rubbed his foot over Dexter's side so that the dog turned over onto his back, slitty-eyed with pleasure.

'Shall I get some nibbles?' Sophie put down the poker.

'What have we got?'

'Olives, crisps, wasabi peas . . .'

'Yes to everything. Only managed a sandwich for lunch. God knows what was in it – tasted like carpet underlay.'

'Poor old you.' Sophie paused to pat Leo's shoulder on her way out of the room. To her surprise, he reached round and, taking hold of her hand, planted a kiss on the palm.

It was late March, the end of the school term. Home early for the Easter weekend, Leo was relaxed and expansive, the mood that had enveloped him after Christmas apparently a distant memory. Sophie had taken great care, in the intervening months, not to irritate him by suggesting anything that would require extra expenditure, so they weren't going away as they usually did. Although he'd been a bit abstracted recently, the prospect of a quiet few days at home seemed to please him, as did the fact that Zac had, despite never seeming to do any work, managed surprisingly good grades in his mock GCSEs.

Returning from the kitchen, Sophie deposited the plate of snacks on the small table beside Leo's chair and took her glass over to one of the windows, where she stood watching the late-afternoon shadows lengthening across the lawn. 'Reverend Barker came over this afternoon, about the CCTV.'

'Is he going ahead with it?'

'Yes, on the side of the tower. He says it won't be intrusive – it's mainly for inside the graveyard and the bit of the driveway that's shared.'

'Well, that's OK. More security for us. When's it going up?'

'About six weeks' time, he said. They wanted it sooner – there's been a lot of vandalism directed at churches recently

– but apparently there's a bit of a waiting list. You wouldn't think people would do that to a church, would you?'

'Don't be naive, Soph. They'll pinch the lead, too, given half a chance.' Leo hitched one ankle over the opposite knee and brushed an invisible speck off his Timberland deck shoe. 'We'll go to the service on Sunday, shall we?'

'I thought it might be nice.'

'Good. What else is happening?'

'Well, Miles and Melissa are coming over for dinner tomorrow – just kitchen sups – Zac's got a rugby match on Saturday and Poppy's got a sleepover at Ottilie's. Imanuela's going down to London for a few days, and I'll have to do a couple of stints in the shop over the weekend, but it's only for a few hours . . . Oh, and we've been invited to drinks at the Powells' on Sunday evening, but I hedged because I wasn't sure if you'd want to.'

'I don't mind.'

'I thought you didn't like Jeremy.'

'I don't, much. He's a bully, and he's always half pissed. Say yes if you want, though.'

'It's just that I feel a bit sorry for *her*, and . . .' Sophie saw an expression of wicked hilarity on Leo's face. 'What?'

'I always think she's going to try and mate with my leg.'

'Leo!' Penny Powell, small, bright-eyed and almost permanently quivering with abject eagerness to compensate for her awful husband, was a lot like a terrier, and the image of her frenziedly humping away at Leo's calf was too much. 'You can't say that,' she spluttered.

'I just have.' Leo looked pleased with himself.

'I suppose it'd be better than mating with *him*.'

'We don't know, do we?' said Leo, airily. 'He might be dynamite in the sack.'

'*Jeremy*? Stop it,' she added, flapping her free hand at him. 'You're making me feel sick.'

'What about Monday, then?'

'I hadn't got anything planned. Thought you'd like some downtime.'

'Sounds good. Any post?'

'I'll get it. Alfie emailed some photos, too. He's got a very pretty new girlfriend.' He'd sent pictures of the two of them standing on a wooden jetty, his arm around her shoulders, and his expression that of a man who'd managed, against the odds, to land an exceptionally large fish.

Sophie felt happy as she went to her study for the letters and her laptop. She must remember to mention to Leo, while he was in this mood, about the trip she had planned to the trade fair at the Business Design Centre in Islington, for the shop. She'd ask Imanuela to babysit so that she could stay up in London and they could go out to dinner or see a film or something. Both, perhaps. Leo'd be OK about it, she thought: he'd barely said a word about the shop since his outburst at New Year – and in any case, they were doing rather well now that business had picked up again after the post-Christmas slump. There was also the matter of their summer holiday – surely, as they'd saved money by not going away for Easter, a couple of weeks in the summer wouldn't be an issue? She'd been wondering about Costa Rica, or possibly Nicaragua.

Leo admired the photographs Alfie had sent – 'I see what you mean, Soph. Good for him' – then began riffling through the small pile of letters, picking out those that interested him and dropping the rest on the floor beside his armchair.

'Fancy a refill?'

'Thanks. God, all these charities . . . Ah.' He shucked a bank statement and scanned its contents. 'That seems about right . . . And there should be a quarterly report from the financial services lot somewhere . . . Here it is . . . Oh, and there's a letter for you, Soph.'

'Is there?' Sophie held out the gin and tonic and, at the same moment, caught sight of the typewritten name and address, heavy letters pecked into the paper.

'Look out, you'll spill it! There you go.'

Holding the envelope in her fingertips as though it might burn her, Sophie retreated to the other end of the room.

'Aren't you going to sit down?'

'Yes, in a minute. Just getting myself another drink.' Sophie found her empty glass and, putting it down on the drinks tray, stared at the letter. Surely the old-fashioned typewriting was just coincidence? The other letters had been returned straight after Christmas. Besides, this one was postmarked Norfolk, and the two other letters had come from further afield. Get a grip, she told herself. Stop being absurd.

All the same, she was glad she wasn't on her own. Taking her drink, she went back to sit opposite Leo in front of the fire, where she took a deep breath and ripped open the envelope. Released, the folded piece of paper seemed to spring open almost before she'd touched it – and, spewed across her neatly typed Christmas letter in frenzied red capitals, was: LEO AND I HAVE BEEN HAVING AN AFFAIR FOR OVER TWO YEARS AND NOW HE'S GOING TO LEAVE YOU. LET'S SEE HOW SMUG YOU ARE THEN, YOU STUPID BITCH.

FIVE

Sophie recoiled as if she'd been hit in the face. LET'S SEE HOW SMUG YOU ARE THEN, YOU STUPID BITCH.

Shock made her gasp. The words seemed to be rising off the page towards her. She closed her eyes to keep them at bay, but as soon as she looked again, they leapt back up into her face. LEO AND I HAVE BEEN HAVING AN AFFAIR. She felt rooted to the chair, as if her entire body had solidified, like cement. HE'S GOING TO LEAVE YOU.

'Soph? Are you all right?' Leo had raised his head from his investment report and was staring at her.

'Yes, fine,' she gabbled. 'Just remembered something.' Struggling to her feet, she fled the room.

It wasn't true. It couldn't be. She stood in the downstairs loo, holding the sides of the basin with the letter still grasped in her right hand, staring down at the plughole, gagging at the bile that had risen in her throat.

It was a lie. It had to be. Leo would never leave her and the children.

He wouldn't. He couldn't.

Oh, God. She was going to be sick.

'Soph? *Soph!* Where are you?'

'Coming!' Sophie rinsed her mouth and splashed water on her face. Snatching up the now water-spotted letter from the side of the basin, she went out into the hall to find Leo standing at the bottom of the stairs, drink in hand.

'Oh, there you are. What's for supper?'

Sophie felt as though she were in a dream. The hall seemed to tip and lurch around her, so that she reached for the newel post to steady herself. Could it be true? He wasn't . . . *different.* Stop it, she told herself. It's nonsense. 'Sorry,' she said. 'Supper . . . I hadn't really thought . . .'

'Never mind. Why don't I go and get a takeaway?'

Sophie looked at him, and then up the staircase. As her eye followed its elegant curve, she experienced the same precarious sensation, and, for a wild, helpless moment, felt as if the whole house might be plucked away into the air by an enormous invisible hand, leaving her cowering, alone in empty darkness.

'Soph?'

'Yes, fine. Whatever you like. I'll just . . .' Sophie made for the safety of her study, leaving Leo bellowing up the stairs to Zac and Poppy about whether they wanted Chinese or fish and chips.

She closed the door and sat down at her desk, smoothing the treacherous paper out on the flat surface. LEO AND I HAVE BEEN HAVING AN AFFAIR FOR OVER TWO YEARS. That would mean – if Leo *were* having an affair, which he *wasn't* – that it had started sometime before March 2014 . . . and the first returned Christmas letter had been at the beginning of January 2014. So – if it *were* true, which it *wasn't* – the dates would fit. If it's not true, muttered a little voice at the back of her mind, why did you react like that? Why didn't you just show the letter to Leo, as you did with the other two? Why are you even thinking like this?

Perhaps whoever it was just fancied Leo – well, they were obviously jealous. Not to mention vindictive. Someone with a grudge? The closest she'd come to an argument recently was having to tell off Megan about the state of the Hamilton De Witt stockroom, but it couldn't be her because she'd only known her since the shop opened in June 2014, and the first letter had arrived six months before that . . . In any case, Megan wasn't on her main Christmas card list – and the idea of her having an affair with Leo was so absurd as to be actually funny. A salty, lippy seaside girl, never without a hangover at the weekend, dive-bombing the boys in the pub and the chippy, squawking like a seagull, knowing everyone, and everyone knowing her.

'Mum?' An arm with several plaited wristbands appeared round the door, followed by Zac's tousled head. 'Dad says what fish do you want?'

'Oh . . . Anything. Cod. I don't mind.'

'OK.'

The door slammed. Sophie heard Zac running down the hall and crashing out of the back door, and then a car engine.

The list. She'd get it out and have a look. Perhaps the Norfolk postmark on this letter meant that the person might live nearby . . . Unless they'd posted it here deliberately, to show her that they were close to home – closing in on Leo, and her, and their life. Except that Leo wasn't having an affair, was he?

HE'S GOING TO LEAVE YOU.

'He isn't going to leave me.'

Sophie retrieved the list from her 'Christmas' drawer and

then, stuffing the letter and its envelope inside, slammed it shut. She must be able to narrow it down. Pushing aside the thought that she'd already attempted this on two occasions in the last two years, and failed, she decided to start by crossing off the names of the people it couldn't possibly be – Leo's sister Charlotte, for example, who lived in Seattle; his cousin in Brisbane; his old secretary, long retired . . .

That got rid of eighteen names, but there were still over a hundred and fifty – and some of them, she now realized, didn't actually ring a bell. Who the hell were Colin and Marjorie Asher and Mr and Mrs Ben Shapcott? And who were Catriona Bickworth, Rowan Ireson and Isabel Melling? Come to think of it, there had seemed to be quite a few more cards to write than usual . . . Perhaps her list had somehow got mixed up with the one on the shop's database, when Megan was updating it.

Shit. She'd just have to leave it until she could ask her about it. I should have put some sort of code on the letters, she thought – pencil marks, or filled the 'O's in. Something different on each one, so she could tell who was sending them back. Why hadn't she thought of that before? Because she wasn't that paranoid, that's why. But now . . .

Was she being naive? She and Leo only spent two nights a week together. The rest of the time he was in London, so there was no lack of opportunity. But there'd have been signs – names mentioned too often, presents given to assuage guilt, evidence of extra care taken with his appearance . . . Surely she'd have known that something was up?

Or would she?

That thing Leo had said after Christmas about her taking

things for granted . . . She'd thought that he was talking about money, but perhaps he'd meant himself.

SMUG BITCH.

She wasn't! She *loved* Leo. She'd been faithful to him and had his children and worked tirelessly to create this beautiful home for them all. Had he mentioned anyone's name a lot recently? She cast her mind back to the conversation they'd just had. Penny Powell didn't seem very likely, and she'd brought up the subject of the Powells herself, hadn't she, asking if he wanted to go over there for drinks. She'd mentioned Belinda, too, but Leo hadn't even remembered who she was, and anyway, she wasn't on the Christmas card list. There was Melissa, of course – but that was ridiculous. Melissa was her best friend, and, in any case, her name often came up in conversation because of the shop. Leo'd talked about some woman at work several times in the last few months, but that was because she'd been giving him a hard time. And it couldn't be her, because she wasn't on the Christmas card list.

Leo hadn't bought any new clothes recently, or not as far as she knew. There might be a whole rail of stuff in the flat in London, of course – although she hadn't noticed anything when she'd been there just before Christmas for *La Traviata* at Covent Garden. He'd belonged to a gym for a long time, and he was always well groomed, so no conclusions could be drawn there. The last time he'd bought her flowers was Valentine's Day, but that was normal. As for sex . . . Sophie winced. The expensive new lingerie she'd purchased in January had misfired badly. She'd forgotten to remove the wrappings from the bedroom wastepaper basket, and Leo, spotting the name on the boxes, had grilled her about how much it had all cost. It was true that they'd made love a few times since then, but it was more friendly and comfortable than actually passionate – but if he'd suddenly started prancing about the bedroom like a stallion, wouldn't that have been more suspicious? She was sure she'd read somewhere that people could get so turned on by a new lover that they started having more sex with their regular partner.

Was Leo fucking someone in London, and coming back here for weekends, treating her as though she were some sort of housekeeper-with-benefits? How fucking *dare* he?

A current of pure rage filled Sophie's body, making her hands shake and drumming in her ears, and she leapt up, bashing her knee hard against the underside of the desk. She'd get herself another drink, and she'd have it out with him as soon as they'd finished eating and Zac and Poppy had gone up to their rooms. Wincing, she hobbled down the hall to the sitting room, where she splashed a large measure of gin and a slosh of tonic into a fresh glass. A thudding noise made her turn, and she saw that Dexter was stretched out on his side in front of the fire, tail thumping lazily on the rug.

There was something about the way the animal fixed his big brown eyes on her, the look of absolute trust and devotion, which made her pause. She stood beside him for several minutes, drinking, feeling the voltage of her anger earthed by her contemplation of his solid, black-furred form.

She was playing right into the unknown sender's hands, reacting exactly how this vile woman hoped she would – which, even if she couldn't see the effect she was having, still meant that she had won.

Leo wasn't having an affair. Of course he wasn't. He was like Dexter, faithful and true. What was it Melissa had said to her, once? *If you two ever broke up, then I'd know there was no hope for the rest of us.*

She downed the rest of her gin and tonic. 'I do love you, Dex,' she told the dog, in a cross between a laugh and a sob. The Labrador thumped his tail again, and then, at the sound of the car coming up the drive, scrambled to his feet and trotted into the hall. Sophie put her empty glass on the tray and followed him. I'm not the stupid bitch, she thought. I've got all of this, and you – whoever you are – have nothing but spite.

SIX

Giving up on sleep at half past two, Sophie switched on the bedside lamp and, turning, leant over to stare at Leo's sleeping face. His eyelids twitched, but she knew he wouldn't wake up – Leo could sleep through anything. He looked peaceful, and also rather vulnerable, with his mouth slightly open and his jaw relaxed.

Sophie observed him minutely: the folds of his upper lids, the cross-hatching of lines at the outer corners of his eyes and the grey threading his light-brown curls. She thought of him standing in the bright kitchen that evening, a white Styrofoam box of fish and chips in each hand, calling for plates, distributing tomato ketchup and licking his fingers, raising a glass of red wine in a toast and pretending to give Zac a clip round the ear for teasing him. Watching him like that, at the centre of the noisy, happy domesticity, with the reassuring scent of warm batter, cooked fish and vinegar, she hadn't been able to believe that his affections lay elsewhere than with her – with all of them – but when she'd seen him stare into space in an unguarded moment, the feeling of doubt had returned.

NOW HE'S GOING TO LEAVE YOU.

She'd got to keep calm. Turning away from Leo, she lay down on her back. Her entire body was aching. As if I'm an old woman, she thought. Well, forty-five wasn't exactly *young*. Whatever she did, however hard she tried, it would be downhill from now on . . . You couldn't stop the clock.

Was that what Leo, at forty-eight, was trying to do? Oh, God – the weary old cliché of the male mid-life crisis. She'd thought the extent of *that* was the classic Porsche Targa he'd bought two years ago and the Silver Pigeon shotgun for his forty-fifth birthday.

Desiring a simpler existence was a sign of a mid-life crisis, as well. She'd read that in an article somewhere. So was thinking life was meaningless – another thing he'd said when they'd had that talk just after Christmas. The article had mentioned other stuff, too, like fretting about your job and feeling that you weren't progressing, that this was as good as it was going to get – which was pretty damn good, in Leo's case, but perhaps his complaining about the woman at work was a symptom of that. And then there was the obvious: sex to ward off death. I can't be on the downward slope, I'm fucking a twenty-three-year-old . . . She would be younger, because they always were. But surely Leo, nothing if not sensible, would accept the intimations of mortality with a rueful grace, not start sniffing round women young enough to be his daughter? It was undignified and it made a laughing-stock of her, too – and there'd be that awful, there-but-for-the-grace-of-God pity from her friends. That would be worst of all.

Unless they already knew. The enormity of the humiliation made Sophie sit up, gasping, as though she'd been drenched in cold water. Another cliché: the wife is always the last to know.

She lay down and turned over, away from Leo. She'd got to stop all this and get some sleep. Things always look much worse than they actually are when it's almost three in the morning and you've got insomnia, she told herself. Be *rational*.

If she confronted Leo with the letter and he was innocent, he'd be dismayed and hurt – 'How could you even think I'd have an affair with someone who'd behave like that, Soph?' She could imagine him saying that, the look on his face.

If she confronted him with the letter and he was guilty, then the moment he realized what the woman he'd been seeing was really like, he'd go off her. After all, however infatuated he might be, he'd surely still have some regard for his wife and children. But then again, he might say he was sorry that she'd found out that way but glad it was out in the open, because that made things easier, and that he'd leave in the morning and be in touch via a solicitor about the arrangements. All that stuff about household expenses – if Leo was planning to ask her for a divorce, he might have been moving money behind her back, liquidating their savings . . .

The house would have to be sold. She wasn't sure exactly how much Leo earned – it was a lot, but not enough for two such establishments, and he'd be bound to want a nice place to live. And then there were the school fees, and Alfie, who'd need money for university. She suddenly remembered the time in the hospital after he was born. She had never known, before, that there could be so *much* love. Holding him for the first time, she'd been overwhelmed, as though her heart might actually burst.

In some ways, she thought, it had been easier to care for the children when they were babies, feeding them, changing their nappies, lulling them to sleep, keeping them safe . . . If Leo left them high and dry financially, and Zac and Poppy had to leave Oddham's for the local comprehensive, she wouldn't be able to protect them then.

And suppose – oh, God – suppose this other woman was pregnant? LEO AND I HAVE BEEN HAVING AN AFFAIR FOR OVER TWO YEARS AND NOW HE'S GOING TO LEAVE YOU. Perhaps that was the reason. That would mean more expense, and Sophie's children would be relegated to second best, with *her* making sure that Leo hardly ever saw them . . .

No. No, no, no. The whole thing was *mad*. Leo was not having an affair. The letter was harassment, plain and simple. She'd call the police in the morning.

Yes, that's what she'd do. Switching off the bedside light, Sophie lay back and closed her eyes.

SEVEN

She hadn't called the police, of course. She hadn't said anything to Leo, either. Several times over the last four days she'd been on the point of it. Once, when they'd been walking down the beach after lunch on Sunday, huddled inside their coats, their feet crunching razor shells on the ribbed sand as they watched Zac and Poppy play frisbee with Dexter, she'd got as far as opening her mouth, but no sound had come out. She'd been about to try again, but the sight of the straggling, wind-distorted trees on the clifftop, and the thought of their clawed roots clutching at the precarious soil, had silenced her.

Now, on Monday afternoon, Leo was upstairs, packing a few things for the journey back to London, and she was in the utility room, spooning glistening chunks of dog food out of a tin while Dexter wriggled and skittered in anticipation.

Was Leo going to *her*? Even with Imanuela coming back this evening, Sophie could hardly follow him down to London to find out, especially now Zac and Poppy had started their three-week break – not to mention the shop being busier than usual, because of all the holidaymakers.

She was glad she hadn't let the whole business spoil the Easter weekend. Oddham's had won the rugby, so Zac was happy, Poppy had enjoyed herself at Ottilie's, and Leo had seemed chilled and genial. There'd been nothing untoward when Miles and Melissa had come for supper, or when they'd gone to the Powells' for drinks.

In church on Sunday, she'd found herself resolving to be a better person, kinder and less acquisitive, if only Leo were not having an affair. Thinking about it later, she realized that she hadn't been praying at all, but bargaining.

A couple of times in the last few days, Leo had asked her if she was all right, and, fearing knowing, pitying looks from the other mothers at the rugby match (that particular horror definitely hadn't looked better in the morning), she'd pleaded a headache. Except, of course – the thought made Sophie drop Dexter's metal bowl on the flagstone floor with a clatter – there was nothing to say that Leo's lover (assuming he had one) hadn't been at the match herself. After all, the letter had had a Norfolk postmark. She might have given the two previous letters to other people to post . . . Sophie tried to remember which of the parents were on her Christmas card list. She'd have to have a look when she came back from taking Leo to the station. And she still had to clear up the business of the possibly mixed-up lists – the shop had been too busy for her to ask Megan over the weekend.

Perhaps she ought to ask Zac – just in passing – whom Leo had talked to at the match. He might think it odd, though, and in any case he was pretty unobservant at the best of times (taps left running, dog shit tracked into the house).

Four days spent alternating between snatching at thoughts

and shoving them away had made her mind ramshackle, unsafe
– words that made her think of the places she and Margot had
lived in her childhood. Books and papers wedged under table
legs. Pictures that swayed crookedly when you walked past
them. Doors that stuck, loos that didn't flush.

That was then, Sophie told herself, and she was never, ever
going back there. She needed to make a plan. Part of her almost
wished Leo gone so that she could make a proper start. She
needed to be objective, to treat it as a project.

She'd already begun by searching Leo's study when everyone
else was out. There was nothing suspicious in his desk, briefcase
or pockets, but that wasn't conclusive, because of course he'd
be careful to keep anything incriminating at the flat in London.
He'd not brought his laptop home with him, but she wasn't sure
if that was significant – after all, if he wanted to communicate
with the woman, he could just use his mobile. Sophie hadn't
had a chance to look at that, because Leo kept it with him all
the time . . . but again, that didn't really mean anything, because
plenty of people refused to be parted from their phones. She
hadn't been able to find any mobile phone bills, though – and,
given that the billing address was the Old Rectory and that Leo
had fixed up a deal for both their phones, that was odd.

She needed to pay a visit to the London flat as soon as possible.
She hadn't mentioned the projected trip to London for the trade
fair – the letter had put it right out of her head – but perhaps
that was just as well. If Leo wasn't forewarned, he wouldn't
have a chance to get rid of anything incriminating. She'd have a
legitimate reason for being there, and she could swear that she
was sure she'd told him about the trip beforehand.

Leo having used her Merc to take Zac to the rugby match, she'd gone to the garage to check the history on the Porsche's satnav and found that it had been deleted. True, he didn't use the car often, and most of the journeys he made were local, to destinations he knew – but he had taken it to London several times in the past year. There was a car park below the flats, and Sophie had assumed that he'd always left the Porsche in there overnight, but perhaps that wasn't the case.

She'd have to come back to that. A glance in the glovebox had told her there wasn't anything suspicious lurking there, and she'd looked under the seats, too, but found nothing. She'd looked in the pockets of his suits, to make sure that there was nothing there – which there wasn't – and—

She'd forgotten Leo's overcoat, which was hanging in the downstairs cloakroom. Sophie put down the tea towel she was holding and ran down the hall to the small room beside the front door. Her fingers, rummaging blindly in the pockets, met nothing except a slightly damp ball of screwed-up tissues. She was about to drop it in the bin when she saw, on the soft white surface of the paper, a pastel-pink smudge.

Not her colour.

Sophie screwed up her eyes against the image of a woman with a lipstick-pink mouth kissing Leo on the concourse at King's Cross Station before he'd boarded the train home on Thursday afternoon. Maybe they'd just had lunch together in the beautiful hotel next door, lingering in the high-ceilinged Victorian elegance over pudding, coffee and brandy (come to think of it, where did Leo keep his credit card bills?). Maybe she'd been tearful about not seeing him for the next five days, and Leo had gently wiped the tears from her face and put them – and the trace of her lipstick – away in his pocket.

'So-oph! I'm ready to go.'

Leo was on his way downstairs.

EIGHT

Melissa looked up from cutting open the tape on the box. 'I'm not sure it's working. I think those photo frames would look better over there, next to the driftwood. We need to mix it up more.'

Sophie stood back and surveyed the window display, frowning. 'Maybe we need a bit more colour. I know we're going for Seaside Naturals, but don't you think it's a bit anaemic?'

'Try one of those in the middle.' Melissa waved the Stanley knife at one of the big azure-coloured ceramic pots Megan had just unpacked. 'Splash of summer sky.'

Sophie fetched the pot, put it in the centre of the display and moved a few bits and pieces around it, but without much conviction. Normally, she loved putting together the different colours, textures and shapes, and she felt confident in doing it – she'd worked at Liberty's before she'd married Leo – but today her pleasure was cancelled out by anxiety. 'Sorry, Lissa, I'm all over the place. Look, do you want a cup of coffee? I need a break.'

'We've only just got started.' There was an undertow of frustration in Melissa's voice. They'd planned to redo the window after the Easter weekend with some more of the new stuff they'd ordered, and the shop was supposed to be opening at midday. Sophie wondered if Miles, too, had been complaining about what it was all costing . . . But anyway, that was about to change. According to Megan, they'd had a record Easter weekend, with things flying off the shelves; she was in the stockroom now, working out what needed reordering.

'I just need a few minutes' break, that's all.'

Melissa pulled out a stack of Breton tops in individual plastic wrappings and started checking the sizes against the description on the box. Leo had once told her, in a tipsy moment, that he thought Melissa was sexy. She was certainly attractive – narrow blue eyes, sharp cheekbones – but in a very different way, Sophie knew, from herself. Not, she thought quickly, that Leo finding Melissa sexy meant anything. She'd always thought Miles was sexy, in a sleepy-eyed, Robert Mitchum sort of way, but that didn't mean she'd have an affair with him, any more than Leo would with Melissa. Anyway, Melissa had no reason to be jealous of her – Miles earned as much as Leo, their house was gorgeous, and their two children (well, not exactly children, because Toby was in his first year at Bristol) were lovely.

Of course it wasn't Melissa. Even if Leo did fancy her, he'd never be that stupid – and Melissa wasn't the type to have an affair. She really had got to pull herself together. Perhaps it would help to share it? She imagined herself telling Melissa about the letters, and Melissa comforting her, telling her it was the sender's problem, not hers. Megan was busy in the stockroom, and Poppy, who enjoyed helping, was combing the beach for suitable pebbles to make a pattern of baby footprints as edging for the Petit Bateau display, so there was no one to overhear.

'Er, *hello?*'

'Sorry, what?'

Melissa, arms full of blue-and-white stripes, was frowning at her. 'Are you OK? You were staring into the distance with a really weird look on your face.'

'It's just . . .' It flashed into Sophie's mind then that talking to Melissa might actually make things worse – she might see it as a challenge, a game of detection, to find out who had returned the wretched things. It doesn't feel like a game, Sophie thought. Not knowing exactly what it *did* feel like – apart from just plain wrong – was what was upsetting her so much, but she suddenly felt that airing aloud the possibility that Leo might be having an affair would give the idea an undeserved authority. 'I've got a bit of a headache,' she finished, lamely.

'Coffee's not a good idea, then. I've got some Nurofen in my bag – and why don't you go and see how Poppy's doing? Fresh air usually does the trick. It's not the end of the world if we open a few minutes late.'

By the time Sophie and Poppy had returned to Hamilton De Witt laden with flat stones and carefully graded pebbles – 'Those are only for the big toes, Mum – the others are smaller, see?' – Melissa had done a terrific job of the main display, and the kids' stuff in the side window, once Poppy had finished with it, looked great as well. Now, sitting in her study after lunch, Sophie figured that she had at least three clear hours to go through the Christmas list. She'd start by eliminating the names duplicated from the shop's database – Megan had finally owned up to problems with the mail merge function, but said she was pretty sure she'd sorted most of it out – and then she'd see if she couldn't come up with a shortlist of potential candidates.

After half an hour's winnowing, Sophie had a longlist of sixteen women in what she'd decided was the appropriate age group (twenty-five to forty-five, because you never knew – look at Camilla Parker Bowles), and Google searches on these had narrowed the field down to four.

Both Lucinda Prekopp and Polly Cosworth were recently divorced and lived in London; Liz Larwood (also London) and Natalie Johnson (Brighton) were both, according to their Facebook pages, single. Polly and Danny Cosworth had been neighbours when they'd lived in Clapham. Lucinda's husband Bill had worked with Leo at his previous company, and Sophie had an idea that Lucinda worked in the City, too. Liz and Natalie, both friends from school, had visited them in Clapham – not often, and not for dinner, but for drinks parties and the like – but only Natalie had come to Norfolk, and that was quite a few years ago. Liz was, or had been, a social worker, and Natalie was now, according to the Internet, the creative director of an independent television company 'dedicated to creating factual entertainment formats, with particular emphasis on health and lifestyle' (in other words, thought Sophie, thinly disguised freak shows).

On the face of it, Lucinda had had the most opportunity to bump into Leo, and it could have gone on from there. She'd be in her late thirties now, and she was certainly attractive. Polly Cosworth didn't, so far as Sophie could remember, have a job, and it was harder to see how her path might have crossed with Leo's, unless . . . She'd been a great one for organizing things, hadn't she? Everything from the local book group to raising money for charity. That last one was a possibility, because Sophie and Leo did attend the odd fundraising do in London – dinners in guildhalls and the like – and there'd been a couple of occasions when she'd not been able to attend so Leo had gone on his own. Polly was a few years older than Lucinda and not – to Sophie's way of thinking, at least – half so attractive, and it was very hard to imagine her having a conversation that didn't revolve around rotas and provisional dates, let alone pillow talk. Leo had told her once that Danny Cosworth had confessed to him that he was addicted to porn. Now, she enhanced the memory with Leo's statement that if he were married to Polly he'd be addicted to porn, too. Leo's voice, as he said this, was so clear in her mind that she couldn't remember if he had actually spoken the words, or if she was making it up – but either way, people could change, couldn't they? Perhaps Polly had started taking pole-dancing lessons and become a fully fledged sex goddess. Divorce had that effect on some women. They changed their hairstyle, dropped a dress size, and went wild.

Liz, Sophie thought, was the least likely of the four. In fact, judging by her Facebook page, she was well on the way to becoming a cat lady. Natalie, with her almond eyes and honey-coloured skin, was an altogether more plausible lover for Leo. She had, Sophie remembered, a bit of a history with married men, and this was confirmed by Google: photographs of her hand in hand, several years ago, with a soap star, and, more recently, with a well-known journalist and broadcaster, when both of them were still – officially at least – living with their spouses. And she'd flirted with Leo. That was the reason – not that she'd ever consciously formulated it in her mind, but there it was – that she'd not invited Natalie to Norfolk a second time.

But – and it was a big 'but' – would any one of them have written those things on the letters and returned them? Perhaps it was someone else entirely . . . Wearily, Sophie turned back to her Christmas list, and was just about to start looking through it again when a door banged, and there was a shout of 'Hello!'

Imanuela, back from the shops. Waitrose, joy of joys, had started to deliver the year before, but some things, like Leo's favourite artisan cheese, could only be got at specialist places, and the au pair had the use of the Nissan runaround. God, it couldn't be her, could it? Imanuela was stunning. Like a lot of Romanian women, she had that whole Sophia Loren thing going on – jet-black hair, slim and voluptuous at the same time. Alfie was crazy about her. And she could easily get hold of one of the Christmas letters.

No, wait. Imanuela had a boyfriend, Marius, and of course she'd only been with them about eighteen months, which wasn't long enough – and her predecessor, Mila from Serbia, had gone back to Novi Sad or wherever it was that she came from.

Perhaps she should attempt to analyse the handwriting? Don't be idiotic, Sophie told herself: when you see red capital letters almost stabbed through the paper, you don't need to be a graphology expert to know they're the work of someone who's angry and resentful.

Anyway, there was no point in sitting here and tormenting herself with ever more ridiculous ideas. For one thing, there was the laundry – a load of sheets to be washed, ready for Mrs P. to iron, and Zac would soon be out of clean rugby stuff, as well.

Her younger son's bedroom was a swamp of dirty clothes overhung with a miasma of testosterone and feet. Having flung open the windows and shovelled the whiffy garments into a laundry bag, she turned her attention to Poppy's room – pin-neat, as always, with the washing neatly folded in the basket – and, as an afterthought on the way downstairs, paused to check the basket in their en-suite. She hadn't expected to see much in there, but she'd forgotten that Leo had brought back a suitcase full of things from London at the weekend. Might as well do it now, she thought, cramming underwear, two dress shirts and a bathrobe on top of the children's stuff and bumping the now-bulging bag behind her down to the utility room.

Shaking it out on the floor, she shoved the first load of washing into the machine and watched it rotate, hoping that the motion of the suds would hypnotize her into a peaceful frame of mind, but it didn't work. She looked at her watch: almost six o'clock – at least an hour until sunset – and went out into the hall. Dexter, who'd been snoozing on the rug, peered up at her with hopeful eyes. 'Come on,' she said. 'Let's have a walk.'

It had rained in the afternoon and the fields and verges gleamed, verdant and lush. Delighted, the dog tugged Sophie down the lane and past the fringe of pine trees to the beach, where she let him off the lead and began walking towards the pewter-coloured sea, while gulls swooped overhead in great arcs.

A man whose wife committed adultery was a cuckold, she thought, but there wasn't a name for a wife whose husband had strayed – presumably because it wasn't considered such a big deal. Why bother to invent a special word, if male adultery didn't really count? Certainly, a cuckold might be an object of pity or scorn, but if a man cheated, the response was more, 'Welcome to the real world. Men stray, of course they do. Life's not a fairy tale.' She thought of the humiliated but stoic wives of politicians she'd seen, standing by their men as the cameras clicked, staying to protect their investment, both emotional and financial – and nobody ever believing it was just the one slip.

Maybe that was true of Leo, too. Supposing there had been others, and their life together had been a lie for years? Perhaps that was the reason he'd wanted the move to Norfolk – more freedom for his fun and games in London. Sophie felt as though she'd been punched. So much for intuition. She could feel her memories begin to curdle – romantic meals, holidays, anniversaries . . .

Wait. She didn't actually know that Leo had been unfaithful *once*, let alone serially. But imagine being divorced and having to be 'out there' again, trying to find someone new . . . At twenty-five, when she'd married Leo, it had all been so straightforward – you fell in love with someone and you married him – but not any longer. How did people even do that stuff any more? Even if middle-aged dating – which, let's face it, was what it would be – wasn't all Tinder and hook-ups, it was still a minefield.

She'd never find anybody, and the children would grow up and leave, and Dexter would die, and Margot would die, and she'd be left entirely alone. It was years since she'd had salaried work, and the courts were getting tougher with divorce settlements nowadays, with women being told to get a job once the children had grown up, like that millionaire's wife last year. That case had been in the papers because it was a landmark ruling. She'd be fifty-two by the time Poppy finished school – she could retrain, of course, do a degree, or . . . or what?

This wasn't supposed to happen to me, she thought.

Calling out to Dexter, who was pouncing joyfully on the wavelets, she turned and began to walk back inland. She could hear the calling of rooks and see, in the far distance, outlined against a sky beginning to bruise with darkness, a solitary tractor.

Seeing the chimneys of the Old Rectory from the lane, she imagined it deserted, the gate on the driveway sagging and shackled to the fence with a rusty padlock and chain, brambles blocking the front door. She saw herself, a pitiful half-thing like a single shoe discarded in a road, left to peer through grimy windows at empty rooms and stained walls with pale oblongs where pictures had once hung.

Stop inventing reasons for self-pity, she told herself. You don't know that's going to happen – and, in any case, if she and Leo *were* to part company, the Old Rectory would have to be sold, and her misfortune would be some other woman's good luck. Sophie imagined the usurper measuring for curtains and creating an 'Ideas' file, and hated her steadily until her train of thought was abruptly curtailed by a sharp tug on the lead.

That was all she needed: Dexter, on the grass verge, was rolling, ecstatic, in the extruded intestines of a car-squashed fox.

NINE

Sophie tied the Labrador up in the yard and headed straight for the utility room to retrieve the dog shampoo. Imanuela was there, standing beside the pile of dirty washing, hands full of purple satin.

'Isn't the washing machine in the cottage working?'

'No, is fine. I was going to put more things in –' the au pair gestured to Sophie's first load of washing, now neatly arranged on the clothes horse – 'but I think this is for handwash.'

'What is it?'

Imanuela held up a pretty slip with spaghetti straps and lace trim. 'Is new?'

'I've never seen it before.' Even as she spoke, she realized she'd made a mistake. Why hadn't she just said yes?

Imanuela consulted the label. 'Yes, wrong size for you.'

Oh, God. Had it come back from London with Leo's stuff? He'd never be so careless – surely, in transferring it all from the laundry basket in London to the suitcase and then into the laundry basket at this end, he'd be bound to have noticed. Although she hadn't noticed when she'd taken it out of the basket, had she? It must be *her*, doing it deliberately, wrapping the evidence carefully inside some innocent garment. One of Leo's dress shirts, perhaps, or the bathrobe. HE'S GOING TO LEAVE YOU.

'Sophie? Are you OK?'

'Yes, fine. Just thinking . . . Maybe Caro left it here.'

'Maybe.' The au pair looked at her doubtfully. Sophie couldn't imagine her mother-in-law wearing the slip, either. Caro was very much a white-cotton-underwear sort of person – although people could be surprising, sometimes, and she and Leo's father had stayed the night a couple of weeks ago, so it wasn't impossible.

'I'll ring and ask her. Or it could be Margot's, I suppose.' This, Sophie thought, wasn't likely either. Her mother was too unorthodox for anything so conventionally sexy. Or, sometimes, for any underwear at all – here, a horribly vivid memory of Margot at a school sports day when Sophie was ten, visibly braless and, as it turned out when she fell over in the parents' race, knickerless as well, made her clench her teeth. 'It must belong to somebody,' she added, lamely.

'But how it get mixed up with this?' Imanuela looked at the mound of dirty clothes at her feet.

'Perhaps Mrs Palmer found it in the guest room and put it in one of the laundry baskets.'

'Or maybe . . .' Imanuela giggled. 'Zac has a girlfriend.'

Sophie forced herself to smile. 'Maybe. Better not embarrass him, though. Put it on the side and I'll sort it out later. Can you pass me some of those old towels? Dexter just rolled in something disgusting and I need to wash him before I let him back in the house.'

Several times over the next few days, Sophie had been on the point of picking up the phone to Leo and asking him to tell her the truth, but she'd always drawn back. Waking at quarter to three on Friday morning, after a couple of hours of fitful sleep, she started to wonder if perhaps she wasn't looking at the problem from the wrong angle. After all, a smudge of what looked like – but actually might not have been – lipstick on a handkerchief was hardly conclusive proof of adultery, was it? And as for the slip: Caro, when asked, had denied ownership, but Margot had said she couldn't remember and become irritable when pressed, so it wasn't impossible that it did belong to her after all, and that it had – at some point in the last few months – been transferred from the guest room to the laundry basket in the en-suite by Mrs Palmer. That's what she'd told Imanuela, anyway – the thought of asking the cleaning lady about it and having to listen to endless speculation about where the bloody thing might have come from was unbearable. Not wanting to risk Leo, or the ever-inquisitive Poppy, spotting it in the utility room, she'd stuffed it in a drawer of her desk when no one was looking. The best thing – seeing that she was unlikely to get back to sleep any time soon – might be, for the moment at least, to stop assuming that the writer was someone who, if she wasn't actually having an affair with Leo, could plausibly be doing so. Maybe she should try looking for another sort of person altogether. An old-fashioned spinster, perhaps, soured by lack of male regard, or someone who was jealous because their marriage had imploded. Come to think of it, there were a couple of people with hard-luck stories in her reading group. Miranda Boxer's husband had left her for a man! Sophie was pretty sure that she wasn't on their Christmas card list, and neither was Emily Upcher, whose husband and business partner had been killed in a car crash and left her up to her ears in debt, but she ought to check for any others.

Creeping downstairs to her study, she'd combed through the Christmas list, but hadn't found Miranda or Emily or anyone else who seemed to fit the bill . . . although she couldn't be entirely sure about this because you couldn't keep up with everyone, could you? Checks on various Facebook pages revealed only pictures of holidays sailing and skiing, meals, parties, and happy families.

Families. A teenager, perhaps? Sending one Christmas letter back one year, thinking it was a laugh, she could believe – but *three*? Unlikely, but not impossible. Printing out a new list – the old one was now an inky hysteria of stars, arrows and crossings out – she began to highlight anyone with children. It wasn't likely to be any of Alfie or Zac's friends, she thought, but she ought to be thorough.

On one of the neighbours' Facebook pages, she found a group photo, taken at their New Year's Day buffet lunch: Leo, with Miles and a few others in the dining room, raising glasses to the camera. Sophie peered at the image. Was Leo's grin as guileless as it appeared, or was he wishing he were somewhere else, with *her*? Perhaps he'd been planning to sneak off upstairs to his study and phone her as soon as the photo had been taken.

Drawing a blank after three-quarters of an hour, she decided to go back upstairs and get her head down. Perhaps some brandy would help. Turning off her laptop, she tiptoed down the hall to the sitting room, turned on the big light, and stared at the rows of bottles in the drinks cabinet. It felt wrong even to be looking at them, but she couldn't help it. Lack of sleep was making her short-tempered with the children, which wasn't fair – after all, they hadn't done anything, had they?

Had they?

No. That really was crazy. OK, Alfie and Zac had both, at different times, expressed disquiet about the Christmas letters ('God, Mum, do you have to?') but they wouldn't do *that*.

Sophie shut her eyes tight and stood quite still for a moment before reaching into the cabinet and pulling out a bottle of Armagnac.

LET'S SEE HOW SMUG YOU ARE THEN.

It couldn't be Leo himself, could it, trying to tell her something she was refusing to see?

I am actually going mad, Sophie thought. It is ten past four in the morning, and I am drinking brandy and wondering if my husband is sending me poison-pen letters. This cannot be happening. I am not this person. We are not these people. None of this is true.

If it isn't true, the little voice at the back of her mind piped up, then why aren't you upstairs asleep?

TEN

In the cab from King's Cross, staring out at rain-slicked streets, Sophie thought about what Leo might be doing at that moment. It would be 8 a.m. in New York – and she knew he was definitely there because she'd phoned his office, pretending to have forgotten which day he'd said he was going. He'd told her about the trip – 'Something came up. It's a bugger, but it can't be helped' – on Friday night, just as they were going to bed. Perhaps it wasn't only business. Perhaps *she* was with him. Maybe they were sitting together, enjoying a post-coital room-service breakfast in matching hotel bathrobes, before Leo went off to his meeting.

Still, Sophie thought, coming down to London was better than sitting in front of her laptop in Norfolk, reading articles with titles like 'Ten Signs that He's Cheating on You'. It had been easy enough to make an excuse to Imanuela about some business for the shop which would take all day, and Zac, on promise of payment, had agreed to walk Dexter.

Moorgate House was a slender glass silo with steel bracing, a stone's throw from Leo's office in Cheapside. After a quick look through the glass panel beside the impressive wooden door to make sure that the concierge wasn't about (she had a vague memory of Leo being jocular with a thickset Eastern European type), Sophie keyed in the date of their wedding anniversary and let herself into the reception area.

The place was decorated in bland, hotel-style bling, with marble tiling. Sophie made for the lifts. Leo's one-bedroom flat wasn't quite at the top – those were impossibly expensive, and had their own private elevator – but the floor-to-ceiling window still commanded a decent view across the City. Often, when they talked on the phone during the week, Sophie imagined him standing in front of it, gazing out at the twinkling skyline. Now, her imagination added another person beside him, her slender hand stroking his arm, slinky and insinuating as a cat.

The lift doors parted. Sophie stepped out onto the landing and began to walk down the corridor, rooting in her bag for the front door key of the flat. Despite being so high up, the sound-deadening carpet and lack of windows made her feel submerged, as though she were in a submarine. Halfway down – Leo's flat was at the end – she stopped, panic beating against the walls of her chest like a trapped bird. What was she going to find? She visualized a narrative told in discarded clothing: Leo's ripped-off tie flung across a chair, a stranger's lace knickers puddled at the foot of the bed, an empty bottle and two glasses carelessly left, and the bed unmade after lovemaking . . .

Imagining corner-of-the-wine-bar chats with a friend – Miles, perhaps – conducted over several months ('You've got to tell her, Leo. Give her the chance to move on'), Sophie stumbled over to the stairs opposite Leo's door – for emergencies, in case a fire broke out and the lift to the penthouses stopped working – and sat down on the bottom step.

'It's all right,' she murmured to herself. 'It's all right.' Of course she wasn't going to find anything. She was just doing this to be sure. And she had every right to be there – she was Leo's *wife*, for God's sake. She took a deep breath and stood, fumbling the key in shaking hands.

Two steps across the corridor. That was all it would take.

'Come on,' she muttered through clenched teeth. 'Just. Do. It.'

She stepped forward – once, twice – and, steadying herself with one hand on the smooth white wall beside the door, inserted the key into the lock and began to turn it.

Nothing happened.

She jiggled it in the lock, but the tumblers didn't move. She withdrew it, and tried again – once, twice, three times. Still nothing.

Leo had changed the lock.

ELEVEN

04.45. 04.46. 04.47. Sophie stared at the numbers on the LCD with peeled eyes. Stretched taut with sleeplessness, she'd given up trying to burrow into familiar, comforting thoughts and memories – the ones involving Leo (which was most of them) were all tainted now – and given up, too, on the manufacture of consolatory fantasies as a soothing pathway to oblivion. Even the one about how her dad had leant over her cot – 'Always remember, Sophie, I love you' – that she'd worked into almost-certainty over the years, from a blurred impression of a man's face and murmurings in the semi-darkness, was no good.

Nothing seemed safe any more – not the beautiful room, with its custom-made furniture; not the house, which no longer seemed like a refuge; not even her own mind, full of sharp edges and dead ends.

The journey home and the evening after it had been a blur. Cold with shock, she'd told Imanuela that she was coming down with something and gone upstairs for a hot bath, but it hadn't helped, and neither had the tumbler of brandy afterwards. She was being excluded from *her own life*. Locked out. She'd ceased to be herself, and become a problem – something to be pitied, but discarded nonetheless.

What if Leo had sold the flat and not told her? On impulse, standing on the pavement afterwards in the rain, she'd called the flat from her mobile and heard Leo's voice inviting her to leave a message, but you could port a landline number, couldn't you? Perhaps, in the last few months, when she'd thought she was calling the flat, the phone had been ringing in a different place altogether. She'd thought of ringing Leo's mobile, too, and had stood unmoving for several minutes, her phone like a grenade in her hand, before thinking better of it. There might be an innocent explanation, but, if so, what was it? If Leo had been burgled and had had to change the locks, he'd have told her.

Wouldn't he?

Now, heart pounding, she scrambled out of bed and ran down the hall to Leo's office. Slapping on the light, she started yanking drawers open and pulling out papers in a feverish scrabble for something, *anything*, that would give her a clue, until the letter-heads, words and figures were a frantic blur in front of her eyes. No longer sure what she was looking for, she collapsed on the floor in a blizzard of crumpled papers and splayed files and lay there, sobbing.

She'd been blind, she'd been stupid. Everything was lost.

'Why are you doing this to us, Leo? Why?'

After a while – she didn't know how long – Sophie struggled to her feet. Leaving the chaos of Leo's study (she'd make an excuse to Mrs Palmer, who was nothing if not nosy, and tidy it up herself in the morning), she stood at the foot of the stairs to the second floor, where the children's rooms were, sniffing back ugly, gulping tears and staring up into the darkness. Zac, she knew, would be sprawled across his bed, duvet half off, dead to the world. Poppy, in her flowered cotton pyjamas, would be tucked in neatly, curled up in a ball. A fierce, protective surge of love made her want to rush upstairs and hug them, promise to look after them, that nothing bad would happen, that—

On the third stair she stopped, imagining their bewilderment, their questions, Poppy's alarm at the sight of her blotchy-faced, red-eyed mother. Besides, what could she tell them she was protecting them *from* if she didn't know herself? The air seemed to vibrate around her, as though an enormous rock had fallen out of the sky and just missed them all.

This was her problem, not theirs. It wasn't fair to burden them. Zac had his GCSEs coming up – nothing must be allowed to upset those – and Poppy was sensitive. Recently, she'd been watching Sophie like a hawk, and there'd been tension at mealtimes, too, not just the vegetarianism but excuses for not finishing what was on her plate and an obsession with sell-by dates.

She retreated to her bedroom, trailed by memories of Margot, sloppy and over-confiding about everything from lovers to friends she'd fallen out with (and there'd been plenty of both), and, later, her cringe-inducing bright-eyed hunger for details about Sophie's boyfriends. Standing in the en-suite bathroom, splashing her face with water in an attempt to regain authority over herself, Sophie felt suddenly detached and watchful. 'You *are* stupid,' she said to her reflection. 'You should have known.'

Almost 6 a.m., and almost light. She might as well go downstairs and make some tea. She fed Dexter, and then, watching him trot happily into the garden, shrugged on a coat to go after him – why, she wasn't sure – noticing, as she did it, that she'd torn her nightdress.

It had stopped raining now, and the early-morning grass looked as though it were boiling, with clouds of vapour rising into the air. Dexter had disappeared into the bushes, so she wandered down towards the swimming pool, the damp grass cold and fresh beneath her bare feet. The pool was still covered (the weather hadn't been warm enough, and she hadn't done anything about the crack in the lining yet), and the thick fabric sagged under a puddle of rainwater. In her mind's eye, she saw it abandoned and derelict, in the same way she'd imagined the house a few days before, algae blooming in a few inches of brackish water at the deep end, the concrete surround fissured and strewn with leaves. Was there anything, she thought, as utterly and entirely pointless as a drained swimming pool? Even more than an abandoned house, it seemed to suggest catastrophe.

She mustn't start crying again. She couldn't afford – in any sense of the word – to fall apart. She'd go back to the house, get washed and dressed, and make a list. For a start, she'd got to sort out the mess in Leo's study, and she needed to take Zac, once she'd managed to chisel him out of bed, for a haircut. There were clothes to be collected from the dry-cleaner's and she really must do something about the pool ... And, at the weekend, she'd get hold of Leo's flat key and have a duplicate cut.

As she turned to go back up the slope to the house, she saw

that Poppy, standing at her bedroom window in her night-clothes, was staring down at her. Sophie was too far away to make out the expression on her face, but she could feel her gaze – serious, intent.

TWELVE

Leo came back on Friday at lunchtime, straight off the red-eye from JFK ('Christ, Soph, I'm getting too old for this') and closeted himself in his study – now restored to its usual state – to send emails. By the time she'd unpacked his bag – nothing unusual there – dealt with a problem at the shop, found Zac's iPod for him, helped Imanuela fold up a pile of sheets ('Is Mr Leo all right?') and given Poppy a lift to her friend Cressida's house, her head was aching with the effort of being normal.

She and Leo had supper in the kitchen – when Zac headed upstairs with his plate, she didn't have the energy to argue – and she'd asked the usual questions about the New York trip and been given the usual answers. After they'd discussed the repair to the pool ('Bloody hell, Soph – how much is *that* going to cost?'), Leo watched *News at Ten*, and, when it ended, announced that he was going to bed.

'Do you want me to bring you a cup of tea or anything?'

'No, it's fine. I'll just finish this.' Leo picked up his whisky glass, which had about half an inch in the bottom, and turned to look at her. For a moment, she thought he was about to say something else. Was he going to tell her now? Time seemed to stop, crouched and tensed, ready to spring.

'I'll be out like a light.' He gave her a lopsided smile and left the room.

Sophie sat on the sofa for five minutes finishing her wine, then slipped off her shoes and went upstairs to check on Zac. Immersed in a world of bright, noisy violence on his computer, he didn't look up as she drew his curtains.

'Just another half hour, OK?'

'Sure. 'Night, Mum.'

Closing the door, she had a sudden memory of undressing him when he was little, pulling a vest over his head, tickling him and making him giggle. If someone had told her back then that one day she'd be creeping about behind Leo's back, looking for evidence of adultery, she'd have giggled too, and been incredulous. That sort of thing happened to other people, not her.

Yes, said a small, mocking voice in her head, and you always wanted to be like other people. Well, now you are. This is what it's like.

On the first-floor landing, she nudged open the door of their bedroom. In the almost-darkness, she could just make out Leo, humped under the duvet, snoring gently. Knee-jerk irritation that he could just go straight to sleep like that, when she'd not had a halfway decent night's sleep for a week, gave way to relief. She'd go into his study now and look for his key. A surreptitious feel inside the pockets of his hung-up overcoat earlier in the evening had told her that it wasn't in there, and the study was the only other place it could be. The two guest rooms separated it from their bedroom, so there was no risk of waking him. She'd get the duplicate made tomorrow and return it straight afterwards.

Five minutes later, having drawn a blank with Leo's briefcase and laptop bag, Sophie turned to the garment bag hanging from a hook on the back of the door. Unzipping it carefully, she exposed the front of the charcoal wool suit jacket and slid her hand inside to explore the pockets. She pulled out first a balled-up hanky – that could go in the wash – and then the key with its leather key ring. Good.

She was about to zip up the garment bag when she heard movement from upstairs – Zac, coming down to the bathroom. Her first thought was that he mustn't find her in here, closely followed by the feeling that it was her house and she could bloody well go where she liked, and in any case there were any number of innocent explanations, such as Leo needing clean handkerchiefs for work . . . She glanced down at the crumpled white cotton in her hand, and in a single, jagged second in which time itself seemed to snap in two – before and after – realized that, nestled inside the folds of material like a tiny, shining snake, was a necklace with a pendant in the shape of a ring.

Not hers. Obviously expensive – looking closer, she could see, on the side of the ring, the letters T. & Co. and a date, 1837. Tiffany's. Not a present intended for her, either – the clasp of the necklace was broken. She recoiled, fingers stiff as flippers, and the thing slipped from her hands. She stared at the silver trail across the rug at her feet, fancying, almost, that it might convulse and glide towards her. Just for a moment, she had a sense of relief – now she *knew* – followed by panic, as blind and enveloping as if someone had thrust a bag over her head, when she heard the door of the kids' bathroom open.

Whatever else happened, Zac must not see this. Heart racing, she scooped up the necklace. Stuffing it, and the hanky, back into the pocket of Leo's jacket, she yanked up the zip of the garment bag. For a moment, she could hear no sound at all except the blood pounding in her ears, and then the unmistakable creak of the bottom step told her that Zac was going back upstairs to his room.

Shoving the key into the pocket of her jeans, she put out the light, closed the door and then walked – slowly, carefully – along the corridor and down the stairs. The sitting room was exactly as she'd left it: lamps switched on, her empty glass on the little table beside the sofa, the cushion slightly indented from where she'd sat on it, Dexter lying in the same position on the rug.

Nothing was different, nothing at all.

She blinked, astonished.

THIRTEEN

After three hours wide awake in the dark, with Leo's snores punctuating thoughts that scurried between absolute, lead-lined certainty that he was having an affair and faint hope of a completely innocent explanation, Sophie remembered the sleeping tablets. They'd been prescribed when, some years before, she'd damaged her knee skiing and it had taken ages to heal, but she'd not used more than a couple.

The kitchen seemed appallingly bright with light and fury as she stood, bare feet on cold tiles, clutching the blister pack in her hand. The idea that she should have to drug herself because this bloody woman was intent on ruining all their lives was abhorrent. Imagining the necklace upstairs, curled in Leo's pocket, Sophie wanted to grab it, shove it under his nose and scream for an explanation – but what if Leo told her it was all true and he was leaving but hadn't found the right moment to tell her?

She put the pills down beside the sink and picked up a plate from the draining board. For a moment, it seemed to vibrate in her hand, and she wondered how it would feel to hurl it to the floor, almost seeing, as she looked down, the impact and the flying shards. How dare Leo tell her she was spending too much and then splash out on a Tiffany necklace for his mistress? And that satin slip – which she'd bet wasn't Margot's at all, and which was still, she now remembered, stuffed in a drawer in her desk – must have cost quite a bit, too. Well, she wasn't having it in the house. If Leo's mistress, whoever the hell she was, thought she was marking out her territory by contriving to sneak her clothes into Sophie's home, she had another think coming.

She barged into her study, flipped on the light and retrieved the thing, then dashed back into the kitchen, yanked the scissors out of the dresser drawer and, in a frenzy of cutting and ripping, reduced it to shreds.

'There.' She flipped up the lid of the pedal bin and buried the pieces at the bottom of the pile of rubbish. 'All gone.'

She poured herself a glass of water and, leaning against the draining board, picked up the plate again, weighing it in her hand. She'd bet Leo had bought the woman other things, too – flowers, chocolates, theatre tickets . . . It would serve him right if she smashed every piece of china in the kitchen.

Then she pictured herself having to clear it up afterwards.

After a while – how long, she wasn't sure – she returned the sleeping pills to the back of the cupboard and walked, like an automaton, back up the stairs to bed.

'Don't use the tea towel!'

Zac, about to dry his hands, stared at her in mild astonishment. 'Chill out, will you? It's not like it's the end of the world.'

'I didn't say it was,' snapped Sophie. Brittle with exhaustion but unable to keep still, she tore off sheets of kitchen roll to wipe spilt milk and chocolate powder off the kitchen table. 'Use the hand towel. That's what it's there for.'

Zac reached for the hand towel, dropping the tea towel on the floor in the process. Dexter ambled over and sniffed at it.

Sophie stomped on the bin pedal and dumped the handful of used kitchen roll inside. 'Oh, for God's sake! Pick it up and put it in the laundry basket.'

'It's fine, Mum.'

'It isn't fine, it's been on the floor. Just do it.'

With agonizing slowness, Zac bent over, picked up the tea towel, and put it on the draining board.

'Not there! The laundry basket. It's in the utility room, in case you've forgotten.' Zac wandered over to the fridge, yanked the door open and stared inside. '*Now*, Zac.'

'I'll do it in a minute. When I've done this.'

'Done what?' Sophie looked up from the dishwasher. 'You're just staring into the fridge.'

'I'll do it.' Poppy got up from the table.

'No, Poppy. Finish your breakfast. Zac's got to do it.'

'I don't see why,' said Zac, without turning round. 'Poppy just said she'd do it.'

'That's not the point, and you know it. It—'

'Any coffee?' Leo, looking refreshed, appeared in the doorway, hearty, rubbing his hands together.

'I'll get it, Daddy.'

'No, Poppy. I'll do it.' Sophie put a capsule in the Nespresso machine. 'You eat your breakfast.'

'It's OK, I'm full now.'

'You've only had half a slice of toast.'

'I had something before you came down.'

'Did you? What?'

Poppy rolled her eyes and got up from the table. 'Cereal. I washed up the bowl, OK?'

'For heaven's sake, Soph, don't fuss. It won't go to waste.' Leo pulled Poppy's plate towards him and took a bite of her toast and Marmite before shucking the *Telegraph* from its plastic wrapper.

Poppy shot Sophie a triumphant look and, ducking under Zac's arm, took the milk from the fridge.

'Can you wash your mug, please?'

'I was just getting this for Dad's latte.' Poppy gave Sophie a look of injured innocence and poured milk into the frother.

Zac closed the fridge door and took a swig of apple juice from the bottle.

'Please use a glass.'

'OK, OK.' Zac went to fetch one, holding the open bottle carelessly and leaving a trail of drips across the floor.

'Zac!'

'What?'

'You're slopping it everywhere. Where's the lid?'

'I don't know, do I?'

'You've just taken it off!'

'It's all right, Mum.' Zac spoke carefully, as if humouring a potentially dangerous lunatic. 'It's not like I've lost it or anything.'

'Well, get it. And wipe that up.'

'Wipe what up?'

'The *floor*!'

Zac stared down at the tiles with an expression of wonder on his face, then looked up at his mother. 'What's wrong with it?'

'It's covered in bloody apple juice!' Sophie grabbed the kitchen roll and slammed it into Zac's chest, shoving him backwards so that he lurched, spilling juice down his jeans. 'That's what's wrong with it!'

She'd spoken far louder than she'd intended, and everyone stared at her, even the dog. For a long moment no one said anything, and, feeling tears pricking her eyes, Sophie turned towards the sink. Behind her back, she knew, Leo, Zac and Poppy were now staring, with various degrees of bewilderment, at each other. Then, as she dabbed at her eyes with the back of her hand, Zac – presumably after some unspoken direction from Leo – exhaled a long, put-upon sigh. 'Fine. If that's what you want.'

When Sophie turned round again, Poppy had disappeared, Leo was absorbed in his newspaper and Zac, having dropped a length of kitchen roll on the floor, was pushing it around with the toe of one slab-like trainer.

A perfectly ordinary Saturday morning.

Except it wasn't.

The rest of the weekend was the same. On Sunday, Zac had kindly brought Sophie a cup of tea as she'd sat in her study, trying to sort through invoices for the shop, and informed her that he'd lost his watch. He'd gabbled it quickly on his way out of the door, clearly anticipating a row – it was the third watch in eighteen months – but rage had given way to weariness. Sensing this, he'd stopped in the doorway. 'So can we get another one?'

Sophie'd put her elbows on the desk and rubbed her hands over her face. It felt stiff, and a bit sticky, and so did her hair. 'Can't you just use your phone?'

'I need a watch for exams.'

'There's a clock in the room, isn't there?'

'To make sure I'm on time. Don't you want me to pass them?'

'Of course I do. I'm just not sure you do – you don't seem to have done any work in the last fortnight.'

'I have! I've been up in my room, and—'

'Yes, playing *World of Warcraft*.'

'Not *all* the time.'

'Just most of it.'

'That isn't true! If you're going to start—'

'I'm not starting anything, Zac. I haven't got the energy.' For a vertiginously insane second, she'd felt tempted to add that, on the scale of loss, a watch came a long way below a father. 'Look, we'll deal with it later, OK?'

Zac gave her an uncertain look. 'OK . . . You won't tell Dad, will you?'

Sophie sighed. 'No, I won't tell Dad.'

At which point, Leo had appeared and said, 'Won't tell Dad what?'

The two of them had shouted at each other in the hall while Sophie sat in despair on the other side of the door, watching the rain sweeping against the windows, and the row had continued, on and off, until it was time for her to take Leo to the station. He'd insisted on helping Zac search his room for the missing watch, and the discovery of a packet of Rizla papers ('They're not mine!') in the mulch of underwear, damp towels and dirty crockery had sent him through the roof. Later, Poppy's favourite mug had slipped from her fingers while she was unloading the dishwasher and smashed on the kitchen tiles. The shards had seemed like an omen – everything so fragile – although Poppy had seemed more upset by Sophie's distress than by the smithereens on the floor. She'd insisted on helping to clear up the mess and had bloodied her hand. Seeing the sleeping tablets in the cupboard as she rummaged for the Elastoplast, Sophie had made a mental note to take one before bed – no sense in having a nervous breakdown from lack of sleep on top of everything else.

Still, she reflected on the solitary drive back from King's Lynn, she'd managed to copy the key to Leo's flat and drop the original back in his pocket. Now, she thought grimly, it was just a question of getting down to London again – and then she'd know exactly where she stood.

FOURTEEN

Sophie stopped at the foot of the stairs opposite the front door of Leo's flat and rummaged in her bag for the key. In the event, it had been easy enough to find a day to come to London – Leo was (or said he was) at the races at Kempton Park with one of his clients. She had a legitimate excuse because they did actually need things for the shop, and Melissa had been happy for her to go to a wholesale place in Surrey they'd found that sold wrought-iron garden ornaments, and choose some pieces for the Hamilton De Witt shelves.

Leo had seemed just as angry with her as with Zac over the Rizla episode, haranguing her on the phone ('One of his friends might be *dealing*, Soph, and that stuff's a lot stronger nowadays') and telling her to 'have a word' at Oddham's. They'd argued, and all the time she'd felt like saying, if you think the odd spliff is bad, what do you think he'll do when you go off and live with this woman you've been seeing behind all our backs?

She thought of this now, as her trembling fingers closed around the small piece of metal. How dare he accuse her of bad parenting when he was about to *walk out* on his own children? When she'd asked why he couldn't phone the school himself if he was so concerned about Zac, he'd said, 'I can't do *everything*, Soph.' No, she'd felt like saying, because you're far too busy fucking that spiteful bitch, aren't you?

She hadn't said that, though, or anything like it. While there was still room for a scintilla of doubt, she was prepared to let sleeping dogs lie, but . . .

Two steps, and she'd be in front of the door. You were prepared to do it once, she told herself, and you can do it again. For a moment, the silence seemed to thud in her ears, and then there was another sound, real this time. Footsteps, muffled by carpet, coming from the other side of Leo's front door – and then the click of a latch.

All but throwing herself at the emergency stairs, Sophie scrambled upwards, out of sight, stumbling onto her hands and knees as she made the turn. Luckily, there was a dividing wall between the flights rather than banisters, and, hidden behind it, she stopped, crouching, heart pounding. There was a bumping noise – something hard falling against a wall – then the sound of someone sorting through a bunch of keys.

Stiff with caution and hardly daring to breathe, Sophie leant forward, craning her neck to peer round the end of the wall. All she could see was a black wheelie suitcase lying on its side by the open door of the flat. Leo had one like it – but then, so did she, left at the hotel when she'd checked in earlier, and so did millions of other people, and—

'There's nobody out here!' A woman's voice. English, well-spoken, amused. *Her*. Leo, also invisible, said something in return, but Sophie couldn't catch the words. The woman laughed. 'I know, but I'm going to miss my train. 'Bye, darling.'

The sleeve of a trench coat came into view. A strap and a buckle on the arm, and then the rest – mid-length, smart, Burberry perhaps – with slim legs in black trousers, black ankle boots with high heels, and there was the whole woman, bending over to right the wheelie case, glossy auburn waves curtaining her profile. As she straightened up, tossing her hair off her face, Sophie instantly drew back behind the dividing wall, but not before she'd caught a glimpse of pale, freckly skin, delicate features and a generous mouth.

Hunched round the corner, on the bottom stair, she thought: I know you. You've been in the shop.

The slight squeak of plastic wheels told Sophie that the woman was on her way to the lift, but she didn't dare move in case Leo appeared. Unless, of course, he'd settled in for the day – the day he'd told her he was spending at the races. It seemed odd that the woman hadn't stayed with him, but perhaps they'd had to change their plans.

She is beautiful, Sophie thought bleakly, and ten years younger than me, at least. My whole life, reduced to a cliché.

Pain, like a block of ice, lodged in her chest. HE'S GOING TO LEAVE YOU. Best to have it out in the open. No more guilty afternoons.

The world slowed, stopped.

Later, emerging from the block of flats, Sophie put on her dark glasses, even though there was no sun.

FIFTEEN

She'd wanted to charge down the emergency stairs and bang on the door with her fists, to confront Leo, to shame him, to tell him about the returned Christmas letter – 'This is the kind of woman you're infatuated with' – but she'd done none of those things. Leo hadn't emerged from the flat, and, in the end, she'd crept away to sit, numb and silent, in a coffee shop near St Paul's Cathedral, staring into space over a cup of green tea. After a while she left and hailed a taxi to take her back to the hotel she'd booked. It was a new boutique place, somewhere in Clerkenwell ('Award-winning cocktail lounge and quirkily opulent dining room' – anger at Leo had justified the price), but she spent most of the evening sitting on the edge of the bed, barely noticing the antique furniture, the 200-thread-count linen or the view of the Shard.

After a perfunctory phone conversation with Imanuela, she took her laptop out of its case and opened the Christmas list file. Mottram. That was the name. Sean and Jessica Mottram. Leo knew Sean from the City – hence the sending of Christmas cards. The Mottrams had a weekend place in Norfolk, a couple of villages away from the Old Rectory, and Sean's name came up occasionally in connection with shooting. That, of course, was why she'd seen Jessica in Hamilton De Witt – and, now she thought about it, she'd seen her at the odd social gathering, too, although they'd never exchanged more than a few words. Jessica Mottram, who'd come into Sophie's shop and smiled at her, when all the time . . . LEO AND I HAVE BEEN HAVING AN AFFAIR FOR OVER TWO YEARS AND NOW HE'S GOING TO LEAVE YOU.

It was just possible, she supposed, that Leo hadn't bought the purple satin slip for Jessica. It would be on the large side for her (although that wasn't in itself conclusive, because Leo had never been any good at sizes when it came to buying lingerie), and also, she hadn't yet entirely ruled out the idea of its being Margot's. However, there was no getting away from the fact that he'd bought her the Tiffany necklace. Maybe they'd picked it out together in New York, then gone back to the hotel afterwards, his hand on her thigh in the cab, and had sex on a bed like the one she was sitting on now. She imagined their faces against the expensive pillows, radiant, gasping. Bile rose in her throat, making her stumble to the over-bright bathroom with its iridescent mosaic tiles, lurching against the freestanding bath to bend, bitter-mouthed, over the basin.

Afterwards, she ordered the second most expensive wine from room service and googled Jessica's name. There was a website: Jessica Mottram, UK travel writer. The home page ('About Me') was dominated by a large photograph in which Jessica was seated behind a desk in a sunny room, smiling from behind a mask of immaculate make-up, her bright hair falling in soft curls. *My first job was working in a City trading room* (presumably where she'd met Sean, thought Sophie), *but happily I quickly came to my senses and launched myself into the world of journalism* . . . There were links to articles about city breaks in Reykjavik, Riga and Belgrade, none particularly recent, and photographs of Jessica variously skiing, riding a camel, and 'testing her skills' on a River Cottage cookery course.

When not travelling, I divide my time between London and Norfolk. A search on Google Earth revealed a charming detached cottage with, by the look of it, at least three bedrooms. She obviously doesn't *need* to work, Sophie thought. And she's already got a husband. Who the hell did she think she was, calling Sophie a smug bitch?

The following day, hung-over and gravel-eyed from lack of sleep, Sophie took the train to Guildford to buy garden ornaments. The various birds, animals and sundials were lovely – even in her crapulous state, she could see that – and she ordered some of them for the shop, although glancing through her scrawled notes on the train home she wasn't entirely sure which, or how many. The only one she could remember with any clarity was a large astrolabe, a framework of rings marked with Roman numerals, with an arrow shooting diagonally through it as though fired from an invisible bow. It was an early form of modelling objects in the sky, according to the details, with the earth or the sun as the centre. Quite what the arrow was supposed to represent Sophie wasn't sure, but it looked good, and that was what mattered.

She arrived home at half past eight, to find Poppy doing her violin practice and Zac watching TV in the sitting room while Imanuela searched the house for his mobile phone. Too tired and dispirited to call Melissa or even remonstrate with her son about putting his feet (still in trainers) on the brocade sofa, she pleaded exhaustion, carted her suitcase upstairs, and went straight to bed.

Several times over the next three days, Sophie took detours from her usual routes to the shop and the school to drive past the Mottrams' cottage. Outside the village itself, it stood on its own at the end of a narrow lane where the trees, now in leaf, met overhead to form a green tunnel, so that Sophie felt as though she were driving underwater. Once, she stopped in a gateway on the other side of the adjacent T-junction and sat staring at the place. The countryside around her seemed curiously intent, as though it were watching and listening – the trees, the grass, the cows, everything.

The cottage was pretty – Victorian Gothic, a gingerbread house; somewhere that Sophie wouldn't have minded living herself. It stood in the middle of a plot of land, with a gravel parking space at the front, screened from the gardens by trees and watched over by a discreetly placed CCTV camera. Seeing a sleek silver car there – an Audi, Sophie thought – she imagined Jessica inside the house, plotting to take Leo away from her, and then imagined entering the place when Jessica was out, examining her clothes and jewellery, opening the fridge to see what was inside, perhaps stealing something small and insignificant.

'Don't cry,' she muttered to herself. 'Do anything, only don't cry.'

SIXTEEN

'It's not my birthday, Leo.'

The flowers were ridiculous. An enormous, guilty bunch from Moyses Stevens – a hundred and fifty pounds' worth, at least.

'Two of my horses came in – thought I'd share the good luck.'

How well prepared he was, Sophie thought. No lame 'Just because', or 'Can't I buy my wife flowers once in a while?' but a plausible reason for the gift. They'd not spoken on the phone for the last few days, which had been deliberate on her part – time to collect her thoughts and work out what to do next.

'Are you OK, Soph? You've not been answering your phone.'

'I'm fine. Just busy, that's all. I'd better go and put these in water.'

Looking slightly hurt, Leo trailed her into the kitchen and took white wine out of the fridge while she hunted for a large enough vase. She primped and tweaked the leaves and blooms during the usual catch-up-and-what's-happening-this-weekend conversation, and then, standing back to admire the effect ('The hall table, I think – it's really too big for anywhere else'), she said, 'I thought we might have a dinner party soon.'

'Oh?'

When Sophie had rehearsed this, Leo had immediately jibbed at the expense and she'd imagined a scenario in which she floored him with a retort about there being enough money to buy his mistress a necklace from Tiffany's. Now, the mildness of his response took her by surprise, and although she had never intended to say those words out loud – at least, not yet – she felt herself mentally dropping down a gear. 'Well, it's been a while. Miles and Melissa, I thought, and I've been meaning to invite the Frayns for ages—'

'The who?'

'Cressida's parents. You know, Poppy's friend from school. I don't know him, but she's lovely.'

'Oh, right. Yes. Anyone else?'

'I thought maybe Sean Mottram and his wife. Nice to have different people, for a change.'

She'd said this quite normally and without inflection, but Leo looked, if not actually alarmed, then definitely perturbed. 'I'm not sure, Soph.'

'Oh?' Sophie picked up the vase, more in order to screen her face with the flowers than because she actually wanted to transport the thing into the hall, and then, not trusting herself with the weight, put it back down again.

'Why not? You like him, don't you?'

'He told me he's not really coming up here any more. In fact, I think they're getting divorced.'

Shit. Sophie concentrated her attention on the leaves and branches, fussing them into place. The whole business was evidently further along than she'd imagined. '*She* still comes up here, though,' she managed. 'I saw her the other day, but I didn't stop because I just blanked – couldn't remember what her name was.' Even as she said it, she wished she could take it back, but she wanted to hear Leo say Jessica's name out loud, to hear how it would sound in his mouth, how—

'Jessica.'

The word landed, three flat syllables, between them. Sophie kept her eyes on the flowers, not wanting to see Leo's expression.

'Maybe she's living up here? If they're separated, I mean.'

'I suppose so. Sean didn't say.'

'What does she do, anyway?'

'Journalist of some sort, I think. Or she used to be.'

'So he's still supporting her?'

'Must be.' Leo swallowed a mouthful of wine.

With willed composure, Sophie turned the vase round and considered the display from the other side. 'But he's not going to do that forever, surely? There aren't any children, are there?'

Leo shook his head. 'I think he said something about her trying to get a book published. This is good – is it the stuff we got from the new wine merchant in Holt?'

Oh, no you don't, thought Sophie. 'So she's writing a novel, is she?'

Leo shook his head. 'Biography. Historical thing.'

'Sounds interesting. We could always invite her on her own. And we can have Reverend Barker. Jessica's very attractive, of course, but it wouldn't be matchmaking because I think he's probably gay – just to balance things up.'

Leo frowned. 'Bit odd, though. I mean, it's not as if you know her, is it? You couldn't even remember her name a minute ago. If you want to invite Reverend Barker and you need a woman to make up the numbers, why don't you invite what's-her-name – you know, that dog walker friend of yours?'

His tone was entirely reasonable. Sophie felt wrong-footed. He was good at this; practice, she supposed. 'Belinda, you mean? I *could* invite her, but I'm not sure she'd be terribly comfortable.'

'Oh? She seems quite . . . well, you know.'

Sophie understood that the 'well, you know' covered a multitude of bases. Belinda had obviously fallen from grace in financial (and therefore also social) terms. A bad divorce, Sophie thought, although Belinda had never volunteered any information and she'd never felt their relationship was such that she could actually ask – but she was well-spoken and looked as though she would probably scrub up all right and could be relied upon not to cause embarrassment vis-à-vis table manners, conversation and the like. However, Belinda wasn't the object of the exercise. 'We don't *have* to have a dinner party,' she said. 'It was just a thought, really.' Picking up the vase again, she carried it into the hall.

Standing in front of the console table, readjusting the foliage with automatic hands, Sophie thought about the conversation. Jessica might want it all out in the open, Sophie thought, but Leo clearly didn't. Presumably he thought that he could have his cake and eat it, and none of Jessica's threats and ultimata had worked, which was why – her source of income about to dry up with the divorce – she'd resorted to informing Sophie about the affair via the returned round-robin letter. Maybe she was, even now, sitting in her pretty cottage and imagining a showdown which would end with Leo's arrival on her doorstep, chastened, suitcase in hand.

Sophie nipped off a dangling leaf with a twist of her fingers. Two could play at that game, she thought. Jessica was the one she needed to speak to, not Leo. She imagined herself, calm and articulate like someone in a clever play, explaining to Jessica that Leo had no intention of leaving her, that she wasn't worth either the damage he'd do to his beloved family or the compromises he'd have to make to his lifestyle.

Sophie took a deep breath and straightened her shoulders. Jessica might be ten years younger, but she clearly didn't realize that possession was nine-tenths of the law. Once she realized the extent to which the odds were stacked against her, she'd surely back off – and if Sophie could give her an eyeful of just what Leo would lose by choosing her over his family, so much the better. That shouldn't be *too* difficult – and she'd make it top of the list for next week.

SEVENTEEN

Sophie felt her strength and resolve, carefully husbanded throughout the weekend, begin to waver as she drove down the lane to Jessica's cottage on Monday morning. Dexter was in the back – most of the beaches were off limits to dogs after April, so there would be nothing unusual about taking him for a walk in the woods – and all she had to do was contrive a meeting, but how?

Saturday and Sunday had been largely uneventful. Imanuela had managed to find Zac's watch and Poppy had passed her ballet exam. Alfie had emailed (there seemed to be a problem with Skyping from Borneo), sending photographs of himself clowning around with his friend Marcus on a beach in Pulau Mantanani. She and Leo had had another conversation – actually rather a fun one – about turning their cottage into a holiday let. Sophie had initiated it, reasoning that letting Imanuela go (or at least saying that she might be able to manage without her) would be a gesture of good faith, and that a joint project might bring them closer together. Anything that focused his thoughts on home, rather than on Jessica, had to be worthwhile – and once Jessica was safely out of the picture, the enterprise could be shelved.

Turning right at the T-junction, Sophie looked over at the cottage. No car on the gravel at the front, so Jessica must be out. She pushed away the feeling of anticlimax – the woman was probably only shopping or meeting a friend or something, and anyway, Dexter, whose tail was thumping rhythmically against the side of the boot-liner, needed his walk. Having parked the car in the same gateway as before, she led the Labrador down the road until she found a footpath that led to a small wood.

The dog was happy enough to scuffle about amongst the trees and do battle with fallen branches while Sophie stood at the edge of the wood in a patch of late-spring sun, staring out across the fields to the flint-faced houses in the distance and, beyond them, the sea's calm expanse of wrinkled blue. This is my life, she thought. I won't give it up for anyone.

'Penny for them.'

Jerked out of her thoughts, Sophie half jumped, half turned, unbalanced on the rutted path, clutching a fence post for support.

'Didn't mean to startle you.' Belinda: a slender jumble of tumbling black hair, brightly coloured scarves, dangly earrings, old Barbour and narrow jeans. Beside her, Robbie, her Border collie, was hunched, pinpoint attention on something inside the wood. 'Hang on.' Belinda slipped the lead and the dog sped off, rippling, lowered almost to the ground, between the trees. 'Gone to round up yours, I expect.' Fixing Sophie with a stare almost as penetrating as Robbie's, she intoned, 'There will be order in the universe.'

Disconcerted, Sophie took a step back, catching the arm of her sweater on a protruding bit of wood.

'Sorry, that was meant to be a joke. I think it's Robbie's mission statement.'

Belinda, Sophie now remembered, had said this several times before, and in much the same way. Now, she said, 'Here, let me help,' and started fiddling with Sophie's sleeve.

'It's OK, you don't—'

'No, no, keep still. Don't want to make a hole . . . There. No harm done. Were you on your way back? I saw your monster Merc in the lane . . . We've only just started our walk.'

A blink-of-an-eye computation told Sophie (*a*) that Belinda, unless she'd brought her own car (assuming she'd got one), would probably expect the offer of a lift home if they walked together and think it odd if she didn't get one; (*b*) that Jessica might well not have returned yet; and (*c*) that everything must appear as normal as possible, even if it wasn't.

'We've only just got here.' For a horrible moment, Sophie thought she might actually burst into tears, and masked it with a minute inspection of the sleeve of her jumper. Belinda said nothing, but feeling her watching, Sophie kept her eyes on the thin wool until the about-to-cry feeling had passed. 'Thanks. The jumper, I mean. It's fine.'

Belinda frowned at her. '*It's* fine, but are you? You seem a bit . . . I don't know, not quite right.'

'I'm fine, honestly.'

'Honestly?'

'Really. Just . . . you know, the usual stuff.'

'What sort of stuff?'

For a split second, she was tempted to confide. Belinda was a good listener – Sophie was always rabbiting on to her about what Leo and the children were up to, wasn't she? Also, she had an idea that Belinda might have lost her husband to a younger woman, so she would be bound to be sympathetic.

Dismissing the idea, she forced a grin and said, 'Life, really. I think I need Robbie to put my universe in order.'

'Herding the children, you mean?'

'Yeah . . .' Reinforcing her claim that it was no big deal with a medium-sized laugh, Sophie added, for verisimilitude, 'Actually, I think I might have a touch of hayfever.'

Belinda looked surprised. 'Bit early for that, isn't it?'

'I suppose so, although I can't think what else it could be. Anyway, how are you?'

'Oh, you know . . .' Belinda shrugged. 'I survive. Where were you going? I was planning to go through here –' she indicated the wood – 'and up to the common. I said I'd drop in on a friend who lives over there.'

That took care of the issue of the lift, anyway. 'We'll walk up there with you. Dexter needs some exercise. I'm afraid he got a bit short-changed over the weekend.'

It took them about three-quarters of an hour to get to the top of the common, where Belinda went off to see her friend, leaving Sophie and Dexter to walk back on their own. Dexter, Sophie thought, liked Robbie because Labradors were disposed to like everybody, but he clearly found both the sheepdog's propensity to treat other creatures as recalcitrant members of an imaginary herd and his general intensity rather wearing. It wasn't dissimilar to her own feelings about his owner. Belinda was nice enough, but she'd asked disconcertingly often – apropos of nothing in the conversation – if Sophie were *sure* she was all right, and there were only so many times you could bat that sort of question away without things getting uncomfortable.

It was warmer now, and Sophie took off her jumper, knotting it around her waist. As they came to the end of the footpath and turned back into the road, she spotted, over Jessica's hedge, the top of what looked like the silver-coloured Audi. Pausing to check her reflection in the wing mirror of her Mercedes, she tightened her grip on Dexter's lead and walked down to the T-junction, turning left to pass the lawn at the side of the cottage.

She could hear, through an open window, the faint sound of a radio, which meant that Jessica must be at home. This part of the garden was enclosed by a picket fence and she was strolling along beside it, trying to look nonchalant, when it occurred to her that, by concentrating on psyching herself up to confront Jessica, she'd neglected a crucial step in her plan. Simply banging on the door and haranguing the bitch, no matter how much she wanted to do so, would be counterproductive. She needed to put Jessica off her guard and then make her feel guilty, and behaving like a vengeful harpy was not the way to achieve either.

Walking a dog along the road was a perfectly legitimate activity, but she could hardly loiter in the lane in front of Jessica's house until the woman happened to emerge. What, actually, was she going to do?

EIGHTEEN

Dexter solved the problem for her. He'd been ambling along at her side, pausing occasionally to sniff beneath the wooden palings, but now he whirled round, bristling, the fur on his back raised in a crest of indignation. Yanked suddenly sideways as the dog bounded forwards, dragging her through the half-open garden gate, Sophie spotted the tabby a split second before it spotted them. She let go of the lead and watched as the cat, closely pursued by the furiously barking dog, streaked across Jessica's lawn and clawed its way up the poplar tree by the back of her garage in double-quick time.

'Dexter! Dexter!' Sophie stood just outside the gateway and yelled at the top of her voice. She knew there was no risk of the Labrador returning to her – at this point, he wouldn't have taken a blind bit of notice even had she been waving a fillet steak. The barking continued as, frenzied now, the dog bounced up and down beneath the tree while the cat, out of reach, clung to the trunk, ears clamped flat to its head.

'Dexter! Stop it!' Why hadn't Jessica appeared? The radio was audible, so surely she wasn't wearing headphones. Unless she was deaf or something. That's all I need, thought Sophie. She half walked, half ran into the garden and, standing as near to the cottage as was plausible under the circumstances, carried on bellowing at the dog.

Jessica must have come out of the back door, because she appeared, at a controlled run, from the far side of the building. She looked every bit as elegant and slender as Sophie had remembered, in a simple taupe-coloured tunic and skinny jeans, with a silk scarf twisted round her neck. Hand-painted, thought Sophie, wondering if Leo had given it to her.

'What's going on?' Jessica had to shout over the din made by Dexter, whose barking had gained such momentum that Sophie guessed it might be several minutes before he could be prevailed upon to shut up.

'I am sorry. Dexter, stop it!' Sophie ran towards the Labrador, who dodged her easily. 'Oh, dear. I was trying to hold on to him –' Sophie gestured at the trailing lead – 'but he practically dragged me through the hedge. He's got rather –' a rueful lift of the eyebrows, here – '*strong views* on cats.'

Sophie had thought that Jessica might be annoyed, but she just laughed. 'Oh, well. It's not my cat, just one that comes in the garden sometimes. Anyway, I'm sure it'll be OK.'

'But we can't just leave it. Cats can get stuck, can't they, if they panic? Dexter! Stop it!' Sophie made another swipe for the dog's collar, causing him to bolt behind a tree. 'For God's sake – come here, you wretched animal.'

Jessica watched while Sophie managed to grab Dexter and drag him from under the tree. Vibrating with fury, he struggled to get away from her as she hauled him towards, and then through, the garden gate. 'I'll just stick him in the car,' she shouted to Jessica. 'It's only down the lane – then I can give you a hand getting the cat down.'

Pretending she hadn't heard Jessica say, 'No, really, it's fine,' behind her, she bundled Dexter off down the road and loaded him, still protesting loudly, into the back of the Merc.

'Bless you, Dex,' she murmured, jogging back to Jessica's cottage. It was the perfect excuse – even if the cat and Jessica had both vanished from the garden, it would be only polite, after all the hoo-ha, to knock on the door, ensure that the animal had made it to the ground unhurt, and apologize formally. It even, astonishingly, felt almost like a normal situation, and, in the minute or so it took to get back to the cottage, Sophie had pretty well convinced herself that she'd let go of Dexter's lead entirely by accident.

In fact, the cat and Jessica were both where she'd left them: the animal flattened against the tree trunk, claws extended, looking paralysed with fright, and Jessica observing it from the lawn, twisting a glossy auburn wave of hair around a slender finger.

'You really didn't need to come back,' she said. 'It'll come down when it's hungry.'

'But what if it really is stuck? I am sorry about all this, but I do feel responsible. I don't suppose you've got a ladder, have you?'

'I have, but I imagine it'll go up even higher if we start climbing after it.'

'Well . . .' Sophie looked around the garden with what she hoped was an air of well-meaning helplessness. 'Perhaps I could just stay here until it comes down? I mean, I'd hate the poor thing to get hurt when it was my dog that made it go up there in the first place.' Encouraged by the 'we', she was banking on the fact that Jessica would be bound, if only from politeness, to stay with her.

'Fair enough. Let's give it a few minutes, anyway.'

Sophie thought Jessica seemed pretty relaxed. No excuses about having to get back to work or anything, and no indication that she'd recognized her, either. There were photographs in the flat, Sophie knew, showing them together – although she supposed Leo probably hid them somewhere when the two of them had their sordid little trysts . . . A sudden power surge of pure rage jolted her. I'm the woman whose husband you're fucking, she wanted to shout. I'm the woman whose letters you're defacing with threats, you vile bitch, and you don't even know who I am. 'Perhaps we ought to ignore it for the time being,' she said. 'Give it a chance to get down by itself. I'm sorry, I feel I ought to know who you are. Have you been in our shop?'

'Shop?' Jessica looked genuinely puzzled.

'Sorry. Hamilton De Witt. It's in Burnham Market.'

At least, Sophie thought, Jessica had the grace to look taken aback at this.

'I'm the Hamilton bit. Sophie.'

'Oh.' Jessica's smile didn't quite reach her eyes. 'Jessica Mottram. I have been in your shop a couple of times, yes. Lovely things.'

'Mottram?' Sophie frowned for a second, as if in thought. 'Your husband goes shooting with Leo, doesn't he? Sorry,' she added, as an afterthought, 'I should have explained. Leo's *my* husband.' She beamed at Jessica, then frowned again. 'But I thought . . . I mean, aren't you in London during the week? Is he taking time off?'

'Sean?'

'Yes. He's up here, is he?'

For a second, Sophie thought Jessica was about to tell her to mind her own business, but she said, 'No. Actually . . .' She looked down for a moment, prodding the grass with the toe of her (obviously expensive) loafer, then added, 'We've separated.'

'Oh . . . I'm sorry. I didn't mean to be . . . you know, to intrude.'

'That's all right. It was mutual. I know people always say that, but it was. It's fine, really.'

Fine because you've got your claws into my husband, thought Sophie. Sean had obviously discovered the affair and dumped her, and she was using Leo as her back-up plan – because, unless you were J. K. Rowling, you didn't make money from writing books, everyone knew that. 'Still,' she said, with a grimace, 'not much fun for you. But now that we've met – properly, I mean – why don't you come over for tea or a drink or something? We're only a couple of miles away.'

Jessica looked doubtful. 'That's very nice of you, but I am quite busy at the moment . . .'

'What do you do? Sorry, I should have asked.'

'Well, I'm a journalist, but at the moment I'm writing a book.'

This, Sophie felt, was said with an annoyingly calculated degree of modesty, but she made a show of being impressed, widening her eyes in delighted surprise and crying out, 'How wonderful! Is it a novel?'

'Biography.'

'Oh, I love biographies. I've just been trying to persuade our reading group to do . . .' Sophie tried, and failed, to remember the subject of the last biography she'd read. 'To do something like that, but they're obstinate about sticking to fiction. Who's it of?'

'A woman called Elizabeth Chudleigh. Duchess, eighteenth century.'

'What made you choose her? I mean, was there a particular reason?'

'Well . . .' Jessica did the grass-prodding thing again, and then, giving a half-laugh, said, 'Scandal, really. She was tried for bigamy.'

'Heavens! Was she guilty?'

''Fraid so. She ended up leaving the country.'

'She sounds fascinating. I'd love to hear more about her – do come over, won't you? I mean, you must have to get out once in a while, and it can't be good to spend so much time on your own, not at the moment. How about Wednesday afternoon? Would that work?'

'Well . . .'

'Tell you what.' Sophie fumbled in her handbag for a note-book. 'Why don't you give me your email address? Then we can sort something out.'

'OK,' said Jessica, weakly. 'Let me write it down for you.'

'That's great. Don't look now, but I think the cat's on the move.'

It was, slowly slithering backwards down the tree trunk until it reached the bottom, whence it shot the pair of them a filthy look before disappearing into the bushes.

*

'OK, Dexter?' Sophie settled herself into the driver's seat and, pulling down the sun visor, inspected her face in the vanity mirror.

'I'm Jessica and I'm writing a book,' she simpered. 'It's about some woman called Elizabeth Chutney who screwed around, so we have a great deal in common.' Changing her expression to one of exaggerated interest, she said, with loud, bright fierceness, 'How fascinating! I don't think I've ever met a writer before – not one who's sucking my husband's cock on a regular basis, anyway.'

The unexpected coarseness of her language surprised her – that wasn't how she talked – and the words seemed to reverberate inside the expensive leather interior, making her almost as embarrassed as if she'd been overheard. After a moment, she felt slow, hopeless tears welling up, and, blinking, stared hard into the hedge. Come on, she told herself. You can do this. After all, you've got this far . . . Now get on home and fire off a nice, friendly email to Jessica.

NINETEEN

Sophie returned home to find a large white van, a courier company's logo on its side, parked in the driveway. Judging from the body language, it looked as though Imanuela was having some kind of stand-off with the driver, who was a beefy type with a mulish expression. She came over, looking anxious, as Sophie got out of the car. 'I told him you're not here right now, but . . .' She rolled her eyes.

'Well, I am here *now*, anyway. What is it?'

'Delivery for Mrs Hamilton.' The driver jerked a thumb at the van. 'Boxes.'

'But I haven't ordered anything.' Surely Leo hadn't got her some absurdly lavish guilt offering to supplement the flowers. What kind of idiot did he think she was?

'Well,' said the driver, 'all I know is what it says on the docket.'

'I told him,' said Imanuela. 'Wrong place. Is for the shop, not here.'

Sophie took the proffered piece of paper. The sender was given as Iron Works, with an address in Guildford. The bloody garden ornaments. She'd been in such a state that she must have put down the wrong delivery address. 'The shop's only a couple of miles down the road,' she said to the driver. 'Could you take them there? I'd be happy to come with you in my car, so you know where it is.'

'Sorry, love. No can do. The instructions said to deliver them here, so . . .' He shrugged, then folded his arms for emphasis.

'OK.' Turning to Imanuela, Sophie said, 'Well, we'd better put them in the hall until I can get them to the shop.'

'Right.' The driver marched back to the van and threw open the back doors. There seemed to be an astonishing number of cardboard boxes – she'd obviously bought more items than she remembered. At least they were clearly labelled: weather-vane, sundial, heron, hare, and the like, with, at the back of the van, a larger box, presumably containing the astrolabe. Perhaps it wasn't such a mistake having them delivered to the house, she thought, as she helped to ferry the boxes indoors. She could photograph some of the things in the garden and upload the pictures to the Hamilton De Witt website. Come to think of it, there was no reason why some of them wouldn't work just as well indoors. With the right background, they'd look quite striking . . . In fact, she'd make a start straight after lunch. The email to Jessica could wait an hour or so – it was probably good not to send it straight away because it wouldn't do to look too keen. Casual and friendly was what she had to aim for, with no suggestion of anything needy or stalkerish.

'Can you take that one through to the sitting room?' she asked as the man brought the box containing the astrolabe into the hall. 'It's the second door on the left.'

*

'Why does it have an arrow going through it?' Imanuela stood back to admire the astrolabe, which they'd unpacked and placed on the coffee table.

'No idea. Can you move it forward and round a bit? The angle's not quite right. I want to get the flowers in the fireplace into the shot as background.'

'Ay ay ay, it's sharp.' Imanuela sucked the tip of her finger. 'Dexter, don't touch.' She gave the inquisitive Labrador a little shove with her knee, so that he backed away. 'So, OK . . . Is that better?'

'I think so.' The wrought iron looked great, Sophie thought, against the mass of pink and white roses and peonies in the large bowl she'd positioned in the middle of the hearth. 'Come and see.'

Imanuela came to stand beside Sophie. 'Yes, it's good.'

'I'll do some pictures, and then we can photograph the other things in the garden, if you want to make a start taking them out there.'

Three hours later, having talked to Melissa and uploaded the best of the photos onto the shop's website, Sophie settled down to write the email to Jessica.

Sorry for invading your garden.

It was important to keep things light, even jaunty, without even a hint of secondary meaning, no matter how hard Jessica looked. Sophie wondered if she should use an emoji after 'garden' to keep the tone light. The monkey with its paws over its mouth seemed the best visual 'oops', but perhaps that wasn't what it was supposed to mean because it was one of the three wise monkeys. Jessica might translate 'Speak No Evil' as Sophie's coded way of saying that she knew she was the sender of the returned letters.

Better not to risk it. An emoticon might be OK, though – more sophisticated, because typographic and not ready-made. Which one, though? Was there even an emoticon for slightly cheeky recognition of minor embarrassment? It appeared to be :$, but Jessica might not understand this and think it was a typing error. Perhaps just a simple exclamation mark, then.

No. Jessica was a writer, and writers didn't like exclamation marks. Besides, she didn't want to come across as shouty or over-eager. Stop overthinking it, she told herself. Be straightforward. Right:

Sorry for invading your garden, but lovely—

Wrong word. Too strong.

Sorry for invading your garden, but very nice to bump into you. Hope you're still on for tea on Wednesday. Say 3.30 p.m.?

Yes, that was good; it made it sound as if 'tea on Wednesday' was a definite arrangement and the only thing unresolved was the time of arrival. Her choice of Wednesday had been deliberate – Imanuela had the whole day off and usually went somewhere in the car, often staying out for most of the evening as well; Zac had nets after school; and it was Ottilie's mum's day for collecting Poppy and the others.

What else? A spot of friendly flattery . . . *Your book sounded fascinating and I'd love to hear more about it.*

Yes, that worked. Any writer – especially one who wasn't published yet – would be bound to go for that. She read the message again and, satisfied, added her name at the bottom and pressed Send.

Good. Job done – and just in time to collect Poppy from her violin lesson. Pleased by her own efficiency, Sophie picked up her handbag, called out to Imanuela, and left the house.

TWENTY

Sophie checked her emails regularly for the rest of the day, but there was no reply from Jessica, and nothing when she checked her inbox on Tuesday morning, either. Jessica's website didn't give a phone number and Directory Enquiries were unable to provide one. She'd definitely sent the email to the address that Jessica had written down – and it couldn't have been wrong because it hadn't bounced back. She could hardly go back to the woman's house and chase her up . . .

It suddenly occurred to Sophie that perhaps Jessica was in London right now, in bed with Leo, having a postcoital discussion about whether or not she should accept the invitation. She could just imagine Jessica being hypocritically sympathetic to her – *I can't, darling. I'd feel terrible. After all, it's not her fault, is it?* – and Leo trying to keep calm as he thought about his two worlds colliding.

Stop it, she told herself. You can't afford to think about that – you don't even know that it's happening. She needed to focus on something else, like making a start on schlepping the wrought-iron ornaments over to Hamilton De Witt. Driving and lugging the boxes about would be just the job to distract her from checking her phone every few minutes.

Four hours later, she had managed to transfer half the boxes to the Hamilton De Witt storeroom (Melissa'd been aghast at how much stuff she'd bought, but mollified by the photographs Sophie had uploaded, which really did look fabulous). The rest of the boxes were still stacked along the side of the hall at the Old Rectory, which had annoyed Mrs Palmer. She hadn't been any too keen on the 'doobry' on the coffee table in the sitting room, either, claiming that the arrow could 'have someone's eye out'. Sophie had placated her with custard creams and the promise that there wouldn't be any people of appropriate height (about three foot six) in the house before the astrolabe and boxes were removed. It would be good for Jessica to see them, Sophie thought – they were proof that she did actually have a job and was therefore an equal. *If* she saw them ... Sophie had kept her resolution not to check her phone every few minutes, but there'd been nothing by lunchtime, and now it was gone two o'clock.

Leaving her phone behind, she loaded Dexter into the car for a deliberately long drive culminating in a breezy walk to a ruined abbey on a headland, where she watched as he ran in and out of stone stumps and arches that led to nowhere, sniffing for rabbits. Staring out at the small, choppy waves, Sophie thought of Belinda's cottage slowly collapsing into the sea. Then she thought about Margot. The last few times she'd phoned her mother, the conversation had been repetitive and straggling, with Sophie trying to conceal her impatience. All offers of help – to shop for Margot, or have her come and stay – had been rebuffed with an irritation that, during their last conversation, had erupted into anger when Sophie brought up the subject of the purple satin slip. Now that Sophie considered it, it had been a while – several weeks, in fact – since Margot had called *her*.

She wandered about, the furze and marram grass catching at her legs, and imagined herself living in Margot's cottage and trying to care for her mother as she became increasingly chaotic, losing things, words, memories, and control of her bodily functions, while a triumphant Jessica took *her* place, in *her* house, with *her* children.

She arrived back home at four to find an email from Jessica: *Yes, that's fine. See you tomorrow. J.*

Clearly, she'd decided to brazen it out. Perhaps she hadn't told Leo at all. Maybe she was even thinking of her visit to the Old Rectory as a sort of reconnaissance mission.

That must be it, thought Sophie. Still, it didn't matter what the reason was, because Jessica was going to be given her marching orders. Now, it was just a matter of booking a blow-dry and a manicure for the following morning – it was important to look her best – and working out how to send the bloody woman packing.

TWENTY-ONE

At half past two, Sophie had a bath and dressed with care. Should she go for Boden Mum – fun, spontaneous, sexy-but-not-alarmingly-so – or something a bit more sophisticated? She needed to look well-turned-out but relaxed enough to make Jessica feel too sharp-edged, too urban, and not a real part of Leo's world. In the end, she plumped for a swishy skirt and a figure-hugging cashmere cardigan, leaving the top buttons undone to show just a hint of cleavage. The troughs of sleeplessness under her eyes from two restless nights going over and over exactly what she would say to Jessica were more of a problem, and had to be grouted with Touche Éclat. Still, the result wasn't too bad at all, and the discreet but gorgeous earrings – an anniversary present from Leo a few years ago – finished things off nicely.

She'd already set the scene in the kitchen, where she planned to take Jessica first, with a jug of spring flowers, a plate of florentines and Choco Leibniz, and a few well-placed props (Poppy's ballet shoes, some schoolwork of Zac's, and Leo's yachting magazine) lying about; signs of family life – the life Jessica wanted to destroy – being lived. Perhaps, she thought, looking around, she ought to bring the dog's bowl through from the utility room, as well ('Leo and I couldn't imagine life without Dexter – the kids absolutely adore him'). The Labrador followed her, paying close attention, and then, no food being forthcoming, curled up beside the Aga. He was fairly clean, having had a bath the previous week, and the freesias in her arrangement smelt lovely ... What else was needed? Sound, perhaps. Classic FM.

SMUG BITCH, indeed. Sophie almost – but not quite – wanted to laugh. Now she just needed to close the door to the freezer room – it wasn't dirty or anything, but they really should have had it spruced up when they'd got the kitchen redone – and everything would be ready.

The sitting room looked fine, too. Unsure how to fill the minutes before Jessica's arrival, Sophie wandered about, fiddling with flower arrangements and fussing with ornaments until, at twenty to four, the doorbell rang.

'Hello! Glad you could make it!'

Sophie heard Zac's voice in her head ('Dial it down, Mum') as she stood back to allow Jessica to enter. She was as stylish as before – crisp white shirt, elegant jacket, cigarette pants, pointy-toed kitten heels, a Mulberry bag, and the same trench coat Sophie had seen her wearing outside Leo's flat, which she hung up in the cloakroom.

'Wow! Love your house. Must take a lot of upkeep.'

'Well –' Sophie gave a little laugh – 'it's not particularly cheap.' So Jessica really is on a recce, she thought. She actually thinks she's going to be moving in.

Jessica looked round the hall. 'Beautiful, though.'

'Well, you know. *We* like it, anyway. Come on through.'

'And this is lovely, too.' Jessica gazed around the kitchen with open enthusiasm. 'That's Dexter, isn't it? Caught any cats lately?'

Dexter, who for once had not accompanied Sophie to the front door, sat up and thumped his tail lazily on the tiles.

'Well remembered! The name, I mean. Hang on, I'll just switch off the radio and make some tea. We can have it in the sitting room, and Old Greedy Guts over there can stay in here, otherwise he'll pinch all the biscuits.'

Sophie put the tray of tea and biscuits on the coffee table next the astrolabe, and Jessica sat down on the sofa and began to examine the ornament. 'What's the arrow supposed to be pointing at? The pole?'

'Could be, though I've got no idea which pole, or which direction it ought to be pointing. I bought it for the shop, really, but I'm thinking I might keep it. As long as Leo likes it, of course.' She beamed at Jessica and pulled up an armchair. 'Milk?'

'Please.' Jessica's expression hadn't changed when she'd mentioned Leo, but then, Sophie thought, the woman was an expert at deception.

After quite a bit more about the shop, and an awful lot about Elizabeth Chudleigh, Duchess of Wherever-it-was, there was a pause. The tea in the pot would be cold by now, and Sophie thought that if she offered to make more there was a chance that Jessica would decline and leave (after all, they'd been chatting about nothing much for the best part of half an hour). It was now or never. 'Your duchess doesn't seem to have had much of a conscience, does she?'

Jessica raised a beautifully plucked eyebrow. 'That's a bit harsh. Social mores were different then – a divorce would have been a terrific scandal.'

'But surely bigamy was even more of one? And she'd perjured herself, hadn't she, swearing that she hadn't been married before.'

'Yes, but nobody was that bothered until her second husband's nephew wanted to challenge the will – so really, you could argue that it came down to money, not morals.'

'But even if he did want the money, she was still a bigamist, wasn't she? She wasn't legally married to the second husband . . . Good job it's easier nowadays, really. Divorce, I mean.'

'Yes, isn't it just?' Jessica's tone was sardonic.

'God, sorry. That was . . . I mean, you and Sean – it must be a sore point at the moment.'

'As I said, it was mutual.'

'Nevertheless –' Sophie ignored the touch of *froideur* and continued, as sympathetically as she could manage – 'it must be difficult. And, as you say, things often do come down to money, unfortunately. I know quite a few woman who've been left . . . well, pretty much high and dry, when their husbands went off with younger women – of course, it's different if you have children, because then obviously you get the house and money and so on, but for people who don't, especially if one earns a lot and the other doesn't . . . I mean, journalism, writing – obviously, it sounds *terribly* glamorous and I'm sure it *is*, but I know it doesn't usually pay very well. And there's so much financial insecurity

these days – for everyone, I mean. I know this place looks . . .'
Sophie glanced around the room. 'You know . . . but Leo's always
telling me that we're only one pay cheque away from disaster.
As you said, the upkeep, and you wouldn't believe the school
fees. Of course, it's not just us, it's the same for lots of people
we know. Take the shop, for instance. Melissa and I have been
working all hours to build up the business, ever since we started,
but it's not breaking even yet, and heaven knows when we'll
actually be able to pay ourselves anything.'

Jessica had sat very still for most of this, with the appearance
of paying great attention. Now, her gaze flitted uneasily about
the room before settling on the empty teacup in her hands. 'I
suppose it must be difficult, but surely you're in a better position
than most people.'

'Oh, I know,' said Sophie. 'And I'm certainly not complaining
– that would be ridiculous. But what I'm saying is, if anything
were to happen, well . . .'

'But . . .' Jessica pushed a strand of hair behind her ear,
exposing a discreet diamond stud that looked suspiciously like
something Leo would choose. 'It's not going to, is it?'

'Isn't it?'

'Well, why should it? Are you worried that Leo's going to lose
his job or something?'

God, but you're good, thought Sophie. You ought to be on
the stage. She took a deep, self-controlling breath, and said, in
the calmest voice she could manage, 'You know that's not what
I'm worried about. What you're proposing to do is theft – taking
what isn't yours – and I have the evidence.'

The last sentence seemed to writhe, worm-like, in the air for a moment before Jessica's eyes opened wide and she flushed, fumbling with the teacup so that it clattered against the saucer. She opened her mouth and closed it again, like an actress who'd forgotten her lines and was desperate for a prompt. 'I don't know what you're talking about.'

'You know exactly what I'm talking about.'

'I have no idea.' Jessica stood up, reaching for her handbag. 'I think I'd better go.'

'Really?' Sophie stood up too, and marched round the coffee table to face her. 'Is that all you've got to say?'

'Yes.' Jessica took a step back. 'I don't know what you think you know or have evidence of, but it's not really any of your business.'

'*What?*' The woman really was unbelievable. 'Of course it's my business.'

'Look,' said Jessica, in an infuriatingly reasonable tone. She put out a hand to touch Sophie's arm. 'I know it doesn't look good, but things—'

'Get your hands off me!'

Jessica backed away again, bag on arm and palms up in a placatory gesture. Now, she was directly in front of the coffee table. 'Whoa! Calm down. It's not as if you're in love with him, is it?'

That was the moment, Sophie thought afterwards. As if a switch had been thrown. 'You really are—'

'Sophie, *please*. Look, I'm going to leave now, and I think it would be best if—'

'You're not going anywhere.' Sophie advanced on Jessica, who was now shielding herself with her handbag. They were so close now that Jessica's face – the cheeks and eyelids Leo must have kissed a thousand times, the mouth that had encircled his cock – was a blur. 'How dare you say I don't love him!' Taut with fury, she jabbed Jessica's shoulder repeatedly with stiff fingers, pushing her backwards so that she was hemmed in by the coffee table, armchair and mantelpiece. 'How! Dare! You!' she spat.

Jessica gasped, jerked her head away and stuck her arms out to push the armchair backwards and escape. Sophie lunged at her. Exactly what happened after that, she wasn't sure: a frenzy of flailing arms, clutching hands and scratching nails, during which she was aware of effortful sounds – breaths and groans – as well as a thud when the armchair toppled over and a splintery crack when the side table followed, but no actual words. She remembered dragging Jessica back as she tried to clamber over the capsized furniture and hitting her across the face as they tussled, just before Jessica barged into her, knocking her to the floor.

As Sophie scrambled onto her knees, Jessica loomed over her for an instant, shouting inarticulately, swinging her handbag and kicking out with her pointed shoes as she tried to get past. Sophie thrust herself forward, rugby-tackling Jessica round the knees so that her legs buckled and she fell sideways onto the coffee table, catching Sophie's cheek with her elbow as she went and scattering the china.

Sophie sensed, rather than saw, this happen. For some moments she remained quite still, face down on the floor, hearing first noise, then silence, and feeling a fierce, burning pain in her cheek. As she clambered upright, using the sofa for support, she heard a sigh behind her, followed by a faint gurgling noise. Turning, she saw first Jessica's legs, awkwardly angled as though she were a marionette dropped from a height, and then her torso, arched over the coffee table so that the back of her head was resting on the wooden surface, chin pointing upwards. The position was an odd one, made odder by the fact that, unbuttoned, the two sides of Jessica's jacket had fallen open, exposing the garment's yellow silk lining and obscuring her shoulders and back from view.

Jessica's face was turned very slightly towards her, and Sophie saw, in her eyes, an expression of stupefied astonishment.

'Jessica.' There was no response of any sort. 'Jessica!'

Oh, God. Sophie's heart seemed to be actually throwing itself against the walls of her chest. She looked round the room. Nobody else there. Of course there wasn't – but the air seemed somehow sharper, the colours deeper, and the silence thrummed in her ears. 'Jessica!'

Still no response, not even the motionless animation of a living-but-unconscious body. Possibilities jostled in Sophie's mind. A seizure? A heart attack? An embolism? Should she try and get her into the recovery position, or would moving her do more harm than good?

Hearing a faint scraping noise, Sophie walked round the coffee table and saw, sticking out from underneath Jessica's splayed jacket, the wooden base of the astrolabe. Gingerly, she lifted the cloth, and saw the rings and – to her horror – the shaft of the arrow with its delicate wrought-iron fletchings.

Sophie gasped and stepped back, her shoulders colliding with the mantelpiece, her entire body feeling as though it had been filled with iced water.

In falling, Jessica had impaled herself. Judging from her

position and the sculpture's, and her utter absence of vital signs, the arrowhead, entering through her back, must have embedded itself in her chest, close to – and maybe actually puncturing – her heart.

TWENTY-TWO

Turning away from Jessica, Sophie saw, in the mirror above the fireplace, a dishevelled woman with wild eyes and a bruise spreading across her cheek. For a moment, she failed to recognize herself. The portion of the room – above waist height – that she could see reflected in the mirror looked normal, even serene, with everything in its place. It was all OK. She'd turn round and find the furniture set to rights, the teapot and cups back on the coffee table and Jessica sitting in the armchair.

Staring into her mad reflected eyes, she counted – very slowly – up to ten. Now, she told herself, she was ready. Now she'd turn round.

She turned. Jessica was still there, in the same contorted position.

She had to *do* something. Stumbling past the overturned, splintered furniture, she made for the kitchen, and, sweeping elastic bandages and tubes of vitamins out of the way with her arm, grabbed the emergency first aid kit out of the cupboard and rushed back to the sitting room, slamming the door on Dexter when he tried to follow her.

She knelt beside Jessica, and, keeping her eyes averted from the slack, sideways face, upended the contents of the plastic case on the carpet and started pawing through it. 'It's all right, Jessica. I'm here. Everything's going to be OK,' she muttered. For a second, she felt like an actor playing a scene in a medical drama. The doctor, competent and calm, working methodically . . . But what was she supposed to *do*? She stared helplessly at the packets of eye pads, the foil heat-blankets in their wrappers, the zinc oxide tape, the ice bags – all of it great for sports injuries, but utterly useless now. 'Jessica, stay with me.' That was what people in films said in these situations, wasn't it? 'Stay with me, Jessica, we'll sort you out, we'll get help . . .'

Get help? Sophie froze, one hand clapped against her mouth. This was Leo's mistress – the woman who was going to take him away from her. If she called an ambulance, the police would have to be involved. They'd see evidence of a fight and think she'd done it deliberately, and then . . . No. She couldn't get help. She'd have to sort it out herself. 'Jessica! *Please*, Jessica!'

She wasn't breathing. Desperate, Sophie tugged at her arm, then recoiled in horror as Jessica, implacably inert, slumped over towards her. There was a noise like nails scraping down a blackboard, and, when Sophie crawled round to look, she saw that the base of the astrolabe, dragged across the coffee table by the movement of Jessica's body, had left a deep gouge in its polished wooden surface.

It was already too late. Jessica was beyond help.

They'd charge her with manslaughter at the very least, maybe even murder. She'd lose everything. Leo would never speak to her again, and he'd turn the children against her . . . She'd go to prison for years and when she finally got out she'd have to live on benefits – assuming that there were any benefits by that time – in some ghastly hostel full of drug addicts and deranged people. She had a sudden, vivid picture of herself, obese and pasty but hollowed out inside by years of misery, clad in a worn-out tracksuit and sitting on the step outside a concrete unit, waiting to be let in for the night.

No. Jessica was dead, and there was nothing she could do about that, but—

The mantel clock – Edwardian mahogany and inlay – suddenly came into focus in front of Sophie's eyes, the hands pointing to four and five. It took her a moment to compute: 4.25 p.m. Ottilie's mum was always punctual, which meant that she had *just over half an hour* to get rid of Jessica's body before Poppy was dropped off.

You can do this, she told herself. Think.

First, she needed to pull the arrow out of Jessica's back. She'd never be able to move her if she were attached to a lump of iron.

She'd need something to soak up any blood. Dexter scratched at the kitchen door as she ran past it to the utility room for newspaper to spread across the coffee table and the surrounding carpet. Brushing the various bits of first aid kit aside, she had vague thoughts – blurry impressions gleaned from various TV shows – about DNA, and decided she'd better clear all that up first, in case it got contaminated. How accurate the TV shows actually were, she didn't know, but it was best to be on the safe side. Scrabbling feverishly to stuff all the various boxes and packets back into the first aid case, she spotted a pair of nitrile gloves – to prevent fingerprints, of course – and, ripping the bag open with her teeth, put them on.

The newspaper in place, Sophie knelt as close to the coffee table as she could, and, taking hold of the base of the astrolabe in one gloved hand, pulled as hard as she could whilst shoving Jessica's body away from her with the other, keeping her eyes shut. For the first few seconds it seemed to be going well, but then there was resistance, as if the arrowhead had – Sophie swallowed hard – caught on something inside Jessica. She imagined cartilage covering the meat of an organ – please let it not be bone, because then she'd never get it out – being ripped open as the arrow was jerked backwards. Shutting her eyes even tighter, she yanked the base of the astrolabe as hard as she could. After a few goes the arrowhead came loose and, with a horrible sucking sound, it was out. Sophie let go of both the astrolabe and Jessica, and heard two thuds as they fell back onto the coffee table.

Cautiously, she opened her eyes. Jessica's top half – still face up, but this time flat – was lying on the coffee table, the rest of her sprawled on the carpet. On her white shirt was a small red stain, just above her heart. The arrow, Sophie thought, must have penetrated all the way through. She was surprised by how little blood there was – she'd been expecting pints of the stuff – but, apart from on the arrowhead and the upper part of the shaft and a bit on the table, there was hardly any.

That made things easier, anyway. The mantel clock said nearly 4.35 p.m. Sophie raced into the hall, grabbed the end of the Chinese rug and towed it back into the sitting room. It was a long one, fairly narrow, and – as had been proved when Dexter puked on it – easily cleaned. She'd just have to hope that blood would come off as successfully as vomit did, and that she could manage to keep Jessica face down, because the wound in her back would surely be considerably larger and messier than the one on her front.

She lined up the rug alongside the coffee table – 4.37 p.m. now – then grabbed hold of Jessica's shoulders and, twisting her over, heaved her off the table so that her upper body landed on top of the exophthalmic Oriental dragons. Next her legs – it was easy enough to pull them onto the rug – and then Sophie gathered one tasselled corner round each of Jessica's ankles and, holding them firmly, began to tug, walking backwards towards the sitting-room door.

Sophie was strong and fit – spinning classes and Pilates had seen to that – but Jessica was astonishingly heavy, with her head down and hair flopping forward with each step Sophie took. One of her arms dropped off the rug and trailed awkwardly across the floor, catching itself in the doorway so that Sophie had to lower her burden in order to release it. This done, she stood in the hall, hesitating. It was 4.40 p.m. now – only twenty minutes left. Whatever she was going to do, she needed to do it quickly. Take Jessica out through the back door and hide her in the garage? Someone might see – the yard, being behind the house, wasn't visible from the road, but Imanuela might come back early. She usually went out in the evening when she had a day off, but today might be the exception, and Sophie hadn't thought to ask what her plans were. The pond? No. As well as being further away from the house, it was definitely visible from the road – besides which, she'd never be able to get her out again, and the water level got pretty low in dry summers. Upstairs was out of the question because she'd never manage it in time, and so was the utility room – too many people going in and out – and the downstairs loo because it couldn't be locked from the outside.

She was wasting time. A cupboard? There wasn't anything big enough downstairs that locked ... Dexter, still shut in the kitchen, gave an aggrieved yelp from behind the door, making her jump.

The kitchen. Of course. She was being stupid – the answer was practically staring her in the face.

TWENTY-THREE

Dexter wagged and sniffed around Jessica as Sophie dragged her, in a series of increasingly desperate and back-wrenching jerks, across the kitchen and into the freezer room, where she shut the door in the dog's inquisitive face.

Apart from the row of coat hooks by the door into the garden, the freestanding chest freezer was the small room's only furniture. It was big – five feet long and three feet high – and three-quarters full of food. Grunting with relief, she dropped Jessica and the rug on the floor, and then, lifting the thick white lid, plunged her hands into the icy fog to pull out frozen peas, ice cream, prawns, fish fillets, legs of lamb, sliced bread, chicken stock and cling-filmed pieces of old wedding cake, and drop them on the flagstones.

Jessica would have to go right at the bottom. She'd need folding up a bit, Sophie thought grimly, but she'd fit, and there ought to be enough room left over for quite a lot of the food to go back in on top. It was a shame that the thing didn't lock, but at least it was a solution.

With hands burning from the ice, Sophie hauled Jessica and the rug as close to the freezer as she could manage. The shoes would have to come off first – that was simple enough – and then ... Careful to bend at the knees, Sophie put her hands under Jessica's armpits and, struggling into an upright position, lifted the body up with her. It sagged against her, making her lurch backwards against the side of the freezer, and the drooping head with its mop-like, hanging hair swung towards her, bumping her cheek.

She closed her eyes and clenched her teeth. Oh, God. She wasn't going to be able to do it.

She *had* to do it. Opening her eyes, Sophie squinted over Jessica's slumped shoulder at her watch: 4.50 p.m. *Ten minutes left.*

She shuffled to one side so that Jessica fell forward, her torso hanging over the edge of the freezer. Then, squatting down, Sophie grabbed her ankles and, with an agonizing, muscle-tearing wrench, yanked them upwards so that the body was propelled inside. For a horrible moment, Jessica appeared to be standing on her head, and then her body collapsed downwards, the legs concertinaing so that she ended up awkwardly bunched at the bottom of the space, arms underneath her.

Sophie crawled around the floor, grabbing packets of food and lobbing them back into the freezer, then scrambled up and squashed everything down as hard as she could with the palms of her hands, scooping up a few more of the flatter items from the floor until the thing was completely full.

Numb fingers trembling, she crashed the lid down, then charged back into the kitchen, shoving aside a thoroughly bewildered Dexter, to find the bin liners. The dog sat in the doorway, eyeing her as she ripped one from the roll and started filling it with the remainder of the food from the floor. She'd cart it down to the bin shed at the gate, then get started on removing all traces of Jessica from the house. Hauling the bulging plastic sack along beside her, Sophie threw open the side door – and saw Jessica's silver Audi, parked on the gravel drive and clearly visible from both the road and the churchyard.

Shit. Dumping the bin liner in the doorway, she galloped back through the kitchen and down the hall to the key cupboard at the back door. She'd have to put the thing into the double garage with Leo's car – unlike the other garage, that one was always kept locked and no one would have any reason to go in there until the weekend. Praying that Imanuela wouldn't turn up, Sophie swiped the fob from the hook, raced out of the back door and across the yard and jabbed the key into the lock. A bolt of pain shot across her lower back as she stooped to yank up the heavy retractable door – why hadn't they got electric ones, for Christ's sake? – and she tottered backwards, grimacing, as it swung up and backwards to reveal – No, no, *no!* – Leo's Porsche, parked smack in the middle of the available space.

She'd have to move it, otherwise Jessica's car wouldn't fit.

The Porsche key wasn't on its hook in the cupboard – Leo must have left it in the study. Sophie raced down the hall and hurled herself up the stairs, crying out as she tripped and her knee smacked squarely into one of the risers, then hobbled down the corridor, wincing from the pain.

The key was on Leo's desk. Sophie snatched it and belted back down to the garage to reverse the car out into the yard and repark it. She never normally drove the Porsche, which was manual, not automatic, so she lost precious, frantic seconds

gear-crunching it into reverse. She got the car out of the garage
OK, but, on the way back in, she heard a thump and a scraping
noise – without sensors to warn her, she'd aimed the thing too
far over and the rear wing had collided with one of the metal
storage racks screwed into the wall.

No time to worry about that now. What was done was done,
and she had – oh, fuck – just over *five* minutes to hide Jessica's
car, lug the bin bag full of surplus food down to the gate and
sort out every other bloody thing. Shit, she'd left herself no room
to get out. Pulling up the handbrake, she clambered across to
the passenger seat, flung herself out of the car and shot back
into the house.

The sitting room. Jessica's handbag. Praying that she'd put her
car key in there and not in her jacket pocket, Sophie scrabbled
through the contents of the expensive leather satchel until –
thank you, God – her fingers closed over something oblong and
chunky.

Jessica's Audi was automatic. Sophie got it round the corner
and into the garage next to the Porsche in under a minute,
then slammed down the retractable door, locked it, and dashed
back round the side of the house to leave the various keys on
top of the freezer before sweeping up the full rubbish bag and
running down the drive to dump it in the bin shed. Sprinting
back through the side door to the freezer room, she tripped
over Dexter, who was sniffing at something on the flagstones.

Sophie careered sideways and fell heavily, catching the underside of her chin on the corner of the freezer as she went down,
one knee landing with a crunch on something agonizingly
sharp. Swearing, eyes stinging with tears, she struggled upright

as the dog, tail between his legs, shot out of the side door and into the garden. Head ringing, one hand on her jaw and the other on her knee, which, thanks to the previous collision with the stair, was now throbbing, she looked down and saw that what she'd landed on was Jessica's left shoe. The right shoe was several feet away, beside the hall rug. For a second, she stared at the thick material, stupefied, wondering what the hell it was doing there, and then she picked up the shoes and limped into the kitchen, where she opened the pedal bin – almost full, thank God – and shoved the kitten heels as far down into the rubbish as she could manage.

4.58 p.m. She needed to get the rug back into place in the hall – Dexter would have to take the blame for any marks – and she still had to sort out the sitting room, or, at the very least, wipe the blood off the astrolabe and hide Jessica's handbag. Grabbing a J-cloth, she ran it under the tap, then limped into the sitting room, where she wiped the ornament as best she could and stood it back on the coffee table so that its base hid the gouge in the wood. Righting the armchair, she looked about her: next must be Jessica's handbag, and there were still the broken side table, the newspaper, the first aid kit and the china to deal with – two cups would be a dead giveaway – and Ottilie's mum was going to pull up at any minute . . . Picking up the handbag, she pushed it inside a cupboard in one of the alcoves, and then, with everything piled onto the tea tray and the newspapers gathered together under one arm, stumbled back into the kitchen.

The newspaper and J-cloth went straight into the bin, together with the leftover biscuits, and she loaded the china into the dishwasher – hand-painted stuff didn't usually go in there, but faded flower patterns were the least of her problems now – shoved a tablet into the dispenser, and pressed the On switch.

After that, she dealt with the rug. Just the side table to worry about, now. Gasping – her knee felt as though it were actually *on fire* – she returned to the sitting room, collected the tipped-over table and its snapped-off leg, and took them across the yard and into the other, unlocked garage, where Leo kept the elderly long-wheel-base Land Rover that served as his shooting syndicate's game wagon. After depositing the pieces right at the back, behind bicycles, plastic storage boxes and half-empty paint tins, Sophie made it across the yard and into the house, stripping off the nitrile gloves as she went, just in time to hear Poppy's key in the front door, the sound of Dexter's barking and girls' voices, an explosion of laughter . . .

Oh, *shit.* She'd completely forgotten that Cressida was coming for a sleepover.

Unable to face either her or Poppy, Sophie hurried into the kitchen, where she thrust the gloves in the bin and collapsed onto the nearest chair.

She heard twin thumps as the girls dropped their schoolbags onto the floor. 'Mu-um!'

Not in here, *please* not in here . . . 'I'm a bit busy, Poppy. Why don't you go straight upstairs and change?'

'OK!' Poppy's voice was a joyful sing-song. 'We'll be down in a minute!'

'OK!' Sophie echoed, doing her best to inject her voice with the same level of enthusiasm.

Footsteps gave way to silence as the girls dashed upstairs, and Sophie put her elbows on the table and her head in her hands.

This cannot be me, she thought, closing her eyes. Not me, not now. It must be somebody else entirely.

I must not panic, she thought. Poppy's 'down in a minute' invariably meant 'down in fifteen minutes' – probably longer, as Cressida was with her – and Zac wouldn't be back for about an hour, so at least she had a little time in which to compose herself.

A sudden pressure on her leg made her start, and, looking down, she saw that it was Dexter, his chin resting on her thigh, big brown eyes yearning. The dog wants his dinner, she thought in amazement. The world carries on.

TWENTY-FOUR

In the utility room, doling out the dog food while Dexter watched, Sophie's sense of unreality intensified. I cannot have done *that*, she thought. I cannot have done what I just did and be here now, calmly feeding the dog.

But she *had*, and she *was*; and – for everyone's sake – everything must continue exactly as normal.

Sophie checked the sitting room: all correct except for a stain – tea, she thought – on the carpet. Tugging the rug slightly to the left in order to cover it, she made a mental note to get the professional carpet cleaners in as soon as possible. Once Zac, Poppy and Cressida were safely in bed, she'd go over the whole room with a damp duster in case Jessica had left fingerprints. Sophie couldn't remember if she had used the downstairs loo, but it would best to damp-dust that, too, to be on the safe side, and the hall table, and of course the front door, because there'd be prints on that, and—

A tinny, insistent noise interrupted her thoughts. It didn't sound like her ringtone – in fact, she wasn't even sure where her mobile was.

Jessica's phone. She must have told Leo that she was coming

131

here, and now he was ringing to see how it had gone. On her knees in front of the alcove cupboard, Sophie plunged her hand into the leather satchel, dreading seeing her husband's name on the screen, but there was only a number. Not Leo's mobile . . . Unless he had a special phone just for calling Jessica – but if so, she'd have the number in *her* phone, wouldn't she? Sophie waited to see if the caller would leave voicemail, but whoever it was must have disconnected during the answerphone message, because there was nothing.

Ought she to turn the phone off? No . . . A woman having an affair with a married man would be permanently 'on call', wouldn't she? Sophie found the volume button on the side of the phone and set it to Mute, then stuffed it back into the bag and shut the cupboard door.

Upstairs, in the en-suite bathroom, she stood in front of the mirror and took an inventory. The bruise on her cheek would have to be covered up, and there was a mark on her chin, too. The clothes would have to go – they didn't look too bad, considering, just a bit of dust and grime from where she'd brushed against things in the garage, but keeping them was too much of a risk. As she washed her hands she saw that, sometime during the afternoon, she'd broken a nail. Still, as long as the top of it was inside one of the nitrile gloves or somewhere in the house and not actually – Sophie shuddered – tangled up in Jessica's hair or something, it would be OK. Stripping off, she bundled up the skirt and cardigan to be taken downstairs and disposed of, and then, wincing, tugged the jeans she'd been wearing that morning over her injured and swollen knee before pulling on a jumper. Better take off the fancy earrings, too, while she was at it – Poppy always noticed things like that. The make-up proved more difficult, but there wasn't time to do a really thorough camouflage job. Still, she could always claim that she'd tripped over in the sitting room – that would account for the absence of the side table, too, and, if anyone were to spot it, the stain on the carpet.

She ran a brush through her hair and forced her face into a smile. It looked not only peculiar, but unfamiliar. Or perhaps that was what she actually looked like, and she'd never realized before.

She stood on the landing for a moment, the balled-up clothes in her hand, listening to the sounds from above. Giggles, followed by a puppyish yelp and Poppy's voice, raised in mock accusation – something about a hairbrush. They'd be up there a while longer, Sophie thought, and went downstairs to empty the kitchen bin, praying that Imanuela would not return and decide to come into the house.

Sophie heaved the bin liner containing Jessica's shoes as well as her own cardigan and skirt into the plastic wheelie bin, on top of the bag full of surplus frozen food. At least *that* would all be gone tomorrow morning, when the dustmen came. She leant against the front gate for a moment and looked up at the house. In the soft, still light of early evening, beneath the huge sky with the birds wheeling in the distance, it looked so solid, so elegant . . . so right. NOW HE'S GOING TO LEAVE YOU. LET'S SEE HOW SMUG YOU ARE THEN, YOU STUPID BITCH.

Suddenly, Sophie felt hysterical laughter bubble up inside her like a hot geyser. Don't, she told herself, sharply. If you let go now, you'll never stop.

The dangerous hilarity was abruptly curtailed by a glance in the direction of the church. There, mounted halfway up the tower, was the hooded electronic eye of a surveillance camera, which began to swivel, very slowly, in her direction.

When had *that* been put up? The vicar had told her just before Easter that it would take about six weeks because of the demand, but maybe there had been cancellations. Perhaps they'd done it while she was in London, and Imanuela had been out, or not noticed. Sophie retreated to the side of the bin shed. Surely it wouldn't be able see her there? Reverend Barker had said the thing covered just the graveyard and the shared part of the driveway in front of their gate, so she ought to be OK – not that putting out the rubbish the day before the bin men came was in any way odd, of course . . .

Jessica's car would be on there.

Sophie felt sick. CCTV was sophisticated nowadays – no longer those blurred, slabby black-and-white images, but sharp ones, in colour. Even if the camera had been at the wrong angle to have captured one or both of the registration plates, it would have picked up Jessica sitting behind the wheel. Would Reverend Barker check the tapes before recording over them, or was it all digital now? Perhaps he could even look at the film on his laptop. But either way, surely he wouldn't bother to check the footage unless someone had vandalized the gravestones or tried to nick the lead. Except . . . it was new, so he might be checking it regularly for the first couple of months to make sure that it was working – and she'd have to get rid of the Audi. What if she could be identified from the pictures, driving a car belonging to a missing person?

You can't think about this now, she told herself. There's the evening to get through first.

Five steps away from the side door, she heard a piercing scream from inside the house, and then another.

TWENTY-FIVE

Sophie felt as though she'd been electrocuted. Stiff with apprehension, on legs that would barely obey her, imagining Poppy staring down through the icy mist at Jessica's frozen face, she groped her way along the side of the house to the freezer room.

It was empty. The noise was coming from the kitchen.

'What's going on?'

'Look!' White-faced, Poppy was pointing to something on the other side of the table.

Sophie felt almost liquid with relief, and then, in the next second, appalled at herself when she saw Dexter lying on his side in front of the fridge, skeins of bright-orange drool hanging from his mouth. Wincing, she dropped to her knees beside the dog. 'My God, Dexter! What's he eaten?'

Poppy's face crumpled. 'I don't know, Mum. We just came in and found him like that.'

Cressida appeared, carrying Dexter's bowl. 'I think he needs water, Mrs Hamilton – I got this from the other room.'

Sophie stroked Dexter's head. 'Come on, old boy, have a drink.' To her surprise, the dog thumped his tail on the tiles, then sat up and tried to stick his head under her arm, leaving an orange smear on her sleeve. 'Well, he doesn't seem too bad.'

'But that stuff on his mouth!' Poppy sank down on the floor beside her. 'And what's *that*?'

'Where?'

'There!' Poppy pointed at something silver on Dexter's lip.

'It's OK, just tinfoil. Must have been from whatever it was he ate. Can you get some kitchen roll?'

Dexter got up, shook himself, and nuzzled her vigorously while she swabbed his chops. Had she missed anything when she'd picked up all the frozen stuff? Sophie glanced around and saw, poking out from beneath the door of the fridge, a gnawed and punctured tube of Berocca, its lid nowhere to be seen. She must have knocked it onto the floor when she was getting the first aid kit from the cupboard.

She clawed for the tube with one hand while fending off Dexter with the other, and discovered that it was empty. 'Well, he certainly won't be short of vitamin B!'

This time the laughter exploded from her, uncontrolled, until her stomach hurt. With feeble hands, she tore off a ragged length of kitchen roll to wipe her eyes. Poppy and Cressida stood side by side, looking down at her warily.

'Oh, dear. I'm sorry. Still –' Sophie scrambled to her feet while Dexter, completely unfazed, wandered out into the hall – 'he seems to be OK.'

Poppy stared anxiously after the dog. 'Vitamin B won't hurt him, will it?'

'No, darling.'

'But he might have had masses. Don't we need to take him to the vet?'

Sophie shook her head. 'I'm not an expert, but I'm pretty sure you can't overdose unless you have an enormous amount. He'll be fine, I promise – maybe a tummy upset, but nothing more.' This isn't real, she thought. There's a dead body not fifteen feet away. She shook her head, trying to drag herself back into the present.

'. . . because we've got to do the cooking for tomorrow.' Poppy and Cressida were staring up at her expectantly.

'What cooking?'

'*Mu-um!* I told you about it last week. For the bake sale. You said you'd help us.'

'OK . . .' Dazed, Sophie made another effort to pull herself together. Concentrate, she told herself. Be *normal*. 'What is it you need to cook?'

'Tarte Tatin. You promised you'd defrost the pastry.'

'Did I?'

'Yes! You said you'd take it out last night.'

'I'm sorry, I forgot. Can't you make something else?'

Poppy shook her head. 'It's all organized now.'

'Well, I can always ring –' Sophie tried to remember the name of the woman who taught Food Tech, and failed – 'the school, and explain.'

'No, Mum!' Poppy's voice rose in exasperation. 'Everyone's doing something different, and we've got to do tarte Tatin. I *told* you.'

'If we take the pastry out of the freezer now,' said Cressida, helpfully, 'we can put the bag in a bowl of water until it's a bit soft, and then unroll it. When my mum did that, it only took about an hour to defrost.'

'Oh.' Poppy cheered up immediately. 'That's OK, then. I'll get it.' Sophie grabbed her daughter's arm as she started towards the freezer room, and Poppy flinched, pulling away from her. 'Ow! Mum, that really hurt.'

'Sorry, darling. Just hang on a minute. Have you got the recipe?'

'It's here.' Cressida brandished a sheet of paper in a plastic sleeve.

Sophie scanned the page. 'It says to use puff pastry, but it's perfectly OK to use shortcrust, and we can easily make that from scratch, so—'

'It says *puff* pastry, Mum. We have to follow the recipe, and it says it's fine to use ready-made stuff.'

'I'm sure Ms . . .' What was the bloody woman's name? 'Your teacher – I'm sure she wouldn't mind.'

'She will! We'll lose marks if we don't do it properly, and it'll be your fault. I'm going to fetch it.'

'Poppy!' Feeling as though she were about to have a heart attack, Sophie leapt in front of her daughter, blocking the door to the freezer room. 'Calm down, OK? I'll fetch the pastry. I've just reorganized the freezer and I don't want it all messed up again.'

Poppy stared at her. 'But if you reorganized it, why didn't you take the pastry out, like we said?'

'I meant to, darling, but I forgot.' Oh, God – what if the pastry was one of the things that she'd thrown away? She imagined herself rummaging through the bags in the bin shed – caught, if she were unlucky, which she surely would be, on the CCTV. Seeing that both girls were now regarding her with careful, adult expressions, she added, 'It's been rather a difficult day, that's all.'

'Are you all right, Mum?'

'I'm fine. Right. So . . . Why don't you two start assembling the things you need, and I'll get the pastry, OK?'

Neither girl moved. 'Mum?' Poppy's face was now full of consternation. 'What's happened?'

'Nothing!' The word came out too quick, too bright. 'Everything's fine. Just a stupid mistake about the pastry, that's all.'

'But . . .' Poppy advanced towards her. 'Your face. You've got a bruise. I couldn't see before because you've put make-up on it.'

'I tripped over, that's all.'

'Where?'

'Where what?'

'Where did you trip over?'

'In the sitting room.'

'What were you doing?'

'I tripped on one of the rugs.'

'And you hit your head?'

'Yes! What is this, a quiz?'

'You're not concussed, are you?' said Cressida.

'No, I'm fine.'

'You're being a bit . . . well, strange.'

'Honestly, Poppy, I'm fine. Just let me get this wretched pastry, and you can get on.'

Poppy frowned. 'Perhaps you ought to sit down. I could make

you a cup of tea. Cressida could find the pastry – she's really careful about things.'

'No!' She hadn't meant to shout, but both girls recoiled. 'OK, OK . . . Why don't you put the kettle on and get the ingredients together, and I'll fetch the pastry, and then you can tell me what you'd like for supper.'

Without waiting for an answer, Sophie went into the freezer room. Neither girl spoke, but she could feel the beams of their scrutiny, sharp and precise as lasers, on her back.

Please let it be in here, *please* . . . Sophie pawed through the jumbled packets of frozen food, trying not to imagine what was underneath, until she discovered – thank you, God – a box of puff pastry. She shut the freezer lid just as the side door opened and Imanuela appeared, carrying shopping bags.

'I just come to fetch something before—' Imanuela stopped, staring at Sophie. 'You're OK? You hurt yourself.'

'It's fine. I just tripped.'

Imanuela took a step towards her. 'It looks bad. Can I do something? Help you?'

'That's very nice of you. It was just a stupid accident, really. I'm sure I'll be fine.'

'I can make supper, if you like.'

'Well . . .' Sophie felt torn between relief at not having to think about food – not just supper, because Imanuela was a good cook and would undoubtedly pitch in to help with the tarte Tatin, if necessary – and anxiety at having yet another pair of sharp eyes on her.

'Is fine. Don't worry.' Imanuela deposited the bags – Uniqlo and Topshop – on the floor, and was about to go into the kitchen, when she stopped, staring at a spot on the flagstones just beyond Sophie's feet. 'You dropped your keys.'

'What?'

'Car keys. On the floor.'

Sophie looked down, but Imanuela had already picked them up. 'Mr Leo's Porsche, and another one . . .'

'That'll be for the garage.' Of course, she'd put them all on the top of the freezer, hadn't she? They must have got knocked off when she'd bashed into it, falling over Dexter. 'I was looking for something in there this afternoon.'

Imanuela raised her eyebrows. 'You drive Mr Leo's car?'

Sophie bared her teeth in what she hoped was a grin. 'No, I wouldn't dare. I just needed to look inside.'

'Something is here, as well.' Imanuela peered down between the end of the freezer and the wall, and then, kneeling, inserted her arm sideways into the narrow space. 'I think I can get it . . . Yes . . .'

'I don't know what that one is,' Sophie gabbled. 'Must have been one we lost ages ago.'

'Not key, bin liners . . .' Imanuela held up the roll. 'What they are doing here?'

'It must have been when I tripped. I meant to put a new one in the kitchen bin.' Imanuela looked confused. 'I was holding them,' Sophie rattled on, 'I came out here because I heard a noise, and Dexter came too, and we got a bit tangled up in the doorway.'

Imanuela frowned up at her for a moment and said, 'You think there is another key down here?'

'No, I just – because you said about keys . . .' Shut up, Sophie told herself, as Imanuela felt about in the space again. You're making it worse.

Imanuela withdrew her arm and straightened up. 'There is a key. Here. For car.' She turned over the key fob. 'For Audi. Look. You have Mercedes and Porsche, not Audi.'

Sophie felt as though she were about to faint. 'I suppose somebody must have left it here.'

'But . . .' Imanuela looked at her doubtfully. 'If they leave car key, how they drive away?'

TWENTY-SIX

Sophie sat on the edge of her bed, head in hands, feeling sick. Imanuela, who seemed to have swallowed whatever crap she'd managed to come out with about the unspecified visitor having a spare car key, had suggested she lie down for a while – 'I call you when supper ready, OK? No problem with girls cooking, don't worry.'

They'd agreed on pasta for supper, so there was no reason for anyone to go near the freezer, but she'd told Imanuela and the girls different stories about tripping over, hadn't she? Stupid, stupid! She couldn't even remember what she'd said. And Poppy, interrogating her like that . . .

Head throbbing, she reached into the drawer of the bedside table for paracetamol. Fishing out the packet, she spotted a drawing – by Poppy, then aged four – of a princess (stick arms, triangle frock, crown), labelled, in wobbly capitals, *My Mummy*. How simple life had been then, she thought. Crayoned pictures on the fridge door and no dead body in the freezer or incriminating car in the garage.

How the hell was she going to get rid of them? Sophie got up and went into the bathroom to wash the pills down with water from the basin tap. Just get through this evening, she told herself. Everything else could be figured out later.

Except . . . Jessica's trench coat was still hanging up downstairs. That needed to be removed now, before somebody spotted it. Not Cressida or Zac, but Imanuela, who always noticed clothes, or eagle-eyed Poppy. Too risky to take it down to the bin shed now, but she could hide it in her study, a mere three paces across the hall from the cloakroom, and get rid of it tomorrow.

She tiptoed cautiously onto the landing and halfway down the stairs. A yelp of laughter from the kitchen, and the sound of clattering pans, told her that the cooking was under way. So far, so good. Legging it down to the hall and into the cloakroom, Sophie grabbed the trench coat, bundled it up and was just about to slink into her study when Imanuela appeared from the kitchen.

'You OK?' she called. 'You drop something.'

'What?' Sophie looked wildly around. Jessica's scarf, which she hadn't previously noticed, was lying, a puddle of abstract pastels, on the front doormat. Fumbling with the wadded-up coat, she bent to pick it up, but once again Imanuela was there before her. (How, for God's sake? The hall, from kitchen to front door, must be at least seventy feet long.)

'Pretty.' Imanuela stroked the silk. 'Is new?'

'Yes. I bought it when I was in London.'

Imanuela sniffed. 'New perfume, too. Not the normal one.'

'I felt like a change,' said Sophie, weakly.

'Very nice. What name?'

'Name?' echoed Sophie. 'Do you know, I can't actually remember.'

Imanuela's face was solemn. 'You're tired, Sophie. Why don't you go to bed? I can do this . . .' She gestured towards the kitchen, then held out the scarf.

Making a physical effort not to snatch the thing, Sophie said, 'What about Zac? He'll need something to eat, too.'

'I can do it. Really.' Imanuela looked at the coat stuffed under Sophie's arm. 'For dry-cleaning? I can take in the morning, if you like.'

'No, no . . .' Sophie backed away, clutching the slippery cotton. 'You're doing too much already . . .'

'Is no problem.'

'Really, it's fine. I can deal—' The phone trilled in the study. 'Look, I'd better get that.'

'. . . and that's the only appointment they could give me, and it's in Norwich, and on top of that I've got to collect Cressida's riding boots from the specialist repair place because there's a horse show at the weekend, which means that I'm not going to be back in time . . .'

Sophie, phone wedged between shoulder and ear, straightened up from stuffing Jessica's coat and scarf into an empty drawer in the filing cabinet, and began scrabbling in the top drawer of her desk for the key while Cressida's mother continued to detail the complicated logistics of her household. The bloody thing had to be in there somewhere. It wasn't as if anyone else came into her study, but there was always a first time, and she couldn't take the risk. She ought to put Jessica's handbag into the filing cabinet, too, because anyone might open the cupboard in the sitting room and find it. She should do that now, in case anyone went in there to watch television later on ... And Imanuela would be bound to notice that the side table had disappeared, and ask about it. She groaned.

'Sophie? Are you all right?'

'Yes, sorry. Trying to do two things at once. All a bit hectic this evening, what with the bake sale and everything.'

'That's what I was asking you about. Can we swap?'

'Swap?'

'It's my turn, but they need picking up half an hour early, and I'm not going to be back in time.'

'Oh, yes ... Right.'

'So can you do it?'

'I suppose so. Or Imanuela can. Don't worry, we'll sort it out between us.'

Cutting short the effusive thanks, Sophie returned to the cloakroom and looked around for something big enough to conceal Jessica's handbag for the journey from sitting room to study.

'Shit, shit, shit!'

Kneeling in front of the alcove cupboard in the sitting room, shoving Jessica's handbag into an empty rucksack she'd found in the cloakroom, Sophie started, banging her elbow painfully against the open door. For a panicked moment, she had failed to recognize the hulking, hooded stranger who stood, his back to her, on the rug in the centre of the room.

'Have you seen my iPod, Mum?'

'You haven't lost it *again*?'

'I haven't *lost* it at all. It was here, and somebody's taken it, and – hey!' Zac pointed at the partially concealed rucksack. 'That's mine, too! How am I supposed to get anything done when you lot keeping nicking my stuff?'

'I haven't nicked it. I found it in here and I was just about to put it back in the cloakroom, OK?'

'Why was it in *there*?'

'Probably because you put it in there.'

Zac gawped at her. 'Why would I do that?'

'I have absolutely no idea, but you must have done. Anyway, it doesn't matter.' Seeing his shrugged shoulders, she mentally thanked God for disorganized teenage boys – had the rucksack been Poppy's, she'd never have got away with it. 'Where did you last see your iPod?'

'It was on that little table . . .' Zac looked around the room, baffled. 'Now the table's gone, too. What the fuck's going on round here?'

'Don't use that word. The table's gone because I had an accident this afternoon. I tripped over it, and it broke.'

'Imanuela said you'd fallen over, only she said you were in the kitchen.'

'That was when I tripped over the dog.'

'So you fell over *twice*? Were you pissed?'

'Don't be ridiculous.'

Zac's stare was coolly appraising. 'You look like you might have been. Did you break my iPod as well as the table?'

'Of course I didn't! It wasn't even on there.' Or had it been? She couldn't remember. 'But if you're so certain you left it in here, perhaps it's on the floor or something.' Holding the rucksack – which now contained Jessica's handbag – Sophie got up to look under the furniture, while Zac flumped, glowering, onto the sofa.

'I wish you'd look after your things.'

Zac watched while she made a show of inspecting the room. There was no iPod in immediate view, and – thankfully – nothing incriminating, either. After a few minutes' poking around, she spotted the small white casing, headphones still attached, under the cabinet by the fireplace, and bent down to reach it. It must have fallen there, or been kicked, during the tussle with Jessica.

'The screen's broken.'

'How about "Thank you, Mum"? Are you sure it wasn't like that before?'

'Mum!' Zac's expression was guileless, hurt. 'It probably won't even work now.'

'Why don't you try it and see? I'll just put this –' Sophie indicated the rucksack – 'back in the cloakroom.' Without waiting for a response, she ran out of the room and down the hall to her study, where she dumped Jessica's handbag in the filing cabinet with the coat and scarf – God, she *must* find that key – before bunging the rucksack in the cloakroom and returning to the sitting room to find Zac hunched over, jabbing furiously at the little screen.

'Not working?'

'Nothing.' Zac flung the iPod down on the sofa beside him and looked up at her with an expression of despair.

'Well . . . Is there a guarantee or something? Perhaps we can get it repaired.'

Zac made a growling noise. 'You have to send them away

for that. It takes ages, and they might not even be able to fix it.'

'Look,' said Sophie. 'I'll take it back to the shop and if they can't fix it, I'll get you another one, OK?'

'Really?' Zac sat up straight. 'Like, tomorrow?'

'Maybe not tomorrow, but I'll try and do it by the weekend.' After she'd got rid of a car and disposed of a body. This couldn't be happening. It was like some terrible dream. 'Better not say anything to your dad, though.'

'OK.' Zac gave her a complicit grin and bounced off the sofa. 'Imanuela's probably got supper ready by now.'

'Have you got homework?'

'Yeah, but it's not important,' he said airily over his shoulder, and lolloped off to the kitchen.

Sophie stared after him. Normally, she'd have been on Zac's case about the homework, but, right now, she agreed with him.

She stood listening to the voices from across the hall, feeling as though she'd plummeted from the top of a high building and was halfway down, clinging to a ledge by her fingertips, while life went on, oblivious, on the insides of lighted windows. Swaying slightly, she picked up the broken iPod and left the room.

TWENTY-SEVEN

After some further rummaging in her desk, Sophie finally located the key to the filing cabinet, locked it, and sat down on the floor with her back to the mahogany drawers. The coat, scarf and handbag would be safe for the time being. Like the car and – here, Sophie closed her eyes tightly to block out the image – Jessica herself, their disposal would have to wait until everyone had left the house the following morning. Mrs Palmer didn't come until at least two o'clock on Thursdays, but she'd need to get Imanuela out of the house, too.

Struggling to her feet, Sophie went into the hall to survey the remainder of the boxes containing the wrought-iron ornaments. The astrolabe would have to stay put until she'd sorted out the scratch on the coffee table, but a journey to the shop in the Nissan would see to the rest, and (assuming that she could find the receipt) she could get Imanuela to sort out the iPod, as well. That would necessitate a trip into Norwich, meaning that the au pair would be out of the way for the whole morning . . . 'And,' she smiled at an imaginary Imanuela, 'why don't you take the rest of the day off to make up for this evening?

There's no need to hurry back if you want to do some more shopping.'

That would do it.

'I think I will go up to bed, if that's . . .' The words died on Sophie's lips as, standing in the kitchen doorway, she saw that Imanuela and Poppy were bending over the open dishwasher. At the table, Cressida was peeling apples while Zac, head down, was shovelling pasta into his mouth as if his life depended on it.

'You're not meant to put the hand-painted stuff in the dishwasher, Mum. *And* it was only half full when you switched it on, so it's a waste of energy.'

'Sorry, darling. I obviously wasn't thinking.'

'You don't even use this stuff –' Poppy held up one of the hand-painted cups – 'unless people come.'

'No, I know.'

'But there are two cups,' her daughter persisted, 'so someone else must have been here.'

'Just Melissa. We had stuff to talk about, for the shop.'

Poppy appraised Sophie, head tilted to one side, eyes shrewd. 'Are you *sure* you're OK, Mum?'

'Yeah . . .' Zac raised his head from his supper. 'You're being weird.'

Now everyone was staring at her, including Dexter. Imanuela's face puckered with concern. 'You need a doctor, maybe? When you fell, if you hit your head . . . Zac said you fell over in the sitting room, too.'

'Just a stupid accident. Really, I'm fine.'

'Are you sure you're not concussed, Mum?'

'Yeah,' said Zac. 'You could be. Who's the prime minister?'

'Oh, for heaven's sake . . .'

'You never do stuff like that.' Zac jabbed his fork in the direction of the dishwasher. 'You're not going senile, are you?'

'Says the boy who can't keep track of his possessions for more than five minutes.'

'Well, now we know where I get it from, don't we?'

'Zac!'

At Imanuela's rebuke, her son's triumphant expression was immediately replaced by a sheepish one. He's starting to fancy her, Sophie thought, just like Alfie did. 'I'm not senile – at least, not yet – but I am exhausted, and I've got a headache. So, if you don't mind . . .'

Once more Sophie sat on the edge of her bed, but this time she was cold to her very core and shaking too badly to get undressed. She pulled the bedcover towards her and, wrapping it around herself, sat, teeth chattering, unable to think. After a while – she wasn't sure how long – she put out a hand to the bedside phone to call Leo. She ought to tell him that she'd tripped and broken the little side table. Perhaps she could say that the scratch on the coffee table had happened at the same time . . . But – the memory flew at her, causing her to jerk backwards – how to explain the scratch (or worse) on the rear wing of the Porsche? She'd have to repark the thing in the middle of the garage after she'd got rid of Jessica's car and claim she had no idea how the marks had got there.

She couldn't face telling Leo about any of it now. But what if he rang her? She hadn't spoken to him for a couple of days.

Not since Sunday, in fact. Sophie inched away from the phone, which looked somehow tense, as if it were ready to spring off its stand and jump at her face like a demonic jack-in-the-box. How was she going to get rid of Jessica's car, anyway? Imanuela had seemed happy enough with the proposed arrangements for tomorrow, but – assuming the coast was clear, and she could manage to drive the Audi across the patch of grass between the garden and the road in order to avoid the CCTV – what the hell was she going to do with it after that?

She should have called for an ambulance. OK, so they probably couldn't have saved Jessica if the ornament's arrow had pierced her heart, but it might have been chalked up as an accident. After all, if she'd actually *intended* to kill the woman, she could have used Leo's shotgun. As it was, she wasn't even sure where he kept the keys to the gun safe – the firearms inspection man had told him he wasn't allowed to share the information. But Leo would never believe it wasn't intentional, even if she managed to convince the authorities, because what were the chances, really, of a woman having a random meeting with someone who was – supposedly unbe-knownst to her – about to waltz off with her husband, and then that person just *happening* to have a fatal accident while under her roof?

In any case, it was too late to think about any of that now. If she could only succeed in dumping the Audi somewhere without being noticed, there was no reason why it should ever be connected with her. Leaving it outside Jessica's cottage was too risky – she'd seen the CCTV in the parking space at the front of the house – and, for the same reason, so was driving it to Norwich and leaving it in a multi-storey car park. God only knew how many cameras she'd end up on if she tried that. The countryside was altogether a better bet: if she left the car in a field with the key in the ignition, there was a good chance someone would steal it, and that would mean – assuming it were ever recovered – that it would be the thief's fingerprints and DNA the police would be concerned with, and not hers . . . because, of course, the obvious thing to do would be to stick Jessica in the boot.

Tomorrow was Thursday. Leo would be home on Friday afternoon and by that time, everything (save the broken side table and the scratch on the Porsche, both of which would have to be explained away) needed to be back to normal. Cressida's mum was doing the school run in the morning, so that was OK, and she'd told Imanuela that Melissa wanted the stuff at the shop for 9 a.m., which meant that she'd have until 2 p.m., when Mrs Palmer arrived, to sort everything out, and – shit! *She* was supposed to be doing a stint at the shop. She'd just have to call Melissa and tell her she was coming down with something. She'd probably get away with Melissa mentioning that to Imanuela, because of 'falling over' this afternoon, but what if Imanuela said something to Melissa about her having come over for a chat about the shop? If that happened, she'd just have to bluff it out – claim that she must have been concussed after all.

That would be OK, Sophie thought. The problem was getting back after dumping Jessica's car. She didn't want to draw attention to herself by calling a taxi when she was in the middle of nowhere. If she went out in the Merc to do a recce for a suitable field and took Dexter with her, then she could park it somewhere nearby, walk back with the dog, and then – Sophie swallowed hard – load Jessica into the Audi, drive it to the chosen field and leave it with the key in the ignition, before coming home in her own car.

How long did it take a human body to freeze, though? If Jessica were stiff by tomorrow, she might not fit, and Sophie could hardly drive along with the boot secured by string and the woman's legs and feet sticking out like planks. Part of her wanted to laugh hysterically. The other part was rigid with horror.

She'd got to do it. She had no choice.

'Somebody help me,' she muttered. 'God, Jesus, anybody . . . Help me.' Remembering Jessica's eyes, amazed and dead, staring at her, she put her head in her hands. 'Oh, God, what have I done?'

TWENTY-EIGHT

Jessica's eyes were wide open as her head broke through the layers of frozen food, ice crusting her lashes and hair, lips blue and face mushroom-white, frantic mottled hands scrabbling and clawing as she surfaced. The bags and cartons crackled and crunched, falling to the floor in a brittle cascade as she emerged, one stiff limb at a time, and—

'No!' Sophie thrashed in terror, tangled in the bedclothes, sweating, still half dormant, before her eyes opened and she took in the bedside lamp, which was still on, and the book and glass now lying on the carpet. Heart thudding, she sat up and looked warily around her. The curtains were closed and, but for the pool of light cast by the lamp, everything was dark and quiet.

05.12. Very soon, it would be light. She wondered who would report Jessica as missing. Leo, perhaps, or the husband, Sean – assuming they were in the throes of divorce, he'd need to be in contact with her. Or maybe a parent. How soon would the police take action? After all, she wasn't a child, or particularly vulnerable. But, when they did start looking for her, presumably the affair with Leo would come to light. He'd be questioned, maybe even suspected . . . Surely he'd have to tell her. When he did, she'd just have to pretend she'd had no idea. Act astonished and hurt. Even if Jessica *hadn't* told Leo that she was coming over for tea, she might have noted down the time and date of her visit somewhere – a diary or wall calendar. Sophie would just have to claim that she'd never turned up, and that she didn't have her mobile number – at least, she thought, the last bit was true. There was the email exchange with Jessica on her own laptop, but she could delete that – in fact, she'd do it now.

She got out of bed and leant over to pick up the glass and book, noting, as she did so, that its pages were soaked with water and there was a dark stain on the carpet.

For God's sake! She hurled the wet paperback in the direction of the wastepaper basket and stomped into the en-suite bathroom, defeated and furious. None of this was her fault. *She* hadn't had an affair or threatened anyone's marriage, and now here she was, having to lie to everybody and act like a criminal. It wasn't fair.

Except . . . She should have shown Leo the letter in the first place, and then he would have seen Jessica for what she was and broken it off. I'm an idiot, Sophie thought miserably. I should have trusted Leo to do the right thing. He loves me.

But she hadn't felt sure enough of that to show him the letter, had she?

What if Leo was devastated when he discovered that Jessica had disappeared and left her anyway?

No. That was *not* going to happen.

This resolve propelled Sophie into the shower. Afterwards, she dried herself, dressed in yesterday's jeans and jumper and spent a frustrating few minutes plastering make-up over the now ripe bruises on her cheek and chin. Once downstairs, she deleted the email exchange, and then, unsure what to do next, stood uncertainly in the middle of the hall while Dexter, who'd heard her moving about, scrabbled at the other side of the utility-room door.

She hadn't smoked in almost twenty years, but she suddenly wanted a cigarette. It was out of the question because there were none in the house. Actually, she wouldn't have put it past Zac to have some secreted in his room, but she could hardly wake him up and ask. Second best would be a cup of tea. She'd have to go into the kitchen at some stage, but the thought of the freezer being right next door was too much, at least for the moment.

She went back into her study and stood looking around. The bin men came early, and she could get rid of Jessica's coat, scarf and bag now, before anyone else was up, if she was quick – but she ought to let Dexter out first, before he started barking and woke everyone. She was about to do this when she noticed, on the floor beside the filing cabinet, a set of keys – for a house, by the look of them – attached to a key ring in the shape of a capital 'J'. They must have fallen out of the pocket of Jessica's coat when she'd bundled it into the filing cabinet, and she'd somehow missed them.

Crossing the hall to the cloakroom, Sophie shrugged on her suede jacket and pocketed the keys before letting a prancing Dexter out of the utility room and accompanying him through the back door.

Head down, following the scent of some night creature, the dog ran down the sloping lawn towards the swimming pool.

Sophie watched him for a moment, then walked round the side of the house towards the pond. It was a large one, and with the sun just coming up, the reeds, stones and plants that surrounded it were partially shrouded in mist. Sophie reached the edge, hesitated for a second and then, in a swift, instinctive movement, lifted the keys out of her pocket and flung them into the dark water.

Splash. Gone.

A second later she reeled as Dexter, barrelling past her, launched himself through the air in pursuit of the imaginary stick, sending up a wave of spray as he smacked down on the surface and began swimming round in energetic circles. She called to him, but the dog, intent on retrieving something – anything – paid no attention.

She walked back to the house, hoping he'd follow. If she shut him out he would start barking in earnest, and that was bound to bring Imanuela out of the cottage. She'd just have to hope he'd be distracted for long enough for her to get Jessica's things down to the bin shed.

She stood in the hall, fighting off the image of Jessica, miraculously risen from the freezer like some appalling ice-covered zombie, standing in wait for her in the kitchen. Taking a deep breath, she pushed the door open with her fingertips and saw that everything was tidy, as it had been left by Imanuela and the girls. All quite ordinary, with nothing untoward or sinister.

'It's all right,' she murmured. 'Everything's going to be all right.' She went to the study and was about to put Jessica's stuff into a bin liner when it occurred to her that, before she disposed of the handbag, she ought to look inside for the phone.

That way – assuming that the thing wasn't locked – she might be able to find out if Jessica had texted Leo, or anyone else, to say that she was coming for tea. There might be a diary, too, and if it contained anything incriminating she ought to destroy it, rather than merely throwing it away . . . Although of course Jessica had a laptop, didn't she? That would be at her cottage, with God knew what on it, including an email from Sophie, and she'd just chucked the keys into the pond. Shit.

She was an idiot. Slow down, she told herself. Think clearly.

Opening the handbag, Sophie emptied its contents onto the rug. As well as the smartphone, a strip of Nurofen capsules and small packet of tissues, there was a Marc Jacobs wallet, a pair of Michael Kors sunglasses, a lipstick and compact – both Chanel – and a Smythson pocket diary. Nothing but the best, thought Sophie. Maybe she should put the bag in the car, as further temptation for a thief.

The phone was locked. Sophie opened the diary. A week at a glance with no room for anything personal, and the entries seemed to be mainly jottings of appointments and meetings. Flipping through, Sophie couldn't find any mention of Leo, which must mean that the references were in code. She thumbed through to the Tuesday (impossibly, only nine days ago) that she'd seen Jessica coming out of Leo's flat when he was supposed to be at the races, and saw the letter 'M' with a vertical arrow from the previous day's space. 'M' for Moorgate House, meaning she'd stayed the night there? Leo's middle name was his mother's maiden name, Makepeace, so it could be that, or perhaps it was something entirely different, a name she'd given him to make him a new person when he was with her. Angry tears pricked Sophie's eyelids. He hadn't been hers to name. Glancing back through the pages, she saw dozens of 'M's – sometimes lunch, sometimes dinner, sometimes with the arrow that must surely denote an overnight stay . . . including the period when Leo was in New York, so she must have accompanied him there. What Sophie had imagined about the Tiffany necklace was the truth.

Hands shaking, she turned over the page to the current week and saw her own name and address in the space for Wednesday, followed by the single word 'Tea' and, in the space below it, 'M – 8.30 p.m.'

Jessica was supposed to be meeting Leo that very evening.

TWENTY-NINE

Finally, at 8.15 a.m., Sophie had the house to herself. She was just clipping on Dexter's lead to take him out to the Merc when the front doorbell rang.

Reverend Barker was tall, craggily handsome, and, but for the garb, more like a Hollywood cowboy than a vicar. Sophie's first thought on seeing him was that he must have noticed something suspicious on the CCTV, but what? At least he didn't seem to have noticed the bruises under her make-up, so she must have made a better job of it than she'd thought . . . Stop it, she told herself. Focus on what the man's actually saying.

'. . . and I'm sure you've seen the website.'

Sophie blinked at him.

'For the Summer Fair.'

'Oh . . . yes.' She nodded enthusiastically. 'Yes, of course. We're all looking forward to it.'

'I know you said that it would be OK for us to store some tables and chairs in your outhouse nearer the time, but I'm afraid there's been a mix-up and they've been delivered a fortnight earlier than we expected. It was the suppliers' mistake, not ours, but they are doing us rather a favour, so we can't really ask them to take the stuff back and redeliver it, and of course we don't have anywhere to put it in the meantime, so . . .' He looked at her expectantly.

'So . . . ?' Sophie tried to mask her dismay with vagueness. 'Sorry, I'm not sure I understand.'

'Could we bring them over this morning? I know it's very short notice, but you don't need to be here or anything. Leo showed us the outhouse, so – if you wouldn't mind giving me the key – we wouldn't need to bother you at all.'

That was all she needed. 'I'm rather busy at the moment, but perhaps a bit later on . . . What sort of time were you thinking of?'

'Would around half eleven be all right? We've got the use of a van, but I'd like to get it back to the owner as soon as possible – he's very kindly stepped in to help, but he's got some work on this afternoon and he needs it.'

'Could you make it a bit later? I won't be back in time.'

Reverend Barker frowned. 'Well, as I said, if you don't mind giving us the key . . .'

'That's the thing.' Sophie forced a little laugh. 'I'm not actually sure where the key *is*. And,' she added, seeing that the vicar was about to make a helpful suggestion, 'I can't ring Leo to ask him because he's at a conference all day and he'll have his phone off, so . . .' Widening her eyes, she made a helpless, what-can-I-do gesture.

'Well . . .' The vicar frowned again and Sophie willed him to say that he could just as well stick the chairs and tables in the vestry or his own garage or anywhere else at all. After a pause he said, in a considered, reasonable tone, 'There's nothing to stop us bringing the things here at, say, midday, and unloading them, is there? Even if the forecast's right and it does decide to rain this afternoon, all the stuff's plastic, and if we left it out of the way somewhere –' he gestured vaguely towards the back of the house – 'then we could come back and put it all inside once you've got hold of the key.'

Shit, shit, *shit*. Closing the front door, Sophie leant against it for a moment while Dexter sat staring up at her, anxious for his walk. She'd had no choice but to admit defeat, and now she had two hours less than she'd originally thought. She knew perfectly well where the key to the outhouse was – in the key cupboard with all the others – so that wasn't a problem, but . . .

Keys. She hadn't put the garage one back in the cupboard. What had she done with it, and where the hell were the keys for the Audi and the Porsche?

After twenty frantic minutes racking her brains and searching, Sophie had managed to locate all three keys in the drawer of her bedside cabinet, and, having left them lined up on the kitchen table, was driving out of the Old Rectory gate with Dexter in the back of the Merc. The dashboard clock read 08.50, which left her just over three hours to dispose of Jessica and her car and get back home in time for the vicar and his helpers. Whatever the forecast, she thought, glancing up at a blue sky dotted with puffy, flat-based cumulus clouds, at least it didn't look like rain at the moment. She decided to go in the direction of the nearest village to Jessica's house. It was only about three miles away, which was a bit too close for comfort, but she needed to be able to park the car somewhere inconspicuous and walk back home with the dog in under an hour in order to give herself enough time to (oh, God) manoeuvre Jessica into the boot of the Audi before driving it to the designated spot.

The village near Jessica's house wasn't a particularly large one: two rows of ten or twelve Victorian workers' cottages lining the main thoroughfare, modern bungalows dotted at intervals down the lanes leading off on either side, and a pub with a bad reputation. Sophie drove past all these, past Jessica's cottage, past the gateway to the field where she'd parked the previous week and past the small wood where she'd walked Dexter, before slowing down. The opposite side of the road was no good – a vast, open expanse, with straight lines of greeny-blue sugar-beet leaves running away to the horizon – but the fields on the far side of the wood were more promising. The first two were paddocks – ponies and dismantled jumps contained within new-looking post-and-rail fencing and chained, padlocked gates – but around a bend in the road was a messy hedge and an open gateway, the ground churned up by hooves – cows, Sophie supposed, although none were visible.

She pulled up and got out to look. Behind the hedge was a stack of bales covered in a sheet of black plastic, and, in a corner, a jumble of rusting agricultural machinery. The whole field had a slummy look, as if nobody bothered much about it.

Good enough. Now to find somewhere to park. Turning the car round, Sophie drove along slowly until she came to Jessica's cottage. On the opposite side of the T-junction was a stand of trees set slightly back from the road, partially hidden by a bedraggled fence which had fallen down at one end. It was a large enough space for the Merc to fit through, and, because the trees were at the edge of a big field, she didn't imagine that anyone would disturb or even notice it. Running along the other side of the field, Sophie remembered, was a footpath, which, as well as not being visible from the road (the fewer people who saw her, the better), would provide a shortcut for part of the way home.

09.22. So far, so good. Sophie set a brisk pace down the single track that ran between the barbed-wire edging of the field and a Forestry Commission plantation of uniform dark-green conifers, with Dexter lolloping happily behind. After about ten minutes' walking, she began to feel hot. It wasn't just the exertion, but the air itself, which seemed to have become heavier and more sultry. She was about to take off her suede jacket when she heard, from somewhere behind her, a cheery shout of 'Yoo-hoo!'

Heart sinking, she turned to see Belinda and Robbie striding towards them. Was the bloody woman lying in wait for her, or what? Dexter, she noticed, did not seem keen to engage with the collie. After a cursory glance, he slunk away down the path. Sophie knew exactly how he felt, but there was nothing for it. 'Goodness,' she said, brightly, 'you two do get about, don't you?'

Belinda's bangles clanked as she adjusted the bright scarf tied around her hair. 'I like to give Robbie a bit of variety. How's the hayfever?'

'The . . . ? Oh, yes. I got some antihistamines. All under control.'

'That's good. But . . .' Belinda peered at her. 'What have you done to your face? Are you OK?'

'Oh, yes. Fine.' Sophie managed a little laugh. 'My own stupid fault – I tripped over Dexter. I know – it sounds like something a battered wife would say – but it's actually true.'

Belinda raised her eyebrows. 'Are you going to walk round the plantation? We could come with you.'

Sophie adopted what she hoped was an expression of pleasure. 'We're on our way back now – stuff to sort out at the shop – so I'll have to peel off when we get to the road, but that would be nice.'

Belinda looked puzzled. 'I thought you must have come in your car.'

'Not this time.' Sensing that more was required, she added, 'I worry about Dexter putting on weight. Labradors are so food-orientated . . . Do you know, he actually managed to get into a tube of Berocca yesterday, and ate the lot. When I saw the orange foam round his mouth I nearly had a heart attack.'

'I'm not surprised. He's all right now, is he?'

'Seems fine. I mean, look at him.' Dexter, fifty yards ahead, was busily sniffing along the base of the fence, tail waving.

A discussion about dogs and their strange habits got them all the way along the side of the woodland to the road, and – thank God – didn't require much concentration on Sophie's part. She put Dexter back on the lead and was about to wind things up ('Lovely to see you, best get back') when her mobile started to ring. Flapping a hand at Belinda with a moue of apology, she fished it out of her jacket pocket and saw that the words *Mrs Palmer* had come up on the screen.

'Cleaning lady. Sorry, I'd better get it.'

'OK.' Instead of leaving her to it, Belinda remained on the

grass verge, the collie at her feet, both of them staring at her with alarming intensity.

'Well, I mustn't keep you.' Sophie half turned away, hoping Belinda would take the hint, but she didn't move. 'Hello?'

'Sophie?' Mrs Palmer's voice sounded distorted, as though she were standing at the bottom of a well. 'I'm just here, looking in the freezer—'

There was a sudden noise like sails flapping in a high wind and the line broke up in a series of hiccups.

THIRTY

Sophie froze, blood roaring in her ears, feeling as though she were about to faint. 'Sorry, Mrs Palmer.' The words felt odd in her mouth, as though she were chewing them. 'I can't hear you. Can you repeat that?'

'I need to know what to do with it all.'

'I don't understand.'

'What to do with the food.'

Keep calm, Sophie willed herself. Act normally. Find out what's going on.

'I don't understand. Where are you?'

'Here. He's just left the bags, and—'

'You're at the Old Rectory? But—'

'I'm here early because of the hospital appointment.'

'Hospital?'

'This afternoon.'

Mrs Palmer *had* told her, a few weeks ago – it was part of the ongoing saga of her cankles, something to do with water retention – and she'd completely forgotten. 'Yes, of course.'

'I need to know what to do about the frozen stuff.' Oh, God.

She was talking about the Waitrose delivery, automatically re-ordered for this morning, and also forgotten – not having looked at her mobile, Sophie had missed the texted reminder. 'I've had a look in the freezer, but there's no room. It's a fair old muddle in there, and I can tidy it up, but—'

'No!'

There was a sharp intake of breath on the other end of the line, and then, all at once, Sophie was aware of silence, solid as a wedge, between her and everything else, and of Belinda's eyes boring into her back.

'Sorry. I mean, that really isn't necessary – too much trouble. If you could just put the bag with the things for the freezer in the kitchen sink, I'll sort it out when I get back.'

'But what if it starts thawing out? Can't refreeze it, not if you don't want to make yourselves ill.'

Sophie managed an unnatural-sounding laugh. 'I shan't be that long! I really don't think we'll be at risk of food poisoning. In fact,' she continued, before Mrs Palmer could object, 'I meant to phone and tell you not to come today. I've got rather a lot of organizing to do – I'm sure you've noticed that there are still a lot of boxes in the hall – so I didn't feel it was worthwhile. I mean,' she added hastily, 'I'll pay you and everything, because obviously it was my fault, but I really don't think it's worth your staying – and I'm sure you'd like to get off, what with the hospital and everything.'

There was a short pause as Mrs Palmer digested this, during which Sophie could feel waves of incredulity coming off Belinda. 'Well, if you're sure . . .'

'Yes, absolutely. I'll be able to manage. Really, it's fine.'

'All right, then. Do you want me to set the alarm? It wasn't on when I got here.'

'No, don't worry. I'll be back very shortly. Look, I'll see you on Monday afternoon. Hope it all goes well at the hospital.'

Sophie turned back to Belinda and, ignoring the raised eyebrows, said, 'Looks like I'd better get cracking. Honestly –' she rolled her eyes theatrically – 'I'd forget my head if it wasn't screwed on. Just have to hope it isn't early-onset senility!'

Belinda's expression indicated that she thought this a distinct possibility, but all she said was, 'I'll let you go, then.'

Sophie practically ran down the verge in the direction of home, not daring to turn her head in case she saw Belinda staring after her. As she rounded the corner, the light, fluffy clouds began to darken to the dense grey of rocks, and five minutes later the rain started, the first tentative drops soon turning into a downpour.

By the time Sophie reached the Old Rectory, it was just gone eleven o'clock. Soaked and sweating, she stood in the porch, head down, rooting in her bag for her keys. The search yielding nothing, she tried the pockets of her suede jacket – and immediately her fingers closed around notched metal edges. Except—

They weren't her keys, but Jessica's. The set she'd lobbed into the pond a few hours earlier had been her own.

THIRTY-ONE

Sophie shook her head in despair. She'd worn the suede jacket yesterday morning and she must have forgotten to return her keys to her handbag. And – *of course* – she'd left the keys for the garage and the Audi on the kitchen table, thinking that she'd have to get back into the house not only to leave Dexter (although he could perfectly well have been locked in the garage for an hour or so) but also because she'd planned to transfer Jessica to the boot of the car . . .

Oh, God. This *really* can't be happening, she thought. I'm *Sophie*. I'm supposed to have a nice life. Oh, said a small, malicious voice inside her head. What makes *you* so special? And then: You don't think there's more where this came from?

Fighting the urge to cry, Sophie walked round the house to the back door, a puzzled Dexter at her heels. Imanuela's car wasn't back. She must have gone into Norwich, which meant that she was out of the way, but it also meant that she wasn't around to let Sophie into the house. Time was ticking away and even though it was still raining heavily she didn't think the vicar would be put off. He'd said the chairs and things were plastic, and if he planned simply to unload the stuff and leave it, he might even be early.

Moving Jessica was too much of a risk, Sophie decided. The important thing was to get the Audi off the property – everything else could wait until after the vicar had left.

She gazed through one of the kitchen windows. Everything inside looked so neat and bright and *right* – the Nespresso machine, the bowl of fruit and the post, stacked on the table by Mrs Palmer, next to the keys that she needed. For a moment, she imagined herself inside the room, cooking, absorbed, looking up from her work now and again at the rain beating against the windows. That's what I could be doing, dry and safe, she thought. Being outside, looking in at her life and knowing that she'd sabotaged it – knowing about the thing in the freezer, out of sight in the room next door – and that she'd have to commit an act of vandalism to get back inside the house, was indescribably unsettling.

At least she'd asked Mrs Palmer not to set the alarm. She fetched a loose brick from the pile behind the garage – leftover from when they'd had the barbecue built – and slammed it through the lower pane of the window in front of the sink. Reaching carefully past the spiteful shards sticking out of the edge of the frame, she undid the latch.

She collected a small stepladder from the unlocked garage and climbed inside, ineffectually hushing Dexter's hysterical barking, then clambered over the draining board and lowered herself to the floor.

Ten past eleven. Stuffing the keys from the table into her purse, Sophie ran down the hall to exchange her sodden jacket for a raincoat with a hood and one of Leo's baseball caps – for the CCTV as well as the rain – then dashed into her study to yank Jessica's handbag out of the filing cabinet, before opening the back door with the spare key from the key cupboard and hauling a soaked and still-barking Dexter inside. She was about to lock the door when she remembered about fingerprints. And footprints, and – if all those *CSI* programmes were anything to go by – probably bum-prints, too. She'd thrown away the bloody nitrile gloves, hadn't she? Cursing, she heeled off her welling-tons, raced upstairs for a pair of leather gloves and grabbed a packet of facial cleansing wipes from the en-suite bathroom, too, just to be on the safe side.

Dexter, now thoroughly confused, skittered backwards in front of her as she went to the kitchen drawer where the bin liners were kept – they'd be fine to sit on, but she needed some-thing smaller to wrap her feet . . . To distract the dog, she pulled a box of Shreddies out of the larder and emptied the contents on the floor. Then, yanking the Cath Kidston plastic-bag holder from its hook behind the door, she tugged her boots back on and belted out to rub some mud over Jessica's number plates before donning her sunglasses and setting off.

The rain smacked Sophie in the face as she opened the door of the Audi and staggered out onto the muddy grass of her chosen field. It was now coming down so hard that, even with the wipers going, it had been difficult to see more than a few hundred yards ahead, and, driving too fast in the unfamiliar vehicle, she'd had two near misses with oncoming cars.

The Audi, she thought, would be largely hidden from the

road by the thick, messy hedge, but she hadn't wanted to drive too far into the field in case the rain kept up and the thing got too bogged down to be driven away by anyone who fancied nicking it. She'd deleted everything from the satnav, checked the boot and glovebox, and left the keys in the ignition, and Jessica's handbag – minus the diary and the mobile, which could be disposed of on the way home – on the passenger seat.

Now, her boots still encased in their plastic bags and the pockets of her mac stuffed with the bin liners she'd sat on and the face wipes she'd used to eradicate all trace of herself from the car, she slithered across to the gate and peered along the road. No people, and – as far as she could see – no traffic. Head down, she hurried along the road to the copse where she'd hidden the Merc.

Once she'd taken off Leo's baseball cap, stripped the plastic bags off her feet and backed her car – with some difficulty and a lot of ominous scraping noises – out from between the trees and onto the road, Sophie felt fractionally calmer. She'd done OK so far, hadn't she? Perhaps it was going to be all right after all. The clock on the dashboard said 12.03, and the vicar had said midday. She'd call him, tell him she was running late. Steering with one hand, she scrolled through the numbers on her mobile with the other, peering through the rain and swiping wipers at the road and then down at the screen and then back again until the car hit a pothole and the phone flew out of her hand and into the footwell. Scrabbling for it, she failed to notice the cyclist and only just managed to miss him, his smear of a face, mouth wide open in outrage, mere inches from her wing mirror as she shot past.

Shit. If she hit someone, she'd be in real trouble. She'd better park in the next village and phone, then – in any case, she'd got to get rid of Jessica's mobile and diary. She'd wrap them in the plastic bags she'd used on her feet to disguise their shapes, and then she'd put them in poo bags and stick them in one of the bins. Better remove the diary page with her name and address on it first, just to be on the safe side. Ripping it out, she tore it into tiny shreds and shoved them into her pocket to be disposed of later.

A responsible dog-owner, she thought as she crossed the road to the bin outside the post office. What could be more normal than that?

Sophie tried the vicar twice, but he wasn't answering. Driving out of the village, she wondered if she should have left a message but she hadn't trusted herself to do it without sounding panicky. It's OK, she told herself. A simple arrangement, nothing more. She'd told him she'd be out, so he'd just think she was held up because of the rain. As long as she behaved as if everything was normal, she'd be fine. She just needed to concentrate on getting home in one piece, and everything would be all right. It was only quarter past twelve now, and in another twenty minutes – maybe less – she'd be back at the Old Rectory. All she had to do was to keep calm.

Paying close attention to the road, Sophie made it home in seventeen and a half minutes, arriving just as the rain stopped. Turning into the driveway, she saw the vicar's borrowed van . . . and, parked beside it, a police car.

Her mind a sheer drop of uncomprehending panic, she pulled up, descended from the Merc, and began walking towards the two vehicles.

THIRTY-TWO

'A break-in?'

'I'm afraid so.' The vicar, looking more like a cowboy than ever in a long Driza-Bone coat, put his hand on her arm. 'It was like this when I arrived – they must have used the ladder to get in – so I called the police. They're just having a look round the garden.'

Sophie stared at the smashed window, almost hysterical with relief. It seemed astonishing that she'd forgotten about breaking it, but she had, completely. She hadn't put the stepladder back in the garage or removed the brick, which was still lying under the window. Turning, she saw that she'd also forgotten to shut the door of the other garage after taking the Audi out, and the Porsche was in full view.

'Amazing they didn't steal it,' said the vicar.

Sophie turned back to the house. Inside the kitchen, Dexter, front paws up on the draining board, seemed to be grinning at her with horrible complicity. In the sink – and fortunately out of his reach – was a Waitrose carrier with a bag of frozen prawns sticking out of the top. The key to the Porsche, marked with its distinctive logo, lay on the table.

*

'Seems all right out here.' The male officer, who was solid and imperturbable and whose name Sophie had immediately forgotten, stood in front of the back door while his female colleague stood a few feet away, head turned like a bird preening itself, muttering into the radio attached to her shoulder. 'Now, if you could wait out here while we go inside, we'll have a look round.'

'I'm sure it's fine,' said Sophie. 'Just a . . . just kids, or something. I mean, I'm sure there's no one in there, and . . .' Realizing that everyone was staring at her, she began fumbling in her bag for the keys.

'It doesn't look as if they've made too much mess,' said Reverend Barker. 'Or not in the kitchen, anyway. Seems odd they'd choose a place with a dog, though. You'd think it would be too much of a risk . . . Although,' he added, pointing at something by the kitchen table, 'it looks as if they placated him with those.'

Looking closer, Sophie saw the empty box of Shreddies, now severely mangled, lying on the flagstones in a muddy jumble of smeared paw prints. Her own footprints were also in evidence, on the draining board and crossing the floor to the hall door. Sophie looked down at her wellingtons. Surely the police wouldn't want to compare the treads for elimination purposes?

Why hadn't she said immediately that she'd broken into her own house? After all, people must do it all the time when they'd forgotten their keys. Too late now. She should have said something – invented an emergency which meant she'd had to rush off and leave the smashed-in window – but what if the police had followed it up and found out she was lying, or Reverend Barker had mentioned it to Leo or something? Her fingerprints would be all over the stepladder and the brick as well, wouldn't they? But they'd expect that, she told herself, because it was *her* house. It wasn't as if the police were going to find anyone inside, or any evidence of damage or theft, so they'd probably just chalk it up as a mystery and she could pretend to be as baffled as everyone else that nothing had been nicked and they could forget the whole—

The back door opened and the female officer appeared, holding Jessica's keys. 'We found these in the hall – are they yours?'

Sophie stared at them, trying to quell a thrashing panic which made her feel that, at any moment, she might do or say something quite insane. 'Our cleaner,' she gabbled. 'The J on the key ring – her name's Jackie. She must have dropped them this morning.' They must have fallen out of the pocket of the suede jacket when she'd swapped it for the mac.

'Your cleaner was here?'

'Yes. A mix-up – she usually comes in the afternoon, but she had a hospital appointment, and I'd meant to put her off, but I forgot. She phoned me from here, and I told her to go home.'

'What time was that?'

'About ten o'clock. I was walking the dog.'

'And she went home after that, did she?'

'Yes, she must have done.'

'How did she lock up, without these?' The woman officer stared at Sophie, weighing the keys in her hand.

'Those must be somebody else's. Somebody that she cleans for, I mean. She works for lots of people.'

'I arrived at around twelve,' said Reverend Barker. 'I'd have called your mobile,' he told Sophie, 'but my phone got broken a couple of days ago. I've got a new one, but I don't seem to have managed to transfer all the numbers.'

'Wouldn't your cleaner normally turn the alarm on before she left?' asked the policewoman.

'Yes . . . I said not to, because I was coming straight back.'

'And you came back when?'

'Just now.'

The officer frowned. 'When you brought the dog back. You said you were taking it for a walk when your cleaner phoned.'

'Yes, sorry. About eleven, I think.'

'And when did you go out again?'

'Straight after. I had some shopping to do.' Seeing the officer's frown deepening, and remembering the Waitrose bag in the sink, she added, 'Extra stuff.'

'And everything was OK then, was it? When you came back with the dog?'

'Yes, fine.'

'But you didn't put the alarm on?'

Sophie shook her head. 'I must have forgotten.'

'Well, that narrows it down, anyway.' The officer turned to Reverend Barker. 'Your CCTV might have picked something up.'

Sophie's stomach lurched. 'But they'd come through the garden, wouldn't they? I mean, they'd hardly drive right up to the house.' At least she was no longer wearing the baseball cap or sunglasses.

'You'd be surprised.' The policewoman stared at her. 'Are you all right? Your face is bruised.'

'Yes, I'm fine.' Sophie tried to sound brisk and matter-of-fact. 'Silly accident.'

'When did it happen?'

'Yesterday. Honestly, it's nothing.'

The policewoman looked at her intently and Sophie tried to think of something to say, but failed.

The vicar cleared his throat. 'Have you found anything else? Signs of an intruder, I mean.'

'Not downstairs. My colleague is checking the upper floors.'

'Do you think we could come in?' Sophie attempted a smile. 'I mean, I'm a bit damp, and—'

'When we've finished. Won't be long, now. Will your dog be OK about me checking the room off the kitchen?'

'Yes, he's fine, but there's nothing in there, so—'

The police officer held up a hand. 'I shan't be a moment. Big freezer, is it? You'd be surprised how often the contents get stolen. It's shops, usually, or external freezers, but I'll need to take a look.'

THIRTY-THREE

Sophie watched through the broken window, as, in apparent slow motion, the policewoman walked across the kitchen, deposited Jessica's keys on the table and registered the key for the Porsche. Then she turned towards the window, and Sophie thought she was about to say something, but she seemed to think better of it and went towards the freezer room, instead.

It was like watching a farce, only it wasn't the lives of imagined characters that were about to implode, but Sophie's own, and there was absolutely nothing that she could do to stop it. She glanced up at the sky and saw that the rain clouds had been replaced by a vivid, innocent blue.

I ought to make a run for it, she thought, but, dizzy and oddly weightless, as if she might actually just float away at any moment, she stood still, clutching the windowsill for support.

The police officer was pushing open the door to the freezer room and going inside. It's not real, Sophie thought. It can't be. She poked her head in through the broken window and craned her neck, trying to see what was happening.

'You probably shouldn't be touching any of that,' said the vicar. 'You might contaminate it.'

Sophie ignored him. She could just see one end of the freezer, the lid still closed. It didn't *feel* real – but then, in the last twenty-four hours, she seemed to have become a different person altogether. And now, this different person was about to be arrested for murder.

'Do you want some help unloading your shopping?'

'What?' Now the police officer's hand was resting on the white surface. The rest of her was hidden from view by the wall of the kitchen.

'Shopping,' said Reverend Barker. 'From your car. You said you'd gone out for some extra stuff.'

'Oh, yes . . . No, that's fine. It's only one bag.'

The policewoman's fingers beat a light tattoo on the lid of the freezer and then – Sophie gasped, involuntarily – they slid under the lid, levering it upwards. What if she glimpsed, through the frosted gaps between the iced-up packets of food, an ear, a finger, a single, staring eye?

Sophie watched as she raised the lid until it was upright. Then she moved slightly to the left and Sophie could see one uniformed shoulder and the knot of hair at the nape of her neck as she leant forward to inspect the freezer's contents.

Time suspended itself and the air seemed almost to solidify, so that Sophie remained rigid by the window, unable to move or even think. She closed her eyes and braced herself, waiting for the blow to fall.

'Seems to be all there.' The policewoman was suddenly in front of her, standing beside the draining board in the kitchen. 'Not sure where you're going to find room for that lot, though.' She indicated the Waitrose carrier in the sink. 'You're full up as it is.'

The male officer appeared in the kitchen doorway. 'There's no one here and it doesn't look as if anything's been disturbed, either. You might want to go and see for yourself, though.'

Sophie nodded, fearing that if she tried to say anything she might start weeping uncontrollably with relief and gratitude, and went inside. Upstairs, she walked mechanically from room to room, in case the officers and Reverend Barker were listening from the hall, and returned, saying, 'Everything seems fine.'

After questions about whether she'd checked for passports and jewellery and other valuables – yes, yes and yes – there was a brief discussion, initiated by Reverend Barker, about finger-printing and checking the CCTV – 'Not a good use of resources under the circumstances. I'm sure you understand, sir.' After information about crime numbers and victim support that Sophie barely heard, the officers left. Reverend Barker's two helpers – who, it appeared, had been sitting in the van all this time – unloaded the tables and chairs, while he made her a cup of tea and said things about glaziers and insurance and what a nasty shock but how lucky they didn't steal anything. Sophie shoved Jessica's keys into her handbag and sat, numb and exhausted, at the kitchen table, trying to think of things to say in response. Reverend Barker had been surprised when she'd immediately produced the key to the outhouse, and Sophie had the feeling that her 'silly me' routine, begun a beat too late, hadn't been convincing.

The kitchen clock said 1.45 – the police had been there for

over an hour – and she had to go and pick up Poppy and the other girls half an hour earlier than usual, which meant leaving at 3.30 p.m. That wasn't enough time to get the window fixed, even if the glazier came out immediately. Just as long as she remembered to remove the frozen food from the sink – otherwise Imanuela, helpful to a fault, would be bound, if she came back and found it there while Sophie was out, to start reorganizing the whole freezer in order to make it fit.

Eventually, at half past two, after more cups of tea, the Reverend Barker and his helpers left. Sophie stuffed as much of the frozen food from the Waitrose bag as she could into the fridge – they'd be bound to eat most of it over the next few days – and buried the rest at the bottom of the kitchen bin, before trudging upstairs to change out of her damp clothes.

There was no chance of getting rid of Jessica today. No chance tomorrow, either, because she didn't want Melissa asking questions about why she wasn't in the shop, and, it being Friday, Leo would get a taxi from the station and be back by five. He'd have to be told about the 'burglary', of course, but it was essential to get the place sorted out before he arrived.

By 3.20 p.m., she'd fixed some cardboard over the broken window, cleaned up the kitchen and managed, by agreeing to extortionate fees, to engage the services of a glazier, a French-polisher and a carpet cleaner for the following afternoon.

Good. If she drove like the clappers she'd only be late picking up the girls by about ten minutes – not enough to cause comment, except from Poppy, and she'd be able to blame it on the break-in. She was at the back door, car keys in hand, when the phone rang in her study and, fearing it might be one of the tradespeople with a change of arrangement, she ran back down the hall and snatched it off the stand.

'Is that Sophie?' said a no-nonsense female voice. 'Sophie Hamilton? It's Frances Wingate. I live next door to your mother, dear.' A stocky, Barbour-jacketed figure with a Hermès scarf and hard, dun-coloured hair assembled itself in Sophie's mind. Mrs Wingate wasn't Margot's type at all, which probably accounted for the fact that Sophie had encountered her perhaps three times in all the years her mother had lived at her current address. 'You're not to worry, but Margot's had a bit of an accident and I'm afraid she's broken her wrist. I've taken her to the West Suffolk at Bury St Edmunds – we're there now, almost finished – and I can take her home, but you'll need to come, dear, because she can't be on her own. I know you talk on the phone, but I'm not sure how recently you've actually *seen* her . . .' There was a pause while the unspoken accusation crackled on the line.

Sophie clung to the phone, biting her lip to stop herself from actually screaming. She'd never get rid of Jessica's body with Margot blundering about the place. 'She's very shaken,' continued Mrs Wingate, 'and she's got much more confused in the last few months. Keeps insisting that everything's fine, of course, but it obviously isn't. We can't keep on putting our heads in the sand about this, I'm afraid.'

'She never seems to want my help,' said Sophie, feebly.

'Well, dear,' said Frances Wingate, briskly, 'you'll just have to insist, because there's no alternative. The hospital were very clear that she mustn't be by herself, and someone will need—'

'Mrs Wingate, I understand that, but I have to collect my daughter from school now, so—'

'But you'll come over straight after that, will you? I can take your mother home but after that I have to go out, so you'll need to get here by six at the latest.'

Sophie put the phone down and looked wildly around her. Where the hell was Imanuela? Fuck. She'd taken the rest of the day off, hadn't she, after she'd gone into Norwich about Zac's iPod – they'd sorted it out last night, which seemed about a century ago.

She'd have to call Imanuela from the car and tell her to come back. Pushing past Dexter, who'd followed her down the hall and was now staring up at her with hopeful eyes, she rushed out of the house.

THIRTY-FOUR

There was a bottle of fabric conditioner in her mother's fridge. Margot's housekeeping had never been up to much; the Bohemian persona she'd cultivated, coupled with an entirely genuine lack of ability, had seen to that, but this level of disorganization was, Sophie thought, unprecedented. The kitchen was not only cluttered but actually dirty, with a sticky floor and a smell of rotting food.

Having fed Dexter and delivered a garbled explanation about the 'break-in' and Margot's accident, Sophie had left the just-returned Imanuela making supper for Poppy and Zac and, driving dangerously fast, had managed to get to her mother's cottage by ten to six.

Margot had abandoned her usual air of being swept along in the breathless drama of her life. Subdued, grey-faced and frail, she was sitting at a table piled so high with newspapers, packaging and crockery that there was barely room for the mug of tea she wasn't drinking.

'She's been living out of tins.' Mrs Wingate, standing in the middle of the room as if she didn't want to be contaminated, addressed Sophie as if Margot wasn't there. Which, to be fair, she wasn't, not really – after greeting Sophie, she hadn't spoken again but had sat with a faraway look as if trying to retrieve a memory. Now, she appeared to be entirely preoccupied in delving, with her good hand, inside the carrier bag at her feet. Close to, she smelt faintly cabbagy, like unchanged water from a flower vase. 'Neglecting herself. And the nurse couldn't get any sense out of her about what medicines she's supposed to be taking. She really can't carry on like this.'

'I can see that.' Sophie continued checking sell-by dates and emptying the fridge. She couldn't just whisk Margot away, leaving the house in its current state, and Imanuela would be fine on her own for a couple of hours. Sophie had left her with instructions about what to cook, so there was no risk of her poking about in the freezer, and besides, the au pair had volunteered to make up a bed for Margot in one of the guest rooms.

'I've been trying for weeks to persuade her to go to the GP, but she refuses. Afraid of the diagnosis – thinks she'll be prevented from driving or having any sort of independent life.'

'She's only sixty-nine,' said Sophie, defensively. 'It might not be . . .' She dropped her voice. 'Senile dementia.'

'Well . . .' Mrs Wingate gave her a disbelieving look. 'She's definitely got *something* wrong with her. You need to face facts, dear.'

I've killed someone, thought Sophie. I have a corpse in my freezer. Those are the facts.

After Mrs Wingate had left, in a flurry of instructions about prescriptions and fracture clinics and the risks of dehydration, it took Sophie over an hour to get her mother ready to leave. With only the two of them there, Margot stopped fussing with her carrier bag and became fretful about Sophie throwing away the contents of the fridge. She insisted on taking everything out of the bin in order to subject it to minute examination, and asked Sophie so many times to check that the back door was locked and the electrical appliances unplugged that it was all she could do not to yell at her.

Margot barely spoke on the way to the Old Rectory, but returned to pawing through the contents of the carrier that she'd refused to let Sophie put in the boot with her suitcase and the bags of retrieved food she'd insisted on bringing. When they stopped at a junction, she began scrabbling at the passenger door with her good hand, trying to get out, and when Sophie leant over to stop her, Margot cringed away, crying out and tugging at the safety belt.

'Margot, it's all right. It's me. You're quite safe.' Her mother gazed at her with fearful eyes. 'It's Sophie. Your daughter.' Margot had never wanted Sophie to call her 'Mum'. Being able to use the word now, she thought, might have made it easier to remind her mother who she was.

'Yes . . .' Margot's face slackened. 'I'm a nuisance,' she added, humbly. 'I'm sorry.'

'You're not a nuisance. It's fine.' Except it isn't, thought Sophie, and it never will be again.

Margot turned away and began fidgeting with her carrier bag again as a line of container lorries rumbled past them. Sophie looked out of the window, over the fields towards the invisible sea beyond, where the tide was going out. What am I going to do? she thought helplessly. What the hell am I going to do?

*

When they arrived home it was a quarter to nine, overcast, blustery and coming on to rain again. Sophie pulled up at the side of the house and sat in silence for a moment, wearily trying to marshal her thoughts into some semblance of order. She needed to sort out Margot's medication, get her off to bed, see to Zac and Poppy, phone Leo and explain – but explain how? As if Margot and the 'break-in' weren't bad enough, there was the scratch on the Porsche. Perhaps she could blame it on the imaginary burglars. That would entail admitting that she'd left the garage door open, but she could always say that what with the rain and the furniture for the fair and . . . And Reverend Barker might mention to Leo how lucky it was that his car hadn't been stolen, what with the key left on the kitchen table, and suggest they look at the CCTV together. *And* there was the business of the broken side table, and the lies she'd told on the spur of the moment, half of which she couldn't even remember . . .

Her mind churned pointlessly until Margot put a hand on her knee. 'Is everything all right, dear?'

'Sorry. Let's get inside before the heavens open, shall we?' To her left, Sophie saw Imanuela standing in the doorway, one hand on Dexter's collar. 'You stay there and I'll come round and give you a hand.'

'I found this.' Margot pushed something small and flat into Sophie's hand. 'I thought it might be important.'

It was a business card with an email address and a telephone number: *Jessica Mottram: Travel Writer & Author.*

THIRTY-FIVE

Sophie's stomach lurched. 'Where did you find that?'

'Down the side of the seat. You must have dropped it.'

It must have fallen out of Jessica's diary when she was bundling it up in the poo bag to throw away. 'It's nothing, but thanks.' Forcing a smile and praying that Margot hadn't noticed the name, she stuffed the card into the pocket of her jeans. 'Come on.'

Feeling too exhausted to argue about whether or not alcohol was a good idea, Sophie settled Margot on the sitting-room sofa with the glass of whisky she'd requested. Having dismissed Imanuela with effusive thanks and assurances that she could take things from there, she lugged her mother's suitcase upstairs and started unpacking. Margot's medications seemed to have multiplied since Christmas, so that now the packets and dosette boxes covered most of the bedside table. Sorting it all out would have to wait, she decided, shoving the last of her mother's underwear into a drawer. She popped one of the painkillers the hospital had prescribed out of its blister pack – Margot hadn't complained about her wrist, but it must surely be hurting – and went back down to the sitting room.

Poppy, lounging on the rug with Dexter sprawled across her legs, was telling Margot about the break-in. 'Did you tell Dad we were burgled, Mum?'

'We weren't really,' said Sophie. 'I mean, they didn't take anything.' She gave Margot the tablet and a glass of water and sank into the nearest armchair. 'I'll phone him in a minute.'

'You look really tired, Mum. Do you want something to eat? Imanuela made lots, but Granny says she's not hungry.'

It was surely significant, Sophie thought, that Margot, who normally objected to being called 'Granny', didn't seem even to have noticed. 'I'm not hungry, either,' she told Poppy, 'but a glass of wine would be nice.'

Sophie thought that Poppy, ever ready to be censorious, might object to this, but she just said, 'OK. Red or white?'

'White, please. There's a bottle in the fridge. Where's Zac?'

'In his room. He says you're going to buy him a new iPod.'

'We're getting it fixed, that's all.'

'He's hopeless.'

'I know.'

They looked at each other for a moment before Poppy shoved Dexter off her legs and began scrambling to her feet. Halfway up she stopped, and, shuffling round the coffee table on her hands and knees, reached under the armchair opposite Sophie's.

'What on earth are you doing?'

'Look!' Poppy stood up and held out her hand. In the middle of her palm was one of Jessica's diamond stud earrings.

'Didn't realize I'd lost it.' Sophie heard the wobble in her voice and clenched her fists to stop herself snatching the thing.

'It isn't yours. You've got some like it, but they're not the same.' Trust eagle-eyed Poppy to spot that, thought Sophie. 'Must be Melissa's.'

'I don't see how—' Just in time, Sophie remembered that she'd told Poppy that Melissa had been there the day before. 'Yes, I suppose it must. I'll take it into the shop tomorrow.'

Poppy frowned. 'Hasn't she phoned you about it? It looks really expensive.'

'I suppose she's been too busy,' said Sophie, blandly. 'Why don't you hand it over and fetch me that wine you promised? I'm shattered.'

Poppy left the room and Sophie lay back in the chair and closed her eyes. The earring must have been loose, she thought. It must have come out when she'd pulled Jessica onto the hall rug to drag her out to the freezer. The bloody woman's leaving bits of herself everywhere, thought Sophie; the butterfly back of the earring must be on the carpet too, somewhere – unless it was caught up in Jessica's hair.

Margot was talking now. 'I said, maybe it belonged to one of the burglars.'

'I don't think it's very likely, do you?'

'You never know. There *are* women burglars. I think you should give it to the police.'

'So do I, Mum, if it's not Melissa's.' Poppy came back with Sophie's wine. 'It might be a clue – even if it wasn't a woman, they could have taken the earrings from somebody else's house, couldn't they, and that one fell out of their pocket or something. Why didn't the police do fingerprints, anyway?'

'They're under-resourced, darling. They can't do everything.'

'All the same, though . . . And why didn't they steal anything? They could have had your jewellery, couldn't they?'

'Would you rather they'd taken stuff?'

'Course not!' Poppy gave Sophie a scornful look. 'And actually, it can't be Melissa's because Mrs Palmer would have hoovered it up, wouldn't she? Except . . .' Poppy paused, thinking. 'Why wasn't she here? Doesn't she come on Thursday afternoons?'

'She had a hospital appointment. And anyway, it might be Imanuela's, or someone else's.'

'It isn't Imanuela's,' said Poppy. 'I'd remember.'

'Yes.' Sophie sighed. 'Of course you would.' She wasn't the only one Poppy watched – every detail of the au pair's wardrobe was noted and assessed, too. 'Let's just see what Melissa says, shall we? Have you finished your homework?'

'Nearly.'

'Well, it's gone half past nine so you might want to do that before you go to bed – because I need to talk to Margot about the arrangements, OK?'

Sophie pressed the Off button on the phone, helped herself to more wine from the bottle on the desk and sat listening to the rain. It had taken the best part of two hours to sort out what Poppy and Zac needed for school and get Margot – fretful, querulous and apologetic by turns – off to bed, and then phone Leo. This last chore had gone better than she'd expected. Leo had been annoyed when she'd given him her edited version of the 'break-in' ('For Christ's sake, why didn't you set the alarm?'), but sanguine about her 'accident' and the broken side table ('As long as you're OK, Soph – tables mend easier than bones') and about

Margot coming to stay – or possibly live – with them ('Bound to happen at some point'). Grateful to him for not making a fuss, she hadn't had the heart, or the courage, to tell him about the scratch on the Porsche. Now, sitting alone with her wine, she wondered if she should have taken the plunge – but what if he'd remembered parking the thing in the middle of the garage, not the side? If he did, she'd have had to confess that she'd moved it – except that she couldn't think of a single reason why she would have needed to do so.

She was too tired to think about it now. Instead, she considered the conversation she'd just had. Leo hadn't sounded worried or preoccupied – which was odd, considering that he'd been planning to meet Jessica the previous evening and she'd neither turned up nor sent a message. Had she, perhaps, cancelled earlier in the week? That could be it, Sophie thought, although, if it were the case, she'd forgotten to cross it out in her diary.

She ought to check whether Jessica's disappearance had been reported yet. It was unlikely – she wasn't a child, and it was only just over twenty-four hours – but all the same . . . She turned on her laptop and googled *Jessica Mottram*, but there were no news items. She'd check on Jessica's car tomorrow.

Since she still had the keys to Jessica's cottage, it would be a good idea, assuming the coast were clear, to remove her laptop. If she could manage to get into it – Jessica might be one of those people who automatically saved their passwords – then she'd be able to delete her email exchange with Jessica as well as working out the state of play with Leo and discovering whether anyone else was anxious about the woman's whereabouts. If she couldn't get into the emails, she'd get rid of the thing – the fewer pieces of potential evidence, the better. She'd do it at lunchtime, on the way back from the shop. Just to be on the safe side, she'd put a cardboard box from the Hamilton De Witt stockroom in the car: if necessary, she could claim to be delivering something to Jessica – she'd create a delivery note for a couple of samples now, and, if it became necessary, explain to Melissa that she hadn't invoiced because she was hoping for a larger order – and the box would be handy to hide the laptop in, as well. Yes, that was a plan – and she'd be back in plenty of time for the tradesmen.

THIRTY-SIX

Sophie had expected Jessica's study to be picturesquely untidy, with heaps of books and papers, like the photographs illustrating those 'Where I Write' articles you sometimes saw in the Sunday papers. She was surprised to find no clutter at all – the small number of paperbacks were neatly shelved, and the only thing on the vintage kneehole desk was a vase of peonies.

Melissa seemed to have swallowed the business about her feeling unwell – the bruises, about which she'd been solicitous, had helped – and Sophie had remembered to go through the charade of showing her the earring. Jessica's car was no longer in the field where she'd left it. She'd driven past as slowly as she dared, but there had been no angry farmer, no police, nobody, and nothing but a splattered catastrophe of bloodied feathers on the tarmac in front of the gateway, squabbled over by a trio of crows.

So far, so good. Having parked her car in the little spinney she'd used before, she'd walked briskly down the road, cardboard box tucked under her arm as an alibi, entered Jessica's garden and, hands shaking, had pulled on a new pair of nitrile gloves – purchased, with several other items in order not to attract any attention, at an out-of-town DIY store – before opening the side door of the cottage. Now, having closed the curtains so as not to be seen, she searched the desk drawers, but, aside from a couple of memory sticks, which she stuffed in her pockets, she found nothing that might incriminate her. There was no calendar on the pinboard, either, just a print of a woman in eighteenth-century clothes that Sophie guessed must be Elizabeth the slutty duchess of Devonshire or wherever it was.

A quick tour of the other downstairs rooms didn't turn up anything, either. The kitchen looked shiny and new and the rest of the place was well appointed and pretty, although there was some evidence – unexpected gaps and not quite enough furniture – of things having been recently removed, presumably by Sean. Sophie put down her cardboard box on the console table in the hall and hesitated in front of the winking red light on the base of the cordless phone. Was Leo's voice in there? Hand hovering over the receiver, she imagined the stored endearments.

Get on with it. A moment's fiddling told her there was one new message. Trembling, she pressed the button.

'Dear Customer, our records show us you still haven't claimed . . .' She blinked at a polished nautilus shell on a stand while a woman's voice quacked about PPI refunds, then pressed Delete. A different woman told her that there were no saved messages.

She went upstairs and stopped on the landing. The half-open doors – glimpses of carpet, tiles, the side of a basin – looked ominous. The air around her seemed to thicken and hum, and a creaking floorboard made her gasp and flinch. Holding her breath, she inched forward and pushed the first door gingerly with her fingertips.

Guest room. Another guest room. Shower and loo. All tasteful, tidy spaces that might have belonged to her or any one of her friends. At the end was the master bedroom with its en-suite bathroom. Had Jessica and Leo done it here, on the French-style bateau bed? She imagined the pair of them, in hours snatched from weekends with her and the children, making love before climbing naked into the freestanding Victorian roll-top bath and holding each other in a soapy embrace.

There were two white cotton waffle bathrobes hanging on the back of the door. Rather on the short side for Leo, Sophie thought. He preferred something altogether more capacious – but then, he'd been a different person when he was with Jessica, hadn't he? Perhaps he was sitting in a meeting right now, pretending to concentrate, or staring vacantly at the numbers on his computer screen, wondering where she was.

She searched the cabinet in the bathroom and found a shaving kit, a bottle of an unfamiliar cologne and a spare toothbrush, but there was nothing remotely masculine folded up in the chest of drawers or hanging in the wardrobe. The bedside cabinet on Jessica's side (tissues, vitamins, and a couple of paperbacks with photos of women staring out to sea on the covers) had, in its drawer, a strip of contraceptive pills with five missing. Sophie picked it up and turned it over, frowning. Jessica certainly hadn't *looked* pregnant, but then some women start to show later than others . . . It was easy enough to miss a pill. She imagined Jessica in the en-suite, staring at the blue line on the pregnancy test with a triumphant smile on her face before sauntering downstairs to her study to deface the round robin and send it back to Sophie. NOW HE'S GOING TO LEAVE YOU.

If Jessica had been pregnant, that would mean Sophie had killed two people, one of them Leo's child. But Jessica might not have told Leo she was pregnant, she thought. She might have been waiting until it was too late to do anything about it. Or maybe she *had* told Leo and they'd had a row because he'd wanted her to have a termination – said he wasn't prepared to leave Sophie and the children – and she'd returned the letter out of spite . . .

Sophie walked round to the other side of the bed. The top of the bedside cabinet was bare, but the ghosted memoir of an old-school villain lay on the rug. There were a couple of other books, too, partially hidden by the gleaming wooden bed frame – true crime things, their titles dripping blood. Maybe Leo had left them there – although they didn't look like his sort of thing. His reading matter was usually confined to dry-looking hardbacks about politics or military history. Perhaps, she thought sadly, I don't really know *what* he likes.

Where the hell was Jessica's laptop? Sophie looked round again and spotted the corner of something hard, dark and flat poking out from underneath clothes draped over a Lloyd Loom chair. There it was. Maybe Sean still had keys to the cottage and she hadn't wanted him to come in and find it – which might also explain why Leo hadn't left a message on the landline. These thoughts, coupled with the sound of a car in the distance, broke the spell.

She rushed down the stairs and shoved the laptop into the cardboard box. She had just locked the front door and peeled off the nitrile gloves, and was turning to go down the garden path when—

'Yoo-hoo!'

Belinda and Robbie were staring at her from the other side of the picket fence.

THIRTY-SEVEN

Caught off balance, Sophie stumbled on a flagstone and almost dropped the cardboard box. What if Belinda had seen her locking up or taking off the gloves?

'Sorry!' At least the wretched woman's tone was brightly unsuspicious. 'We always seem to be creeping up on you.' Robbie actually was creeping. Flat to the ground, he inched towards her as though she were a straying sheep, eyeing her with mistrust.

'Hey, Robbie,' she said, trying to keep her voice casual. 'Enjoying your walk?'

Robbie, his stare unwavering, didn't acknowledge this.

'Jessica not in?'

'Apparently not.'

Belinda looked from Sophie to the cottage. 'The downstairs curtains are closed.'

'I suppose she forgot to open them. I didn't know you knew her.'

'Not very well – or not any more, anyway. Another life.' Belinda's bangles clanked as she batted the years away with a dismissive hand. 'You know.' She stared at Sophie expectantly. 'So . . . No Dexter?'

'He's at home. I was just bringing this over.' Sophie patted the cardboard box. 'From the shop. Jessica ordered it but we only had the display ones left and the delivery people messed up, so the stock's only just come in. I was passing, so I thought I'd bring it over – save her the journey.'

'What is it?'

'Ohhh . . .' What? What was supposed to be in the box? Sophie stared down at the cardboard, trying to remember. 'Just some Moroccan tiles. Accent tiles – she wanted to see if they'd work in the bathroom,' she gabbled.

'You could put a note through the door and leave them in the woodshed.'

'She hasn't got a woodshed.'

'It's round the other side, where she parks her car.'

Where the CCTV is, thought Sophie. The police will look at the footage, she thought, and that'll be the last sighting of Jessica – getting into her car, two days ago, to come to the Old Rectory. As long as no one knew where she was going . . . 'No, it's fine. I'll come back.'

'They'll be quite safe.'

'I know, but we left something in someone's barn a couple of months ago and it got pinched, so . . .'

Belinda was frowning and, for a moment, Sophie thought that she might be about to argue, but she said, 'I'm glad I bumped into you, actually. Are you going back home now?'

'Well, yes.'

'You couldn't give us a lift, could you? Only, I've hurt my ankle. Tripped over yesterday, walking Robbie – just after we'd seen you, as a matter of fact. I'd have come in my car, only it's at the garage. I thought I'd be OK by now, but I was obviously too ambitious.'

'I can take you to the GP, if you'd like.'

Belinda shook her head. 'I'm sure it'll be fine if I keep the weight off it for a bit. Where's your car? I didn't see it anywhere.'

'Just down the road. Tell you what – why don't you stay here and I'll fetch it?' Without waiting for an answer, Sophie began walking back towards the T-junction. She'd just have to hope that Belinda didn't see her go into the spinney – the last thing she needed was questions about why she'd parked the car in there.

'This is me.' Belinda gestured towards a cobbled alleyway just off the village green that Sophie remembered from giving her a lift before – a row of tiny, flat-fronted Victorian cottages tucked behind the larger, more prosperous-looking houses. 'Have you got time for a cup of tea?'

'Better not.' Sophie switched off the ignition. 'You know how it is – the "To Do" list never gets any shorter.'

'Yes, but you're always really organized. That's why I was a bit surprised the other day – you seemed so agitated.'

Sophie forced a laugh. 'Just a mix-up. It was all a bit fraught because my mother managed to break her wrist, so she's staying with us at the moment. There's always *something*. Shall I give you a hand getting out of the car?'

Belinda didn't move, and Sophie saw that an elderly woman, thin and faded as a pressed flower, was making her slow way along the narrow pavement at the side of the Merc.

'Why don't I get Robbie out of the back first?' She was about to open the door when her mobile rang. Imanuela, she thought. Margot. The freezer. Jessica.

'Hadn't you better get that?'

'It'll go to voicemail.'

'I don't mind – and we'll have to wait in any case.' Belinda nodded towards the passenger window. The elderly woman was standing in front of it, both hands on the crook of her stick, catching her breath. 'It might be important.'

'Right.' Sophie gritted her teeth and rooted in her bag for the phone. 'Hello?'

'Sophie?' Imanuela sounded anxious. 'Please, I have to speak to you.'

THIRTY-EIGHT

Blood thudded in Sophie's ears and, for a moment, she couldn't hear, much less understand, what Imanuela was saying.

'. . . so he is early and he needs the payment—'

'Imanuela? Sorry, I didn't catch all that. Are you talking about the glazier?'

'The . . . ?'

'For the window.'

'Kitchen window, yes.'

'He was supposed to come this afternoon.'

'Somebody change their appointment. You want to talk to him about the money?'

Having provided the necessary credit card details – giving out this information in front of Belinda was, frankly, the least of her problems – Sophie ended the call.

'Everything OK?'

'Yeah.' Sophie dropped the phone back in her bag. 'Someone broke in yesterday afternoon. It's no big deal.'

Belinda raised her eyebrows. 'Sounds quite a big deal to me. Did you lose much?'

Sophie shook her head. 'They didn't take anything. It was weird.' Having repeated this several times, she found she now almost believed in the phantom burglars.

'Don't you have an alarm?'

'Yes, but I forgot to set it. Too busy worrying about Margot.'

'Margot?'

'My mum.'

'Oh.' Belinda looked at her for a long moment, not bothering to hide the recalibration. I know, Sophie wanted to shout. I don't look like the kind of person who calls her mother by her first name but it isn't my fault and for your information the dead body in my freezer isn't my fault either and will you please stop asking questions and just get the fuck out of my car?

'Well, you're jolly lucky.' Belinda's cheerful tone was so entirely at odds with the snarling inside Sophie's head that, for a long moment, she couldn't think of a reply.

By one o'clock she was alone in her study, Jessica's laptop on the desk in front of her. Margot had elected to stay in bed, the glazier had left, Imanuela had gone to the cottage to have lunch and the French-polisher and the carpet-cleaning firm weren't due for another hour. She had Jessica's email address, but the password was another matter, unless – *please, please* – she kept herself signed in ... Turning on the laptop, Sophie keyed in the code for the Wi-Fi, brought up the search engine, typed in 'hotmail.com' and was rewarded with an email page containing seven new messages in the inbox. *Re: Insurance* was clearly from Sean, *Re: Your Membership Enquiry* looked as if it was from a health club, *We'd love to see you . . .* was from a French email address, and

Make your money go further with our Best Buys from Which? and something from an art magazine about a free exhibition catalogue were obviously junk. That left two from me@mfdw.freeserve.co.uk. The subject of the first, sent the previous day, was *Where are you?* The second, *WTF?*, had been sent at 11.57 that morning.

Sophie's index finger hovered over the mouse. Would Leo be able to tell that someone had read his emails? And, since she was using their Wi-Fi, would the police computer people be able to tell, even without having Jessica's actual machine, that the emails had been looked at from the Old Rectory IP address, or whatever it was called? Perhaps just typing in the code to get online was enough to let them know who'd accessed Jessica's emails, in which case they'd know she was guilty even if she didn't open the things, wouldn't they?

Snatching her hand away from the keypad, Sophie pushed her chair back and sat, weak and clammy, fighting to stay calm. No, that couldn't be right. They'd only know about the IP address if she actually answered the emails. She'd seen that on some TV drama – it had been how they'd caught the killer. But if she just *looked* at the emails, then cleared all of Jessica's personal data so there was nothing to connect her with the machine (she was pretty sure the Internet would tell her how to do that), before dumping it somewhere, she'd be in the clear.

Hitching the chair back to the desk, she directed the cursor at the first email and double-clicked.

Where are you? I've been here for three hours, waiting. This isn't like you. I'm sorry we rowed the other night but you know how difficult it is sometimes. Please call me as soon as you get this, however you're feeling. I just need to know you're all right. xxx

Not even an initial, thought Sophie – but then, he doesn't need to, does he? No doubt who it's from. Had the row been about Jessica having tea with her? She closed the email, marked it as unread, then double-clicked on the second one.

What the hell is going on? I haven't heard from you since Tuesday, and I've just had a call from a Norfolk plod to say that your car was nicked by a bunch of pissheads and crashed on the A1067. They say they haven't been able to contact you and they want to 'interview' me, whatever the fuck that means. CALL ME AS SOON AS YOU GET THIS. Miles.

Miles?

THIRTY-NINE

Miles. A depth charge inside her, filling her mind with noiseless incomprehension as she gasped, hollowed out by shock.

me@mfdw.freeserve.co.uk. Miles De Witt. The 'f' must be a middle initial – Francis or Felix or something.

It's not as if you're in love with him, is it? Jessica had thought that her anger was on Melissa's behalf. That was why she'd looked so taken aback when the pair of them were in her garden and Sophie had mentioned Hamilton De Witt.

On the wall beside her desk were a group of family photos, including one of Miles, Melissa, Leo and herself at a restaurant, taken the previous year. It had been his and Lissa's twenty-first wedding anniversary. She could picture Miles now, happy and tipsy, making an impromptu speech. 'I still can't believe she married me,' he'd said, and called her his 'guardian angel'. They'd always seemed happy, and Melissa had never indicated that anything was wrong. That either meant that she genuinely didn't think that anything *was* wrong, or that she did, but hadn't felt that she could voice it. Surely she could have told *me*, thought Sophie. But, said the little voice in Sophie's head, you didn't tell her about the letters. In fact, she remembered, she'd made a deliberate decision not to say anything.

Leo must have been lending the pair of them his flat, and it had been Miles's voice she'd heard, not his. Male solidarity, she supposed. They'd *had* all those imagined talks in the corners of wine bars, but with the positions reversed . . . But Miles had a flat of his own in London. And what about Jessica's car? The only reason the police would have for contacting Miles was if the car were his – if he'd bought it for her.

Sophie scrolled down, looking for other emails from Miles's address, but there were none, and the 'Deleted' box was empty. A habit of secrecy, Sophie thought, if Jessica hadn't trusted Sean not to look. That didn't explain why she'd saved the password, of course, but perhaps she changed it regularly.

Miles hadn't mentioned the handbag in his email, but the police had obviously tried to contact Jessica, so presumably it had been discovered in the car. Sophie googled A1067, remembering too late that she ought to have been doing it on her own computer.

The A1067 near Fakenham remains closed in both directions after a car crashed into a brick wall. Firefighters had to use hydraulic rescue equipment to free three people from the vehicle, a silver Audi, after the wall collapsed on top of it. One man was airlifted to the Norfolk and Norwich University Hospital by the East Anglian Air Ambulance, and another man and a woman were taken to the hospital by ambulance. All three are believed to be in their twenties.

Miles's pissheads, Sophie thought. Perhaps the police hadn't been able to do more than ascertain that the handbag didn't belong to them.

She scrolled down to an earlier report of the crash on the *Eastern Daily Press* website.

Emergency services were called to the scene of the accident at 2.25 a.m. Three people have been cut out of the vehicle, at least one of whom is said to have serious injuries.

The airlifted one, thought Sophie – and 'serious' probably meant 'life-threatening'. Fakenham was only ten or twelve miles away, so if they'd pinched the car on the way home from the pub, they must have been driving around in the rain for a couple of hours, at least.

She imagined the cans being passed around, the bravado and laughter turning to screams as the driver, blinded, perhaps, by headlights coming the other way, had miscalculated and the car had skidded on the wet road. She saw, in her mind's eye, the wall rearing out of nowhere before their eyes, the impact, the buckling and rending of metal, the crushed and mangled limbs, and then the silence before everything was bathed in the blue flickering lights of the police cars and the firemen set to work with their tools.

Sophie gazed at the words on the screen until they blurred together. I did that, she thought, numbly. It happened because of me.

FORTY

Sophie welcomed the French-polisher and the carpet cleaners, made them tea and left them to sort themselves out. She called the fracture clinic and made an appointment for her mother, while Margot, woken from sleep, sat at the kitchen table in her dressing gown, her face crumpled and vague. Sophie prepared soup and toast and coaxed her to eat; fed Dexter; dispatched Imanuela to fetch the dry-cleaning and had a complicated phone conversation with Ottilie's mum about the tennis tournament at Oddham's – the girls would need to stay on for extra practice twice a week, necessitating changes to the rota for the school run. All the time, images jostled each other in her mind: Jessica's laptop, stuffed behind the filing cabinet in her office; the police questioning Miles; the crash; the young man who'd been air-lifted to hospital lying in intensive care . . .

Poppy arrived home at half past four and they had a row about whether or not she could attend pottery classes, in the middle of which the French-polisher appeared and said he'd need to come back and finish the work tomorrow and no one must use the coffee table this evening. Sophie helped him move it into the dining room, where the rugs from the hall and sitting room were drying, tented over chairs. Halfway through, Zac arrived home from nets, left a trail of kit across the hall floor and let Dexter out of the utility room so that he got in the way and caused her to drop the table on her foot.

Her big toe felt as if it might be broken. She saw the French-polisher off and hobbled back to the kitchen. Poppy was in tears. Zac was staring into the crammed-to-capacity fridge and complaining that there was nothing to eat. Margot was rooting in the bin, pulling out the packets of food Sophie had hidden at the bottom and dropping them on the floor, where Dexter was enthusiastically tearing into a tray of mince.

'What the bloody hell are you doing?'

Margot straightened up, her face stiff with hurt and disappointment. 'You threw my food away.'

'I didn't! Your stuff is in the fridge. Go and look.' Sophie scrabbled on the floor, grabbing things and shoving them back into the bin. 'All of this needs to be thrown out.'

Margot seized a tea towel with her good hand and beat at Sophie as if she were trying to put out a fire. 'Stop it! Stop throwing my food away!'

'I'm *not*! This is ours, and it's past its sell-by date.'

'This isn't.' Zac inspected the plastic wrapping Dexter had ripped off the mince. 'It says the nineteenth.'

'Well, the others are. Dexter, drop that!'

'This one says the nineteenth, too.' Poppy had dried her eyes and was holding up a bag of sweetcorn.

'For God's sake! Just put it all in the bin. Even if it isn't out of date, it's started thawing, which means we can't refreeze it.

Dexter!' Sophie tugged at the plastic tray that was hanging out of the dog's mouth.

'That's just if it's meat or fish and you didn't defrost it in the fridge. Or ice cream, because it goes funny. We did it in Food Tech.' Poppy bent down to pick up a bag of fruits of the forest. 'I can put these things in the freezer.'

'No!' Sophie gave the tray a desperate yank and Dexter let go abruptly, spraying the tiles with chunks of half-defrosted meat, then lunged for a tub of salted-caramel ice cream that Margot had dropped beside the bin. Shooting Sophie a look of guilty triumph, he raced off into the hall, almost colliding with Imanuela, who'd just appeared in the doorway with an armful of dry-cleaning.

'Ay ay ay.' The au pair's eyes were wide. 'What happen?'

'*She* says –' Poppy gestured at Sophie – 'that we have to throw these away.'

'Yes, we do.' Sophie spoke through gritted teeth. 'Because there's no room in the freezer. Just give them to me, Poppy.'

'I can make room.' Imanuela deposited the dry-cleaning over the back of a chair.

'See? We shouldn't waste food.' Vindicated, Poppy held out the bags to the au pair. Sophie intercepted and, after a brief, wordless tussle, retrieved the sweetcorn and fruits of the forest and staggered back, clutching them to her chest. Her foot was throbbing and her throat felt compressed, as though invisible hands were squeezing her windpipe. Everyone was staring at her. Margot and Poppy had retreated to opposite ends of the room, looking fearful, and Zac stood in the middle, grinning and shaking his head. I must look completely mad, she thought.

Pulling herself together with an effort, she said, 'All right. They can go in the freezer, but I'll do it, OK? Margot, why don't you sit down? Zac and Poppy, go and rescue the ice cream, or what's left of it, and Imanuela, why don't you sweep all this mess up and make us a cup of tea?'

Nobody moved as she walked into the freezer room, pulling the door to behind her. The huge white chest seemed to glow before her eyes, as though it were full of some appalling radio-active substance that would turn her bones to lace. Opening it as little as possible, she shoved the two bags inside, pressed them down hard and slammed the lid shut. Eyes closed, she stood there, swaying slightly. Keep calm, she told herself. Breathe. She heard, as if in a dream, the sound of a car pulling up in front of the gate. The taxi. Feet crunching on gravel. Leo.

A second later, the door from the kitchen was nudged open, and Dexter crept round it, looking guilty, with Poppy behind him, holding the ravaged ice-cream tub. A second after that, Leo appeared through the outside door, briefcase in hand. Before anyone had time to speak, Dexter extended his neck in a retching motion, opened his mouth, and was spectacularly sick on the flagstones.

Poppy looked from Sophie to Leo and back again. 'So,' she said, in a conversational tone, 'is it OK about the pottery classes?'

FORTY-ONE

Sophie poured vegetable stock into the pan of pea and asparagus risotto she was preparing for a late Sunday lunch. Margot was upstairs lying down, Zac and Poppy were busy in their respective rooms, and Leo was in his study. He'd been ensconced there for most of Saturday as well, absenting himself from meals, citing work as a reason for not involving himself in the household schedule. In many ways, this was a relief, although the inevitable ructions about the dent and scratch on the Porsche – unable to sleep, she'd crept out to look at the car at 5.30 a.m. and found the damage was worse than she'd previously thought – couldn't be put off forever. If they'd still lived in London, it would have been parked in the road and the scrape could have been chalked up to a side-swipe from a passing van, but not here. Leo's preoccupation, she thought now, must be the reason that he hadn't even appeared to notice that the coffee table was missing from the sitting room.

Sophie felt dazed, powerless to control the thoughts that scurried round and round in her head then whirled away as if directed by centrifugal force, each scenario worse than the one it replaced. Leo had weighed in on Poppy's side about the pottery classes, necessitating another long conversation with Ottilie's mum about further changes to the rota for the school run. Zac had managed to drop a teaspoon down the waste disposal unit. Margot, getting up in the small hours to use the bathroom, had opened the wrong door and, confused, had blundered into their room by mistake so that Sophie, waking to the sight of a white, drooping wraith at the end of the bed, had almost had a heart attack. The world is relentless, she thought, wonderingly. It just carries on.

Standing at the stove, she eyed the door to the freezer room, firmly closed after her in-and-out dash-and-rummage for a bag of frozen peas. Leo's old Barbour and Dexter's spare lead were hanging on pegs next to a hessian carrier with 'Bag for Life' written across it in large green letters. How was she ever going to get Jessica out of the house?

A noise in the hall made her turn. Leo was standing in the doorway, the Porsche key in his hand. 'Something's come up, Soph.'

'Can't it wait?'

'Not really, no.' Leo looked down at his feet, weighing the key in his hand.

'But lunch will be ready in twenty minutes.'

'Eat without me – I'll pick something up on the way.'

'On the way where?'

'Sorry.' Leo backed away. 'It's urgent.'

'Leo, before you go, I need to explain—'

Too late. He'd turned on his heel and, before she knew it, he was striding across the yard towards the garage. Sophie ran to the window and saw him raise the door, realizing, as he did so, that she hadn't repositioned the Porsche and that therefore he wouldn't be able to get into it without levering himself across the passenger seat. Surely, she thought, he'll realize that he didn't park it like that.

She watched in stupefied amazement as, without even glancing back towards the house, he yanked open the passenger door of the car, struggled awkwardly into the driver's seat, reversed out at speed and shot away in a spray of gravel.

It must be Miles, Sophie thought. She returned to the stove and recommenced stirring the glutinous rice. Could it be possible that the sender of the returned letters thought that Miles was Leo? That would mean, of course, that it hadn't been Jessica, because if Miles had, for some reason, been masquerading as Leo, he would hardly have put his own name to the email he'd sent her.

No. Leo's affair had to be something entirely separate – apart from the fact that he and Miles had, presumably, swapped adulterers' notes – and she was no nearer discovering the culprit than she had been six weeks earlier. How extraordinary, she thought. That realization ought to have provoked at least some sort of emotional response, but now she felt nothing except a sort of detached wonder at her numbness.

'Where's Dad gone?' Zac shambled into the kitchen. 'He was driving like Lewis Hamilton with a rocket up his arse.'

'I don't know, darling. He said it was an emergency. Work, I suppose.'

Zac frowned. 'So is he going back to London?'

Sophie realized she didn't know the answer. Had he said he was going back to London, and she'd somehow missed it?

But surely he wouldn't take the Porsche, unless ... Unless what? 'I don't think so,' she said, lamely, 'or he'd have told me.'

'Didn't he?'

'No.'

'You're being weird again. Have you two had a row or something?'

'No, we haven't. Can you lay the table?'

Zac, who was leaning against the sink, didn't move. 'I mean,' he said, carefully, 'if you were getting divorced, you'd tell us, right?'

'What are you talking about? Of course we're not getting divorced.'

'Well, I don't know. It's all getting a bit strange round here.' Sophie saw that he seemed, if anything, to be rather pleased by this.

'I'm just worried about your grandmother, that's all.'

'Yes, but you weren't worried about her the other day, when you kept falling over, were you?'

'I didn't "keep falling over". Don't be silly.'

'And,' Zac eyed her suspiciously, 'I'm sure I didn't put my rucksack in the sitting-room cupboard.'

'Well, *somebody* did. If you're not going to lay the table, can you at least go and tell Margot and Poppy that lunch is ready?'

Zac lolloped over to inspect the contents of the pan. 'Can I have pizza instead?'

The clock on the bottom right-hand side of Jessica's computer screen read 16.15. Zac, Poppy and Margot having returned to their respective rooms after lunch, Sophie had checked Jessica's laptop for further emails from Miles, but there were none. There were no further news updates about the crash on the A1067, either.

She turned off the laptop, returned it to its hiding place behind the filing cabinet, and sat, slack with fatigue, staring out at the front lawn. For no apparent reason, she found herself remembering her grandparents' bungalow in Bexhill-on-Sea. She'd often stayed there during school holidays, parked by Margot when she was off on some adventure or other with her latest man. Sophie'd liked the order and the regular meal times, having her own room and being fussed over, but her absolute favourite thing had been walking down the avenue at dusk, before curtains were drawn. The flickering, bluish light from the televisions had made the rooms behind the net-curtained picture windows look calm and soothing, like a row of fish tanks. Strolling past the front gardens with their rockeries and dwarf conifers, towards a supper of fish fingers with mash and peas followed by banana custard, she'd felt as if nothing bad could ever happen.

She closed her eyes. The gardeners would be coming tomorrow, so there'd be no chance of moving Jessica, even if she knew what the hell to do with her. She must be frozen stiff by now, Sophie thought. Unyielding, she'd be a human plank. Burial in the garden was out of the question – Dexter and the gardeners – and so was the churchyard, because of the CCTV. Even supposing she *could* get Jessica across the back seat of the Merc – which was, she thought, about five and a half feet wide, around the same height (or rather, length) as Jessica – or into the Land Rover, where could she take her? She'd never manage to manhandle her into a wood or a ditch without being spotted, and as for the sea – even if she could somehow disguise the body as something else and get it onto the yacht, she wasn't at all sure that she could manage to sail the thing by herself, and someone at the marina might notice and mention it to Leo, and—

The sound of tyres crunching on gravel made her open her eyes again. Leo was back.

'I need to get back to London.' Leo's voice was toneless, distant. Sophie had followed him up to the study, where he was shovelling paperwork into the pocket of his laptop bag. He looked flushed and, standing beside him, she caught the smell of whisky.

'What's going on?'

'Problem at work.'

'Really? So what were you doing—'

'I'm sorry, Soph, but I really don't have time. The taxi's on its way.'

Dismayed, Sophie shook her head. 'I'd have taken you.'

'Honestly, it's fine. I've messed up your weekend enough as it is.'

'It's not *my* weekend, Leo, it's *our* weekend, and the children can perfectly well look after Margot. Let me cancel the taxi and—'

'Really, Soph. I've said it's fine, and it is.' He turned his back on her and started rummaging in one of the desk drawers.

'Look, if this is about the car, I'm sorry, but—'

'What about the car?' Leo didn't even look up from his search. 'The wing. The scratch.'

'I'm sure the garage can deal with it.'

'Yes, of course.' A dizzying surge of relief made Sophie clutch at the back of the desk chair for support. 'I'll take it in, shall I?' she went on. 'I'm sure it won't be difficult to repair and I can collect it, so—'

'Fine.' Leo trousered whatever it was he'd been looking for and picked up his laptop bag. 'I have to go.'

Sophie followed him downstairs and outside to the gate. 'Leo, I'm worried. Can't you give me *some* idea of what's going on?'

Leo, already elsewhere, glanced at his watch. 'The taxi'll be here in a minute.'

'But you'll phone me later, won't you?'

'If I get the chance. Look, there's no need for you to wait. Go back inside.' He turned away and stared up and down the road. 'Where is the bloody thing?'

He barely seemed to notice when Sophie kissed him. His face felt like rubber against her lips, as if it were a latex mask.

Defeated, she walked back to the house and found her mother sitting at the kitchen table, slow tears trickling down her cheeks.

After half an hour of weepy apologies from Margot ('I'm such a nuisance to you, darling') Sophie managed to jolly her into the sitting room and settle her in front of the television. She dumped the congealed risotto in the bin – lunch had not been a success – and was about to pour herself a glass of wine when she heard a car turning, too fast, into the drive. A few seconds later, Melissa's Lexus braked sharply outside the kitchen window.

Sophie's stomach lurched. Miles. The police. Melissa must have found out about Jessica. What on earth was she going to say to her?

FORTY-TWO

'He's always on at me about spending money, and three months ago he bought her a fucking *car*!' Melissa's eyes were swollen and her face scoured pink with crying. 'Hers had broken down or something. And I can't believe he sold the flat without telling me,' she said, gulping wine. 'He said we couldn't afford both mortgages and he was worried about being overexposed. Lying *bastard*.'

Sophie didn't think she'd ever heard Melissa swear before. She'd been sitting at the kitchen table for over an hour, crying and raging by turns as she rehashed the events of the weekend – the police turning up; the joyriders finding Jessica's car in the field and crashing it; Miles's admission that he'd been questioned in London; the halting, sheepish confession of adultery; the claim, not believed, that he'd been about to end the affair; the shouting and recriminations. Zac and Poppy, curious, had appeared in the kitchen doorway and been shooed away.

'Leo went out just before lunch,' said Sophie. 'Wouldn't tell me where – just that it was an emergency. He must have been going to meet Miles.'

'Miles said they'd used Leo's flat. You didn't know about it, did you?'

Sophie shook her head in what she hoped was a convincing display of bewilderment. 'I had no idea – and Leo didn't say anything about any of this when he came back this afternoon. He just packed up his things and said he had to get straight off to London, so perhaps he'd arranged to meet Miles at the station.'

'I'm surprised he didn't tell you.'

'I'm not,' said Sophie. 'I mean, not that he doesn't tell me stuff, but . . . you know. Men stick together about things like that. Where's Miles been living during the week, anyway?'

'He's renting a room from his sister's ex-husband in Wimbledon. I suppose it wasn't convenient to take *her* there all the time. I didn't even know he and Simon were still in touch. For all I know,' Melissa added, downing the rest of her wine, 'he's been seeing her when he's up here, too – telling me he's going out in the boat and then nipping round to her house.'

It crossed Sophie's mind that maybe Miles had sold the flat because he was going to buy a place for him and Jessica and present it as a fait accompli, but she said nothing. In fact, afraid of betraying herself by her knowledge, she'd said as little as possible since Melissa arrived, but fortunately silence, and the odd 'I'm so sorry, I don't know what to say', had been taken as a normal reaction to the extent of Miles's duplicity. By focusing all of her attention on Melissa, she'd found that it was possible, for several minutes at a time, to block Jessica's frozen corpse – less than ten feet away from them – out of her mind. At least, she thought, if Miles had known that Jessica was coming to tea with Sophie, he hadn't mentioned it to Melissa, or she'd have said something by now.

'I'm so stupid!' Melissa wiped her eyes. 'All this was happening and I didn't even realize.'

'Of course you didn't. Miles was keeping it secret, wasn't he?'

'Yes, I know, but I should have paid more attention. Things weren't great between us. We weren't really communicating, but it wasn't . . . Oh, I don't know. I thought it was just a bad patch, that things would work themselves out.'

'You never said anything.'

'Well, you know how you ignore your feelings and hope things'll go away. Or perhaps you don't. You and Leo are so rock solid. We used to be like that, but . . .' Melissa shook her head.

If only you knew, thought Sophie. 'Everyone has problems, Lissa. I just wish you'd told me.'

'I should have. God, I feel such a fool. When the police came to the house asking for Miles on Friday afternoon, I was just . . .' Words failing her, Melissa shook her head. 'And then they asked about the car and I had no idea what they were talking about, and then they said they needed to speak to Jessica Mottram and did I know where she was.'

'That was because they'd found something with her name on it in the car, was it?'

'Yeah, her handbag.' Melissa refilled her glass. 'One of the joyriders told the police. And they said she'd left her key in the ignition, which is even weirder. They told Miles not to go anywhere, which must mean they think he's got something to do with her disappearing.' She put the bottle down and stared into space. 'Perhaps they think he put those kids up to stealing her car as a cover-up, or something.'

'But . . .' Sophie gathered herself together. '*You* don't think that, do you?'

'I don't know what I think.' Melissa's voice was bleak. 'But I don't really see how he could have been up here with her because he was in London all week, at work. If he'd suddenly vanished from the office, they'd have noticed, wouldn't they?'

'It might not have been during the day, though.' How strange, Sophie thought as she said this. She felt completely outside herself, as though she were behind a pane of glass, observing something that had nothing to do with her.

'But,' said Melissa, 'if he'd got the train to King's Lynn and hired a car from somewhere to go and meet Jessica at her house, it would be pretty stupid to deny it, because it'd be on his credit card, wouldn't it?'

'He could have paid in cash.'

'For the ticket and the hire car?'

'Well, only if he was planning to . . . you know . . . *do* something to her. Do the police have any idea *when* Jessica left the car in the field? Assuming it *was* Jessica who left it there, I mean.'

'I don't think so, but it couldn't have been there long, could it? The farmer would have noticed. Miles kept saying he was worried about her – her state of mind – as if he expected me to feel sorry for her! What about *my* state of mind? He obviously doesn't give a fuck about that. Well, I don't care why the conniving bitch left the car in the middle of a field. I hope she's drowned in a slurry pit.'

Sophie hadn't thought of a slurry pit. It might actually work, if only she could get Jessica there in the first place. She'd prob-ably have to cross a field, though – perhaps more than one – and even the Land Rover might get stuck in the mud. It would leave tyre tracks, too, which might stand out as unusual amongst the wider treads of agricultural machinery, and—

'Sophie?'

'Sorry. I was just thinking about why you'd leave your car in the middle of a field like that. Perhaps she had to pee?'

'But if you're *that* desperate, you just stop at the side of the road and nip behind a tree or something – and anyway, that field's only about a minute's drive from where she lived, so why didn't she wait?'

'Do you think she's dead, then?'

'What do you mean?'

'You said "lived".'

'I don't know, do I?' Melissa blew her nose. 'And I wouldn't care, either, except it means that Miles is in trouble. Actually –' she took a large gulp of wine – 'the way I feel at the moment, I wouldn't care about that, either, except for what it might do to me and the children. God, Sophie, you're so lucky. Leo would never go behind your back.'

Sophie made what she hoped was a non-committal noise. 'Where's Lucy? Does she know about this?'

'Lucy? Oh ...' Melissa struggled to remember her daugh-ter's whereabouts. 'She's off on some weekend under-sixteens lacrosse thing – staying with a friend tonight, thank God. And Tobes is in Bristol. If Miles wants them to know what he's been up to, he can bloody well tell them himself. He's the one who's fucked everything up.' She let out a long, shuddering breath. 'What the hell am I supposed to do?'

'Nothing, for the moment. Wait till things calm down a bit, then see how you feel. I mean, OK, Miles had an affair with Jessica, and obviously that's not good, but there might be a perfectly innocent explanation for her disappearing like that. She might just turn up – perhaps she had some sort of mental breakdown and just . . . I don't know . . . wandered off, or something. People do. Or maybe it was carjacking.'

'This is Norfolk, not Johannesburg! And carjackers would take the car, not the person.'

'No, but it might have happened elsewhere, and she's still out there, lying in a ditch.'

'But she'd be right by a road, and someone would have spotted her.'

'Well, perhaps the car was stolen from outside her house – before it was dumped in the field, I mean – and she'd just left her bag in there by mistake.'

'Yes, but she'd have reported it, wouldn't she?'

'Not if it happened after she went missing.'

'What, so she just walked off down the road without her handbag, and got lost?'

'Have the police searched her house?'

'They must have done, but they can't have found any clues or they wouldn't keep asking Miles where she is.' Melissa drank more wine. 'People don't just disappear into thin air. Not people like us, anyway.'

This isn't real, Sophie thought. It can't be. I can't actually be having this conversation. 'Perhaps she committed suicide. You said Miles was worried about her state of mind.'

'Only because she hadn't been in touch with him and then she disappeared. Anyway,' she added bitterly, 'why would she want to kill herself? She was too busy getting her hooks into Miles to be depressed, wasn't she?'

'Perhaps Miles *was* going to end it.'

'Yeah, right,' said Melissa scornfully. 'He was going to end it, so he bought her a car.'

'Yes, but you said that was three months ago. Things might have changed.'

Melissa shook her head. 'You didn't hear the way he was talking. "Oh, I'm so worried about Jessica." Well, *fuck* Jessica! I hope she *is* dead in a ditch.'

'I know. I'm sure I'd feel the same way if it were Leo – but Lissa, keep your voice down. Poppy and Zac might hear you. Assuming Jessica *isn't* dead – because there's nothing to say she is – what about Sean? Could Jessica be with him?'

'The ex-husband? Do you know him?'

Shit. Still, there was no sense pretending, especially since she'd discussed the Mottrams with Leo. 'Leo's mentioned him. From shooting. And I know her by sight – she's been in the shop a couple of times.'

'When? Why didn't you tell me?'

'Because I didn't know there was anything *to* tell, Lissa. Honestly. I had no idea . . . You do believe me, don't you?'

Melissa stared at Sophie for a long moment, then said, 'Yes. Of course I do. I'm sorry. It's just . . . It's like being in a nightmare but you can't wake up because it's real. Sean Mottram's in Australia at the moment – a work thing. Jessica told Miles.'

'Well, what about parents or siblings? They might know where she is.'

'It's just her. Miles said her mum and stepfather live in the Dordogne.'

That explained the French email address, thought Sophie. 'Well, maybe she's gone to see them.'

'Leaving her car in a field with her handbag in it?' Melissa's voice rose an incredulous semitone.

'Well, perhaps she'd transferred her stuff to another bag.'

'Not all of it, or the police wouldn't have known who she was, would they?'

'Some of it. All I'm saying is, there might be an explanation which has nothing to do with Miles at all.'

'The police don't think that. They kept asking him about her laptop – if he'd got it.'

'Why would he have it?'

'I don't know! But it's obviously disappeared.'

'How do they know she even had a laptop?'

'Because she's got an email address. Miles gave it to them. Anyway, she's a writer, so of course she'd have a computer.'

The police were probably hacking into her emails already, thought Sophie. Would they be able to tell that they'd been opened and re-marked as 'Unread'? She'd got to get rid of that laptop. No chance of getting it out of the house tonight, with Melissa – who was clearly going to have to stay over – as well as Margot, Zac and Poppy, so it would have to be tomorrow. She'd better get rid of Jessica's memory sticks, too, while she was at it.

'For all I know,' said Melissa, 'the police are wondering if *I* did it.'

'That doesn't make sense, Lissa. You didn't even know about her.'

'Supposing they don't believe that? They probably think I'm a . . . you know, what they say in those police things on TV . . . a Person of Interest. And I *should* have known, Sophie! Why didn't I realize? Miles tried to make out he'd only been seeing Jessica for a few months, but eventually he admitted it's been going on since last July.'

Almost a year, thought Sophie. LEO AND I HAVE BEEN HAVING AN AFFAIR FOR OVER TWO YEARS . . . Unless Miles was lying – and, from his point of view, there was surely no point in not telling the truth now – then it was conclusive: the returner of her Christmas letters could have nothing to do with Jessica.

'What if they arrest Miles?' Melissa wailed. 'What am I supposed to do then? God, Sophie, I can't believe this. Everything's *fucked.* I mean, how did any of this even *happen*? How am I supposed to *cope*?'

'Mum?' Poppy appeared in the doorway, holding the phone and looking embarrassed. 'Sorry, but it's the vicar.'

'Oh, OK. Just give me a sec, Lissa.' Sophie took the phone and went out into the hall. 'Hello?'

'Mrs Hamilton? I hope this isn't an inconvenient time, but I just wanted to let you know that I've been looking at the CCTV.'

Sophie's heart sank. 'Heavens,' she said, in what she hoped was a cheerful tone. 'You needn't have gone to all that trouble. After all, nothing was stolen. We've had the window repaired, and everything's fine.'

'That's good, but I thought I ought to check. I spotted a car – an Audi, I think – leaving your house at twenty-one minutes past eleven.'

Sophie felt as though she'd been punched. 'That must have been while I was out.'

'Well, that's the strange thing. I can see you walking back with the dog – that was about eleven o'clock – but then you don't appear to go out again. I'd assumed the person in the Audi must be a visitor, although you didn't mention one – you can't see the face clearly, because they're wearing a hood and a cap and sunglasses – but when I went back through the footage from the morning, I couldn't see the car *arriving*. All I saw was you driving out in your car at about ten to nine.'

'I had to take it to the garage.'

'Sorry, I'm confused. I thought you said you'd gone shopping.'

'That as well. It was only a small thing with the car, and they said it would be done in a couple of hours so I thought I'd take the dog for a walk, then bring him home – it was raining like anything – and get a taxi back to the garage to collect it.'

There was a pause, during which Sophie held her breath, before Reverend Barker said, in a puzzled voice, 'But I didn't see you walking down to the road – for the taxi, I mean.'

'No . . . I was in the garden. I saw the taxi coming and hopped over the fence. It's easy enough,' she added, brightly. 'I do it all the time. It was jolly kind of you to check your CCTV, but really there wasn't any—'

'This other car's a bit of a mystery, though. Did you have a visitor the day before? Someone who'd stayed the night?'

Sophie hesitated. He obviously hadn't looked at the footage

from Wednesday yet, but there was every chance that he might, and if he did, he'd see the Audi arrive with Jessica in it. What should she say? 'I . . . I . . .'

'It's just that I'm not very familiar with this gadget yet.' Reverend Barker sounded slightly sheepish. 'I'm afraid I've somehow managed to delete all the footage prior to Thursday morning.'

Sophie felt breathless, as though she'd run a race. 'Oh, well,' she said quickly, 'maybe it was a friend of Imanuela's – that's our au pair – and I didn't notice the car because it was parked round the side of the cottage.'

'It might be a good idea to ask her. As I said, I didn't get a good look at the driver, and it was difficult to make out the number plate apart from a couple of letters at the end, but I read an article recently about how burglars sometimes case places – if they're stealing to order – and come back, so I thought I'd better let the police know, just in case.'

Sophie leant against the wall, clutching the phone to her chest, feeling the sweat in her armpits and along her spine. She couldn't envisage a conversation between the vicar and Imanuela about the au pair not only not having had any visitors but also finding the Audi's key down the side of the freezer, but the police might put two and two together, and then . . .

Sophie took a deep breath and, squaring her shoulders, returned to Melissa in the kitchen.

FORTY-THREE

How could she have got it so wrong?

Sophie had been too distracted to draw the bedroom curtains and, after a few hours' fitful sleep, she lay awake and watched the pale light creeping towards the windows. Having put away the best part of two bottles of wine, Melissa had finally, long after the rest of the household was asleep, allowed herself to be helped upstairs to the second guest room, where she'd collapsed, sobbing, on the bed. Now, Sophie could hear her stumbling towards the bathroom in the corridor, and wondered if she were going to be sick.

If only she could put the clock back. Please, God, let me start again. I didn't mean to, it was an accident. I didn't *know* . . .

Bloody Miles! Why did he have to have an affair? It wasn't her fault the wretched man had had a mid-life crisis. If only Leo had *told* her – but then he wouldn't, would he, knowing that she'd tell Melissa?

What if the police did arrest Miles? There was no reason for anyone to think that Sophie had had anything to do with Jessica's disappearance, except – the thought catapulted her out of bed and she stood on the carpet, dry-mouthed with anxiety

– that Belinda had seen her at Jessica's cottage, and Belinda knew Melissa. She'd been at their party, handing out canapés. Melissa had never mentioned Belinda, though, and she and Miles didn't have a dog, so that couldn't be the connection . . . Perhaps Belinda was employed by a catering service. She's on her own, Sophie thought. She must do something for a living.

The phone beside the bed started to ring. Leo? He hadn't rung the previous night and she'd made no attempt to contact him.

'Hello?'

'Sophie, I'm sorry.' Miles's voice. Sophie sat down with a bump on the stool in front of the dressing table. 'I know it's early, but is Melissa there? She's not answering her phone.'

'She's probably turned it off – and yes, she is here. She's asleep.'

'Is she all right?'

'What do you think?'

'No, OK, that was a stupid question.'

'Yes, it was. Miles, she's in *pieces*. What's going on? Have you heard anything else from the police?'

'Only that the bloke who was driving Jessica's car – I'm sure Lissa's filled you in about what's happened – died last night. The woman's sticking to her story about finding the car in a field, but I don't think they believe her. *I* don't believe her.'

'What about the other passenger? Melissa said there were three.' Had she said that or had it been in the news report? Never mind – she probably wouldn't remember.

'In a coma. They're going over the Audi with a toothcomb, but I don't see how they're going to find any evidence because it's completely trashed. None of this is anything to do with me, Sophie, I swear it. I know I've been a complete idiot, but I wouldn't kill anyone.'

'Where are you now?'

'At Simon's. My ex-brother-in-law. They're taking statements from everyone at work, and . . . Look, you have to believe me, I've got no idea what's going on.'

'Miles, I . . .' Sophie stopped, shaking her head, with no idea of what she'd been about to say, and stared at her reflection in the dressing-table mirror. I look normal, she thought, with astonishment. Tired, yes, but quite ordinary. None of this is my fault, she wanted to shout.

'It's OK,' Miles was saying, 'you don't have to say anything. Sophie, I love Lissa. I don't expect you to believe that, but I do. I never wanted to hurt her.'

'Perhaps you should have thought of that before.'

'Yes . . . yes, I should. But I was going to end it. I know Lissa doesn't believe that, but it's true. I just . . . I hadn't . . .'

'. . . got round to it?' Sophie finished. 'I'm not the one you need to convince, Miles.'

'I know. God, I've been so stupid. I'm so grateful to you for looking after her, Sophie. Can you ask her to give me a call when she wakes up – if she can bear to speak to me, that is?'

'Did Melissa stay the night?' Poppy was cutting a slice of toast into tiny pieces.

'Yeah,' said Zac, taking his head out of the fridge. 'She was hammered. What was all that about, anyway?'

'None of your business,' said Sophie, glancing at Imanuela, who was making up a breakfast tray for Margot.

'It's OK.' Zac grinned. 'We'll ask Lucy. We've run out of peanut butter, by the way.'

'Have something else, then. And please don't ask Lucy. It's nothing to do with you.'

The pair of them asked more questions, but Sophie shook her head mutely, too exhausted to argue. After Miles rang, she'd gone down to her study and, after downloading instructions on her own computer, had started the process of wiping Jessica's laptop of all its data. It was possible, she supposed, that some of it might be recoverable if a police IT forensic team – or whatever they were called – got hold of it, but if she disguised the computer as ordinary rubbish and threw it away somewhere, there was no reason why they ever should. There were some stickers on the bottom of it with barcodes and numbers, but those could be soaked off easily enough.

Eventually, after she'd said goodbye to Zac and Poppy, left a note for the gardeners, phoned Megan to explain that she'd be on her own in the shop and given a mystified Imanuela a breezy explanation for Melissa's presence in the guest room ('a row at home – happens to everyone at some time or other'), Sophie escaped to her study. Retrieving the newly wiped laptop, she whipped it upstairs to their bathroom to scrub the barcode labels off before shoving it into a large plastic carrier.

She put Dexter on his lead, grabbed her handbag and was heading for the back door when she was intercepted by Mrs Palmer, who appeared from the kitchen, lugging a full bin liner. The cleaning lady, who enjoyed hearing bad news almost as much as she enjoyed giving it, clearly felt she'd been short-changed by Imanuela in the matters of Margot and the burglary, and wanted more.

'More', coupled with the latest on Mrs P.'s cankles, took almost a quarter of an hour, until Sophie managed to disengage herself by saying she'd take the bin liner down to the gate herself.

Pausing only to check that no one was watching, she loaded the bulging black sack into the passenger-seat footwell of the Merc and, with Dexter installed in the back, drove off down the road. What she needed was somewhere nice and quiet – second homes, vacant during the week unless it was a school vacation, with some building work going on . . . She'd stuff the laptop into the middle of the bag of rubbish, chuck the whole thing into a skip and that would be that.

Half an hour later, Sophie sat on a bench on the coastal path, looking out over the salt marsh while Dexter snuffled his way round clumps of cordgrass. Across the vast expanse of moist green pelt, she could see an abandoned boat, blue paint flaking off its cabin. It was pleasantly warm and, but for the squawks of a few gulls wheeling chalky-white against a sky of solid blue, there was no sound.

She felt safe, at least temporarily, and becalmed. No doubt the knowledge that there was almost no chance of bumping into Belinda and Robbie contributed to this, but it was also to do with the landscape itself: the sense of being right out on the edge, where the land broke up and surrendered to the sea.

She'd managed to keep it together so far. Sophie felt a surge of hope. She had no need to hurry back home: she very much doubted that Melissa, who ordinarily wasn't much of a drinker at all, would be in any condition to be out of bed; Imanuela could look after Margot; and there was absolutely no reason for anyone to go near the freezer. As long as you keep calm you can sort this out, she told herself. You just (just!) need to work out what comes next, and how to do it. Calling out to the dog, she started to walk.

FORTY-FOUR

Sophie wrenched her gaze away from the sharp tip of the arrow, which glinted menacingly in the fierce morning sun. For eight days the temperature had been 30°C – the hot weather, according to the *Today* programme, was set to continue, breaking all June records – and the air felt as though it had been microwaved. Sophie could feel sweat breaking out on her hairline as she forced herself to focus on the other objects in the display. 'Megan did a good job, didn't she?'

She and Melissa were standing in the street, looking into the window of Hamilton De Witt. Outside the newsagent's on the opposite side of the road – Sophie had glanced and looked quickly away, hoping Melissa hadn't spotted it – was an *Eastern Daily Press* advertising board with the headline CONCERN FOR MISSING WOMAN.

If only someone would buy the bloody astrolabe. While multiples of the wrought-iron birds and animals that flanked it had already been snapped up – trade was usually pretty good in half-term weeks – nobody had expressed any interest in the centrepiece.

Melissa nodded, listless. 'Sales seem to be doing OK, anyway.'

'We ought to order more of this stuff.'

'I know. I started making a list but I'm finding it so hard to concentrate – and then I couldn't find the paperwork . . .' Melissa tailed off, looking as though she might cry. In the last couple of weeks there'd been quite a bit in the media (local papers, mostly, but small items in a couple of the nationals) about Jessica, but the police hadn't arrested Miles. They'd interviewed Leo, who, it turned out, had had a drink with Miles on the Thursday evening, but they clearly hadn't picked up on what the vicar had told them about the CCTV, because they'd made no attempt to contact Sophie. By loading Dexter into the car and walking him in places that were at least half an hour's drive away, she had succeeded in avoiding Belinda entirely. She still hadn't managed to come up with a viable plan for getting Jessica out of the house, but, steeling herself one afternoon when Margot was asleep and everyone else was out, she'd managed to fix a thick sheet of black plastic over the food that was directly covering the body, and reorganize the top layers of the freezer in a way that ensured that everything they consumed on a regular basis was immediately visible. She'd also – in the hope that no one would need to open the freezer at all – transferred as much of the popular stuff as she could fit to the freezer compartment at the top of the fridge in the kitchen and told Imanuela to look there first. Sophie had been worried, after the outburst about throwing away her food, that Margot might start rummaging around in the freezer, but as far as she could see, her mother seemed to spend most of her time fretfully burrowing down the sides of cushions for things that she either had, or thought she had, lost.

Sophie's own days had assumed a peculiar sort of rhythm. Every morning, there would be a few seconds' time delay between waking and remembering – a sliver of peace and normality before the plunge, after which her mood would oscillate between bravado and despair. At any given time, half her mind was given over either to trying to work out what to do about Jessica, or to keeping her thoughts about it from taking over entirely. In the evenings came resignation: on not a few occasions, having picked at dinner, she'd sat up late in her study, refilling the glass of wine at her elbow, googling women's prisons and giving herself nightmares. Or she'd decide that the house was dirty and throw herself into a frenzy of cleaning, knowing all the while that she was only giving herself the illusion of being in control. She knew she was brittle, and, despite the extra make-up, looked it, although only Poppy ('Are you sure you're OK, Mum?') seemed to have noticed.

'I think that might be my fault,' she said now. 'The paperwork's probably at home – the wrought-iron stuff got delivered there, remember, instead of the shop.'

'Oh . . . yes.' Melissa looked as if she didn't have the faintest idea what Sophie was talking about. Judging from what she'd said over the past fortnight, she and Miles appeared – despite the fact that both children were refusing to speak to their father – to have reached an uneasy truce. Something similar existed between herself and Leo, who remained loyally scornful of the idea that Miles could have had anything to do with Jessica's disappearance. He'd been defensive about omitting to tell her that he'd facilitated the affair, but, fearful of giving herself away, she hadn't pursued the matter. She also decided to say nothing when he informed her that he'd lost his phone and, due to some inexplicable mess-up with the service provider, had had to buy a temporary pay-as-you-go thing with a different number. (Zac had been more vocal: 'You two lose stuff the whole time and it's never your fault, but if some tiny thing of mine goes missing, it's like I can't be trusted with anything.')

Now, Leo had taken the week off to spend time with Poppy and Zac over half-term, and they were treating each other with scrupulous – almost painful – consideration. It was as though they were two strangers who'd been forced, by some bizarre circumstance, into pretending they were married. He'd spent most of his time outside, cutting the grass with the ride-on mower (a chore he usually left to the gardeners), sorting out the split in the pool lining, dragooning Zac into washing the cars. Now, it occurred to Sophie that she couldn't actually remember the last time they'd had sex.

'. . . and it looks as if you'll have nice weather for it.' Melissa was polishing her sunglasses on the hem of her T-shirt.

'For . . . ?'

'Your Summer Fair. It's on Sunday, isn't it?'

'Yes, two o'clock. Are you coming?'

'I don't think so.' Melissa put her sunglasses back on and looked up and down the street. 'I mean, I know Miles hasn't been mentioned in the papers, so there's no . . . you know . . . *connection* . . . but it's too raw, and all those people . . .'

'Of course.' Feeling herself flooded with the now appallingly familiar sensation of self-hatred coupled with self-pity, and quite unable to look at her friend, Sophie took refuge in rummaging in her handbag. Pretending to spot a message on her phone, she said, 'Sorry, Lissa, I'm going to have to go. Leo's taken Zac and Poppy to sort out some problem with the boat, and I need to take Margot to the fracture clinic.'

'Where's Imanuela?'

'Had to go back to Romania – some sort of family crisis.' Although the fracture clinic appointment wasn't till the following week, this last bit was quite true – much to Sophie's annoyance, although it did mean that there was no chance of the vicar asking Imanuela whether the mysterious Audi belonged to one of her friends. 'Why don't you get off home? Megan's doing fine without us and I can reorder the wrought-iron stuff.'

Driving home between fields that shimmered in the heat, it occurred to Sophie that, Imanuela not being around, she needed to find someone to look after Margot on Friday evening. Leo had somehow managed to get tickets for the four of them to see the Harry Potter play – Sophie had expected Zac to greet this idea with the contempt of one who was fast putting away childish things, but in fact he'd been delighted – which necessitated staying the night in London. Since arriving at the Old Rectory, Margot's mental fog seemed, if anything, to have thickened, so that Sophie felt that her mother was slowly being reduced to intermittently haunting (as opposed to permanently inhabiting) herself. Ordinarily, she'd have asked Melissa for help, but that was out of the question. Mrs Palmer always went to her daughter's on Fridays and Megan was off to some concert she'd been talking about for weeks. Pulling up on the verge, she rang first Ottilie's mum and then Cressida's, with no luck. Out of ideas, she called Leo.

*

Having run through all the possibilities, Leo said, 'What about that woman you're always bumping into when you're out with Dexter? She must be fairly local.'

'Belinda?' Down the line at Wells-next-the-Sea, Sophie could hear the faint clink of halyards slapping against aluminium masts and the lap of waves. She stayed silent, hoping against hope that he'd come up with some other idea, but he said, 'Perfect solution, I'd have thought.'

'I haven't got her phone number.'

'You know where she lives, though, don't you?' *Shit.* 'Just go round and see her. You said she could do with the money, so offer her fifty quid and Bob's your uncle.'

'What if she's out?'

'Stick a note through the door with your telephone number on it.'

'I'm not sure I can remember which house it is.'

'Well, ask one of the neighbours. Look, Soph, I've got to go. I'm sure you'll sort it.'

Sophie stared over the hedge at the grey top half of a concrete pillbox. Like a miniature fortress, she thought. Like a prison. Could she go straight home and pretend Belinda had gone on holiday or something? But Leo might bump into her, and if it came up in conversation, Belinda might reveal that she'd encountered Sophie coming away from Jessica's cottage on or around the time she'd gone missing, and Leo would ask why she'd not mentioned it before, and . . .

It was no good. She'd have to go round there. Sighing, she switched on the ignition and turned the car round.

FORTY-FIVE

'It's the last one.' The woman, who'd answered the door with a toddler straddled on her hip, gestured down the row of cottages.

Sophie thanked her and walked in the direction indicated, the tarmac, softened by the heat, spongy beneath her feet. The little terrace, bright with fresh paint and cheerful window boxes, ended in a rather dilapidated cottage which appeared to be sloping, ashamed, away from its better-appointed neighbours.

She rapped on the door and heard a bark, followed by footsteps and clanking – the bangles, thought Sophie – and then the door was tugged open, revealing Belinda, with Robbie at her side like a sentinel.

'Sophie! Do you want to come in?'

'No, really, it's all right. I don't want to disturb you, but I just wondered if you might do me a favour – I mean, obviously we'll remunerate you and pay for the taxi and everything, but . . .'

She blundered on, over-explaining and repeating things, until Belinda put out a hand and squeezed her arm. 'It's fine, Sophie. Of course I'll help.'

'That's wonderful. I mean, I know you must be busy and I hate to ask at such short notice, but . . .' Sophie gabbled on, unable to stop herself, until Belinda interrupted.

'I'm glad you've come, actually. I wanted to ask – have the police been in touch with you?'

The word 'police' seemed to ricochet around Sophie's brain, so that she struggled to make sense of what was being said. Catching sight of a painting on the dingy wall beside Belinda's head – a still-life of some sort, with food on a plate, sludgy and dim – she had a sudden, vivid memory of the faded, greenish photographs of burgers and ice cream that had remained in the window of the Wimpy Bar near one of the flats where she and Margot had lived, long after the place had shut.

Belinda was still talking, and, after a moment, with a physical sensation in her ears as if the air pressure had changed, the words began separating themselves into identifiable units and making sense.

'. . . so I thought I ought to say something because it might help to give them a bearing on *when* Jessica disappeared – us being there, I mean – because they don't seem to know anything much. It was on the local news about her car being abandoned in a field. One of my neighbours said they'd spotted it, only they couldn't remember which day it was. I realized I wasn't entirely sure about the time I saw you at the cottage, and I thought you might have a better idea so I tried phoning the shop, but the girl who answered said you weren't there and obviously she couldn't give out your number or anything. Anyway, I went ahead and told them, so I expect they'll contact you if it's important.'

'They haven't,' said Sophie, trying to inject the right note of concerned puzzlement into her voice. 'Not yet, anyway. I'm sure they will if they need to. And I'm afraid nobody told me you'd rung the shop.'

'That's all right. I didn't leave my name or anything. Don't look so worried! It's not as if *you* had anything to do with it, is it?'

Sophie forced a laugh. 'It's the heat, that's all. I've been rushing around.'

On the way home, after an exchange of phone numbers, Sophie took a detour past Jessica's cottage. She wasn't sure what she'd expected to see – police tape, perhaps, or even officers – but there was only one car (not a police vehicle, unless it was an unmarked one), parked on the gravel outside the front door. Sean, back from Australia, perhaps, or Jessica's mother, arrived from France.

For the first time, Sophie had a sense of Jessica as a real person with a life and a family, rather than as a problem to be solved. Jessica's life had been cut short, while hers was carrying on. The paroxysm of feeling – shame, horror, pity – made her take her foot off the accelerator so that the car slowed abruptly, pitching her forwards against the seatbelt. She should turn back, confess, stop the people who'd loved Jessica suffering the torture of not knowing and hoping, hoping . . .

No, she shouldn't.

Confessing wouldn't bring Jessica back, and it would undoubtedly wreck not only Sophie's life, but Leo's and the children's, too. There was far too much to lose by admitting either that Jessica was a human being, just as valuable as herself, or that she had – albeit accidentally – killed her and hidden the body. It was quite impossible: for everyone's sake, not just her own.

FORTY-SIX

Staring out at the city at night from Leo's flat – sparkling lights against velvet darkness, skyscrapers, opulence and glamour – always made Sophie feel as though she were in an advert for some luxury product. She supposed she'd enjoyed the Harry Potter play, although it had been very long, and, distracted, she had – judging from the conversation in the taxi afterwards – missed quite a lot of the plot. Now, Poppy and Zac were bedding themselves down in the sitting room, and Leo, who'd been solicitous all day, was fixing her a nightcap.

She'd been checking her phone whenever she could in case Belinda had rung her to say there was a message from the police but, so far, there'd been nothing. If they did want to speak to her, she'd just have to bluff it out . . . And if Melissa heard about her visit to Jessica's cottage, she'd have to bluff that out, too – make up something about a mix-up over addresses.

In an effort to tune out the clamour in her head, she willed herself to think of something – anything – else. She found herself picturing Belinda at the Old Rectory, watching television in the sitting room with Robbie at her feet. She'd said she'd known Jessica in 'another life', hadn't she? It occurred to Sophie now that Belinda might have fallen from a rather higher place than she'd previously imagined. Perhaps her 'other life' had been similar to Sophie's own: a wealthy husband, although probably not a family since she'd never mentioned any children, a big house . . . The description of the place that fell into the sea didn't really fit the bill, but maybe that had come later. She didn't really look the part, though – too cluttered and clanky with all those bangles and scarves, more retired art teacher than City wife (or ex-wife). Still, whatever she had or hadn't been before, how awful to have ended up, in her mid-fifties, living in that dingy cottage, alone . . .

Wait, wait. The way Leo had brought Belinda up in the conversation, back at Christmas, asking about her, and then going mad when she'd suggested offering her a part-time job at Hamilton De Witt . . . He'd said it was because of the extra cost, but perhaps that had just been an excuse. Then there'd been that other time, when he'd pretended not to know who she was – *and* he'd suggested they invite her to dinner. Not to mention making Sophie ask her to look after Margot and Dexter . . .

But surely Leo would want to keep Belinda *away* from Sophie, not bring her into their home? And the Tiffany necklace wasn't Belinda's sort of thing at all; she was more wooden (or possibly even plastic) beads . . . although Sophie didn't actually *know* that, because, apart from that one time at Miles and Melissa's drinks party, she'd never seen Belinda in anything other than dog-walking clothes. Maybe she had a whole other wardrobe, *including the purple satin slip.* But she's at least ten years older than Leo, Sophie told herself. No. It wasn't possible.

Are you sure about that? needled the little voice in the back of her mind. After all, Sophie thought, if someone had told me I was going to be hiding a dead body in my freezer, I wouldn't have thought *that* possible, either. Perhaps it was a clever double bluff. Belinda wasn't on the Christmas card list, which meant that she couldn't be the returner of the letters, but she could easily have discovered the Old Rectory's address. She'd always been very interested in their family life, hadn't she, asking questions as they'd walked along with the dogs – getting a window onto Leo's existence when he wasn't with her, when all the time Sophie'd thought she was just being friendly. And she'd tried to get Sophie in trouble with the police over Jessica – all that stuff about thinking it 'might have a bearing' on what time she had disappeared. And, right now – *this very minute* – she was probably poking around Sophie's house, gazing at everything, opening cupboards and drawers, spraying herself with Sophie's perfume, maybe even trying on her clothes and lying down on their bed and possibly – *No, it is not going to happen so DON'T EVEN THINK IT* – looking into the freezer.

Except: the logistics. Perhaps Leo paid for Belinda to come down to London and stay the night here. Surely Robbie didn't come along with her? Nobody was allowed to keep a dog in Moorgate House, but presumably they were permitted to visit, so maybe he did.

The idea ticking in her mind like a bomb, Sophie inspected the room for dog-height scuff marks on the walls, hairs on the rug beside the bed. There was nothing immediately apparent, but of course the cleaners had been in while Leo was in Norfolk with her, hadn't they? She ought to have a look in the kitchen cupboards, see if there was any dog food, or a bowl—

'I know that look.' Leo came in, carrying two glasses of Scotch. 'It's your Interior Design face – you're itching to get your hands on this place, aren't you?'

'*What?*'

'Let yourself go.' Leo made an expansive gesture. 'I can see it's all getting a bit tired – and it'd be nice to have you here during the week, for once. I miss you, you know.'

'Do you?'

'Of course I do.' Leo handed over the Scotch and put his arm round her, giving her shoulder a little squeeze. He hadn't said anything like that for a long while and Sophie knew she ought to be pleased by it, but it felt stage-managed. Maybe, shaken by what had happened to Miles, Leo had ditched Belinda, and was now trying to salve his conscience by letting her spend money redecorating his flat and giving her a few nights on the town. If that were true, she supposed, it meant her marriage was safe – for the time being, at least. If she could only get rid of Jessica's body, then maybe she could ignore the fact that Leo had had an affair, and everything would be OK. Unless, of course, he and Belinda had agreed just to put things on hold for a couple of months . . .

'I thought we were supposed to be saving money?'

Leo grinned. 'It'll be fine. Just don't cover the walls in gold leaf, that's all.'

When the curtains were closed and Leo asleep, Sophie eased herself out of bed, and, cautious in the dark and unfamiliar surroundings, padded on bare feet into the kitchen, closing the door behind her. There was nothing canine-related in any of the cupboards, and the recycling was free of dog food tins. She went next door to the bathroom, but the cupboards there yielded only cleaning fluids and a neatly folded stack of towels. Where else?

The cupboard by the front door. Mindful of Poppy and Zac asleep in the sitting room, Sophie groped her way down the hall. It was a big cupboard, built in, with enough room inside for her to stand, and an internal light. Leo's coats, regimented on wooden hangers, his shoes in two neat rows, a plug-in fan heater, a couple of umbrellas, a squash racquet, a sports bag . . . And a second sports bag, larger, in the shadows behind the first one.

Sophie knelt down to examine them both. The first contained gym clothes, trainers and Leo's iPod. The second, bulgingly full, was locked shut with a small silver padlock. Sophie felt it. Whatever was in there appeared to be yielding, not rigid – Belinda's toiletries and food for Robbie, wadded round with some of her clothing? Sophie hefted the bag by its handles – fairly heavy, but not excessively so – and examined the lock, wondering if it would be possible to pick it, maybe with a safety pin. There was one in her handbag, which she'd left on the shelf in the hall. She'd just go and get it, and—

Scrambling upright, she put her foot down squarely on the pins of the fan heater's plug. Yelping, she lurched against the side of the cupboard, sending the umbrellas and squash racquet clattering to the floor.

'Soph?' A gruff whisper from the bedroom door. 'What the hell are you doing?'

'Nothing,' she hissed. 'Needed to pee and went the wrong way. Go back to bed – I shan't be a sec.'

*

She'd thought Leo might be asleep, or pretending to be so, when she returned from her cover trip to the bathroom, but his bedside lamp was switched on and he was sitting up, looking straight at her. 'Is everything all right?'

Sophie willed herself to smile, relax. 'How do you mean?'

'Is it Alfie?'

'*Alfie?*'

'You know.' Leo looked suddenly sheepish. 'Gap year, university. Empty nest, and all that.'

Astonishment made Sophie snap, 'An empty nest containing two chicks called Zac and Poppy, in case you haven't noticed.'

'I'm sorry, I just thought . . . Look, Soph, I know you think I don't notice anything, but you've been like it for weeks.'

'Like what?'

'On edge the whole time. As if you're about to burst into tears or something. It's not the menopause, is it?'

'*What?*'

Leo looked even more sheepish than before. 'I just thought . . . when I looked it up on the Internet it said the average age for British women is fifty-one but it can be earlier. Apparently about five per cent of women get it between forty and forty-five, and the side effects can include mood swings, so—'

'Leo, I am aware of the menopause, and if it was happening to me I think I'd be the first to know, don't you?'

'Well . . .' Leo reached out and took her hand. 'What is it, then?' His voice was tentative. Trying to find out if I suspect anything, Sophie thought.

'What's in the bag in the hall cupboard?'

Leo looked puzzled. 'My gym stuff.'

'The other bag. With the padlock.'

For a moment, Leo looked genuinely confused. Then, his hand in hers as still and lifeless as marble, he said, 'I suppose it belongs to Miles.'

'Why's it locked?'

'No idea.' Sophie was unable to gauge whether Leo was lying. She clasped his hand tightly, as if she might sense a current of treachery flowing from him, like electricity. He didn't attempt to disengage himself, but neither did he look her in the eye. Instead, he said, 'He's still coming home at the weekends, so we can take it back for him when we go up tomorrow.'

That didn't prove it was actually his, thought Sophie. Miles, if asked, would presumably cover for Leo as Leo had done for him. Reckless, she said, 'Supposing it's evidence?'

'Evidence of what?' Leo sounded exasperated. 'Miles didn't do anything to Jessica, you know that.'

'Do I?'

Now Leo did let go of her hand and looked directly at her, taken aback. 'Well, of course he didn't.'

'If you say so.' Sophie wasn't sure why she'd said it, or even what she meant by it, but she was angry with Leo. How dare he try and blame Alfie and her non-existent early menopause for something that was entirely his fault? How stupid did he think she was? She lay down and turned her back on him. 'I'm going to sleep.'

*

Leo said nothing. After a couple of minutes, she heard him sigh and lie down, drawing himself over to the other side of the bed. Staring into the darkness, she wondered if he, too, were thinking about the padlocked sports bag lying under the hems of the hanging coats.

FORTY-SEVEN

By the time they returned to the Old Rectory it was almost midday, and the fair was due to start at two. They'd travelled on the train, the sports bag in the luggage rack above their heads and the atmosphere splintery with recrimination – fortunately Zac, plugged into his iPod, and Poppy, nose in a book, didn't appear to have noticed – and collected the Merc from the King's Lynn car park. Turning into the drive, Sophie saw cars and flatbed trucks in the field behind Imanuela's cottage. There were marquees, Portaloos and trestle tables. Stewards, highlighted by their fluorescent yellow vests, were hefting straw bales off a lorry and putting up bunting.

As Sophie emerged from the air-conditioned car into air that was solid with heat, Dexter rushed to greet her. Leaving the dog to be fussed by Zac and Poppy, she turned and saw Belinda and Robbie standing at the open back door. As if they owned the place, she thought. HE'S GOING TO LEAVE YOU. LET'S SEE HOW SMUG YOU ARE THEN.

Mrs Palmer was on the other side of the yard, arms crossed, watching the helpers ferrying tables and chairs from the outhouse. 'I didn't think you'd mind, only we weren't sure when you'd be back and the vicar needs to get everything set up, so – seeing as how I knew where the key was kept . . .'

'That's OK.' Sophie went round to the back of the car where Leo, who seemed to have moved with astonishing speed, was unloading bags. They were all on the ground, except for the padlocked one, which was still in the boot.

Mrs Palmer followed her, still talking. '. . . He'd come himself, only he's ever so busy, but he says can they borrow the portable gazebo for the fortune telling, like last year?'

'Yes, of course.' Leo picked up the drawstring sack containing Poppy's sleeping bag. 'Tell him I'll bring it over in a minute. Zac can give me a hand. Don't bother about that,' he added, seeing Sophie lean into the car and grasp the handles of the padlocked bag. 'I'll put it straight in my car and take it to Miles later.'

He doesn't want Belinda to see the bag, Sophie thought, in case she gives herself away. 'But—'

'It's fine.' Leo's hand closed over hers, tight and deliberate, so that she couldn't make him let go of the handle without them having a tug-of-war in front of Mrs Palmer, who was still hovering. 'We've got enough clutter in the house as it is. Go and see how Margot's doing – I can deal with all this.'

'Can I come in for a sit-down?' asked Mrs Palmer. 'Only what with this heat, my legs—'

'Why don't you make us all a cup of tea, Soph?' Leo's voice sounded falsely hearty.

Sophie wanted to hit him. 'Yes. Fine. Right,' she said tightly, and, gritting her teeth, marched towards the house.

*

Belinda had already switched on the kettle and was assembling mugs when she got to the kitchen, while Margot sat at the kitchen table, the local newspaper spread out in front of her. 'It's all been fine,' Belinda told her. 'I think she's a bit confused – she called me "Sophie" a couple of times – but apart from that, she seems OK.'

'That's good.'

Mrs Palmer, who had followed her inside, sat down opposite Margot with a grunt of satisfaction. Poppy had disappeared upstairs but Zac had his head in the fridge, and Dexter, standing right beside him, was wagging his tail hopefully.

'I'll be doing lunch soon.'

'It's OK, Mum, I just want a snack. There's bound to be food at the thing.'

'All right, but—'

'Do you want some cake?' asked Belinda. *Cake?* What cake? There was no cake – and, even if some had suddenly materialized, who was Belinda to offer it to *her* son in *her* kitchen? 'I've started baking recently,' she told Sophie, 'and I'm not very confident yet so I thought it would be good to have a second opinion.'

'Fine.' Sophie wouldn't, couldn't, look at her. She yanked a small pile of side plates out of a cupboard and set them down with a clatter beside Margot's newspaper. *PUBLIC ASKED TO HELP TRACE MISSING WOMAN*, she read, upside down. Beside the headline was a photograph – Jessica sitting at her desk – that Sophie remembered from her website.

'Great.' Zac closed the fridge door and ambled over to the table. 'Hey –' he stabbed a grubby finger at the photograph –

'that's who you and Melissa were talking about that night, wasn't it?'

Fuck.

'Jessica Mottram, thirty-six,' Zac read, 'has not been seen since leaving her home near Fakenham on Wednesday, May 12. Ms Mottram is described as white, five feet five inches tall, with shoulder-length auburn hair and hazel eyes.' Sophie, hands in the cutlery drawer, clattered the forks together loudly in the hope that no one else would hear what he was saying. 'You know,' her son continued, raising his voice, 'when Melissa came round and got pissed in the kitchen. Me and Poppy heard what you were saying. You blew us off when we asked you about it, remember? But it's all right,' he added, 'we didn't go off to school and tell Lucy that this Jessica woman had had an affair with her dad, or anything.'

There was a sudden and absolute silence. Sophie stared down at the jumbled utensils, not daring to look round.

'What?' said Zac indignantly. 'I just told you – we didn't say anything.'

'*Well* . . .' Turning, Sophie saw that Mrs Palmer's eyes were gleaming. 'The police'll be wanting to speak to Mr De Witt then, won't they?'

'They already have.' Glaring at Zac, Sophie dumped the forks on the table. 'And he's in the clear.'

'Must have been a terrible shock for poor Mrs De Witt.'

Yes, thought Sophie, and it'll be even worse once you've told everyone in sight. 'The less said, the better,' she said.

'Oh, of course.' Mrs Palmer nodded emphatically as she said this, but her expression of greedy love made Sophie think of an alligator eyeing up a herd of wildebeest at the water's edge.

'It's a private matter. Neither Miles nor Melissa has done any-thing wrong – and there is such a thing as slander.'

'Isn't that when it's in the newspapers? Great, thanks.' Zac accepted a large piece of chocolate cake from Belinda.

You *utter* bitch, thought Sophie. Chocolate was Leo's favourite. 'That's libel,' she told Zac. 'Slander is spoken. It's when you make false and damaging statements about people –' she turned to look at Mrs Palmer as she said this – 'and it's a criminal offence.' Actually, she was fairly sure it was nothing of the sort, but anything to stop the bloody woman broadcasting to the entire world.

Margot, who'd been gazing vaguely in front of her, suddenly said, 'You know her, don't you?'

'I know Melissa, yes. We run the shop together, remember.'

Margot shook her head impatiently, then laid her right hand flat on the newspaper as if she were about to swear an oath. 'This one. Jessica. She left her card in your car.'

Why the hell, thought Sophie, did she have to remember *that*? 'I don't really know her. She's been into the shop a few times, that's all. She must have given me her card at some point, and I lost it.'

'Was it her earring, as well?'

'What earring?' Mrs Palmer leant forward.

'The one we found after the burglars came,' said Margot. 'Did you hand it in to the police, Sophie?'

Mrs Palmer's avid gaze darted from Sophie to Margot and back again. 'No . . . We thought it must be Melissa's, remember?'

'Was it?' asked Mrs Palmer.

'No.' What the hell had she done with it after she'd shown it to Melissa? She couldn't remember. Shit, shit, *shit.*

'And what about the slip? The one you kept asking me about – was that hers?'

'Oh, yes!' Mrs Palmer's eyes gleamed. 'Imanuela told me about that.' Of course she did, thought Sophie. 'It's quite a mystery.'

'What's a mystery?' Poppy appeared with a pile of old paperbacks for the book stall.

'This slip that turned up in the washing,' said Mrs Palmer. 'Purple satin, all fancy, and no one knows whose it is. Very odd to have strange underwear just turn up in your house like that – I mean, you wouldn't know what was going on, would you?'

'Nothing's been "going on".' Sophie rolled her eyes. '*Honestly.*'

'What did you do with the slip, Mum?'

'Threw it away.' She shrugged, hoping the show of nonchalance was convincing. 'What was I supposed to do with it?'

'You should have given it to the police, Sophie,' said Margot, as Mrs Palmer tutted in self-righteous agreement. 'And the earring, too. It might help them find Jessica.'

I will not scream, Sophie told herself. I will *not* scream. 'No, it won't, because neither of them are hers – and, before anyone says anything else, I know they can't be hers *because she has never been in this house.* OK? Now, can we *please* stop having this ridiculous conversation?'

There was a pause, during which Sophie could feel the room pressing in on her as if the space had somehow collapsed, before Zac murmured, 'It's fine, Mum. Chill out, OK?'

*

Later, flinging quoits at a variety of undesirable objects at Poppy's urging, it occurred to Sophie that, during the entire exchange, Belinda hadn't said a single word.

FORTY-EIGHT

From the kitchen, Sophie could hear the shouts from the field, the dismantling of stalls and the revving of cars and lorries as they tilted and swayed across the rutted grass to the gate. It was a quarter to seven, just starting to cool down a bit. Zac and Poppy had stayed behind to help, and probably wouldn't be back for some time. Belinda and Robbie, who'd got separated from them during the afternoon, must have got a taxi home by now, and she'd eventually managed to shake off Mrs Palmer with her endless questions and barely concealed prurience. Margot, who'd had a quick look round the fair before retreating back inside, was lying down in her room. Dexter, who'd got second prize in the dog show and disgraced himself by trying to eat the rosette, was now sitting close beside her as she loaded the dishwasher, waiting for his dinner. Leo, who'd managed to disappear for most of the afternoon, was drinking wine and reading the paper on the terrace.

Nothing else had gone wrong after the conversation about the earring – she must find the bloody thing – and all the 3 a.m. premonitions she'd had about generators failing and people wanting to store ice cream in the freezer had been groundless.

Nevertheless, she felt as though she'd been on stage all afternoon, and was supremely relieved to find herself alone.

She couldn't remember what she'd been wearing when she'd asked Melissa about the earring. She'd better check all her pockets. Handbags, too. She'd get rid of it, and if Margot remembered it and asked again, she could always claim she'd lost the thing.

She fed Dexter, then went down the hall and into the cloakroom. Leo had left Poppy and Zac's sleeping bags by the door. Sophie looked down at them. They were supposed to be waterproof, weren't they? That was the reason they'd been so expensive. If they could keep out water, she thought, then presumably they'd be able to keep it *in*, too. If she could just get Jessica out of the freezer and into one of them, she'd be easier to transport on the back seat of the car, and a lot less conspicuous . . .

The earring wasn't in any of her coat or jacket pockets. Sophie ran upstairs to their bedroom with the intention of rooting through her handbags and the jeans she thought she'd been wearing the day she showed the earring to Melissa. She was just about to open the cupboard when Leo's voice floated in through the open window.

'. . . So if you could hang on to it for the time being . . . I can bring it over tomorrow, if that's OK.'

He's talking about the padlocked bag, Sophie thought. He has to be.

'Yes, and I'm sorry about that, but—'

Was he talking to Belinda? Sophie took a sharp breath and, pressing her fingernails into her palms, moved gingerly forward to look down at the terrace.

'I know, but—'

Leo was silent for a few moments. Sophie could see the top of his head – she'd never noticed before that his hair was starting to thin at the crown – as he paced up and down on the flagstones.

'Thing is, I told her it was yours.' He's talking to Miles, Sophie thought. She watched Leo nodding – sympathetic agreement – and imagined Miles saying that he was in quite enough shit already, thanks, without any more complications. Why *was* Leo bothering him with it, anyway, when he could just phone Belinda? Maybe he was worried that Sophie, being suspicious, might follow him round to her cottage when he returned the sports bag. 'It's quite above board,' Leo was saying now, 'just not a good idea to keep it here. No need to mention it to Melissa. I know how difficult things are at the moment . . .' Leo moved further away, and Sophie lost the rest of what he was saying.

She stood quite still, heart hammering, and watched as he turned and retraced his steps, still talking. 'Thanks – I owe you one.'

Ending the conversation, he stood for a moment looking out at the garden and then, before Sophie had time to react, turned back to the house and looked directly up at the bedroom window. She stepped back into the shadows, but it was too late. He'd seen her.

Sophie closed her eyes, breathed in, and breathed out. When she opened them again, she saw that Leo was standing quite still, hands spread wide in a gesture of supplication, staring up at her.

*

He knew she'd heard – not all of the conversation, perhaps, but enough. He turned away abruptly and began walking towards the back of the house. He's leaving, Sophie thought. He's actually going to get in the car and go.

She made it downstairs, half running, half falling, and found him in the yard, opening the garage door.

'What's going on, Leo?' She grabbed his arm as he backed away from her, eyes wide with alarm. 'I want to see what's in that bag.'

'Sophie, *please* . . .'

'Never mind please, what the hell do you think you're playing at?'

'It's not what you think.' His voice was tight.

'Really?' Sophie shouted. 'What is it, then?'

'For God's sake keep your voice down.'

'Don't tell me to keep my voice down. I want to know what's happening, and I want to know *now*!'

'Just let go of me, OK?'

'Only if you give me the car key.'

'Sophie . . .'

'Give it to me!'

'For God's sake.' With his free hand, Leo dug into the pocket of his chinos. 'Here.'

Sophie let go of him and snatched the key. They stood looking at each other for a long moment before Leo said, in a voice devoid of expression, 'What do you want me to do now?'

'Open the garage door.'

She stood quite still as he did as he was asked, careful to keep out of her reach.

The Porsche was parked in the middle of the space. Sophie stared at its gleaming metal rump.

'It's in the passenger footwell.'

'Right.'

One eye on Leo, Sophie retrieved the bag. 'Where's the key to the padlock?'

'I've got it.'

'Give.' Sophie held out her free hand.

'Sophie, I can explain. Just give me a chance – but not out here.'

'I want the key.'

'Really, you don't want to do this here.'

'Don't tell me what I want!'

'OK, OK.' Leo made calming-down motions with his hands.

'And don't do that! I'm not some toddler having a tantrum.'

'Sorry. But can we go somewhere more private? I'll explain everything, I promise.'

Sophie took a deep breath. She could see the sense in this, but she didn't want Leo to assume control of the situation. 'OK,' she said, finally. 'But I'm keeping the bag, and the car key.'

They stood at the end of their bed, the sports bag on the floor between them. 'I'm not having an affair, Sophie.'

'Oh, really? You must think I was born yesterday.'

'Really. I'll prove it to you.'

'Go on, then.' Sophie sat down on the bed. 'I'm listening.'

'Just give me a minute.'

'To think up an excuse?'

'No. I promise, Sophie. I can explain.'

He picked up the bag and left the room. She heard a door slam in the corridor. Too close for his study – one of the guest bedrooms, perhaps, or the bathroom.

These might be the last moments of their lives together as a family. After this, it would be solicitors wrangling over money and strained conversations on the phone to make arrangements that would grow fewer and fewer as the years passed and the children grew old enough and mobile enough to make arrangements of their own. And that's assuming I'm not in prison, she thought dully.

She lay back on the bed, feeling used up and blank. After a minute or so, she had a sudden memory, precise and vivid, of the whole family being on a beach when Poppy was little – not in Norfolk, because they hadn't lived up here then, but during a weekend in Southwold or Aldeburgh. Poppy had toddled off into the sea and Leo had run after her to scoop her up before a wave knocked her over, and she'd shrieked with joy as he'd lifted her and carried her back on his shoulders. It seemed a lifetime ago.

Perhaps Leo was on the phone to Belinda right now – unless there really *was* another explanation. Remembering his words to Miles – 'It's quite above board' – she wondered if he were in trouble at work. Vague memories of the Enron scandal floated to the surface of her mind: debts hidden in shadow companies, executives swept up in a blizzard of dodgy balance sheets, columns of fake figures with no substance behind them, pension funds that existed only on paper . . . Maybe the sports bag was packed with evidence of some massive accountancy fraud. She imagined Leo, haggard and disgraced, facing a battery of microphones and television cameras. She was pretty sure that quite a few of the Enron people had gone to prison, some of them for several years.

Of course, accountancy fraud didn't explain the broken necklace or the purple satin slip, but it might well explain Leo changing the lock on the door of his flat – paranoia – and the supposed loss of his phone – theft by, say, an investigative journalist hot on the bank's trail – and it could certainly be the reason behind his nervousness about their finances. But then again, he'd just given her carte blanche to do up the flat, hadn't he? Perhaps, figuring that the house of cards was about to come tumbling down around him, he'd become completely divorced from reality . . .

Sophie gave up and lay staring at the bedroom ceiling.

After some time – five minutes, ten, more? – she heard footsteps in the corridor outside. This is going to be it, she thought. This is the moment. There's nothing I can do to stop it happening.

The footsteps passed the bedroom door. Too quick for Margot – Zac, perhaps, or Poppy.

More time elapsed. Cars passed on the road outside. An alarm sounded as a van reversed. A door banged, somewhere downstairs. Sophie carried on gazing up at the ceiling, unthinking, immobilized and leaden. Raising her arm to look at her watch felt as effortful as lifting a kettlebell.

Twenty minutes had passed. At least, she thought tiredly, Leo hadn't told Miles he was having an affair (assuming that he actually was having one and wasn't about to be arrested on a fraud charge), and she'd not told anyone about the last returned Christmas letter. She wondered, tiredly, why – if it were an affair – Leo had kept quiet. After all, he'd known about Miles and Jessica.

What had she been doing in here when she'd overheard Leo on the phone, anyway? She couldn't even remember. Dazed, she got up and wandered around the room, touching things.

She'd just picked up Leo's alarm clock when the bedroom door opened. It was a cheap plastic thing, which, for some reason, he preferred to his phone. Afterwards, she remembered that detail, as though it were in some way significant.

She didn't drop the alarm clock, or scream, or make any sound at all. She just stared.

FORTY-NINE

The first thing she saw was the slip. Satin and lacy, like the one Imanuela had found mixed up in the laundry, except that this was white. The second thing was the Marilyn Monroe-style wig. The third was the garish make-up. The fourth was the pair of shiny red stiletto shoes. The last thing she noticed in this lightning-fast inventory was that the person sporting this regalia of femininity was Leo.

'Is this some sort of joke?'

'I didn't think you'd believe me unless I showed you.' Leo moved towards her, wobbling like a foal on high heels that made his calves bulge. Looking at his face, Sophie recoiled from the smeared crimson lips and trowelled-on eyeshadow.

He was utterly grotesque. She backed away, skirting round the end of their bed, a solid core of ice-cold, implacable fury in her chest. How dare he? 'Well, now you *have* shown me, and I still don't believe you. If you really think that pretending you're a transvestite is preferable to being honest about the fact that you're having an affair, there's something seriously wrong with you – and I'm insulted that you'd imagine, even for a second, that I'd be stupid enough to believe you,' she spat. 'Oh, I bet you and Belinda had a great laugh cooking this up – shame she didn't show you how put on make-up without turning yourself into Coco the Clown while she was at it, but never mind – but now you've had your fun, you can just take all that crap off before someone sees it and then you can tell me the truth!'

Leo stared at her. If he was pretending to be mystified, Sophie thought, he was doing a world-class job – but then, she thought sourly, he'd had plenty of practice. 'Who's Belinda?'

'Your *mistress*.'

'I haven't got a mistress.'

'Come off it, Leo.'

'I don't even know who you're talking about.'

'Yes, you do. You even suggested she stay here – *in our house* – and look after *my mother*.'

'The *dog woman*? You thought that I . . . that she . . .' Leo shook his head. 'No. Really, no. Look, I don't blame you for being angry, but I'm not pretending, not about this.'

'Of course you're pretending! And what do you mean, you don't blame me for being angry? I've got every *right* to be angry! How dare you treat me like this?'

Leo took another couple of jerky steps towards her. 'Sophie, I promise you—'

'Get away from me!' Turning, Sophie ran into the en-suite bathroom and locked the door.

'Sophie, please. Come on. We need to talk.'

'No, Leo, *we* don't need to talk. *You* need to tell the truth. And I'm not coming out until you're properly dressed.'

'That's what I'm trying to tell you.'

'Oh, what?' Shaking, Sophie grasped the edge of the basin,

staring down at the shiny porcelain. 'That you *are* properly dressed?'

'Look, if you'll just let me explain . . . Please open the door. I'll lock the bedroom door so no one can come in.'

There was a pause, and she heard him crossing the room. When he returned, he said, 'I'm sorry. I know I've done this all wrong, but please come out. I need you to understand.'

'I understand, all right. You're having an affair.'

'No, I'm not. I swear it. You have to believe me.'

'I don't *have* to do anything, Leo.' Sophie lifted her head and stared at her reflection in the mirror. It is me, she told herself, stupidly. I am looking at myself, so I must be here. But how could she be here, like this, with Leo, like *that*, on the other side of the door? The certainty that he'd been having an affair with Belinda crumbled away to nothing. Of course it was ridiculous. She couldn't understand why she'd ever thought it. But this . . . *this* . . .

I want to start again, she told herself. Go back, and start again.

'Sophie?'

'All right. Give me a minute. I want . . .' What did she want? To tidy herself up, for one thing. To compose herself. Not to look blotchy and frantic, as she did now. She reached for her comb and make-up, and, as carefully as she could manage with trembling hands, repaired her face.

'OK,' she said, finally. 'OK.'

Leo was sitting on the end of the bed, his legs stuck out awkwardly. The sports bag, its padlock open, was lying on the floor at his feet.

Sophie held up a warning hand as he made to get up – 'Don't come any nearer' – and went over to sit on the chair in front of her dressing table. Turning it round to face him, she said, 'Well?'

Leo cleared his throat as though he were about to make a speech. 'I've never been unfaithful to you and I'm not having an affair. I wanted to keep this separate from you. I was ashamed, I knew you'd be upset, and I certainly didn't want the children to know. I thought I could sort it out by myself. I never intended to tell you.'

'So . . .' Sophie could feel the salted-caramel ice cream she'd eaten at the fair come up into her throat. Forcing herself to swallow, she turned so that she was facing the window. 'Why are you telling me now?'

'The police are getting a warrant to search the flat. They've already taken my computer and my phone.'

This, Sophie felt, was a manageable subject; almost – at least compared to what was actually in front of her – an abstract one. 'So you didn't lose your phone?'

Leo shook his head. 'They took it after the second interview – that's when they said they wanted to examine the things.'

'I didn't know you'd had a second interview.'

'I know.' Leo sighed. 'I'm sorry. They seem to have got the idea that I'm in on it, somehow – because of Miles using the flat and my giving him an alibi for Thursday evening.'

'That's ridiculous. You must have a credit card receipt, and anyway, the waiters at the wine bar or wherever it was will remember you being there, won't they?'

'That's just it. We were at the flat. Miles came over. He

couldn't understand why Jessica hadn't come to meet him on the Wednesday and he couldn't get hold of her.'

'But that means Jessica was missing before Thursday, doesn't it, so you can't have had anything to do with it.'

'They don't believe him, Soph. And there's stuff on my computer. Things I've bought, websites . . . And photos on the phone. Of me.'

Sophie whirled round. 'You mean you got dressed up in all this stuff and took *selfies*? Are you completely out of your mind? Anyone could have seen – someone at work, or the children, or . . .'

Leo hung his head. 'I know. Believe me, I know. It was really stupid – at least I should have got a different phone, but I just wanted . . .' He made a choking noise and, for a horrible moment, Sophie thought he was going to cry. 'I wanted to have a record of it, that part of me. And now the police'll see it. I thought you'd be bound to find out, because I knew you were already suspicious, and at least this way I'd have told you myself.'

'I see.' Sophie went back to staring at the window frame. There was a chip, really quite a big one, in the white gloss paint. 'Is that why you started going on about the menopause the other night? If I'd said yes, would you have told me it was affecting my brain?'

'I just thought there might be another explanation, that's all.' Leo's voice was quiet, almost a mumble.

'I can see it would have been convenient – but tell me, what were you doing when Miles and Jessica were in your flat? Bringing them tea in bed, dressed up as a French maid?'

She heard a rustle as Leo shifted slightly. 'They don't know anything about it. I wasn't even at the flat when they were there – it was during the day, or when I was out in the evening or away on a work thing.'

'So what were you going to tell Miles was in the bag?'

'I don't know. I hadn't got that far. Look, Soph, I'm sorry. I know I've done this all the wrong way – how I told you, I mean. I just thought, if you saw . . .'

Sophie made herself turn her head and look at him. He was patting the wig self-consciously, in the sort of gesture she'd seen actresses make in old films . . . And not only actresses – his mother patted her hair like that, too. 'God, Leo . . .' The salted caramel rose up again, blocking whatever she'd meant to say next, and she fought it back down, tears pricking her eyes.

'I know it's not easy for you to accept. I know that one of the reasons you were drawn to me was because I was conventional. Not like Margot. I know that was important to you, Sophie, and I understand it – and, whatever it looks like, I love you. I honestly thought, when we were married, that all of this –' he gestured again – 'would go away, and it did; for a while, anyway, but there was always this *feeling*, this other part of me . . . And then I thought, if I just kept it private . . . I used to buy things and try them on when you were out. When we lived in Clapham I hid them in the attic. And then I'd feel disgusted with myself and throw everything away – "purging", they call it – and tell myself I'd never do it again, but I'd always end up getting more. It's easier in the flat. I keep the things locked away so the cleaners won't find them, or if it's something that needs hanging up, I put it in a garment bag, and if they ever look inside they must think they're yours—'

'*Mine?* You mean dresses and things?'

'Yes.'

'Have you ever tried on *my* clothes?'

Leo stared down at his lap and smoothed his slip for a moment. 'No.' The word came out as a croak, and he didn't raise his head.

'I need you to look at me and say that.'

'Only your nightdress. The black one.'

'The birthday present, you mean?'

Leo nodded. 'Just a couple of times. When you've been in France with Melissa, buying stuff for the shop, I've slept in it.'

'Supposing Poppy'd come in, or Zac?'

'I always locked the door.'

Sophie leant over and began rummaging furiously in the chest of drawers. Yanking out the nightdress – a slippery satin affair from La Perla, which, now she thought about it, was on the large side – she wadded it up and threw it at him. 'Go on, take it. You obviously bought it for yourself, and I'm never wearing it again.'

Leo stayed quite still as the nightdress landed on his chest and slithered to the floor at his feet.

'Anything else?'

Leo's Adam's apple, not usually noticeable, bobbed as he swallowed. 'Nothing.'

'Are you sure about that?'

'Yes. Honestly.'

'You said you were doing this when we got married. How long has it been going on?'

'Since I was a child. The first time it was a pair of Mum's tights. I saw them lying on their bed – I'd seen her put them on so I knew how she did it, and I put my foot in and rolled them up my leg. I don't know why I did it. I suppose I was curious. I liked the feeling of it. I used to try on my sister's stuff, sometimes – party dresses and things.'

'Did she know?'

Leo shook his head. 'I was very careful. I never did it when I was away at school, or at university, but when I first went to work in London and had my own flat I'd buy lingerie and pretend it was for a girlfriend, or a silk robe or something like that. I liked the fabrics. The way they made me feel.'

'Excited, you mean? Turned on?'

'Ye-es . . . but it isn't just about that. It's . . . I can relax. If I've had a difficult day at work – if something's gone wrong – then I can put it aside when I put the clothes on. It's a different part of me. The ritual of it, putting on the make-up, the clothes – it's soothing.'

'So are you saying you can't relax when you're here with us? You know, Leo, if you want to embrace your feminine side, there's always plenty of ironing.'

'It's not like that.'

'Why doesn't that surprise me? There is *slightly* more to being a woman than wearing a frock and simpering, you know. Having periods, for instance. Having children.'

'Of course I know that. I don't want to *be* a woman, Soph. I just want to . . . I can't really explain it to you – I can't even explain it to myself. I read stuff on the Internet about cross-dressing – forums and things – because it helped to know that I wasn't the only one. Then I'd get disgusted with myself for doing that, and I'd stop . . . and then I'd start again and I'd want to take it a bit further, so I'd buy some more things . . . But always online. I've never been in a shop.'

Sophie felt cold inside and quite still, as if some internal motor had ceased to function. 'Have you ever gone outside dressed up as a woman?'

'Never. I wanted to preserve the fantasy. I'd imagine it, walking down a street or having a drink somewhere. I've always known I couldn't pass – that's what they call it when people think you're a real woman.'

'But you *want* to pass. Do you want attention from men, too?'

'Are you asking me if I'm gay? Because if so, the answer's no. You know that.'

'Do I? And you wouldn't actually need to go outside, would you? You could find someone on the Internet and invite them over.'

'I'd never do that. I've always been faithful to you.'

'No, you haven't. You're right about me being suspicious. I did think you were having an affair, but this is actually worse, because you're having an affair with yourself. You don't need another woman, Leo. You don't even need me. You just need a wardrobe full of frocks and a mirror. The other woman is there all the time, inside you, waiting to come out. She's part of you.' Sophie put her hands over her face. Her head was pounding like the sea.

'Do you want something? I could get you some water.'

'No.' Sophie turned and groped on the dressing table for a tissue. 'I told you. I don't want you to come near me.'

'Look, Soph. We don't need to mention it again, ever. Not if you don't want to. As I said, nobody else knows – I mean, I'm not

Grayson Perry, am I? I work in the City, for God's sake, not the arts. My firm only started letting women wear trousers to the office about twenty years ago. If they found out about this, I'd probably lose my job – and even if I didn't, I'd be a laughing-stock.'

'So put up and shut up, is that what you're saying? But even if we don't talk about it, I'm hardly going to forget it, am I? And what about when we're in bed? Have you been turned on by me all these years, or have you been fantasizing about yourself in a negligee?'

'Sophie, I love you. When we're together, it's just us.'

'How can I be sure of that? I've been married to you for almost twenty years but obviously I've got no idea of who you actually *are*, Leo. How do I know that you . . . that *Leonora* isn't there as well?'

'Not Leonora.'

'Oh, God! You've actually given her a name.' Seeing that Leo was about to speak, Sophie put up a warning hand. 'Don't tell me! I don't want to know.'

'OK, OK. I know it's difficult—'

'*Difficult!* It's impossible. Can you even hear yourself? You've had your entire life to get used to this and you can't explain it, and yet you expect me to come to terms with it in five minutes.'

'I don't expect that. I told you, I'd never have mentioned it except for what's happened – but it's not as if I've killed anybody, is it?'

Breathing hard, Sophie stared down at the vomit in the basin. Leo, leaning against the bathroom door, pushed a towel into her hand.

'Thanks.' Sophie turned on the tap to flush away the splatter. 'Was that why you changed the lock?'

'Changed . . . ?'

'At Moorgate House. You changed the lock.'

Leo's eyes opened wide. 'How do you know about that?'

'I told you, I thought you were having an affair.'

'OK. I locked myself out one night. The concierge wasn't around, and I couldn't get hold of the cleaners, so I had to get a locksmith. One of those emergency people. I must have forgotten to tell you. It wasn't important – just a stupid mistake.'

'A mistake. And what about the necklace I found in your pocket? The broken one.'

'I bought it in New York.'

'From Tiffany.' Sophie reached for her toothbrush. 'And Imanuela found a purple satin slip in the laundry. We didn't know whose it was.'

'So that's where it went . . . I'm sorry, Soph. I had no idea it was there. I've always been so careful. What did you do?'

'I threw it away. I thought it belonged to another woman – a real one. You know, Leo, last Christmas you were complaining about how much this house costs to run. How much have you spent on your wardrobe over the years?'

'I've never stopped you having the things you wanted. Or the children.'

'That's not the point. You were talking about how we were haemorrhaging money. That was the word you used: *haemorrhaging*.'

'Things haven't been going well at work, Soph. I should have told you, but I didn't think you'd understand . . . I'm worried about my job.'

'You're right about me not understanding. Things aren't going well at work and you're worried about your job and the next minute you're off buying yourself fancy lingerie and jewellery from Tiffany – and what was all that about me redecorating the flat? Was that just . . . throwing me a bone to make yourself feel better about all this?'

'If it's the money that's bothering you, then—'

'Of course it isn't! Well, not just that. It's everything. You, looking like *that* . . . It's not what I signed up for, Leo. It's not *fair*.' I wish it *had* been Jessica, Sophie thought wildly. I could have coped with that. I *did* cope with that. 'And now I've seen it – now I know about it – I can't just unsee it and unknow it. I married a man, not a woman. If that's what I wanted I'd be a lesbian, with a proper woman as a partner, not some sort of . . . Aunt Sally. And even if I never see you looking like this again, I'll always know that that . . . that *thing* . . . is there, waiting for you to take it – and I'm not calling it "her", because it isn't – out of its box. And yes, I know we're supposed to be non-judgemental nowadays and respect other people's choices and all the rest of it. That's fine when it's theoretical, but not when it's actually happening to you. I'm not all right with this, Leo, and I'm never going to be.'

'I don't want to lose you, Soph. I just thought—'

Whatever Leo had been about to say was cut off by the sound of something heavy crashing to the floor somewhere below and the clattering of metal, closely followed by a shrill and terrible scream.

FIFTY

Halfway down the stairs, the appalling smell hit Sophie's nostrils, causing her to stop abruptly, one hand clutching her throat. Leo, hard on her heels, cannoned into her, almost pitching her over the banister. 'For God's sake,' she hissed. 'What are you playing at? Go and put on some proper clothes.'

There were more screams, this time accompanied by a volley of barks, all coming from the kitchen. They stared at each other wide-eyed for a second before Leo, bouffant wig askew and hand clapped over nose, staggered back towards the bedroom.

The smell, overwhelmingly putrid, scoured Sophie's nasal membranes, eyes and the back of her throat. Gagging as she ran towards the noise, she stepped on a metal pole just inside the kitchen door and her feet shot out from under her. Dexter barrelled towards her as she clutched at the kitchen table to stop herself landing flat on her back. There seemed to be several poles, of varying lengths, scattered round the floor – someone had obviously dropped the disassembled gazebo.

'Mum!' Poppy appeared through the freezer-room doorway, T-shirt pulled up over her nose. 'Go and look! There are actual *maggots*! We're all going to die of food poisoning. I'm going to be sick.'

Sophie didn't need to look. Cheeks bulging, Poppy fled past her as she shoved the dog out of the way and scrambled upright. She ran into the freezer room and slammed the lid down over the sea of foul-smelling grey and black slush, but the odour remained, clinging, acrid as smoke, to their clothes and everything around them. Margot, hunched against the wall, appeared to be choking, and Reverend Barker was doubled over in the garden doorway, retching into his handkerchief. Sophie tried not to breathe as she bent her head to look at the wall behind the freezer and saw an empty socket with the plug lying on the floor beside it.

How long had it been like that? Why hadn't she checked? Leaning over, she grabbed the plug and smacked it back into the socket. That, at least, would halt the decay.

'The fuck is that smell?' Zac appeared in the kitchen doorway with Dexter skittering round his legs, sniffing the air. 'It's like something died in here.'

I barely looked, Sophie thought. With the ice melted, some part of Jessica might have emerged through the layers of polluted food and been spotted. Poppy had said something about maggots, but that could be because there was meat in there . . . Sophie glanced from Margot to the vicar and back again, but neither one looked capable of speech. If they said they'd seen anything, she could always deny it – surely no one would be mad enough to suggest opening the freezer up again for another look?

'Someone unplugged the freezer.' The words seemed to

process out of her mouth, orderly and calm. 'I imagine it was quite a while ago,' she added, in a measured, reasonable tone, 'judging by the smell.'

Zac's face was greenish-white. 'It's disgusting. What are you going to do about it?'

'I am going to get your grandmother out of here.' Sophie put an arm around Margot, who groaned and clutched at her. 'You can open some windows.'

Before they could move, there was further metallic clattering from the kitchen, accompanied by shouts – Leo, clad in the shirt and chinos he'd been wearing earlier. 'What's going on?'

'The freezer's been unplugged.'

Leo raised the lid a couple of inches, then dropped it. 'Jesus! How the hell did that happen?'

'No idea. Can someone *please* open some windows?'

'Right.'

Leo turned to go back into the kitchen, but Zac blocked his path. '*Dad?* Have you been wearing make-up?'

FIFTY-ONE

For a second, Sophie felt completely breathless, as if the air had been squeezed out of her by a giant hand. Leo had removed the make-up, but not thoroughly enough: his cheeks bore mascara smudges and his eyelids the glossy remnants of eye-shadow. As he opened his still-too-red mouth and then closed it again, Poppy reappeared, her face buried in one of Sophie's lavender bags. 'Mum, have we got any air freshener? You can smell it right upstairs, and . . . Dad? Why are you wearing make-up?'

'Yeah, *Dad*. What's that about?'

As Leo's mouth opened again and no sound emerged, Sophie said lightly, 'Oh, that was me.'

Zac stared at her. 'You were putting make-up on Dad?'

Sophie managed as much of a shrug as she could with Margot clinging to her. 'We were messing around.'

'You mean . . . for *fun*?'

'Yes!' Sophie made a face at him. 'Even old people have fun sometimes, you know.'

Zac, she saw, was actually blushing. 'Oh, God. TMI.'

'Well, you did ask. Now, let's get those windows open before we all suffocate. And there's some air freshener in the utility room, Poppy. It's in the cupboard under the sink.'

Sophie manoeuvred Margot through the kitchen and sitting room and onto the terrace. The smell wasn't quite as strong there, but it was still astonishingly – although not quite as eye-wateringly – prevalent. She left her mother gasping in a chair, and went upstairs to douse a silk scarf in perfume to wrap around Margot's face. She felt strange – light-headed, although that could have been the effect of the stink – yet composed. She looked down at her hands, which were quite steady. The worst has happened, she thought in wonder, and I am equal to it.

Five minutes later, Leo and Zac had opened most of the downstairs windows, but all that seemed to have done was let in flies. They formed a frenzied merry-go-round above the freezer as the vicar departed, muttering queasily that he hoped the problem wouldn't be too difficult to clear up. Poppy, having used up the air freshener, was busy spraying the place with every odour eliminator she could find, so that Dexter, sneezing, had given up snapping at the flies and fled into the garden. The family followed, with Poppy periodically turning, like a retreating sniper, to aim more spray in the direction of the house.

'It was him, Mum,' she said, throwing herself on the grass at the bottom of the slope. 'Zac.'

'Was it?' Sophie stared back up the garden at Margot, who seemed to have wrapped the entire scarf around her head, completely obscuring her face.

'No, it wasn't!' Zac slumped down beside Poppy. 'That is so fucked.'

'Zac! That's not necessary.'

'Well, it is. Why do I always get blamed for everything?'

'Because it's your fault,' said Poppy. 'It was when you got him to wash the cars, Dad. He had his iPod dock out by the door where the freezer is and I saw the cord. He must have plugged it into the freezer socket and forgotten to plug the freezer back in.'

'That was . . .' Sophie thought back, 'Monday, wasn't it?' Seven days of heatwave – no wonder the place stank. She'd been so concerned with keeping people away from the bloody thing that she'd never thought to check if it was still switched on. 'It's a *double socket*, Zac. Why didn't you just use the other one?'

'Dad was charging his cordless screwdriver. I couldn't take that out, could I?' said Zac, virtuously. 'He wouldn't have been able to use it.'

'You could have moved it to another socket instead of unplugging the freezer.'

'Look, Mum, I'm sorry, OK? And anyway, if Poppy saw, why didn't she check I'd plugged it back in?'

'Because I didn't know about Dad's screwdriver being plugged into the other socket – and I didn't think that even someone as stupid as you could be *that* stupid, that's why.'

'Stop going on about it.' Zac lay back on the grass with an air of exhaustion and closed his eyes.

'Mum! You're not just going to let him get away with it, are you? He's trashed the freezer and stunk out the whole house and—'

'We'll deal with it later, OK?' It was the first time Leo had spoken since they'd gone into the garden. His voice was loud and harsh. 'Not now.'

'Fine,' muttered Zac, eyes still closed. 'One little mistake . . .'

'What did you want from the freezer, anyway?' Sophie asked.

'Just ice cubes.' Poppy looked hurt. 'The tray in the freezer bit of the fridge was empty. I was getting us a cold drink.' She jabbed Zac with her foot, hard. Sophie pretended she hadn't noticed.

'Leave me alone!'

Poppy kicked him again and Zac bounced to his feet and glared down at her. 'You're such a bitch.'

Leo breathed out, hard. Sophie looked at him, and then at her children. Zac was looming over Poppy, who was huddled, head down, as if expecting a blow. 'Pack it in, the pair of you. I'm going to make sure Margot's OK.'

Margot, her head still shrouded in the scarf, was unresponsive when Sophie asked if she could fetch her anything. Having tried for several minutes to get her mother to speak, or even look at her, Sophie gave it up and went back down the slope. Poppy and Dexter were by the pond and Zac was slouching, hands in pockets, towards the house. The studied casualness of his movements made Sophie certain that he was off to his room to sneak a cigarette, but that was the least of her problems.

Leo was sitting alone on the grass, his arms around his knees, staring straight ahead. Silently, she sat down beside him. Without turning to look at her, he said, 'Thanks for rescuing me, Soph.'

'It's OK.'

'I love you.'

'Yes.'

'Can you say it?'

Sophie turned to look at his profile. She could see crumbs of make-up in the creases round his eyes, traces of lipstick at the corner of his mouth. How can I say I love you when I don't know who you are? she thought. Perhaps she had simply constructed 'her' Leo out of a need for security and a good life. All those years, she'd been so certain: of her place in the world, of how she should behave, of how things were supposed to unfold, what she deserved . . . And she'd been so sure that Leo was having an affair.

Here, now, it all seemed utterly without meaning. Jessica, floating in a murky soup dotted with stray peas and oven chips, cells breaking down, solid becoming liquid. Everything you thought you knew.

FIFTY-TWO

'I don't know, Leo. I don't know anything any more.'

They sat in silence. Sophie hunched forward, resting her forehead on her knees and closing her eyes. The world, vast and empty, thrummed in her ears.

When she raised her head, after a length of time that could have been a minute or an hour, Leo was gazing at her. Turning to look back at the house, she saw that Poppy was helping Margot back inside. Zac and Dexter were nowhere to be seen.

'Say something, Soph. Please.'

Sophie stared at him. He'd obviously been wiping his face because the residue of make-up was largely gone and a grubby-looking handkerchief was balled up in his fist.

'Anything. Call me a selfish bastard or whatever you like, but talk to me.'

'I've been stupid.'

'No, you haven't. I'm the one who's stupid. I'd never do anything to jeopardize us, Sophie.'

'But you did.'

'I didn't think I had a choice. The business with Miles ... What else could I do? All I want is to be with you.'

'To be with me and to dress up as a woman.'

'I won't do it any more.'

'But you can't stop, can you? You said you'd tried in the past, but you always buy more things.'

'I know, but this time I'll get rid of everything. Or you can get rid of it, if you like. Take it to a charity shop, or—'

'No.'

'Sophie, *please*. Just give me a chance.'

'No, I mean I think you should keep it.'

Leo stared at her. 'But you said—'

'I know what I said.'

'But—'

'But things have changed.'

'What, because the freezer's buggered and the place smells like a charnel house? I don't see what that's got to do with . . . with what we were talking about. I know it's a pain in the neck – and right now I'd like to throttle Zac – but we'll get someone in to clean it out and everything'll be back to normal. As far as the house is concerned, at any rate.'

Sophie put her shoulders back and took a deep breath, feeling as though she were preparing for a high dive. Even as she opened her mouth to launch the words, she didn't know if she could actually say them.

'Leo.'

There was still time to lie, to dissemble, to turn it into something else.

'I need to tell you something.'

Make something up. Something. Anything.

'It's about the freezer.'

Still time, still time.

'Jessica Mottram. Her body – it's in there.'

Too late.

FIFTY-THREE

Leo laughed. It wasn't actual laughter, but the uncomfortable chortling that politicians sometimes make when they're asked questions they can't answer, and the bubble of relief – she'd actually told him – burst in Sophie's chest. Something of this must have shown on her face, because Leo abruptly stopped the noise he was making and said, 'Oh, Christ. You're serious.'

'Yes.'

'Ohhhh . . . kay. Right. I see.' Leo's voice was wary, as if the words themselves were a dark corridor leading to an unknown horror. 'Well, no, I don't see. Was Melissa involved?'

'Melissa? Oh . . . no. I thought Jessica was having an affair with *you*. But it was an accident, Leo.'

'Even if it was, you can't just . . . you can't . . . I mean—'

'I didn't have any choice.'

'You had to kill her? But you said it was an accident.'

'It *was* an accident. I didn't have any choice about putting her in the freezer.'

Leo opened his mouth to say something and then shut it again, shaking his head. 'Right,' he said, finally. 'You'd better tell me what happened – and what on earth gave you the idea that I could possibly be involved with Jessica.'

'So . . .' said Leo, when Sophie had finished explaining. 'There was no attempted burglary.'

'No. It was me. So was the scratch on the Porsche. You'd parked it right in the middle of the garage and I had to take it out to get Jessica's car in – so it would be hidden overnight – and then put it back afterwards. I couldn't put her car in the other garage because it doesn't lock, and I couldn't risk anyone seeing it.'

'Oh.' Leo blinked. 'What scratch?'

'I told you just before you went back up to London. After you'd been out to meet Miles – if that's where you went. You didn't tell me.'

'Yes, it was. He was all over the place, out of his mind with worry and convinced the police were going to arrest him at any minute. Which they still might, of course . . .'

'Don't remind me. When Melissa came round here, having to listen to her talking about Miles and Jessica was just . . . I can't tell you how I felt. And then the vicar rang up and started going on about how he'd looked through the CCTV footage. He'd managed to delete quite a lot of it by accident, thank God, but he saw me driving the Audi away. Don't worry, he didn't recognize me – I was wearing a hoodie and sunglasses – but he's convinced that the "burglars" were casing the joint so he'll probably be keeping an eye on it from now on.'

'Christ, Soph . . . Why didn't you just show me the bloody letter in the first place?'

'I was going to, but I kept putting it off. You seemed so distant, and I kept thinking about the way you were talking at Christmas, as if we – me and the kids – were some sort of encumbrance. I thought you wanted to ditch us and get yourself a different life. And then Imanuela found the slip in the washing and I discovered you'd changed the lock, and then I found the broken necklace in your pocket . . . And then seeing Jessica come out of the flat like that. What was I *supposed* to think?'

Leo sighed. 'I'm sorry, Soph. It was true what I said about the rat race, all the . . . the *stuff* everyone's got to have. You get the life you want, and suddenly you reach a point when you realize you're not going to get any further up the ladder. You see all these other, younger people coming up and you feel . . . I don't know, that it's not your time any more, it's theirs. You've been displaced. Then you start looking around and wondering what it's all *for*. And the more stressed I felt, the more I needed to . . .' He fell silent.

'Escape?'

'Yes. Escape.'

Sophie wondered why he wasn't panicking. It was true that there was nothing, now, that he could do, apart from calling the police. Was all of this a preamble to that? After all, they wouldn't be able to have any more private conversations if she was in custody. 'Are you sure you never went out dressed up? I mean, if whoever returned the letters thought they'd seen a woman leaving the flat, they might have jumped to the wrong conclusion.'

Leo shook his head. 'I didn't. And even if I had – well, they'd have thought I was having an affair with Coco the Clown, wouldn't they?'

'Oh, God – did I say that? I'm sorry.'

'That's OK. I can hardly blame you for being shocked.'

'You were right when you said that I married you because I thought you were conventional. One of the reasons, anyway. But it turns out we both had a secret, didn't we?'

'Were you going to tell me?'

Sophie shook her head. 'It was my problem, not yours. I thought I could manage to solve it by myself.'

'Like I did.' Leo pushed his hands through his hair. 'Fuck.'

'Yes. Fuck.'

'You never swear.'

'I never accidentally kill people and hide their bodies in freezers, either. And you never wear make-up and frocks – or I didn't think you did.'

The silence stretched between them. Sophie noticed that it was starting to get dark. Was Leo gearing up to tell her that he was going to call the police? She turned her head to look back up at the house, imagining it without her. Imanuela could stay on, she supposed, and look after Zac and Poppy, until such time as a housekeeper could be arranged – unless Leo decided to move back to London for good. If that were the case – and she was hardly in a position to object – then new schools would have to be found. Zac and Poppy would have to cope with people knowing what their mother had done. And Alfie, going off to Cambridge . . . And Margot – what would happen to her? And to Dexter? She found she didn't care much what happened to her, because that seemed almost incidental, but she cared – fiercely, passionately – about her family.

Leo was saying something.

'Sorry, what?'

'I said, are you *sure* it was an accident?'

'Yes. I only wanted to talk to her. If I was intending to kill someone in my own home, I wouldn't do it half an hour before the children were due back from school.'

Leo's eyes narrowed, as if in minute examination. Sophie had a sudden vision of bacteria under a microscope: live rainbow sprinkles, twitching on top of a cake.

'No, you wouldn't do that. And I wouldn't do . . . what I do . . . if I could help it.' Leo looked at her, steadily. She looked back, knowing that an unspoken deal was being struck. 'So, the question is: how are we going to get rid of Jessica?'

'You're sure? You'll help me?'

Leo placed his hand over hers. 'We're a team.'

FIFTY-FOUR

Sophie found Margot sitting alone in the unlit sitting room, the scarf bunched under her nose. The full-on reek had dispersed, leaving a fainter, but still jolly unpleasant, miasma. Previously apathetic, Margot was now peevish and distracted, and addressed Sophie as 'Frances' – meaning, presumably, her neighbour Frances Wingate.

Still, Sophie thought, as she piloted Margot up the stairs, perhaps it wasn't surprising. She'd had a terrible shock – but at least the smell wasn't so bad up here. Margot would probably be fine in the morning. Firmly pushing from her the idea of what the morning was likely to entail, she helped her mother undress and get into bed.

Against the pillows, Margot's head looked somehow diminished and, leaning down, Sophie was suddenly aware of the skull beneath the thin skin and the sparseness of the artfully arranged hennaed hair. Margot murmured something almost unintelligible and closed her eyes.

'Goodnight.' As she tiptoed away and closed the door, Sophie thought how odd it was, and how pitiful, that Margot should have called her 'Mummy'. Then – although she had intended to leave them both to it – she went upstairs to check on Zac and Poppy.

On the upper landing she stopped and sniffed. There was something else, mixing with the faint tang of rottenness. Something sweetish and pungent. She flung open the door of Zac's room. He had the window open, but he wasn't quick enough, and stood staring at her, an open-mouthed mixture of indignation and shame. Dexter, who'd been curled up in the middle of his bed, leapt off it and slunk sheepishly past her legs and down the stairs.

'I thought you said those Rizla papers we found in your room belonged to one of your friends.'

'Yeah, they did. And actually it's a good job he gave me this, because that smell was making me really sick.'

'Hand it over.'

'You want some?'

'Of course not! Put it *out*. And give me that, as well.' Sophie indicated the foil container – presumably left over from some takeaway meal – that he'd been using as an ashtray.

'It's *medicinal*, Mum. They've done studies and everything.'

'I'm not going to argue with you, Zac. Just *do* it.'

'All right.'

'You haven't got any more, have you?'

'No. I said, didn't I?'

Sophie decided to believe him, not because she thought he was telling the truth, but because she really didn't – at that specific moment or possibly ever – have the energy to deal with the consequences of not believing him.

'You won't tell Dad, will you?'

'Not if you go straight to bed. School tomorrow, remember?'

'Thanks, Mum. I'm in enough shit already.'

Enough shit. Sophie closed the door, shaking her head. *You have no idea.*

'What's that?' Poppy stared at the foil container in Sophie's hand.

'Your brother's ashtray.'

'He's *so* stupid.'

'Yes, he is. Where did all these come from?'

Poppy was sitting in bed, reading, surrounded by at least fifteen scented candles. Several hundred pounds' worth of melting wax, Sophie thought – quite a few of them were Jo Malone or Diptyque.

'The utility room.' Poppy challenged her with a look. 'I don't see why I should suffer because Idiot Boy stank the house out.'

Sophie opened her mouth to remonstrate about how much the candles cost, then closed it again. None of this was Poppy's fault. 'I know,' she said. 'Do you think I could have a couple for our room?'

For a moment, her daughter's face was a surprised blank. 'Course. I *so* can't believe he did that.'

'Me neither.'

'Will you get someone to take it all away? Only, I don't think I can bear to go into the kitchen, and I can't even think about eating anything.'

Now she's got the perfect excuse to refuse food, thought Sophie. 'We'll sort it out, I promise.'

'Tomorrow? Because I really can't go in there.'

'I'll do my best, OK?'

'OK. Mum . . .'

'What?'

'Is Dad all right?'

'Dad?'

'That thing with the make-up. It was gross.'

Banishing the thought that the deal she seemed to have struck with Leo might include, in his mind at least, permission to sashay about the place in a twinset and pearls, Sophie said, 'We were just being silly. It's been a funny couple of weeks, that's all.'

'You mean about Miles having an affair with that woman who went missing? *Was* she here?'

'No, darling. Mrs Palmer got the wrong end of the stick.'

'But you do know her, don't you? Zac told me Granny said she'd left stuff in your car.'

Unable to look at her daughter, Sophie stared out of the window at the blocky outlines of dumpsters lined up against the stone wall of the churchyard, filled with rubbish from the fair. Reverend Barker had promised that they'd be collected within forty-eight hours. 'You know Granny gets confused.'

'Ye-es . . .' The word was drawn out as if Poppy were considering whether to believe her. 'But it's still pretty strange, someone just vanishing like that. What do you think happened to her?'

'No idea.' Sophie hoped her shrug was convincing. 'I expect she'll reappear and it'll all be a storm in a teacup.'

'You don't think Miles killed her?'

'Don't be silly.'

'It might not be *that* silly.' Poppy sighed. 'Everything's so weird at the moment.' Sophie was about to say goodnight when she added, 'Dad wouldn't do that, would he?'

'Do what? Have an affair or kill someone?'

'Either. Both.'

'No, darling. Of course he wouldn't.'

Poppy's stare took on an alarming intensity. 'But you can't actually *know* that, can you?'

'Well, no, but I'm as sure as I can be about anything. You will blow all these out before you go to sleep, won't you? Dad and I need to have a talk about what's going to happen about the freezer—'

'And what punishment Zac's going to get.'

'That, too. But I'd like to be sure that the house isn't going to burn down, OK?' Sophie gave her daughter a kiss. 'We've got quite enough on our plates already.'

Sophie blew out the two candles she'd taken – Jasmine and Pomegranate Noir – and went to deposit them on the dressing table in their bedroom. Leo's sports bag was in the middle of the floor, draped with the slithery folds of the slip he'd been wearing. The red patent leather stilettos lay next to it. Size 10 at the very least – no one was ever going to believe they were hers. She stuffed them into the bag, zipped it up and shoved it into the bottom of the wardrobe. But he is a good man, she thought as she shut the door. A good man, and a good father.

After checking the guest bathroom for telltale traces of make-up, she went down to the kitchen to consign Zac's contraband to the bin.

Leo, a Cath Kidston antique rose tea towel wrapped suicide bomber-style around the lower half of his face, was opening a bottle of white wine. 'Disco rice.'

'What?'

'What New York bin men call maggots. I heard it on Radio 4.'

'Oh, God. I'll never eat rice again.'

'I don't think I'll ever eat *anything* again. What's that you've got?'

Sophie held up the spliff. 'It's Zac's. I promised him I wouldn't tell you. It's all right, he hasn't smoked much of it.'

'Good.' Leo released the cork. 'We'll have it later.'

Sophie gawped at him. 'You're kidding.'

'I'm not. Not after the day I've had.'

'But you went ballistic when we found Rizlas in his room. And you told me you'd never even smoked dope at university.'

Leo shrugged. 'I didn't think you'd approve, because of . . .' He raised his chin in the direction of Margot's room. 'Your formative experiences. And there's no need to look at me like that – we're already fucked six ways from Sunday.'

'Zac and Poppy know something's going on, Leo. They're both pushing boundaries – Poppy's got my entire stock of scented candles up in her room. They need to know that we're in control of things.'

'Point taken, but we won't be in control of anything if we're banged up in prison, will we? And they're not going to come back down.'

Sophie shook her head. 'I told them not to.'

'Grab those glasses, then, and we'll go into the garden. We've got some serious thinking to do. Fortunately there's nothing urgent at work tomorrow, so I've left a message to say I won't be in.'

Later, upstairs, they undressed and lay down side by side, flat on their backs, not speaking. Sophie imagined the pair of them as two astronauts, waiting for take-off, as separate and unable to communicate as if their heads had been inside polycarbonate globes.

Everything's unravelling, she thought. The dope, which she'd ended up sharing with Leo after a couple of hours' discussion about how to get rid of Jessica, had not only made her feel utterly unlike herself, but had given her a sense of physical dissociation, so that now she floated, unanchored by her body, up into the vastness of the night sky.

FIFTY-FIVE

Even at half past six, the air was thick with rising heat. Sophie felt as if she had almost to push it aside, like a heavy curtain, in order to get out of bed.

'Weather's got to break soon.' Leo padded across to the bathroom, rubbing his eyes. 'And that'll be the summer over.'

'Did you sleep?'

'Not much.'

'Me neither.'

Consciously calm, they showered and dressed with silent efficiency.

The smell had dissipated, but the knowledge of what lay beneath the clean white lid of the freezer next door made the surroundings feel somehow contaminated. Sophie took the breakfast things across the hall to the dining room, but even there, with every single window open, Poppy said she didn't want anything and Zac, who wasn't meeting anyone's eye, said that he wasn't hungry either.

When they'd both left – apparently as relieved to be gone as Sophie was to see the back of them – Leo took the Land

Rover down to the DIY superstore to pay cash for a list of items that included opaque plastic sheeting, parcel tape, heavy-duty bin bags, disposable boiler suits, nitrile gloves and face masks. Having tidied up, Sophie pocketed the sleeping tablets from the medicine cupboard and prepared a breakfast tray for Margot.

Sophie stared down at her mother's open mouth and waxy, dun-coloured skin and, for a horrible moment, thought that she was dead. Margot didn't stir while she replaced three of the pills in the dosette box with the ones from downstairs. They looked similar enough to pass muster, and the double dose should ensure a long enough sleep. Besides which, Sophie thought, there was no risk of anyone disturbing, or trying to disturb, her because Imanuela wouldn't be back from Romania until tomorrow. Alfie was due back in the UK, too, but he'd told her he was going to stay in London with his friend Luke for a few days.

'Margot . . . ?' Margot opened her eyes and, seeing Sophie's face so near her own, flinched. 'It's OK, it's only me.' Her mother stared at her fearfully, clutching the bedclothes. 'I've brought your breakfast. We're going to have to go out, to sort out the freezer – the problem we had yesterday, remember? So it might be an idea if you stayed put for a while.'

Margot had seemed contented enough, after being assisted to the bathroom, to eat and be dosed, although, Sophie reflected as she went back downstairs, it was by no means clear that her mother actually knew who she was except in a general way, as an ally. Wetting her palm under the cold tap in the kitchen and running it round her neck, she wondered if it might not be temporary – the effect of Margot's fall and of being taken from her home. She'd have to discuss it with the doctor, but right now—

Barking from Dexter and tyres crunching on the gravel. Leo must be back, which was good because they'd need to get a move on if they were to be finished and back to normal in all the ways that mattered before Poppy and Zac arrived home from their respective after-school activities at around seven. Sophie ran to help him unload, but when she flung open the back door she saw not the Land Rover but the blue-and-yellow checks of a police car.

Sophie stepped into the yard, closing the door behind her. This is it, she thought. Here, now. How it ends.

There were two men in the car: a driver, in uniform, and, beside him, an older man – grey hair, jowls – wearing a suit. Sophie seemed to be looking at them from a long way away, as though she'd somehow travelled across the garden and into the field, leaving her body leaning against the door, rigid, like a plank of wood.

The man in the suit got out of the car. Sophie watched his mouth move as he spoke – to her, apparently, although none of it appeared to make much sense. The hot, thick air around her seemed to twitch, and static hummed in her ears, so that she caught only random words: 'Sorry to disturb . . . hope not inconvenient . . . making enquiries . . . Jessica Mottram . . .'

His voice was deep and quiet. He must have introduced himself, but she hadn't caught his name. 'I don't know anything,' she blurted. 'I didn't know Jessica Mottram. I mean, I know she's disappeared, because I read it in the paper, but that's all. I don't really see how I can help.'

The white noise between her ears ceased abruptly and the officer's monosyllable, 'No,' plopped into the silence from a long way away, like a stone thrown into a well. What did he mean by 'No'? Was he going to arrest her? She held her breath as he glanced over his shoulder to the driver, who was still sitting in the car, and then back at her. She forced herself to look into his eyes as the words, 'Sophie Marianne Hamilton, I am arresting you for the murder of Jessica Mottram,' sounded in her mind as clearly as if he'd actually spoken them. 'You do not have to say anything unless you wish to do so . . .' That was how it went, wasn't it? She'd heard it a hundred times on TV crime dramas.

This can't be happening, she thought. It isn't real.

It wasn't real. He was saying something quite different.

She gaped at him. 'Sorry, I didn't quite catch . . .'

'I understand that you visited her cottage on Friday the eighteenth of May.'

Of course. Belinda had said the police might be in touch. The surge of relief made her dizzy. 'Did I?' There seemed to be shadows gathering at the edge of her vision. 'I'm afraid I can't remember the date. I've been to her cottage. Not inside, because I was just delivering something from Hamilton De Witt – that's the shop I run with a friend.'

'De Witt? Would that be Melissa De Witt?'

'Yes, that's right.' Of course, Sophie thought. They knew about Miles. Would they think she was part of some sort of plot to get rid of Jessica?

'Did you drop it off?'

'Did . . . ? Oh. No. She wasn't in, so I came away.'

'Can you remember what time that was?'

'In the morning, I think. Or maybe early afternoon . . . I'm sorry, I don't think I can be more exact.' At least, she thought, he didn't seem to have asked if they could come in – although that, of course, might still happen.

The officer regarded her thoughtfully, his head slightly tilted to one side and an expression of impersonal interest on his face, as though they were deep in discussion of some abstract problem. 'Which door did you go to?'

'Door? Oh. Yes. The one at the back.'

'The one that's accessed from Long Lane?'

'Yes, that's right.' She hadn't been spotted going into the cottage, had she? Apart from Belinda, no one had come past on foot while she was entering or leaving, and she was pretty sure there'd been no cars, either. Jessica's cottage had no immediate neighbours, and the thick hedges at the back and side would surely prevent anyone in the fields from seeing what was happening in the garden, even if they'd been high up, sitting in the cab of a machine.

'And you didn't walk round the house to find a place to leave the parcel?'

Sophie shook her head. 'Not our policy. Too many things go missing.'

'Very sensible.' He nodded again, bland and unsuspicious. With any luck, Sophie thought, she'd be able to get rid of the pair of them before Leo came back.

'You didn't leave a note to say you'd been.'

'I'm sorry?'

'A note. Most people put a note through the door if they're trying to deliver something and there's no one in.'

'Yes, I should have. But I'd left my pen in the car . . .' Hearing herself start to gabble, Sophie made a conscious effort to slow down. 'And I was in rather a hurry.'

'But you gave Ms Langdon a lift home.'

'Ms . . . ? Oh, you mean Belinda. Sorry. With people you only see out dog walking – we've got a black Labrador – it's only ever first names. In fact, half the time it's only the dog's name and you have no idea about the man or woman on the other end of the lead . . .' She paused, hoping this would suffice, but the officer stood silently, looking expectant. 'Yes, the lift . . . She'd hurt her leg, and it's not exactly out of my way, so I could hardly refuse. I thought I'd phone Ms Mottram when I got home.'

'But you didn't.'

Sophie frowned at him, wondering how he could possibly know she hadn't phoned Jessica, then realized that of course the police would be able to get records of calls from the relevant phone companies. He must also have known, from looking at Jessica's CCTV footage, that she hadn't walked round to the front of the house. 'I must have forgotten.'

'But you didn't try again?'

'Try . . . ?'

'To deliver the parcel.'

'No.' Sophie gave a weak laugh. 'I should have, but we've been terribly busy and it was only some samples.'

'Would you normally deliver those?'

'Not usually, but when I looked up the address in the shop

I could see that it wasn't too much of a detour, so I thought I might as well.'

'Even though you were in a hurry.'

Sophie gave him a look that she hoped was sufficiently quizzical as to suggest he was making a mountain out of a molehill. 'Well, I suppose I'd assumed she'd be there.'

'Where did you park your car?'

They must suspect her. Otherwise, why keep asking questions? Had she been seen, or had Jessica mentioned their 'chance' meeting and the tea invitation to someone? The sudden thought that Leo might return and shout out something incriminating before she could warn him cut through the babble of 'what if's in her head. She'd just have to hope that she'd be able to excuse herself and rush round to intercept him before he got out of the Land Rover.

'Your car, Mrs Hamilton. Where did you park it?'

She mustn't say in the spinney, because that would seem odd, as though she'd been trying to hide the thing. 'Up by the T-junction.'

The officer raised his eyebrows. 'Bit dangerous, I'd have thought.'

'Yes – that's why I wanted to be quick.'

'Why didn't you go round to the front of the house? You could have parked in the drive.'

'I'd never been there before. I wasn't even sure,' she added, with an air of helplessness, 'if it was one house, or two.'

'But Ms Mottram's address is the main road, not Long Lane.'

Oh, God. Sophie could feel her carefully held smile spasming into a grimace. 'I know,' she said, 'but I'd driven up Long Lane to get there, and a lot of people prefer deliveries to come to the back door, don't they?'

'But if you thought it was a different house . . .'

'I said I wasn't sure!' Hearing the edge of panic in her voice, Sophie added, more quietly, 'It *was* several weeks ago. I mean, I can see how it might be important now, my going to the cottage – because of what's happened – but at the time it was just . . . you know, another errand, so I don't remember that much about it.'

'You seem to be doing pretty well.' Was he being sarcastic? Sophie couldn't tell. 'Was Ms Mottram's car parked at the front of the house?'

'No. Well, it might have been, but if it was I didn't see it. Or I suppose it could have been in the garage.'

'I see. Well, we won't keep you any longer.' There was some other stuff about possibly having to make a witness statement, but Sophie barely heard it.

She stood watching as the police car backed out of the yard, and, once alone, slumped against the back door on legs like water, feeble with relief, her breath coming in gasps.

After a couple of minutes, she heard more tyres on the gravel, and Dexter started barking again.

This time it would be Leo.

Right. Sophie levered herself away from the back door and had just started across the yard to meet the Land Rover when the front of a small, battered-looking car appeared, with—

Oh, God, no. Sophie stood staring, trying to keep the hysteria that was frothing inside her from spilling over.

Please, no. Why now?

That was all she needed. She wanted to scream, to shout at the top of her voice, to rush into the house, lock the door behind her and hide, but none of that would cancel out the fact of Belinda, who'd pulled up and was now emerging from the driver's seat, closely followed by Robbie.

'Could I come in for a minute?'

'Sure. I haven't got long, I'm afraid. We've had a bit of a catastrophe with the freezer – it got unplugged a week ago and nobody noticed. It's all pretty revolting so I need to get on with sorting it out, but yes, come on in.'

This, thought Sophie, would surely be enough to make most people say they'd come back another day, but Belinda just said, 'OK,' and followed Sophie into the kitchen while Robbie herded an obliging Dexter into the garden.

'I'm afraid it's still a bit . . .' Sophie wrinkled her nose, 'from the freezer. Would you like a cup of tea?'

'No, it's fine. Actually . . .' Closing her eyes momentarily, Belinda took a deep breath. 'I've come to tell you something.'

She looked better, Sophie thought now. Tidier. She'd blow-dried her hair, and there were fewer scarfy, dangly things hanging off her. In fact, although she wasn't entirely sure why, Belinda looked vaguely familiar in a way she hadn't before. Leo lied to me, she thought. She's going to tell me that she knows his secret and she can accept him for who he really is and that she's doing this for all our sakes and – oh, God. Had Leo phoned her and told her about Jessica?

*

Belinda was talking. Sophie needed – *really* needed – to pay attention, but somehow she couldn't. She felt grubby, despite having showered, as well as clammy and shaky. 'Wait. I just . . . Sorry, I think I'd better sit down. It's so hot, and . . .' She couldn't finish the sentence. Her thoughts clotted with wordless, terrible panic, she groped for a chair and collapsed into it.

Belinda remained standing. 'I need to tell you . . . I realize it's likely that you'll never want to see me or speak to me again, but it's important that I explain everything. It's not that I expect you to forgive me, or . . . or anything, really, and I know I've got a long way to go, but I just . . . I have to . . .'

'What?'

'It's part of the process.'

'Process?'

'AA.'

AA. Sophie glanced out of the window at Belinda's car. Surely it was working, if she'd driven it? 'I don't understand.'

'Alcoholics Anonymous. The twelve steps. I'm sorry, Sophie, I know this must seem a bit – well, more than a bit – *odd* to you, but I've been going to the meetings for a few months now, and one of the things you have to do is to make amends to people you've wronged. That's why I'm here.'

'I didn't know you went to AA.'

'I haven't exactly advertised the fact. It's just that since yesterday – being here, seeing you with your family – I haven't been able to think about anything else and I thought if I didn't do it now . . .'

'Do *what*?'

'I sent those letters, Sophie. The round robins. I sent them back.'

FIFTY-SIX

Time stretched between them, taut. Sophie heard a car pass along the road outside, then a single, sharp bark from somewhere in the garden. She took a deep, ragged breath. 'You *are* having an affair with Leo.'

'No.'

'That's what you wrote.'

'I know.'

Sophie stared at Belinda. Nothing made sense. Her mouth was dry and her tongue felt like a foreign body that had somehow got inside it, an impediment to speech. 'Why?' The word came out as a rasp.

Belinda started talking with such fluency that Sophie felt sure the words had been rehearsed, not once but many times. 'We've known each other for three years – informally, of course, because of the dogs, but you've told me a lot about yourself. Your perfect life. You have all the luck, and yet you go on and on about your piddling little problems as if they actually *mean* something. Dithering over which cushion covers to buy or which Cambridge college your clever son is going to attend – those aren't problems, they're luxuries. My house fell into the sea, Sophie. *That* is a problem. I was made homeless. *That* is a problem. Where I live now – well, you know what it's like because you've seen it – the roof is leaking and there's mould growing on the walls but the landlord won't do anything and I don't have the money to fix it. *That* is a problem. No one supports me, I have no savings, and such jobs as I get barely cover the food, rent and bills. *That* is a problem.

'The reason you don't know about any of this, by the way, is because you've never asked me about my life. Not one single question. You have no idea what life is like for most people. You live in this . . . this *bubble*, and you think the rest of us want to hear about how well you're doing.'

'I'm sorry the letters made you angry,' said Sophie, cautiously – there was, presumably, a particular way in which Belinda wanted her to respond, and she didn't want to make things worse – 'but I don't understand why you got them. I mean, I know where you live, but I don't actually have your address. I had to ask one of your neighbours which house it was.'

'My ex-husband sends them on.'

'Ex-husband?'

'Ben used to work with Leo.'

'Ben . . . ?'

'Shapcott.'

'But . . . I thought your surname was . . .' Oh, God, what had that policeman said? Something beginning with L. 'Landon?'

'Langdon. I went back to my maiden name when we got divorced.'

Ben Shapcott. A hazy image formed in Sophie's mind of a tall, languid and cynical individual, met at several dinner parties, but when she tried to fill in the space beside him where a spouse should be, she came up blank.

'I realized you didn't remember me,' said Belinda.

'I'm sorry. When I lived in London I was always going to work things with Leo, but I'm afraid they're all rather a blur,' said Sophie. 'The children were much younger then, and it was all a bit hectic,' she added weakly.

'Ben dumped me. Younger model. We didn't have children. I'd wanted to, but he always said he didn't. He must have meant that he didn't want them then, or with me, because Number Two had twins within a year. I'd been a journalist – women's magazines, mostly – but the work dried up. I lost my confidence. I couldn't cope – whole weeks would pass and I would barely get out of bed, never mind leave the house – and I certainly couldn't afford to stay in London. I got *some* money when the house was sold, but there was still a pretty big mortgage so it wasn't as much as you'd think . . . Ben did help me, financially, but obviously that wasn't going to last forever. Coming up here wasn't the best idea. My mistake, but I needed to crawl away somewhere and lick my wounds.

'It's hard when everyone you know is in couples. With a lot of our mutual friends, they – or one of them – would be in the City, or something like that. Some of them had known about the affair before I did – the men, anyway – and they made it obvious that they expected me to fade away in order to save their embarrassment. And a lot of the women reacted as if I was contagious, because I represented a fall from grace that scared them shitless . . . How easily you can slide down to the bottom of the heap. It's funny,' she added, sardonically, 'that as a society, we're always congratulating ourselves on how far we've come now that there's no social stigma around things like illegitimacy and being gay, but try being in my position and you'll find yourself right back in the nineteenth century.

'We'd often been to Southwold and places round there for weekends, but by the time I moved, they were too expensive, so I had to settle for somewhere further up the coast. If I'd done my homework, I'd never have bought the cottage, but I wasn't used to making decisions like that on my own, and I'd started drinking. A lot. The thing about coastal erosion is that it's not a steady process. Sometimes you don't get any problems for years, and then all of a sudden . . . That happened about nine months after I'd bought the thing and of course the insurance shot up – Ben had been paying that, but he said he couldn't afford it any more. The bank wouldn't lend me the money – no regular salary and no collateral worth speaking of – and my family aren't in a position to help.

'Ben always sent on the post. Stuff addressed to me, or both of us – not that there's much of that now, except your Christmas letters. I was angry, Sophie. You and your husband and your children and your perfect life and your entitlement – you never seemed to have a single problem. You were rubbing my nose in it and you *didn't even know who I was*.'

Sophie shook her head, defeated and floundering.

'You expect other people to be interested in your life, but you don't give a toss about theirs. You can't even be bothered to update your address book.'

'I don't know what to say, Belinda. Just . . . I'm sorry.'

'I wondered if you'd tell me about it.'

'About . . . ?'

'Getting the letters returned.'

'Was that what you wanted? For me to confide in you?'

Belinda looked surprised, then frowned. 'I don't actually know *what* I wanted. Just for you to *realize*, that's all. How lucky you are.'

'I . . .' Sophie opened her mouth to protest that it wasn't *only* luck, then thought better of it. After all, if the past few months had taught her anything, it was that, whatever one did or didn't do, life was entirely, appallingly, terrifyingly random. 'But,' she said, 'those postmarks were from miles away.'

'I gave them to people to post.'

'Not the last one – and that didn't come till Easter.'

'I didn't mean to send that. I'd started going to AA by then. It was difficult, but I was keeping it together, at least in terms of not drinking. You were going on and on about Alfie being in Borneo and how well he was doing and it just made me feel like shit. Don't you remember? You only stopped when Dexter tried to run after a cat and I had to help you hang on to him. I know it's not an excuse, but afterwards I went home and I thought, 'I feel terrible and I can't even have a drink and it's not fair,' and then of course I did have a drink, and . . . Well, it went on from there. To be honest, I barely remember writing on the thing, let alone posting it back to you, but it wasn't there when I looked the following morning, so I knew I must have.'

Sophie remembered the occasion. Belinda had grabbed Dexter's lead as he bounced and lunged, while Robbie, unflustered, looked on with cool superiority. 'You did.'

Belinda's stare was inescapable, like a searchlight, and, for a moment, Sophie experienced an irresistible urge to tell her what she'd done – what Belinda's returned letters had *made* her do. 'See?' she heard herself saying. 'See? You think you're the only one with problems.' Instead, she smiled and said, 'It's nice of you to come and apologize, and I do understand, but – to be perfectly honest – I didn't really pay them much attention.'

FIFTY-SEVEN

Sophie stood outside with Dexter, watching Belinda drive away with Robbie in the back, his nose pressed against the rear window. I ought to be relieved, she thought, and wondered at herself for feeling . . . well, nothing at all.

The Land Rover appeared almost immediately. Leo pulled up outside the freezer room's outer door. 'Who was that?'

'Belinda.'

'What did she want?'

'I'll explain later. The police were here, too, earlier.'

'*What?* Why?'

'You know I told you I'd pretended to be delivering something to Jessica's house so I could go inside and get her laptop, and Belinda saw me in the garden so I had to give her a lift home? Well, she mentioned it to the police because she thought it might help them work out when Jessica actually went missing, but she couldn't remember the exact time so she suggested they ask me.'

'So . . .' Leo looked bewildered. 'What did you say to them?'

'The truth – that I thought it was late morning or early

afternoon, but I couldn't really remember. I nearly had a heart attack when they arrived.'

'I'm not surprised.'

'I'll probably have to make a statement, but that seemed to be all they wanted to know ... Except that they know Melissa and I run the shop together, so I suppose they might want to ask me about her – if she knew about Miles's affair.'

'Which she didn't.'

'No – so at least I'll be telling the truth about that. What took you so long, anyway?'

'Sorry. There was a massive hold-up on the A148.'

Sophie knew, without knowing how she knew, that this wasn't true. She pictured Leo sitting in a lay-by somewhere, wondering if he could go through with what they were about to do. She couldn't blame him for that – especially not now he was here. Aloud, she said, 'Do you want to back up to the side door? Not all the way, because we won't be able to get the Land Rover door open.'

Twenty minutes later, with Dexter shut in the utility room, they'd unrolled the turquoise plastic sheeting to cover the flagstones, and they were standing, clad in white polypropylene boiler suits, plastic shoe covers and nitrile gloves, in front of the now-unplugged freezer. Deal with it, Sophie told herself. Treat it as a basic household task, unpleasant but necessary. Leo turned to look at her, his eyes, above the white striations of his face mask, as grave and intense as a surgeon's.

'Ready?'

Sophie took a deep breath, closed her eyes, and nodded. When she opened them again, Leo was raising the lid.

The freezer having been turned back on just over twelve hours earlier, the contents neither looked nor smelt as bad as they'd done the day before, but the sludgy mass, dotted with maggots, was still repellent, and as for what lay underneath . . . Desperately trying to think of something – *anything* – else, Sophie held open a heavy-duty plastic bin liner while Leo, working as fast as he could, removed the packets and boxes and shoved them into it. Despite the attempt at refreezing, the stuff seemed surprisingly limp, sagging cardboard boxes and flaccid vacuum packs flopping in Leo's hands. If the food was like that, Sophie thought, how would Jessica be? She imagined her skin, slimy and half-iced, the fluids leaching from her, the contaminated pulp of her liver, stomach, intestines, and—

Releasing the bin liner and wrenching the mask from her face, she rushed from the room to throw up in the kitchen sink.

Leo came in as she was bending over, heaving, with watering eyes, and rubbed her back. 'Come on, Soph. Keep it together.'

He disappeared as she was wiping her mouth with kitchen roll, and came back carrying two glasses of brandy.

'Are you sure? We're driving.'

'One measure won't put either of us over the limit.'

'All right.' The glass rattled against her teeth.

When the second bin liner was full, he stopped. The smell had gradually worsened as he'd removed the food, so that now it was well on the way to being as bad as it had been the previous evening. Leo remembered something he'd read in a crime novel and fetched Vaseline to smear in their nostrils, but it didn't make much difference.

Eyes closed, dry-heaving, Sophie heard him say, 'OK. We're down to your layer of plastic. Better fetch another bag – that'll need one to itself.'

The thick black sheet shed maggots and ice crystals onto the floor as Leo wrestled it into a manageable wad and stuffed it into the third bin liner. One more layer of food to go, and then it – *she* – would become visible.

'Ohhhh . . . kay.' Leo straightened up and dropped a plastic container of grey mince into the bin liner. 'I can see her.'

FIFTY-EIGHT

Sophie forced herself to look. It was actually worse than her nightmares. Only Jessica's face was visible, framed by Zac's favourite toffee ice cream and an unidentified transparent bag containing grey sludge. She had somehow become lopsided, so that one eye glared out, Cyclops-like, far larger than the other. The lips, which, like the eye sockets, were green-tinged, curled back in a snarl and the skin, dusted with ice like heavy powder, was a clay-like grey.

She recoiled, unable to help herself. Leo grabbed her arm. 'For Christ's sake, Soph. Do you want to land us both in prison? I *can't do this* without your help.'

'That's it.' Leo took the bin liner from Sophie and tied up the top. 'Let's get all these down to the dumpsters.'

'Won't it look odd? The boiler suits, I mean. On the CCTV.'

Leo shook his head. 'The vicar was here, remember? As far as he knows, the freezer broke down so we have to clear it out. It's the logical thing.'

*

'OK,' said Leo, when they'd heaved the last of the bin bags over the lip of one of the dumpsters. 'I don't think we can lift her out – for all I know, she might be coming apart – so we're going to have to tip the freezer over and push her onto the plastic sheeting. There's quite a bit of . . . well, *liquid*, in there, but we'll just have to mop that up afterwards. Are you ready?'

Coming apart. Sophie hadn't thought of that. Standing in the hot sunlight, sweating and clammy in her polypropylene suit, she felt as though she were about to faint.

'Come on, then.' Without waiting for a reply, Leo set off back up the drive to the house. Sophie stared after him. Actually *coming apart.* Oh, God. She couldn't do it. She *couldn't.*

She had to.

'Right, after three.' Leo closed the lid and they faced each other from either end of the freezer. Sophie shut her eyes as Leo counted, and heard sloshing and sliding noises coming from inside as – 'Not too fast!' – they tilted it forward to the floor. The smell, overwhelming, broke over her like a wave and she heard the heavy, soggy thud as Jessica's body tumbled onto the plastic sheet. She heard a muffled groan – Leo, hurrying to the kitchen to vomit in the sink.

Not daring even to glance at what was on the floor, Sophie followed him, the smell like a solid thing in her nose and mouth and bile rising in her throat. 'Was she . . . in one piece?'

'Yes.' Leo wiped his mouth on a tea towel. 'Looked like it, anyway. Thing is . . .' He stared past Sophie to the Land Rover, which was visible through the open doors. 'We're going to look bloody suspicious at the other end, toting a great long parcel wrapped in bright-blue plastic. And it's going to be difficult to get rid of. Hang on.'

'Where are you going?'

'The garage.'

When Leo returned, he dumped two navy-blue nylon sail bags and a coil of nylon rope on the kitchen table and, next to those, a kit box. Sophie stared at it, imbecilic, until the letters imprinted in the ridged black plastic formed themselves into recognizable words.

Black & Decker.

'It's no good, Soph. We'll have to cut her in two.'

FIFTY-NINE

Showered and dressed for a day's sailing, Sophie climbed into the passenger seat of the Land Rover and rolled down the window. The air clung to her like warm, damp fabric – muggy, saturated, unmoving – but the open window was necessary because of the smell, and, in any case, the vehicle was too ancient to have air con.

The flagstones had been mopped with Jeyes Fluid and the freezer disinfected and hosed out and, unless you counted the fact that the lid was up and the thing was empty and not switched on, the room looked more or less normal. Bisecting Jessica had been ... Sophie shook her head in an attempt to jettison the image, but it remained stubbornly in front of her mind's eye.

'Right, that's got rid of all the bits and pieces.' Leo, similarly showered and changed, swung himself into the driver's seat. 'I got some bricks from the pile behind the garage,' he said matter-of-factly. 'We'll need something to weigh the bags down.'

Sophie looked into the windowless back of the Land Rover and saw that, in addition to the two sail bags that lay between the bench seats, there were now three large cool boxes.

'They're inside those,' said Leo. 'Christ knows what people would think if they saw us loading up the yacht with bricks.'

'Good idea.'

As Sophie turned back to face the windscreen, Leo caught her eye and stared at her with an intensity that made her lean back, away from him. 'You owe me.'

'I know.'

'OK, then.'

He started the engine. 'High tide's at half one, and it's quarter past now so we should be all right. So, if we reckon on fifteen minutes to get there, allow half an hour to fetch the boat and get that lot on board, then – assuming the wind's on our side – a couple of hours' sailing before we can offload and a couple of hours to get back, plus sorting out the boat and getting home, that should take us up to about . . . quarter to seven, so we should make it back just before the kids arrive.'

Once they'd got going, the smell – with the windows open – wasn't too bad at all. They drove through the village in silence, but as they turned onto the A149, Leo said, 'I hope I've brought enough bricks. I reckon they weigh about five pounds each, so twelve would be fifty pounds, which is about . . . hang on . . . four stone and three pounds. I should think that half of Jessica would probably weigh about that – well, I suppose the top half might weigh a bit more, because of the head, but I shouldn't think there's much in it. It's really a question of offsetting the buoyancy, although actually I shouldn't think there'd be very much of that, with her being chopped in half . . .'

He could be discussing a problem at work, Sophie thought,

so completely pragmatic did he sound. The demonstration of simple arithmetic, of logic, was important, a means of showing them both that he was taking control of the situation by applying reason. She had a sudden image of him as a schoolboy, sitting at a tidy desk, meticulously writing out his workings on a maths test paper so the teacher could see how he'd arrived at the answer.

'. . . didn't work on poor old Pooky.'

'Sorry?'

'That was its name, wasn't it?'

'The hamster? We didn't chop him in half, did we?'

'Yes. And no, of course we didn't, but we gave it a sea burial, remember? Ended up having to bash the air pockets out of whatever it was wrapped in with an oar, and Poppy in floods of tears.'

Sophie did remember. Poppy, who'd been about six, had been inconsolable, and the boys had become bored and got silly.

'Just need to make sure the same thing doesn't happen this time,' said Leo. 'As far as lifting the bags over the side . . . If we put twelve bricks in each one – we can do that when we're on board – then they'll weigh about eight and a half stone, which should be doable.' Leo nodded a few times, as if in agreement with himself, then lapsed into silence while Sophie thought, with a sense of wonder, of the days when all she'd had to worry about was a dead hamster.

'I had a call from Miles,' Leo said suddenly. 'When I was at the DIY place. The police want to see him again. He thinks they're going to arrest him.'

'How can they, with no body? As far as they're concerned, she could be anywhere.'

'But they're not going to find her, are they? And people do get convicted of murder without the corpse – there was a bloke on a ship who pushed a body through a porthole, and someone else who dissolved his victims in acid, and I'm sure there are—'

'*Don't.*'

'Sorry.' Leo frowned through the windscreen for a moment, apparently bringing all his concentration to bear on driving, then said, thoughtfully, 'Did I really look like Coco the Clown?'

'God, Leo. Not now.'

'I was trying to change the subject.'

'Yes, but . . .' Sophie fell silent. She wanted to cry. This is how it's going to be, she thought, staring out across the fields. He's going to ask for make-up tips, lessons in how to walk in high heels. Maybe he was thinking of dressing-up sessions when she stayed overnight at the flat to plan the redecoration, or perhaps taking it further and attending cross-dressing conventions. She'd seen a documentary about one once – the men primping and mincing, playing at fashion shows, while their wives, sad-eyed and resigned, tried to put a brave face on things.

She'd be one of them. The humiliation of it, the sheer . . . *wrongness*. She couldn't bear it.

'You know,' she said, 'if you want me to be in London during the week to do up the flat, Imanuela will need to stay on to look after things at home. And I'm not sure how much time I'll have – I mean, there's the shop, and—'

'The shop isn't working out financially, Soph. You know that. And decent lawyers don't come cheap. If Miles gets arrested—'

'OK.' Sophie sighed, defeated. 'OK.'

She'd have to bear it. There wasn't a choice.

SIXTY

Sophie stood on the pontoon while Leo took the dinghy out to fetch the *Alzapop*, which was moored in the bay. High above the fishing boats and pleasure craft, seagulls rose and fell in the luminous blue sky, bird-kites in the breeze, pulled on invisible strings. Behind her was the sea wall, where people were walking their dogs, and behind that the narrow-gauge railway with the little train that chugged the mile to the pine woods and the beach. On the quayside, more gulls squabbled over dropped chips and people strolled past the novelty shops to buy shellfish from the kiosk. She didn't think she'd ever felt so absolutely, overwhelmingly alone. She glanced over at the Land Rover, which was backed into one of the spaces by the harbour wall. There was nobody close to it, and, even if there had been, with no windows at the back it was impossible to see inside.

There'd been so many times, during the last few months, when she'd felt at breaking point, but somehow she'd managed to carry on. Now she wondered, with a dull resignation that was barely even curiosity, when she would snap. What did you expect? asked the cold little voice in her head. That everything was always going to be perfect because somehow you deserved it?

The *Alzapop*, white with blue trim, bobbed gently next to the pontoon. Sophie stood back while Leo busied himself tying it up, holding the ropes he gave her and waiting for instructions.

'Go back to the Land Rover,' he said, without looking at her. 'I'll get a trolley – otherwise it's going to be obvious to anyone that all this stuff weighs a lot more than it should.'

She watched Leo walk towards the jumble of buckets and lobster pots at the edge of the car park and stop to speak to an elderly man with a face like the result of a landslide, crevices and ravines of flesh. One of the fishermen, she guessed. She'd seen him before. And there was his grandson – gangly, late teens, cheeks and forehead bubbling with acne – doing something with a nylon net. They seem so unconcerned, she thought, almost with wonder. Their lives are carrying on as normal.

There was an insistent trilling from the bottom of her bag. Alfie. When had she last spoken to him? She couldn't actually remember. 'Hello, darling.'

'Mum? Where are you? I've just got back, and—'

'Got back where?'

'Didn't you see my email?'

'Sorry, it's been a bit . . . Where actually are you?'

'Here, at home. I got back Saturday, like I said, but there was a problem about staying in Fulham because Luke's mum had guests. Then Olly said he was coming up, so I got a lift. I emailed you about it last night.'

'Sorry, darling, I didn't see it. Did you give Olly something towards the petrol?'

'Yeah, course.'

Leo was still talking to the old man. The boy was walking towards one of the wooden sheds – for the trolley, she supposed. She couldn't think of anything to say to Alfie. What if the sail bags had *leaked*? What would they do then? 'I'm glad you had enough money left. Isn't it hot?'

'How long are you going to be?'

'I'm not sure.' Realizing that some sort of explanation was called for, she said, 'I'm with Dad.'

'You're in *London*?'

Alfie, Sophie now realized, was sounding worried, even panicky. 'No, darling. We're here. On the boat, actually. Dad said he'd got to do something to it so he took the day off. And Zac unplugged the freezer by accident so all the food went bad and we've got to sort that out, too.' She gave a breezy little laugh. She was doing quite well, she thought, in terms of nonchalance. 'I'm afraid you're in for a bit of a wait if you've lost your key.'

'It's not that. You need to come back, Mum.'

'Why?'

'It's Margot. You said she wasn't well, so when I got in and there was no one about, I went up to her room to see if she was OK. I thought she was just really asleep at first, but I had another look and I think it's more – I don't think she's breathing.'

SIXTY-ONE

'Christ, Soph! How much did you give her?'

'Only a couple of tablets. Leo, we'll have to go back.'

'Are you out of your mind?'

'If Margot's died, what else can we do? We can't just leave Alfie to—'

'So you're seriously proposing that we go home, *right now, with a dismembered and suppurating body which we will have to leave in the back of the car for God knows how long?*'

'We could get rid of it tomorrow.'

'No, we couldn't. Tomorrow I have a major meeting with people who are coming all the way from California to see me. I can't just blow them off – things are quite bad enough at work as it is. Even if Margot *is* dead – which we don't actually know – Alfie's quite big enough to take it in his stride. He's got to deal with the real world at some point, Soph. You can't wrap him up in cotton wool forever.'

'I'm not trying to, but—'

'But if she's dead there's nothing we can do for her.' Leo climbed into the driver's seat of the Land Rover. 'How did you leave it with him?'

'I didn't know what to say, so I pretended I couldn't hear properly. I told him we were out on the boat and I'd phone again when I could get a signal.'

'Better than nothing, I suppose.'

'What about *your* phone? He knows you're here.'

'It's the new one, remember? Different number. I'm going to move forward a few feet so we can load up and get going.' Leo rubbed his perspiring forehead with his arm. 'There's a storm forecast, and I'd like to try and be back before it kicks off.'

He's compartmentalized everything, Sophie thought, and wished that she could do the same.

She stood at the rail, watching the houses on the seafront get smaller and smaller. The sail bags hadn't leaked, thank God, and they'd managed to get them on board and shove them, and the cool boxes containing the bricks, down into the cabin without drawing attention to themselves or attracting offers of help. She'd managed to follow Leo's barked directions about mooring lines and not trip over anything or get in the way too much. He seemed to enjoy shouting commands – she'd noticed it before when they'd been on the boat. Maybe he thought he was in a war film or something. She tried to square this Leo – at the helm, alert, in charge, the man she knew – with the one she'd encountered the previous evening, and failed. Instead, she tried to ward off all her fears about sailing – having to cede control of her life to the boat and the elements; feeling imprisoned, far from land; the wind that messed up her hair; the spray; the nausea that ballooned inside her even though her stomach was empty; and the lack of knowledge that made it impossible for her to do anything more than obey the very simplest instructions.

Alfie must be mistaken about Margot. She'd thought her mother was dead, hadn't she, that morning, and three sleeping pills couldn't have killed her, unless ... Sophie realized she'd never actually got round to checking exactly what medication Margot was supposed to be taking, and when. She'd just trusted that what had been put into the individual compartments was the correct dosage, but perhaps they were all jumbled up, and Margot could easily have woken up and, confused, taken a second, or even a third, lot. Perhaps there were even sleeping pills amongst them, prescribed by the doctor. Would Sophie's three extra tablets, on top of those, have killed her?

Surely not. Alfie was overreacting. Besides, if he were seriously worried, he could always call an ambulance.

When she got back, she'd make it up to Margot. A fresh start. She'd spent so long running away from her mother in order to be different from her that she'd been selfish. Margot couldn't help how she was, and she, Sophie, should have recognized this and brought her to live with them sooner.

She suddenly remembered being in a hotel in Paris, aged about eight. She'd never been abroad before but she'd been taken there by Margot and whichever man it was at the time. It occurred to her now that she could only have been there under sufferance, presumably because her grandparents had been unavailable for babysitting duties. She remembered quite clearly the whine and clank of the lift, the dark corridors with their mosaic-tiled floors. Being left alone in the evening when Margot and whichever-man-it-was went out for dinner, sitting in bed reading *Miss Happiness and Miss Flower* by Rumer Godden for the ninth or tenth time. She'd liked the contrast of the familiar book in an unfamiliar place. Different cooking smells. The bolster and the square, flat pillows. The bidet. She wished she were back there now with her life stretching out ahead of her, and that none of this had happened . . .

'. . . OK?' Leo appeared at her elbow, his previous words having been swallowed by the clatter of the engine. Just for a second, she regarded him with complete impartiality, as if he were someone she'd never encountered before, and realized, with the shock of returning familiarity, that he looked almost happy.

Happy because he's doing something, she thought. Solving a problem. The relief of having confessed to her probably came into it as well. Maybe, too – although he hadn't admitted it to himself and probably never would – the fact that he had her in his debt, now and forever.

'All right so far, just about.'

'We need to put the sails up now – the wind's good, so it'll be quicker than the engine. If you could bear to make me a cup of something afterwards, that would be nice.'

Sophie looked up at the sky which, to the north-east, was now a swollen, purplish mass – the first sign of the storm Leo had mentioned – and then at the open hatch. Even though the sail bags weren't leaking, there was still a smell and the motion of the boat would definitely make her queasy if she went below. She opened her mouth to refuse, then saw the look on Leo's face – this was actually an order and she wasn't in a position to argue – and changed her mind. 'What is there?'

'Tea or coffee – I don't mind. There's UHT milk. It might be a good idea to bring the oilskins and boots up as well, and the life jack— Oh, *shit*.'

'What?'

'We've got oilskins and boots, but the life jackets are at the chandler's, being serviced. I took them when I came up here with Zac and Poppy to sort the boat out. We'll just have to be careful, that's all.'

'Aren't you having anything?' Leo asked.

'Not a good idea.' Just being down in the cabin had been bad enough – dark, but for the oblong patch of light below the open hatch, the air corrupted and stifling. Sophie had tried not to bump into, or even look in the direction of, the two sail bags, as she'd lurched about opening cupboards whose contents slid from side to side with the motion of the boat.

It was more tranquil with the engine turned off, but the sea was definitely getting choppier. What Sophie always thought of as wrinkles on the surface of the water were starting to rise into white-capped waves; the sky was darkening, and the sails were beginning to vibrate in the wind.

'You know . . .' Leo peered at the binnacle and made a slight adjustment to the wheel. 'With Margot . . . it might be for the best.'

'You mean if she's dead?'

'Yes.' Leo stared at what Sophie thought was a fishing boat on the horizon. 'The alternative could be . . . Well, senile dementia can get pretty grim, from what I've heard.'

Swatting away the thought that he was probably right, Sophie said, 'But what if I killed her?'

'No one's going to think that. Elderly people get muddled up over tablets all the time.'

'I should have been kinder, Leo.'

'Bit late for that. And this is Margot we're talking about, Soph. She's never exactly fitted into your picture of a perfect family.'

He's right, said the little voice in her head. Was Leo, freed by his new honesty, going to wrench open a Pandora's box of uncomfortable truths and lay them bare for everyone to see? The loss of their unwritten contract, as though Leo had physically torn it up and fed it to the waves, left her . . . where? All the landmarks and reference points of their marriage had been so thoroughly jolted out of position that she couldn't orientate herself . . . You can't say that, she wanted to shout. That wasn't the deal.

'Mind you –' Leo challenged Sophie with a look – 'I don't suppose I fit into the perfect family now, either.'

'That's not *fair*!' She knew it sounded childish and petulant, but she didn't care. 'You wanted this family and this life just as much as I did – don't start pretending otherwise.'

Leo stared at her for a long moment, and Sophie waited for a comeback, but instead he said, 'What did Belinda want, anyway?'

'To tell me that she was the one who sent the letters back.'

'Really? Why? I wasn't having an affair with her, or with anyone.'

'I know that.'

When Sophie had finished explaining, Leo stayed silent for such a long time that she began to think he hadn't understood what she'd been saying.

'Unbelievable,' he said, finally. 'So all of this is down to her.'

'Not *all* of it, Leo.'

'OK, not *all* of it. But . . .' He shook his head. 'Christ, what a mess. I don't know whether to laugh or cry.'

'Me neither. I don't feel I know who I am any more.' And I don't know who you are, either, she added silently.

Leo's face softened, and she wondered if he were about to kiss her, and what she would do if he did. Instead, he just looked at her again – as if, she thought, he was searching for something. The old Sophie, perhaps. 'We'll get through this,' he said.

'Yes.' Get through it to what, though? They weren't the same two people, and they never would be again.

'Do you think Melissa will divorce Miles?'

'If he gets charged, you mean?'

'Either way.'

'Well, she was pretty angry. Do you think he was going to end it with Jessica? That's what he told Lissa.'

'He didn't say anything to me, but he didn't say anything about leaving Melissa, either.' Leo adjusted the wheel again. 'He probably hoped he could have his cake and eat it.'

Miles wasn't the only one, Sophie thought. Not wanting to look at Leo, she turned round to look back at the land, but it had disappeared entirely.

They'd been out for almost two hours, and the entire sky had changed – slowly at first, and then with increasing rapidity as the storm approached, from cobalt blue to purple to dense charcoal grey – and the *Alzapop* was no longer rolling but pitching, rising up sharply and dropping back, with a flat slap, onto the water.

It was getting much more difficult to move around the boat. Sophie clutched at things to steady herself and tripped over ropes as the yacht lurched.

'It's coming faster than I thought.' Following Leo's gaze, Sophie saw, slanting from the turbulent sky, an advancing wall of rain. 'Hold on to this.' Leo took his hands off the wheel. 'I should shorten the sails, and I want to make sure everything's secure.'

'What do I do?'

'Steer it into the wind.'

The fishing boat – or whatever it was – was no longer visible on the horizon, and there were no other vessels in sight, just miles of heaving, gunmetal-grey sea. Sophie had absolutely no idea where they were. How far down would you have to sink before the water pressure collapsed your lungs? Dizzy now, sweating and nauseous, she fixed her eyes on the line of the horizon and concentrated on remaining upright.

Leo, unaffected by sickness, was moving purposefully about the yacht, tugging at ropes. He's actually enjoying this, she thought sourly. He gets to be a man of action and save all our bacon and then he can relax in his negligee and fluffy mules afterwards, and I shan't be able to say a word about it. Surely he wasn't proposing to do it in front of the children? What was it he'd said when they'd been talking about Alfie before? *He's got to deal with the real world at some point.* Did the 'real world' include *that*, as well?

He wouldn't.

Would he?

She couldn't think about it now. She'd tackle him about it when they were safely back on dry land.

'Right.' Leo was back beside her. 'I'll take over. You might go down and have a look at your phone – see if there's anything from Alfie.'

Sophie returned her phone to her bag and clambered back up the ladder. 'It's OK. There was a text, sent about an hour ago – he says Margot's fine, but confused.'

'No change there, then. She'll be OK.'

'You said it might be for the best if she wasn't.'

A flicker of impatience passed across Leo's face. 'I was trying to make you feel better.'

'Were you?'

'*Yes.*' He took a hand off the wheel and patted her shoulder. 'It's like I told you – we're going to be all right.'

At least there'd be another chance with Margot, thought Sophie. Pushing from her mind the fact that her mother only appeared to recognize her intermittently and seemed to be lucid only at the most inconvenient moments, and that this was, in all probability, the start of a long slide into the oblivion of utter senility, she pictured the two of them going to Paris for the weekend, sitting in a café by the Seine and talking as they never had before, and then perhaps—

A sudden, bitter upsurge of bile told her that she was definitely going to be sick.

Twenty minutes later, while the wind howled and Sophie's stomach rose and fell as the deck bucked beneath her and the entire sea seemed actually to be tilting, the first fat drops of rain – the beginning of a deluge – were splashing onto the deck. A second after that she heard, in the distance, the percussiveness of thunder.

Leo shouted something above the howl of the wind.

'What?'

'I said, I'm heaving to. We need to do it *now*.' He secured the wheel. He didn't look happy, or even purposeful, but uneasy. I was wrong, Sophie thought. He's not enjoying this – or, if he was, he isn't now. He's frightened. 'Come on,' he said. 'We'll need to put the bricks in the bags while they're still in the cabin – too risky to do it up on deck.'

SIXTY-TWO

'It's going to be bloody difficult pulling these up on deck with the bricks inside, so I'll need you down here to push.' Leo, braced against the door to the forecabin, knotted a rope around the first sail bag and got up off the floor. 'Need to cut the rope first, though – hang on.' He fished a knife out of one of the lockers. 'Then I'll get back up top.'

Sophie stood up, staggered as the yacht gave a great heave, and fell, banging her head on the edge of the table as she went down and collapsing on top of the other sail bag, which yielded horribly, billowing around her like a half-filled waterbed. She lay there for a moment, stunned, and then, scrambling on all fours, wrenched herself away from it.

'Shit!' Leo was back on the floor, his face contorted in pain, and he was cradling one hand in the other. Sophie could see blood seeping out between his fingers. 'Fucking thing slipped – nearly sliced my thumb off.'

'Where's the first aid kit? I'll get a plaster.'

'Leave it. There's no time to fuck about. You've got to *help* me.' He knelt in front of her and took hold of her chin. His own jaw was tight, rigid, and she could feel the wetness of the blood

351

on his hand, and see smears of it across his oilskin jacket. He's lost it, she thought, with an ice-water shock of fear. He's not in control any more.

'Look at me, Soph.' The words were squeezed out between clenched teeth. 'Do you *understand*?'

Sophie raised a trembling hand to push her sodden hair out of her eyes. 'Yes.' It came out in a ragged whisper. 'Yes.'

'OK.' Leo scrambled to his feet, and stood over her, swaying. 'Help me push this over to the ladder.'

Sophie watched as he climbed the steps, holding the end of the rope, his cut thumb bloodying the side rail. 'I'm going to start pulling,' he shouted back to her. 'You need to make sure the bag doesn't get jammed on the way up, OK?'

He stepped over the coaming and disappeared from view. Sophie stared up through the hatch as thunder broke overhead, and a flicker of lightning forked across the driving, horizontal rain. *Please God, let us not be struck by lightning. Please God, make this all right. I'll do anything, anything at all . . .*

Even as the words formed in her mind, she recognized both their futility and their mendacity. It was too late to get back her old existence, the people she and Leo had been. Too late for all the things she should have thought and said and done. It was all way, way out of her control. She struggled to her feet, propping herself against the ladder, head down and shoulders hunched against the rain that poured through the hatch, watching the rope attached to the sail bag jerk over the coaming as Leo took up the slack.

There was sudden colossal thump from above. Leo must have fallen onto his side because a second later his head and shoulders came into view above the hatch, his face a rain-slicked grimace. 'Fuck, that hurt,' he muttered. 'But it's all right. Be all right.'

He's not talking to me, Sophie thought. He's talking to himself. 'Are you OK?'

'Just got to . . .' He groaned and bent over, shoulders bunched, as if he were clutching a limb. Behind him, another electrical burst ripped the sky apart.

'What's happened?' Legs shaking, Sophie began to climb the steps.

'Stay there! Just give me a minute . . .' He tailed off, mumbling, and crawled, or slid, out of view.

Trembling, Sophie hung on to the ladder, unable to move further. What if he'd broken his leg? There was no way she could do this alone. She waited. *Please God, help us . . .*

You're asking for God's help *to dispose of a body*, the voice in her head said sardonically. Really? What are you going to offer in return?

As if on cue came another rumble of thunder, and then Leo's head reappeared. 'Twisted my ankle. Hurts like buggery, but I think I can pull the bag up from here, so get ready to lift.'

He vanished again, and Sophie watched as the rope tautened until the sail bag began to move. The bricks at the bottom banged against her face as she shoved it upwards with shaking hands, almost suffocated by the fabric and the smell.

The rain beating down through the hatch was turning the floor into a skidpan. She fought for purchase on rubbery legs, then slipped, her feet shooting out from underneath her, and landed, agonizingly, on her coccyx as, with a final jerk, the sail bag disappeared onto the deck.

Whimpering, she groped for the bottom rung of the ladder and pulled herself upright, the rain hammering her face. She could see, backlit by lightning, the silhouette of Leo's head as he bent over the sail bag.

'Shall I come up?'

'Stay there. I'm going to get up on the coaming with the sail bag, and then I can push it into the sea from there.'

'Don't you need help?'

'Think . . .' Leo grunted, and Sophie saw the sail bag move past the hatch as he tugged at it. 'I . . .' The bag was in the air now. 'Can . . .' And now she could see Leo's lower legs, partially obscured by the bag as he clasped it in front of him. 'Manage.'

'Shouldn't you at least tie yourself to the boat, or something?'

'Let's . . . just . . . get it . . . done.' Sophie could see the bag moving as, with more grunts and groans, Leo repositioned it to go over the edge – and then she realized, as the boat tilted, that the trailing end of the rope Leo had tied round the bag was looped around one of his ankles.

'Leo, stop!' she screamed. 'The rope!'

The boat tilted again, and Leo tilted with it, tipping towards the water.

'Leo, get the—'

There was an inarticulate shout and Leo's legs and feet were jerked out of sight, and then Sophie's head smashed against the cabin wall as the boat reared up and her feet slipped from the rungs.

Dazed, she scrambled onto her hands and knees, sliding on the wet floor. 'Leo!'

There was no answer, only the storm.

'*Leo!*' Sophie propelled herself forwards, catching her chin on the lowest rung of the ladder. She'd got to get up on deck. Rescue Leo.

Hauling herself up and through the hatch, she collapsed, face down, as the wind tore at the sails above her. 'Leo!' She crawled forwards, clutching at the rails. 'Leo!'

Please, God, let him be all right. Let us be all right. I'll do anything . . . Not good enough, said the little voice. Why should you be entitled to a miracle?

If it was to be a bargain, she must offer something in return. Something specific and concrete. *I'll go to the police. I'll tell them everything. Just let us survive. I'll do it. I promise I'll do it.*

She raised her head. 'Leo! Where are you?'

Waves, as unyielding as if they were solid, slapped her in the face, engulfing her as she peered into the water. Surely he couldn't have been dragged under already? Even a bag filled with bricks would have enough air pockets for a few minutes, wouldn't it?

A sheet of lightning illuminated the whole deck and the sea around the boat and she saw, in a single, bright-white second, his dark head, bobbing a few feet away from the side of the yacht.

'Leo! This way! Swim this way!'

'Help me!'

'Hold on!' Sophie leant over the rail to grab hold of him and, in a single, confused moment, as a huge wave smashed into the side of the boat, found herself, gasping and thrashing, in the sea. Leo seemed to be trying to climb onto her back, and she flailed about, trying to keep her head above the waves. 'Stop it,

Leo! Wait!' She tore at her oilskins and kicked out, trying to get her boots off.

If they could just get back to the boat . . . She gulped, desperate for air as the sea churned around her, battered, winded and swallowing salt water that burned her throat while pain bloomed in her chest. Beating at Leo to stop him forcing her under, she managed to look round at the yacht for long enough to see that the ladder wasn't there. How would they get back on board?

'Get off!' Leo was drowning her. In a blind panic, spluttering and choking, she jabbed backwards with her elbow and connected with something solid. She felt Leo slip away from her as a wave crashed over her head and she floundered and scrabbled, trying to stay afloat.

Alfie. Zac. Poppy. Margot. Dexter.

'Leo!'

Someone would find the sports bag in their wardrobe. The wig, the oversized red patent shoes.

'Leo!'

I'll tell them everything if only you'll let us live.

'Leo!'

I'll tell them everything.

Sophie looked wildly around her, but Leo was nowhere to be seen. The stern of the *Alzapop* came in and out of view as she, and it, rose and fell with the waves. Even drifting, the yacht was faster than she could swim. She watched it pull slowly away from her as Leo's name, torn from her mouth by the wind, was lost in the storm.

TWO DAYS LATER

EASTERN DAILY PRESS

Yacht containing human remains found abandoned

A woman has been rescued from the sea after a 40ft yacht was found abandoned off the Norfolk coast yesterday evening. Fishermen alerted the authorities to the vessel, which appeared to be in difficulties.

When the lifeboat arrived, the crew discovered that there was no one on board, but a bag containing human remains was found. The rescued woman, Sophie Hamilton, is the wife of the yacht owner, banker Leo Hamilton. He has not been seen since the pair boarded the boat, which was moored at Wells-next-the-Sea, two days ago. Traces of blood were discovered in the cabin.

Mrs Hamilton, who was taken to the Norfolk and Norwich University Hospital by the search and rescue helicopter, is understood to be helping the police with their inquiries.

ACKNOWLEDGEMENTS

I am very grateful to Lisa D'Aguiar, Tim Donnelly, Marcela Gheorgheasa, Stephanie Glencross, Jo Green, Nick Green, Jane Gregory, Sue Hall, Jane Havell, Trudy Howson, Therese Keating, Ettore and Eugene Lusardi, Mel McGrath, Fenella Mallalieu, Olivia Mead, Dorinda Ostermann, Peggy Smith, June Wilson, Claire Winyard, Jane Wood and Florence and Gemma for their enthusiasm, advice and support during the writing of this book.